Heady with love … plucking out her hairpins as she twirled in the pelting rain. "If you want that kiss, you'll have to catch me!" she called out.

She could hear Dillon's footsteps getting closer, so she ducked down the next little street to call a truce.

Dillon grabbed her arm. "*Never* duck into an alley," he admonished her. "It's where drunks and despicable beasts lurk."

"Beasts like you, Mr. Devereau?"

"Absolutely." He brushed a raindrop from the tip of her upturned nose—anything to stall, so he wouldn't devour her on the spot. Her hair clung wetly to her shoulders and her damp satin gown outlined her ripe curves. It took a supreme effort not to crush her soaked body against his own.

Charity bobbed up to kiss his cheek and immediately realized her mistake: on a glorious summer night, with a devastatingly handsome man gazing at her, a chaste peck wasn't enough.

She closed her eyes and offered up her lips. He brushed her mouth lightly with his own, then wound his arms around her and kissed her firmly, fiercely, with all the pent-up longing of the past twenty-four hours. She pressed herself against him and surrendered to his warm embrace.

"This is a nice alley," she whispered into his ear. "A nice alley for a nice beast." Her lips met his in a kiss to remember forever.

CHARLOTTE HUBBARD

GAMBLER'S TEMPTING KISSES

ZEBRA BOOKS
KENSINGTON PUBLISHING CORP.

For Mom and Dad, who taught me to believe in myself.

ZEBRA BOOKS

are published by

Kensington Publishing Corp.
850 Third Avenue
New York, NY 10022

First printing: September, 1991

Printed in the United States of America

10 9 8 7 6 5 4 3 2

Chapter 1

"Time to send that preacher packing," Littleton muttered. "I've had all the temperance talk I can stomach for one night."

Dillon Devereau glanced at his partner, who was leaning on the glossy mahogany bar beside him, and smiled to himself. In his black frock coat and gray vest, Abe Littleton resembled a clergyman himself, but he had little tolerance for the men of the cloth who occasionally tried to convert the customers at the Crystal Queen's game tables. "All right, I'll get him out of here. The men aren't paying much attention to him anyway."

As he strolled toward the stage at the far end of the spacious casino, Dillon nodded to the few customers who were looking at him instead of at their cards. The Crystal Queen was one of Kansas City's finest gambling halls, and attracted a clientele who dressed and wagered accordingly. It was his lifelong ambition to own an establishment that rivaled the parlors of New York and San Francisco, and not even the thundering admonitions of Reverend Scott could diminish his pride in his self-made success.

"Throw down your cards! Abandon those whiskey glasses and go home to your wives and mothers!" the preacher commanded in a deep, sonorous voice. "Lady Luck's a fickle heartbreaker, brethren, and I can tell you from my own tragic experience that when you've lost the woman who warms your heart and home, you've lost everything."

When Reverend Scott paused, there were only the murmurings of intent poker players, and the rapid clackings of the roulette wheel in the corner. Dillon stopped beside a green-covered faro table to study the preacher, who was pacing the stage like a caged circus cat, gripping his black lapels as he gazed out over the inattentive crowd. Scott was a natural showman, sporting a thick mane of ebony hair with a sunburst of silver flowing back from his temples. His barrel-shaped chest allowed his theatrical voice to resonate around the room without any visible effort on his part. He was gearing up for the hook, ready to impart a personal testimony that would save souls and send coins clinking into the hat he would pass, but a movement to the right of the stage made Dillon look away from the imposing preacher.

The girl was wearing a dowdy calico dress that revealed a figure far too thin for his liking, yet her direct gaze told Dillon that she'd anticipated his purpose and was about to stall him. He crossed his arms, silently challenging her. She smiled coyly at him, and tossing her long, auburn hair, she climbed the stairs and sat down at the grand piano on the Crystal Queen's stage.

After she played a few soft introductory chords, Reverend Scott glanced impatiently at her. Then he peered into the crowd, spotting Dillon, and narrowed his eyes behind his steel-rimmed spectacles. He pulled a folded sheet of paper from inside his coat and continued his sermon in a solemn voice. "Yes, my friends, my daughter Charity and I can attest to the grievous pain which comes from the loss of a good woman—and may my tale be a lamp unto your feet. You see, a few days ago I received this letter from my wife's sister in Leavenworth, and our lives will never be the same."

Dillon watched, his arms still folded, as Reverend

Scott removed his eyeglasses and straightened the withered page. He knew damn well this was a hoax. Yet some of the gamblers were taking note of Charity's graceful way with the piano, and Devereau enjoyed analyzing a pitch, so he stayed where he stood, listening intently.

"Dearest Noah and Charity," the preacher intoned with the rhythm of the music. "It grieves me to send such unbearable news, but I can't neglect my duty to my dear sister's family. You see, while Marcella was taking some sun and darning our stockings—ever the thoughtful, caring sister despite her debilitating illness—she was abducted from our front porch, in broad daylight!

"My Erroll heard the commotion from his study—looked out to see a huge, dark-skinned Indian slinging Marcella over his shoulder and running to his horse. By the time my husband got out of the house, the savage was galloping toward the river, brandishing a tomahawk with a buffalo's head carved into its handle. He whooped and hollered obscenities at the men who tried to stop his black stallion."

The story sounded like the product of an overwrought female imagination, since the Army at Fort Leavenworth had long ago wiped out any warlike redskins around town, but the description of this particular Indian made Dillon turn and stare at Abe. Abe was staring back, and then he straightened his narrow shoulders and strode resolutely across the room.

Dillon turned his attention to Reverend Scott again, listening with renewed interest.

"The sheriff was summoned, but the brutal savage had a head start," the preacher continued in a voice that was starting to falter. "They—they found pieces of poor Marcella's clothing strewn along the shoreline, and had to ride several miles down the river before they located her body. Erroll said she'd been . . . hacked to pieces . . . and it was all the men could do to gather up her limbs and put them in a box for burial. I was too overcome to attend the funeral, and even now I can barely summon the strength to write you about it."

The gambling hall was enveloped in such a stunned silence that Charity Scott's stifled sob echoed in the room. She glanced apologetically at her father, and after wiping her eyes with the back of her hand, she resumed the quiet hymn she'd been playing.

"This is an outrage!" Littleton whispered as he came up behind Dillon. "Get that charlatan out of here!"

Dillon grasped his partner's elbow to keep him from storming up to the stage. "Wait—let him finish," he replied in a low voice. "We know damn well the Indian he's talking about didn't butcher anybody, and Scott's bound to let enough rope slip in the next paragraph to hang himself."

"But the customers—"

"Shh! They're eating it up!" Dillon gripped Abe's slender arm again, glancing at the rapt faces of the men around them. "After Scott finishes, they'll be talking and drinking—and betting—like there's no tomorrow. Right?"

Abe shrugged out of Devereau's grasp and brushed at his coat sleeve. He looked around the busy game tables, noting that the dealers were using this pause in the gambling to restack their decks, and made no further move toward Reverend Scott and his daughter.

The preacher had been watching the two proprietors; he cleared his throat and maintained his melancholy expression as he slipped the folded letter into his pocket. "My friends, if you have even the faintest glimmer of human kindness in your hearts, you'll understand that I, a man of God, could never fabricate such a bizarre, heartrending story for the sake of milking your pockets. I have taken leave from my pulpit in Jefferson City, and Charity and I are journeying to Leavenworth to console my sister-in-law Magnolia, and to pray over the grave of my dear, departed wife, God rest her soul. We have little money—barely enough for our steamboat passage upriver, let alone a suitable amount to repay Marcella's headstone and burial expenses. If you would be so kind . . ."

Even before Reverend Scott took his broad-brimmed hat from the piano, the customers were reaching into their pockets. And Abe Littleton was bristling. "He's a fake if I ever saw—"

"Nobody's twisting their arms," Dillon whispered pointedly. "Who are you to question their generosity, when they could certainly take their money elsewhere?"

Abe's closely trimmed beard rippled as he clenched his jaw, but at that moment a clear, sweet voice made Dillon Devereau forget about his partner's objections. Charity was playing softly, caressing the keyboard as she crooned the words to a familiar gospel song.

" 'In the Sweet By and By,' " he murmured, and he felt a smile steal across his face as he turned to watch Miss Scott.

"Sentimental claptrap," Abe muttered. "Surely you know better than to fall for that waif's act. She's as phony as her father."

Dillon didn't reply. He was riveted by Charity's soothing contralto, which was a welcome change from most female singers' voices. She rendered the song with a grace and an angelic expression that reminded him of his mother, who would've sung the tune with the same stirring conviction, were she alive. When Reverend Scott's black hat passed by, Dillon deposited a thick wad of bills in it.

The customers at the nearby faro table murmured among themselves and grinned knowingly at him as they dropped in their own contributions.

"You've gone absolutely mad!" Littleton said in a strangled voice.

"Neither of our girls sings half as well," Dillon replied matter-of-factly. "If it's money the Scotts need, I'd let Charity sing for her supper or anything else she wants. She's damn good, Abe."

"And she's a *preacher's* girl, for Chrissakes." His partner shook his head and passed the black hat along without adding to its contents. "Just can't say no to a woman, can you, Devereau?"

Dillon grinned. "I've rarely found a reason to. Now hush. I'm listening."

With a roll of his gray eyes, Abe surveyed the gambling hall and seemed satisfied that once the men chipped into the Reverend's collection, they were resuming their games. As his partner walked slowly between the nearby tables, Dillon again turned his complete attention to the slender redhead on the stage, thinking she would be almost attractive if she dressed more fashionably and did something with the wayward auburn waves hanging down her back.

As though hearing his thoughts, Miss Scott played the final, lingering chords of her song and gazed directly into his eyes. Damn, she was straightforward! And she was indeed as skilled as her father when it came to playing a crowd. Dillon flashed her an encouraging smile, placing his hands in his trouser pockets as though he intended to listen all night. Charity responded by executing a graceful run up the keyboard, and then began a familiar hymn that told Dillon exactly what was coming next. Reverend Scott, who'd been watching his hat pass among the gamblers, now opened his arms wide and began to speak above the music.

"God is indeed everywhere. He dwells here in the Crystal Queen as surely as He does in His heavenly home," his voice rang out fervently. "If any of you have felt the Savior's hand leading you toward His light this evening—"

"That's quite *enough,* Mr. Scott," Abe Littleton's shrill voice came from the center of the room. "You've done your tricks and you've been paid handsomely for them. You may leave by the side door."

Dillon's first impulse was to apologize for his partner's behavior, but he saw a challenge sparkling in the preacher's eyes so he let the confrontation run its course. Charity was playing more loudly now—victoriously, Dillon thought—as Littleton approached her father.

Noah Scott smiled benignly, as though he'd heard no condemnation but rather the answer to a prayer. With his arms spread wide, he welcomed Abe onto the stage. "Brother Littleton, it is truly gratifying to see you, as the manager of this magnificent palace of vice, come forward to confess your newfound faith in the Lord."

"Don't flatter yourself! I've come up here to escort you and your daughter—"

"The love of God can lift us from the deepest seas of sin, above the waves of guilt and degradation—"

"Would you listen to me, dammit?" Abe shouted. "And stop playing that piano!"

The Crystal Queen was suddenly as hushed as a cathedral, and Reverend Scott gazed warmly at the man beside him, as though he were deaf to Abe's insults. "And what is it you wish to confess?" the preacher asked quietly.

Littleton turned toward Dillon, beseeching his help with a frustrated scowl, until he saw the hundreds of elegantly dressed customers watching him from around the spacious, hazy room, some of them snickering. Dillon kept all expression from his face as he returned his partner's gaze, thinking that any response would make him look as foolish as Abe did.

Littleton blinked and quickly reached into his pocket. "I—I didn't get to contribute to your cause. You and your daughter have a safe trip." Before the clergyman could respond to the thick, green roll he dropped into the hat, Abe rushed off the stage, his face inflamed. He disappeared into the storeroom behind the mahogany bar.

After a moment, Charity resumed the hymn she'd been playing, a gospel tune Dillon had recognized as an invitation to come forward before Abe had humiliated himself. When she reached the end of the song and realized that most of the men in the Crystal Queen were again engrossed in their cards, she launched into the refrain, this time singing the words with a lusty spirit that made her soft voice carry to the farthest corners of the room. Dillon saw that even the dealers were looking up from their games with admiring glances, until a slight nod from Reverend Scott signaled her to end the hymn. Charity finished with a flourish on the piano and then folded her hands demurely in her lap.

"We thank you for your time and your indulgence," the preacher said as he raised his arms in a broad, sweeping gesture, "and we'll close with a prayer."

Scott shut his eyes, as did Charity, and while the Reverend pleaded for everlasting mercy on all their souls, Dillon saw that no one but his daughter was paying the preacher any heed. With her head bowed and her face in prayerful repose, Miss Scott looked so fresh and unsullied that the owner of the Crystal Queen felt a sudden urge to protect her from the hardness and vice his livelihood represented, hypocritical as that seemed.

When the benediction ended, Dillon approached the stage and chose his next comments carefully. "You made quite an impression," he said, looking from the clergyman to his daughter with a polite smile. "Most preachers don't have such a . . . compelling testimony. Or a daughter with such a stirring voice."

Noah Scott bowed slightly and began to separate the coins from the bills in his hat. "Even men of God can suffer great tragedies, Brother Devereau, and I honestly don't think I'd have the strength to face this one without Charity. We'll sorely miss her mother. Your customers' generosity is indeed a sign that God hasn't forsaken us in our darkest hour."

Dillon nodded. He detected no insincerity in the woeful pucker the preacher's comments brought to Charity's lips, yet he wasn't sure he trusted Noah Scott. The man was counting his money with a quick-fingered relish that seemed inappropriate to a man of his calling. And why would such a skilled speaker lack the funds for his wife's funeral expenses, when he could've raised hundreds of dollars in the river towns between the state capital and Kansas City, telling about her horrifying death?

Noting how faded Charity's brown calico gown was, and the way it stopped short of her delicate wrists, Dillon wondered why a bereaved clergyman's daughter wasn't wearing black when the preacher himself was stylishly and appropriately attired. He smiled kindly at her. "It's none of my business how much you brought in tonight, but if you'd like to earn more before leaving for Leavenworth, I'd be happy to have you perform here, Miss Scott."

Charity's smile was brief and bewildered. "Oh, I couldn't. The songs I sing are hardly suited to—"

"If you read music, we have stacks of it backstage," Dillon offered. Then he grinned. "And with a voice like yours, I doubt the men would care *what* you sang. Will you at least consider it?"

"I—I don't think so, Mr. Devereau." She glanced nervously at her father. "Papa sent word to Aunt Maggie that we'd be arriving—"

"I told her within the week, not a specific day," Noah interrupted, smiling indulgently at her. He stuck the money in a leather pouch, which he slipped inside his frock coat. "It seems Brother Devereau has just offered you the perfect chance to witness with your music, daughter. Perhaps you should reconsider."

"Yes, Papa," the slender redhead murmured.

Reverend Scott placed his hat jauntily over his silver-streaked hair and then buttoned his coat. "In fact, if he has the time to talk to you right now, I could get us a room for the night. He seems trustworthy enough, for a sporting man."

"I'd be honored to keep her company, sir," Dillon replied evenly. He was used to being considered somewhat disreputable because of his profession, yet coming from this particular preacher, the insinuation was one more item on a growing list of reasons he didn't like Noah Scott. He offered the red-haired girl beside him an elbow, gesturing toward his private table near the rear exit. "Why don't I fetch you some punch, and we'll get better acquainted?"

Charity meekly took his arm, watching her father until he disappeared through the door beside the stage. Then she focused intently on Dillon, her jade eyes flashing with resentment. "I don't really have much choice, do I?"

Chapter 2

Recalling the submissive expression she'd worn only moments ago, Dillon chuckled. "I won't force you to sing, Charity. My offer was intended as a compliment, because you have the loveliest, most provocative voice I've ever heard."

Charity's mouth opened, but words eluded her. She was being escorted between the crowded game tables by the most elegant man in the Crystal Queen: crisp white ruffles peeked out of his frock coat, which was fashioned from brown velvet, and his floral vest was accented with a gleaming gold watch fob. He brushed his blond hair back with long, slender fingers as he smiled down at her. Dillon Devereau was almost *too* handsome, yet his amber eyes were as gentle as an old hound dog's and she heard no hint of condescension in his praise.

He stopped beside his private table, still holding her hand beneath his elbow as he waited for her reply.

"I—I could use that cold drink now," she mumbled.

Dillon grinned as he seated her. "Would the lady prefer that with whiskey or gin?"

"I do *not* indulge in alcoholic—"

"I know that, Miss Scott, and I wouldn't think of spiking your drink," he answered with a chuckle. "I was only teasing. Trust me."

Charity could no more trust Dillon Devereau than

she could fly, yet the dimple winking in his right cheek kept her from stalking out of the room. And as he made his way through the congested aisles, Charity chided herself for acting like such a shrew. He probably *had* been making fun of her, but he'd complimented her, too. And how long had it been since a good-looking man—or *any* man—had shown the least bit of interest in her?

As she awaited her host's return, Charity gazed around the huge gambling hall. The walls were covered with gold wallpaper flocked in a scarlet pattern that was repeated in the elegant swag draperies. The mahogany bar gleamed in the light from dozens of wall sconces; the beveled mirror behind it reflected the room's opulence. And everywhere there was crystal! The chandeliers dripped with prisms that glittered like diamonds; the crystal ashtrays were etched with an intricate design resembling a woman's face.

And in the center of all this splendor, surrounded by green tables where fashionably dressed gentlemen studied their cards and chewed their cheroots, a glass statue rose up from a bubbling marble fountain. She was larger than life, this crystal queen—which made her voluptuous nudity all the more awesome to Charity. When she saw Dillon easing between his customers with their refreshments, she fidgeted with an ashtray so he wouldn't catch her gaping at the statue.

"Still here, virtue intact?" he asked lightly. He placed two tall glasses on the table and sat down across from her. "I hope punch is all right."

"It looks delicious. Thank you." She drank deeply of the rosy liquid, which was tangy-sweet with chips of ice floating in it.

Dillon studied her for a moment, wondering why he felt so drawn to this impoverished-looking girl. "Miss Scott, I—"

"Please, my name is Charity."

With a nod, he sipped his whiskeyed punch. "Charity, I realize I've put you in a compromising position. I didn't intend to offend you or back you into a corner your father wouldn't let you out of. Can you excuse my insensitivity?"

She almost forgot to swallow her mouthful of punch. He'd read her situation perfectly: her father *always* set her up as an example of a virtue so mortally unattainable she wanted to scream. Papa would expect her to be appalled at the goings-on in this opulent den of iniquity, and he'd want a report of how she'd railed against their sins, just as Jesus had overturned the tables of the money changers in the Temple.

Charity also realized that her host would see through any self-righteousness for the act it was. "Mr. Devereau, this doesn't mean I want to perform here—though it's a glorious place!" she added quickly. "I appreciate what you said about my singing. And . . . and I'm sorry I've been behaving like such a jackass."

Dillon choked on a laugh. "If your father heard—"

"It's in the Bible, you know," she said lightly. "But I save it for special occasions."

He leaned back in his chair, pleased that he'd relieved her resentment. Her light drawl tickled his ears and her impish grin made her look carefree and childlike. Since she'd be leaving when her father returned, he decided to learn as much as he could about her aunt in Leavenworth without upsetting her. "I'm sorry you stopped by here under such unfortunate circumstances," he began quietly.

Charity looked away from the sympathy in his expressive eyes. She would *not* blubber in front of this man!

Dillon chose his next words carefully. "Your Aunt

Magnolia must be beside herself, since your mother was her constant companion."

"For the past ten years," she said with a rueful nod.

"And the *way* she went . . ." He observed a slight shudder as the girl across from him widened her woeful green eyes.

"Are there many Indians in Leavenworth, Mr. Devereau?" she asked in a tight whisper.

"I should think not. And I'm sure they've caught *that* one by now," he stated firmly. Resisting the urge to clasp her hand, Dillon continued his questioning cautiously. "You'll be a great comfort to your aunt, Charity. I'm sure her husband's done his best, but women are much better at consoling than men are."

"I—I hope so. This'll be the first time I've ever seen Aunt Maggie." Charity sniffled, and when she saw Dillon's questioning scowl she added, "It was because of Mama's consumption, you see—she was afraid I'd catch it, and Papa insisted he needed me at home, so I've never gone to visit her. Yet I think Mama lived a full life, even if she was practically an invalid. She wrote to us every month, telling how they were sewing for the orphans, and what book Maggie was reading aloud in the evenings. Mama sounded so . . . *happy.*"

Dillon nodded solemnly. "And your Aunt Maggie probably felt better, knowing she'd brightened an invalid's life. Sisters grow very close when they share each other's burdens."

Charity brightened. "They're twins, you know. And they looked so much alike they sat in for each other in school, and their teachers couldn't catch them. And they *lied* for one another!" she added with a giggle. Dillon's dimple winked, which inspired her to keep him entertained for as long as she could, so she'd have memories of his handsome smile during the dreary days ahead. "Would you like to see a picture of them? I have it in my suitcase."

He knew he should be making his collection rounds among the dealers, yet the sudden sunshine in Charity's smile rendered her suggestion irresistible. "Yes, I'd like that, if it won't upset you to show it to me."

Charity quickly made her way toward the stage, before Devereau's sympathy got the best of her. A haze of cigar smoke had settled over the Crystal Queen and the vast gaming room was surprisingly quiet, considering the crowd it housed. Two girls around her own age were setting up for an act, eyeing her haughtily as she opened her luggage. Their blond topknots fell in tight ringlets, and their scanty scarlet costumes molded their figures into such exaggerated hourglasses that Charity wondered how they could breathe, much less perform. She pulled the photograph from between her folded underthings and returned to the table.

"Those are the O'Leary sisters," Dillon said as she seated herself. "They deal faro in the afternoons and sing at night . . . when the customers are too liquored up to notice how they sound."

Charity glanced toward the stage. "If they're so bad, why'd you hire them?"

"They're Abe's nieces."

"Ah." His subtle humor was like a spring breeze blowing through her gloomy life. Fearing she'd bore him if she dwelt on her sadness, Charity put on a smile and handed him the framed photograph. "That's Mama in the chair, and Aunt Maggie standing beside Uncle Erroll."

Dillon recognized Miss Scott's angular features in the women's faces, which were eerily identical, right down to the saucy sparkle in their eyes. Except for being dressed differently, they could've been the same woman. "Your mother doesn't *look* sick."

"That was taken when she was first diagnosed," Charity explained. "They wanted a photograph made in case Mama started, well . . . wasting away. And now my aunt has consumption, too."

Nodding, he gazed into Charity's intense green eyes. "When you get your growth, you'll be every bit as pretty as your mother," he reassured her. "Your father must be very proud to—"

"I'm eighteen, Mr. Devereau, and my *growth* shouldn't be of any concern to *you.* If you don't—"

"I'm sorry. I seem to have twisted my compliment into an insult. Again." Grasping the hand that was about to snatch the photograph away, Dillon did his best not to chuckle. Wounded pride was making Charity's lip quiver like a child's . . . a very sweet, kissable child. "Well—at least you have this to remember your mother by," he said.

Charity pressed her lips together, determined not to cry. Dillon Devereau was so suave she wasn't *sure* he'd been poking fun at her figure, yet how could someone with her sheltered background believe *anything* a gambling man said? At the sound of a raucous duet, she glanced toward the stage to see one O'Leary sister's breasts shimmying above the keyboard while the other shook her backside toward the audience.

Oblivious to the nightly stage act, Dillon was studying the photograph again. Something about the pose struck him as odd, although it seemed perfectly logical that an ill woman would be seated while her sister stood beside her husband. Erroll was a dapper, dark-haired man with a gaze that met Dillon's as though he were staring out of the paper and glass—and across the miles and years as well. Devereau's insides tightened. It couldn't be Erroll Powers—not with a wife and invalid sister-in-law in

Leavenworth—yet the unusual name and the uncanny resemblance couldn't be mere coincidence either.

He cleared his throat. "What does your uncle do, Charity?"

"He's a lawyer. A very successful one, Mama always said." She turned her attention from the bosomy blond sisters to smile at him. "I'm looking forward to seeing their huge house, and strolling through the rose gardens, and—I mean, Mama made it all sound so grand. Seven bedrooms, and a library! Can you imagine?"

Dillon had no trouble picturing the sort of house Erroll would own, and at the risk of revealing too much, he lowered his voice. "What's your aunt's last name, Charity?"

Her brow furrowed. "It's been years since I heard Mama say . . . I—why? Do you *know* them?"

Shrugging, Dillon released her slender hand. "He resembles a man I knew in California, but after all these years . . ." Miss Scott's probing gaze was making him wish he hadn't pursued the subject, and he had to reweave his story quickly. "Come to think of it, his name wasn't even—"

"You don't believe me, do you?" Charity demanded. "You think Papa made that story up, so people would feel sorry for us and donate—"

"I never said any such thing. I was merely asking about your family to make conversation while—"

"Well, *other* people believe it! And it's my *mother* we're talking about," she said vehemently. "So if you're going to make fun of me and call my papa a liar, you can just go to hell in a handbasket, Mr. Devereau."

It wasn't the first time an enraged young lady had sent him to the devil, yet Charity's indignation made him shake with pent-up laughter. She wasn't the sniveling, holier-than-thou preacher's daughter he'd expected, and he sensed that her loyalty to her father was sincere, if misplaced.

"I'm not doubting *you,* Charity," he began in a conciliatory tone, "but perhaps your aunt's condition has affected her reason. The Indians were driven from Fort Leavenworth more than—"

"Aunt Maggie's illness has nothing to do with it," Charity replied crisply. "Uncle Erroll watched that savage carry my mother off. Maggie was merely reporting what he saw, as best she could."

She had him there. Yet Erroll's involvement, not to mention the role of the Indian with the buffalo tomahawk, made the story even more suspect. Dillon stood up slowly, smiling at her. "I've been a poor host, badgering you with questions when you've suffered such a horrible loss," he murmured. "Your father should be back any minute now, so instead of upsetting you, I'll go—"

"No! I didn't mean to—please don't leave me." Embarrassed that she'd broken down in front of this handsome yet confusing man, Charity buried her face in her hands and shook with silent sobs.

Dillon wished he'd never fallen for her alluring voice. She probably *was* playing him for a fool, and with nearby customers watching them, he couldn't very well abandon her. He swung his chair around and sat down to rub her quaking shoulders. "Charity, I'm sorry."

"You shouldn't be. I'm the one causing all the commotion." His hands were warm on her back, and as she smeared the tears from her eyes, she tried to explain her predicament. "I—I'm just tired," she said with a loud sigh. "We've been five days on the river, stopping in the little towns so Papa could preach. It's his duty to proclaim the Gospel wherever he goes, you see. And it sounds awfully selfish of me, but I just want to make my peace at Mama's grave, and sleep in a real bed."

His heart went out to her, and although he realized he was behaving like a first-rate sucker, Dillon pulled her gently into his arms. She nuzzled against his shoulder as he stroked her auburn hair. With a few of the gossamer strands tickling his cheek and her delicate body resting against his, Devereau thought it a crime that Noah Scott was putting his duty to the Gospel ahead of his concern for a grieving daughter. Because of the June heat, Marcella's remains would have been interred immediately—no time to wait for her family to arrive from downstate. But the preacher had extended their trip by two full days to speak along the way, claiming he was too short of cash to repay his wife's funeral expenses. The whole story smelled funny. And as he felt Charity's shoulder blades beneath her faded calico dress, he resented the Reverend's remarks about human kindness and generosity even more.

Charity stirred from the cocoon this handsome stranger had created around her. His velvet shoulder made a fine pillow, and she would have gladly gone on inhaling his bracing, masculine scent—cloves, she thought—but the men around them were starting to pay more attention to her than to the dreadful-sounding song coming from the stage. "Thank you, Mr. Devereau," she mumbled, "but what would Papa say if he saw us this way?"

With her angelic face so close to his, Noah Scott's reaction was the furthest thing from his mind. Dillon loosened his hold on her. "Perhaps you're right. He thought I was trustworthy—for a sporting man—and this won't look good at all."

She had to force herself to stop gazing into his golden-brown eyes. "It *is* pretty terrible."

"Being seen with me? Well, I'll admit a lot of ladies have—"

"No, that singing. I've heard starving cats that sounded better," she said with a tentative smile.

Charity's eyes gleamed like polished jade and he was again caught up in the emotions she displayed so freely. Her laughter was low and melodious, and as the O'Leary sisters reached a dismal finale, he found himself chuckling as hard as she was. "My offer still stands. But I can understand why you want to be moving along."

Her lips parted, yet Charity's words were lost in the wonderment of being so close to a man who seemed genuinely interested in what she said and how she felt. His gaze wandered along her jawline and rested on her lips. Was he going to kiss her?

Dillon saw surrender written all over her beguiling face, and the urge to make love to Charity Scott drove every other thought from his mind. He could invite her to the kitchen for another glass of punch, and then he'd lure her up the back stairs to his apartment. She was so starved for affection she didn't even realize she was holding her breath as she gaped at him. "Sweetheart, would you like another—"

One of the O'Leary sisters shrieked and brought Dillon to his senses. He stood up to look over the heads of his customers, and saw Noah Scott staggering into the Crystal Queen, holding the side of his head as he peered desperately at the faces around him.

"Papa! Oh my God!" Charity rushed from the table and pried her way between the men who were helping her father to a chair. "What happened? Who on earth—"

"Give him some air!" Dillon insisted as he followed her through the curious crowd. Scott's right eye was swollen nearly shut and the side of his face was turning a nasty reddish-purple. That his spectacles had survived the blow was a miracle Devereau decided to speculate about later. "Somebody bring him some water," he ordered. "Reverend Scott, how did this happen?"

The preacher grasped his daughter's hand and looked woefully up at them with his good eye. "Heathens!" he gasped. "As if taking our money wasn't enough, they *hit* me, too. I was entering the Pacific House Hotel to register, when they attacked me from behind."

"Oh, Papa," Charity murmured. She gingerly stroked his hair back from his battered temple and took the damp cloth Abe Littleton offered her. "Hush now, and get your breath. Then you can describe who robbed you, so Mr. Devereau can notify the authorities."

"But I didn't *see* them! The cowards sneaked up behind my back, or I'd have reported them myself."

Devereau had a feeling the preacher wasn't admitting the most pertinent details about the incident, and Abe's glance told him his partner shared his suspicions. Kansas City was a raucous town at night, especially here on Main where the saloons and gambling houses were clustered, but the sight of a man entering a hotel would hardly provoke a scuffle—and the Pacific's burly night clerk would have stopped it.

Charity held the cold compress to her father's swollen eye, gazing at him anxiously. "How much did they take?" she whispered.

"All of it. Just grabbed the pouch from my pocket and left me holding my head." He winced when she touched the cloth to his bruise, and then he removed his glasses and gave Dillon a rueful smile. "Sorry to cause such a stir, Brother Devereau, but nothing like this has ever happened to me. When I catch my breath, Charity and I will be on our way. If you could direct us to the nearest mission . . ."

"I'd be pleased if you'd stay here tonight," he said in a low voice. Dillon sensed the preacher was fishing for just such an invitation, yet he had his own motives for extending it.

Charity's eyes widened. "But this is a—we couldn't stay in a—"

"The Crystal Queen's a gambling hall, Miss Scott, not a brothel. And I'm offering you my private quarters."

"Well, of course it is. I didn't mean to imply . . ." The suave proprietor had a sparkle in his eyes, and Charity realized the devilish Mr. Devereau had just put her in another compromising position. Papa couldn't afford to refuse his hospitality, so she was forced to appear grateful for it despite their host's devious intentions. He could have easily put them up somewhere else, rather than under his own roof, where he could lead her into temptation. "Thank you, Mr. Devereau. You've been most generous," she mumbled.

Dillon fought a grin and looked over at Abe, who was scowling. "Have Samson put fresh linens on my bed and fill the tub with hot water. I'll help Reverend Scott upstairs as soon as he feels able."

With a stiff nod, Littleton disappeared. The men around them returned to their game tables, murmuring among themselves about thieves on the streets and policemen who were never around when they were needed. When he saw that Noah was ready to stand up, Dillon reached for his elbow.

"Thanks, but I'm not a cripple, Brother Devereau. Merely a bunged-up fool for having walked the city streets after dark," Scott muttered while he rose to his full height. He glanced around the vast casino, gripping his lapels as though they'd give him the strength to climb the stairs. "Which way do we go?"

"Your spectacles are in your pocket, Papa," Charity murmured, and she glanced knowingly at Dillon.

"He can't see beyond his nose without them, yet he tries—"

"That's quite enough, daughter," the preacher snapped as he donned the steel-rimmed glasses. "Mr. Devereau is no doubt tired of us interfering with his customers' entertainment. Shall we go?"

Dillon gestured toward the back of the hall, where the private stairway ascended from the kitchen. "I'll have Samson bring your bags," he said, masking his irritation with the low voice he used to control unruly customers. He didn't expect Scott to be all smiles after being robbed—if that was indeed what had happened—but his gruffness toward Charity was inexcusable. And the Reverend was nearsighted in more ways than one if he couldn't see the holes in the story he was spinning.

Charity felt the gamblers' curious glances as she passed between their tables, and after the way Papa had rebuked her, she wanted to disappear into thin air. It was obvious Mr. Devereau thought little of her father and *was* glad to be ushering them out of sight, as though they were poor white trash off the streets . . . which wasn't so far from the truth right now. Charity climbed the carpeted stairs and then stood aside to let Dillon lead them to his rooms.

Noting her gloomy expression, he opened his door and waved Noah in ahead of him. "If you can think of anything you'll be needing, let Samson know," he said with a nod toward the colored housekeeper. Then he took Charity aside and whispered, "I'm sorry if I've embarrassed you somehow. I'll be happy to cover your steamer fare to—"

"You've done too much already." She looked him steadily in the eye, unable to keep the color from rising into her cheeks. "We may not be as wealthy as you are, Mr. Devereau, but we Scotts pay our own way. We'll be out of your rooms bright and early, looking for—"

"If that's Brother Devereau you're talking to," the Reverend's voice came from inside the apartment, "ask him what time you can start work tomorrow. After church, of course."

As the flames rose in her face and her eyes sparked with angry pride, Dillon was surprised he didn't see steam coming from Charity's ears. He gave her a slight bow, biting back a smile. "I'll see you downstairs for breakfast, whenever you're ready."

Shortly before midnight, Dillon watched his partner approach the bar with the strut of a frustrated bantam rooster. He poured another whiskey for himself and one for Abe, putting on his most congenial smile.

"First you allow Scott to solicit from our stage and then you humor *another* of his lies by lending him your apartment," Littleton said in an exasperated whisper. "Those leeches might hang on for days, Devereau."

"I doubt it. No respectable clergyman would sit idle while his daughter earned their steamer fare in a gambling parlor—on Sunday." Dillon sipped his whiskey, chuckling. "But then, we both know Reverend Scott's somewhat less than respectable. How do you suppose he got that shiner?"

Abe downed his shot in one swallow. "I don't know, and I don't give a damn. What concerns me is *you,* letting that girl *moon* over you. She's trouble, Dillon."

"She's eighteen and innocent to the core," he replied with an easy grin. "And a girl named Charity has to have some goodness in her. In fact, I find her rather refreshing."

Littleton snorted. "Charity—that's exactly what

she'll live on all her life. And now that she's in your room, where'll *you* sleep?"

"You're implying I don't know what to do with a woman in my bed?"

"Dammit, Devereau, you let those people make an ass of me, and now they're suckering you. I don't see—"

"Correction—you made an ass of yourself, Abe," Dillon replied. "You can't tell me that with all the revivals you and Voletta attend, you didn't recognize that hymn as an invitation to be saved."

His partner grunted and poured them another round. "I don't go to those things unless I can't get out of it. Nothing but a bunch of hysterical women with too much time on their hands." Abe eyed Dillon cautiously as he quaffed his second shot. "Don't tell me *you're* taking on religion these days."

"I say my prayers, like any high roller," he replied with a shrug. "Maybe *you* could do with a little churching, Abe. I won this hall from you on the flip of a card and a prayer, as I recall."

"Don't remind me," the little man replied sourly. "But mark my words, your luck'll change if you don't show Noah and his dear daughter to the door."

Chuckling, Devereau decided to play devil's advocate to relieve the evening's monotony. "At least the Reverend made no bones about the money being for his own use. He could've said it was for the widows and orphans."

"And you'll justify that con artist's lies before you'll stick up for me? Thanks, pal," Abe jeered. "Nice to know where I stand, compared to—"

"Nice to know my partner can be counted on for a little fun when the evening gets slow." Clapping him on the back, Dillon drained the last drop from his shot glass. "You're probably right, though—I'm starting to go off the deep end. I need a vacation from this place. So I'm planning to escort the Scotts to Leavenworth."

Before Abe could lecture him again, Dillon strolled out from behind the bar and began picking up cash from the dealers at the various tables. When he'd placed the bundled money in the storeroom safe, he ambled toward the stairway, smiling to himself. He needed a clean shirt for tomorrow, and his clothes were in the armoire beside the bed where Charity was sleeping.

After listening at the door, Dillon eased the lock open and slipped inside his dark apartment. When his eyes adjusted to the shadows he saw that Noah was snoring upon the sofa, his mouth hanging slack. Even in the dimness, the preacher's right eye looked as gruesome as a war wound, and Dillon again wondered what he'd done to deserve the beating he received.

He glanced toward his bedroom, glad to see the door was ajar. Devereau removed his boots, and then crossed the parquet floor as silently as a tiger on the prowl. Once inside his bedroom, he paused to savor the sight he'd been imagining for the past few hours.

Charity was bathed in moonlight, stretched gracefully down the center of his bed with her long, slender legs on top of the sheets. She mumbled something and turned onto her back; Dillon remained in the shadows until her breathing was deep and even again. Her muslin nightgown had ridden up her thighs, and as the breeze from the window teased at its hem, he gripped the cool iron footboard to keep himself under control.

The scent of clove soap still lingered, mixed with Charity's own subtle fragrance. Dillon stepped toward her, unable to resist the fragile beauty that stole his breath away as he gazed at her moonlit face. Without even realizing it, he let his hand come to rest on her knee.

A loud, grumbling snort came from the front room, and Dillon stood stock-still. He heard Scott rearranging himself on the sofa, and then all was quiet again except for the pounding of his own heart. He knew he should take a shirt from the armoire and leave, before either of the Scotts awoke and discovered him here. Yet his fingertips followed the curve of Charity's inner thigh, delighting in her softness as they approached her slender hips.

Dillon paused, his hand beneath her gown. He was trembling with anticipation—he, who never *needed* such illicit means of satisfying his curiosity about a woman. It was the risk of being caught that excited him, and yet Charity had whetted his appetite hours ago with her boldly innocent gaze and her low, vibrant voice.

Wavering between depravity and honor, he gave in. His fingers skimmed the delicate skin of her thigh until they found the patch of springy curls. She was still sleeping peacefully. Without the slightest idea what he'd do if she awoke, Dillon eased his hand lower.

Charity's lips parted and she smiled as though she were having the sweetest of dreams. She moaned softly, arching against his palm with an abandon that nearly made him cry out with wanting her. Quickly he withdrew his hand and let her gown flutter down over her legs again, and then he removed a shirt from the armoire. He was almost to the door, his heart pounding wildly, when her restless stirring made him glance back at her.

Charity stretched with the complacency of a napping cat, and then her arm fell toward him, her graceful fingers extended in a silent invitation. "Dillon . . ." she mumbled, and then she nuzzled the pillow.

Devereau rushed past the snoring Noah Scott, snatched up his boots, and didn't breathe until his apartment door was closed behind him. He leaned against the wall, every bit as exhilarated as when a comely San Francisco whore had ushered him into manhood. Charity Scott, for all her prim cotton clothes and strict religious upbringing, had responded to his touch with a wanton wildness that made his pulse roar! He had to possess her—had to probe the redhead's intimate mysteries until they were no longer a challenge, so he would tire of her and get on with his life. Yet as Dillon strolled down the hall, he wondered if he'd ever stop hearing her whisper his name.

Chapter 3

"I will *not* be a part of some—*wiggling*—act!" Charity exclaimed. She yanked at each sequined, feathered costume hanging on the rack in front of her, and then shoved it back into place. Devereau was leaning against the doorway of the small backstage room, obviously amused. "Dressing like a hussy wasn't part of the deal. I agreed to *sing,* not to show myself off."

"And sing you shall," Dillon replied suavely. He ran his fingers over a lavender dress that would flatter her immensely. In his mind he saw its softly gathered neckline dipping over her bare shoulders, but only the sweet young nymph of his midnight fantasies would try it on. The Charity Scott standing before him now was more likely to slap him. Smiling, he walked over to the spinet. "Let's find you a few songs and worry about your costume later. We'll come up with something."

As Charity watched the lithe gambler lift the top half off a pile of sheet music, she was more frustrated than angry. He was right: neither the blue gingham gown she was wearing nor her dress of brown calico was suitable for a performance on the Crystal Queen's stage. She made do with only two outfits each season, and her limited wardrobe was a perennial source of friction—vanity, Papa called it, and he refused to buy her new fabric until her clothing was nearly threadbare. Gazing at her benefactor's colorful cravate, gold brocade vest, and pin-striped trousers made her realize how dowdy she must look to him, which in turn made her wonder why he was taking time to set up her act.

"I can find some music, or I'll ask the O'Learys to help me," she said quietly. "You must have more important things to do, Mr. Devereau."

Dillon patted the round piano stool and took the chair beside it. "I can watch men lose their money any hour of the day or night, but I seldom get to hear someone sing the way you do, Charity."

She frowned. "The Crystal Queen never closes?"

"Nope. Nonstop sport for whoever can afford it."

Charity studied his face before she sat down. He looked fresh and rested, disarmingly handsome in his shirtsleeves. "But when do you and Mr. Littleton sleep? You were both here last night."

"We're night owls," Dillon replied with a chuckle. "I nap during the day, and since Abe has a wife, he usually goes home around midnight and returns after breakfast."

"And Mrs. Littleton doesn't complain? I'd think she'd die of loneliness."

Dillon hid a smile and started thumbing through the music in his lap. "When she gets tired of supervising the servants, she does mission work at her church. And when she feels Abe's neglecting her, she comes in to fetch him. Creates quite a disturbance until he takes her out on the town, and then two or three weeks later she'll come in erupting with frustration again."

"Like a volcano?"

He laughed out loud and selected a few popular ballads. "Voletta the Volcano! That's incredibly accurate, sweetheart." Dillon was still chuckling as he looked into her lovely green eyes. Charity was so naive, yet so innately intelligent about some things . . . and he wished she'd laugh more often.

Seeing that a rather morbid song was next in the pile, he quickly stacked it against his vest.

Charity plucked the sheet out of his lap and read the title. " 'You Never Miss Your Sainted Mother Till She's Dead and Gone to Heaven?' How . . . odd."

"I've heard ballad singers make grown men weep with that one," he replied with a shrug, "but under the circumstances, I didn't think you'd enjoy it."

His eyes had the look of a long-suffering hound dog's again. Why was he being so kind, when she and her father had caused him such an inconvenience? Charity opened the music, and noting its low range and easy accompaniment, she set it on the music rack. The next piece was an old favorite, so without opening it she played a soft arpeggio and began to sing. *"Beautiful dreamer, wake unto me . . ."*

From the first notes, Dillon was captivated. Her voice and hands flowed with a fluid grace; she appeared to be floating above the music rather than thinking about it, and as she sang of starlight and dewdrops, Dillon felt his desire for her stirring all over again. Charity's eyes were closed now and her dreamy contralto coaxed him into the final chorus. *"Beautiful dreamer . . . awake unto . . . me."*

His clear tenor harmony had Charity gazing into a rapt expression that both frightened and fascinated her. Dillon Devereau's eyes shone like gold only inches from hers. His lips parted, and he gazed at her with a silence so eloquent she wondered if he could hear her heart pounding. His face was freshly shaved around his mustache, and she smelled the spicy soap she'd used last night as well as the starch in his snowy-white shirt. His hand was warm on her back, and as his eyes closed for the kiss she desperately wanted, Charity held her breath.

"Dillon! Where on earth *are* you?" a shrill voice

interrupted them from the hallway. "I simply *must* speak with you about—"

Startled from a reverie where Charity was already surrendering to him, he rose from his chair. "Be ready for an eruption," he said with a wink.

The petite woman who bustled through the door filled the tiny room with the overpowering scent of gardenia perfume. Dillon performed the introductions, and Charity knew from the quick, dismissing glance she received that Voletta Littleton would waste little time talking to her.

"You're Reverend Scott's daughter?" she asked as she daintily tucked her parasol under her arm. "How *inspiring,* to be in a prominent evangelist's family. Dillon, I can't tell you how *excited* I was when I heard the Reverend was *here.* I simply *must* meet him! We *can't* let him leave town without inviting him to *preach,* for heaven's sake!"

Charity caught an amused sparkle in Devereau's eye as Mrs. Littleton gushed on. Noah Scott's reputation often caused such outbursts among the faithful, and she smiled politely at these ladies because their generosity put food on the table. Voletta's animated conversation made the tight curls at her temples quiver, along with the ruffle at the neckline of her rose silk dress. She was bustled and beribboned in the height of fashion, yet Charity had to hold her breath to keep from laughing. The two purple birds on Voletta's feathered bonnet pecked each other's heads each time she nodded to emphasize a word.

"If I talk to him *now,* I'm *sure* we can post handbills and erect a tent in time for a revival tonight," she was insisting. "When my friends hear I've talked with *the* Reverend Scott—"

"You'll have to ask the preacher himself about this," Dillon suggested as he steered her toward the door. He gave Charity a quick smile as he offered

Mrs. Littleton his elbow. "Last time I saw Noah, he was in the kitchen with his after-dinner coffee."

When their voices faded in the hallway, Charity fanned the air to clear away Voletta's cloying perfume. She spent the next hour immersed in the music Dillon had stacked on the chair, enjoying the familiar melodies she seldom got to play because Papa insisted upon gospel songs and hymns. Rather than being upset by "You Never Miss Your Sainted Mother," Charity chuckled as she imagined the sentimental style in which it was meant to be sung.

She was experimenting with a conclusion to "Old Folks at Home" when she felt a presence in the doorway. Charity turned to find Mr. Devereau gazing at her. His tawny eyes gave the impression that he could read her mind; she decided not to ask what *he* was thinking about, because she sensed the answer was related to the delicious dream she had last night. "Hello," she murmured shyly.

Dillon smiled. "I hated to turn Voletta loose on your father, but he seemed receptive to the idea of holding a tent meeting. They were talking nonstop, so I didn't figure they'd miss me."

Again he'd chosen to be with her rather than to attend to his casino business, and Charity was pleased. "I think I'm ready to—"

"I *know* you're ready, sweetheart." He sat down beside her, keeping his hands to himself in case Voletta and the preacher burst in on them. "And Mrs. Littleton has solved some of our problems. Your father will collect enough at tonight's revival to pay your steamer fare, and Voletta is sending a dress or two over for you. She's close to your size, so I asked . . . what's wrong, Charity?"

Humiliation bit her cheeks. "You told her I had no clothes?"

"I explained that you'd packed hastily for the trip to your aunt's, and you hadn't expected to perform in public." He reached for her hand, but then thought better of it and laced his fingers over his crossed knees instead. "Voletta was pleased to help—flattered that one of her gowns will grace the stage Noah Scott's to preach from tonight."

Charity sighed, anticipating her father's reaction to this gesture. "Will they arrive in time for me to wear one this afternoon?"

"They'll be here within the hour. We sent one of the kitchen girls after them."

"Thank you," she mumbled.

Once again Dillon resented the way Reverend Scott arrayed himself like a peacock while he kept his daughter looking like an impoverished sparrow. He raised Charity's chin with his thumb until she gave him a reluctant glance. "You'll play and sing wonderfully no matter what you wear, honey," he whispered. "I thought you'd enjoy looking like the fine young woman you are. We can't have the congregation thinking you're about to do a *wiggling* act, now can we?"

His expression was deadly serious, except for the flicker of his dimple, and Charity felt a laugh bubbling up from the bottom of her soul. She shook with it, loving the sound of Dillon's laughter as it mingled with her own. "I talk like a preacher's daughter, don't I?"

Dillon released her chin with a tender squeeze. "No one can fault you for being exactly who you are, Charity. In a world where there's damn little honesty, you're a breath of spring air."

He would have continued his flirtatious banter, but Katrina from the kitchen was entering the little room with two huge boxes in her arms. Dillon rose to take them from her, and he turned to Charity with a grin. "Shall we see how these fit? Unless I miss my bet, you'll be every inch as elegant as Mrs.

Littleton—only prettier, because you carry yourself more gracefully."

Knowing that flattery came as easily to Dillon Devereau as breathing did, Charity still felt a glow spreading through her. She watched him set the boxes on his chair and then her mouth dropped open. He was lifting a gown of deep green satin from the top one with an appreciative whistle.

"Voletta chose well," he said as he held the dress up to her shoulders. "Let's see if the other one suits your coloring as perfectly."

Charity clasped the shimmering gown against herself, marveling at its richness. Never had she worn anything so extravagant, and yet Mr. Devereau's arching eyebrows told her the remaining gown was even lovelier.

"Perfect for a summer afternoon," he murmured as he parted the tissue paper. "The customers will think an angel descended from heaven to sing on our stage."

She sucked in her breath. The cream-colored silk faille floated out of the box in layers that did indeed resemble angels' wings. The bodice was adorned with ivory embroidery, and a row of tiny pearl buttons ran from the collar to the dropped peak at the waist. Charity cleared her throat. "That wasn't her wedding gown, was it?"

"No, no—Voletta fancies herself in light colors," Dillon explained. Noting the way she was clutching the satin dress, he congratulated himself for asking this favor of his partner's wife. "Shall we save the green one for the revival? This silk's more suitable for afternoon."

Charity nodded and hung the gown on the costume rack, arranging its forest-green skirt so it wouldn't wrinkle. It was best not to be too happy about wearing such finery, since Papa would never let her keep the gowns, but . . . silk and satin . . .

luxury she'd never dared to think about even for a wedding dress.

"I'd like you to be onstage in about an hour," Devereau said as he draped the pale gown over the spinet. "Shall I help you change?"

Charity whirled around to face him. "You most certainly will not! If you think I'll let—"

"I wasn't making advances, Miss Scott," Dillon said with a chuckle. "Most ladies have a servant or a sister hold their gown while they slip underneath the skirts. It keeps the fabric from wrinkling."

Although her ignorance embarrassed her—and the suggestion *was* practical—Charity shook her head. "Leave it there on the piano, thank you. And if you come back in less than fifteen minutes, I—I'll take *your* clothes to sing in!"

Devereau laughed low in his throat and turned toward the door. "How can I let such a dare go unanswered? I'll see you in five minutes, sweetheart."

With an exasperated gasp, Charity quickly shed her gingham dress. She had no crinolette to support the dress's voluminous bustle, so her profile would be as hopelessly frumpy as her muslin camisole and pantaloons, but it couldn't be helped. She slipped her arms beneath the billowy ivory skirt until she could stand straight and the dress fell gracefully around her.

She was staring at herself in the mirror, amazed that Mr. Devereau had gauged her figure so accurately, when she saw that the handsome blond was smiling behind her. Charity grabbed the bottom pearl button, wishing she didn't have more than a dozen left to fasten.

"You look lovely," he whispered as he approached the young woman. And as he took in her fumbling fingers, and the wedge of drab muslin beneath her embroidered bodice, and the blush that accented her wide green eyes, Dillon knew he'd remember this glimpse of Charity Scott forever. As though mesmerized, he lifted her auburn waves out of the back of the dress and let them drift over her shoulders.

Charity's breath caught in her throat. Her fingers were trembling so badly she had to pause with her hands between her breasts, staring into Dillon's reflection, because she was unable to do anything else.

Longing to help with her buttons, he crossed the small room and opened a decorative box on the top of the piano instead. "I think the O'Leary girls keep some hairpins here," he said in a voice that sounded strangely tight. Noticing her perplexed frown, he carried the chair over to the mirror. "I admit I'm better at *removing* these things, but between the two of us we'll give you a presentable upsweep. All right?"

She could only nod, fascinated, as he stood behind her with a brush poised over her hair. Did he do this for every woman he knew . . . for his mistresses? Charity sat very still as he brushed sections of her hair into graceful twists, which he pinned at her crown. As he continued around the back of her head, his breath fell on her bare neck and sent goosebumps skittering down her spine.

Who *was* that green-eyed girl in the mirror? And why did her heart beat in triple time when Dillon rested his hands on her shoulders with a satisfied smile? Charity didn't know, but she was more wildly happy than she'd ever been in her life, and she wished this wonderful moment would last forever.

Dillon forced himself to talk so he wouldn't give in to the maddening desire to kiss her exquisite neck. "Charity, I would be honored to—when we get to Leavenworth, I—"

"Well well now, wouldja looky 'ere!" a heavy

Cockney accent rang in the little room. "Dillon's got 'imself a sweet young lady friend, 'e 'as!"

"Aye, and she looks ready to drop 'er drawers, too. Maybe we oughtn't intrude," came the reply.

Charity's cheeks burned when the O'Leary sisters eyed her with knowing grins. They stood before the costume rack, unbuttoning their clothes as Dillon cleared his throat.

"These are the O'Leary girls I was telling you about," he began quickly. "This is Faith, and her younger sister, Hope."

"Pleased to make yer acquaintance," the older blonde said with a chuckle. She let her blouse flutter to the floor and extended her hand to Charity, her ample, camisoled bosom bobbing with her handshake.

"Like we always say," the younger girl quipped, "when yer in a place like the Crystal Queen, if y'ain't got Faith an' 'ope, ye'll soon be relyin' on charity!"

Before Dillon could make amends, his red-haired companion rose to her full height with resolute grace, smiling sweetly. "Where would *any* of us be without charity?" she asked in a low, controlled voice. "Why, some of us rely upon it for our very jobs, don't we?"

Dillon was grinning, ready to applaud, but Miss Scott wasn't finished.

"I'm pleased to meet you," she continued as she offered her hand to Hope. "I'm Charity, Reverend Scott's daughter. But then, you already knew that."

The younger O'Leary's jaw dropped and she turned to find a costume. "Maybe I did, maybe I didn't."

The tiny room grew so silent Dillon thought he heard claws slipping out of their sheaths. He offered Charity his elbow, hoping to avoid a spat. "Shall we gather up your music and go out to the stage now?" he asked lightly.

"I don't need any. Thank you."

Charity walked ahead of him, her pulse pounding victoriously. She paused at the entryway to the Crystal Queen's main salon, taking in the roomful of studious gamblers. Most of the men were sitting at round tables playing poker, or at rectangular green layouts she knew were faro games. Her eyes widened as a newcomer reached up and lovingly fondled the crystal statue's breast before tossing a coin into the fountain at her feet.

"He did that for luck," Devereau explained when he saw Charity's color rise. "But you obviously don't need the queen's help, as neatly as you handled the O'Learys."

Charity smiled at him, her heart swelling when she saw the fond approval in his eyes. "Thank you," she murmured, and before she realized what he was doing, she saw her hand being raised to his lips.

From then on, it was as though she floated in someone else's body. Somehow she climbed to the stage and played the grand piano, but Charity had only the vaguest idea of what songs she was performing. The appluase was scattered, and a few men deposited money in a crystal bowl at the edge of the stage. She glanced up to see Dillon leaning against the bar, gazing steadily at her, and it seemed that the girl in the cream-colored silk must indeed be someone else, to have such an elegant admirer. Smiling to herself, Charity played the introduction to her next song.

Before she'd sung the first line, Dillon straightened with anticipation. A slow smile spread across his face as she crooned "You Never Miss Your Sainted Mother Till She's Dead and Gone to Heaven" in a low, sultry voice that had gamblers looking up from their cards with appreciative smiles. With her neck arched proudly and the pale silk sleeves flowing around her arms, Charity Scott resembled a graceful swan. That she could set aside her grief, after dealing with the O'Learys' rudeness, and assume the role of the virtuous ballad singer every high-class casino featured, only added to Dillon's admiration for her.

As she played the closing chords, a figure in black came through the door beside the stage. Devereau strode toward Noah Scott, determined the reverend wouldn't spoil the mood his daughter had so effectively created. Several customers were making their way toward Charity's crystal bowl now, and the clergyman's dour expression made Dillon walk faster.

"She's done a wonderful job," he said as he reached Scott's side. "I'm paying her double what my regulars get."

"She keeps all of her tips, too?" Noah inquired as he watched the bills pile up in the bowl.

"Certainly. She's earned every dollar."

When Charity looked beyond the throng of smiling gentlemen at the stage's edge and saw her father's grim expression, she knew she'd timed her last number poorly. Before he could chastise her, she launched into a rousing rendition of "Oh! Susanna," inviting the customers to join in with her. Their spirited voices made her feel better, but she knew not to invite trouble. "I really must stop now," she said as she curtsied to them, "because my father and I need to prepare for a revival tonight—and we hope you'll all come. *Thank* you for your generosity!"

The applause was loud and enthusiastic as Charity picked up the overflowing bowl of money. She descended the stairs with one hand on top of it to keep the bills from fluttering off. "I must not've sounded as nervous as I felt," she said happily.

"You were wonderful! They want an encore," Devereau replied as he added his applause to the crowd's.

"Mrs. Littleton has spent the past three hours arranging for a service by the river," Reverend Scott said above the din. "It behooves us to get ourselves in a more spiritual frame of mind, daughter."

"Yes, Papa," Charity said, though she knew her smile still reflected the fun she'd had.

"Let's put your money in my vest for now, and when Brother Devereau pays you—"

"Perhaps Charity should keep it herself," Dillon interrupted quietly. He read the disapproval on Scott's badly bruised face, but he continued as he reached into his pocket. "Considering the way you lost your money last night, it's wise not to carry it all in one place. Thugs might come at you again, Reverend, but who would suspect your daughter had any cash, much less attack her for it?"

Charity tried not to grin as she watched her father's disgruntled expression. When she saw that her handsome benefactor was handing her fifty dollars, she nearly dropped her crystal bowl. "I can't take—"

"Yes, you will," he stated as he closed her fingers around the money. "And under the circumstances, I think I should escort you to the revival tonight. Pickpockets and thieves love a crowd, you know." Reluctantly he let go of her and glanced at Noah. "What time shall I meet you?"

The reverend scrutinized him with his good eye for several seconds. "The service begins at eight."

"Fine. I'll see you right here at seven-thirty."

As Noah Scott's voice rang out over the congregation, Dillon glanced at the people around him. The torchlight flickered in their faces; they were listening so intently they didn't wipe the sweat from their brows or even swat an occasional mosquito. When the reverend paused—something he did often, and effectively—there was only the sound of the tent flapping in the welcome breeze that was starting to blow in from the river.

"Brothers and sisters, the family as we know it—*civilization* as we know it—is on the verge of collapse," Scott declared in a dramatic whisper. "And it's up to us, as God's chosen people, to set the world back on His straight and narrow path to salvation. Your presence here tonight tells me that you've heard His call, and that you've come here to better understand your part in God's eternal plan. We *can* save the world with Christ's help, my friends."

"Amen!" came a shout from the back.

"Hallelujah!" someone else cried.

Reverend Scott gripped his lapels and slowly strode across the makeshift stage, his good side to the audience. "And we'll start right here in Kansas City—gather with the saints by the mighty Missouri River—while my daughter Charity leads us in the fine gospel song of that name."

Charity situated herself at the piano. Her green satin gown shimmered in the flickering light, and as she played through the rousing chorus, Dillon noted nods of approval from the audience. He stood up to join in the singing, again aware of how confidently Miss Scott performed, how she shone with an ethereal beauty when she closed her eyes to let the music carry her with it. And he was more intrigued with her than ever.

But it was her father who stole the show. When the worshipers had settled back into the closely crammed wooden chairs, Noah Scott immediately appealed to their sympathies. With his thick hair flowing back from his battered face, he launched into the tale of his wife's untimely demise at the hand of a brutal savage. Since the audience was made up mostly of women, Dillon heard several gasps when the preacher recounted the gory details about Marcella and continued with the story of the thieves who'd beaten him the previous evening. Scott was pulling out all the stops, imploring the ladies to campaign against the gambling and drinking that caused the moral decay he'd been a victim of, and the disintegration of their own dear families as well.

Devereau wasn't surprised to see that the collection plates were heaped high as they passed down the rows, and no sooner had Charity begun the invitational hymn than the women were flocking to the center aisle. *Like moths to a flame,* Dillon thought when he observed their enthralled expressions. Scott's voice rose theatrically as he blessed each one, clasping her hands between his own and gazing deeply into her eyes. It was animal magnetism, lusty and unrestrained, and Noah was clearly enjoying his work as much as his followers were.

During the next hour the blessings and declarations of faith became steadily louder and more fervent. Despite an occasional outburst of religious ecstasy from the front of the tent, Dillon's attention remained focused on the auburn-haired girl playing the piano. His mind told him that Charity Scott, despite her humble upbringing, was far above him and that their worlds could never be reconciled, but his heart wouldn't let her go. It was foolish for a man of his profession to entertain such notions, yet the memory of her willowy body responding to his touch blocked out all rational thought. He wanted Charity, and he wanted her *now.*

"Mr. Devereau?"

Dillon was startled out of his fantasies by the whispering of his name, and when he realized it was Charity standing in the aisle beside him, he knew that both God and Lady Luck were listening to his prayers. "Yes? What is it, sweetheart?"

She lowered her gaze and whispered, "Papa thinks we should take the money back to your apartment now. There's a storm blowing in, and he's almost finished."

Nodding, Dillon followed her to the stage. He and Noah had agreed to this plan of action on the way to the tent meeting, so after the generous stacks of cash in the collection plates were stashed in a money pouch, he gave the clergyman a wave and escorted Charity outside.

A flash of lightning made her jump. "We'd better hurry. If this dress gets rained on—"

"Plenty of time," Devereau assured her while he tucked her hand under his elbow. "If we rush, you might stumble. I'd have to catch you up and carry you to God only knows where," he added with a mischievous chuckle.

Charity laughed. She was exhilarated from the energy a revival always generated, and as she looked up into her escort's rakish grin, her heart beat even faster. The clouds parted, and the full moon tinted Dillon's hair a pale gold; a streak of lightning gave his face a mysterious glow as he gazed down at her. "Are you really going to Leavenworth with us, Mr. Devereau?" she asked.

Dillon blinked, ignoring the first sprinkling of raindrops. "Who told you that?"

"You did. You mentioned it before the O'Leary sisters burst in on us this morning."

Surprised that she'd remembered such a passing phrase, he draped an arm around her and led her under the balcony of the nearest building. "Don't you *want* me to go?"

His question was a challenge, accented by a deep rumble of thunder above them. Charity placed her hands on his chest, but with his arms coaxing her against his warm, solid body, she knew she was defenseless. Her knees were wobbling as she looked shyly into his eyes, because he was the most dangerous and captivating man she'd ever met.

"If you don't want me to escort you tomorrow, you'll have to give me a very convincing kiss goodbye," Dillon teased.

Charity looked away. "It seems a kiss would convince you of anything you wanted it to—except good-bye."

A few teasing strands of her hair had fallen loose, and when the blowing rain made her cling more tightly, he lowered his face slowly to hers. "Sweetheart, I want—"

A clap of thunder made her bolt, and Charity ducked out from under his arms with a sudden laugh. The rainy breeze was cool and refreshing, and now that her green satin bustle was drenched, it was too late to worry about ruining Mrs. Littleton's gown. She dashed out into the street, surging with a playfulness she hadn't felt since she was a child. Dillon was staring at her, yet she began plucking out her hairpins as she twirled in the pelting rain. "If you want that kiss, you'll have to catch me," she called out.

Devereau hesitated for only a moment, yet it gave her a head start. Charity was scampering up the street like a squirrel, her hair flying behind her as she lifted her skirts. He couldn't recall ever chasing a woman—and certainly never a woman who frolicked in the pouring rain—yet as his clothes became soaked his laughter raced ahead of him to mingle with hers. Damn, she was quick! Half a block ahead of him, and too feisty to slow down.

Charity shook her wet hair back from her face, breathless from running and laughing so hard. She had no idea where the Crystal Queen was, and the buildings on either side of her looked alike in the moonlight. Devereau's footsteps were getting closer, so she darted down the next little street to call a truce.

Dillon grabbed her arm. "*Never* duck into an alley," he panted as he pulled her onto a storefront porch. "It's where drunks and despicable beasts lurk, just waiting for such a tender young thing to stumble in."

"Beasts like you, Mr. Devereau?"

"Absolutely." He brushed a raindrop from the tip of her upturned nose—anything to stall, so he wouldn't devour her on the spot. Her hair clung wetly to her shoulders and she was gasping for breath, still giggling as she looked up at him, and it took a supreme effort not to crush her soaked body against his own.

Charity bobbed up to kiss his cheek and immediately realized her mistake: on a glorious summer night, with a devastatingly handsome man gazing at her, a chaste peck wasn't enough to remember him by.

Dillon's insides turned to mush when she closed her eyes and offered up her flawless, rain-splotched face. He brushed her lips lightly with his own; she was pressing against him with her eager innocence until he wound his arms around her and kissed her firmly, with all the pent-up longing of the past twenty-four hours. With the slightest coaxing, she opened her mouth and allowed him to savor the deeper secrets of her willing lips.

When he finally released her, Charity looked up with a tremulous smile. "That didn't taste like good-bye to me, Mr. Devereau."

"It wasn't."

"But you said—"

"I'm liable to say anything, if it gives me the chance to hold you this way again," Dillon whispered against her ear. "Now kiss me once more, sweetheart, and then we'd better think of a damn good story to tell your father if he's already at the Crystal Queen."

Chapter 4

"Daughter, I forbid you to have any further association with Devereau. He's trouble."

Charity gripped the steamboat's railing and stared unseeing over the wide Missouri River as they chugged away from the Kansas City dock. How did Papa *know?* Dillon had hung their drenched clothing in the backstage room to dry and she'd been in bed last night before Papa returned from the revival. Had a romp in the rain and two kisses visibly changed her?

They were powerful kisses, she mused as she avoided her father's probing eyes. *Wonderful kisses . . . magical kisses.*

"I'm saying this for your own good, Charity," he insisted gruffly. "As far as I can tell, he has no business in Leavenworth, save to lead you astray. To a hustling, conniving professional gambler, an innocent girl like you is no challenge at all—easily impressed by his wealth, and just as easily brushed aside when he's stolen your virtue. That's all he's after, daughter. I don't want to see you hurt, so until he's out of our lives, you will not so much as *speak* to him without my being present. Is that understood?"

Charity's mind churned with resentment, because Papa always treated her like a child—was prejudiced against *any* man who so much as engaged her in conversation. "Why are you just now coming to this conclusion?" she asked bitterly. "You considered him trustworthy enough night before last when you went looking for a hotel."

"Don't sass me. I won't have it." Her father lifted her chin, forcing her to meet the dark, uncompromising eye that shone behind his glasses. "I know what evil lurks in men's hearts, Charity, and Dillon Devereau is Satan's own doorman. The only reason he escorted us to the tent meeting last night was so he could make eyes at you. I saw him—"

"Did you want someone to steal our money again?" she challenged. "Would you like another shiner, to match the—"

Her father's sudden grip on her shoulders cut off the rest of her sentence. His nostrils flared and he lowered his voice to a hiss. "You see? His flattery and money have already wormed their way into your soul. You'd do well to spend the rest of our journey in prayer, daughter. Asking God to clear away your idle fantasies and to give you the strength to face the grief and sorrow that await us at your Aunt Magnolia's."

Knowing the trip upriver would take several hours, Charity glumly allowed her father to lead her to a bench at the boat's bow. Other passengers were already eyeing them, and she knew better than to inspire his temper when he had an audience. Was it only last night she'd run giddily through the rain and been kissed for the first time? As the humidity made her brown dress stick to her back, she wondered if she'd ever feel so free and happy again.

After arranging their luggage in the steamer's cargo hold, Dillon came up on deck and searched the crowd. Reverend Scott was easy to find, surrounded by a knot of women who were hanging on his every word and clucking over his unsightly eye. And there was Charity, hands folded in her calico lap, looking like a pauper's daughter instead of the fairy princess he'd beheld yesterday. He slid onto the wooden bench and slipped his arm around her waist. "You'd be cooler with your hair up, honey. Shall I help you?"

Aching with the memory of how tenderly he'd brushed her hair before she played at the Crystal Queen, Charity sighed. "I'm not supposed to talk to you unless Papa's here. He says you're trouble."

"He's right. Trouble of the randiest sort—but always a gentleman, Charity." When he saw her gaze fall forlornly to her clasped hands, he added, "Surely he didn't suspect anything last night? We were at the Queen at least an hour before he was."

Charity shook her head, avoiding his gaze.

"Then he has no right to . . ." Seeing the slight quiver in her lower lip, Dillon let out an irritated sigh. It was Charity who had no rights, at least where her domineering father was concerned, so rather than upset her further, he saved his choice comments for Reverend Scott. "When I speak to him about this, I'll—"

"No! He'll think I . . . you'll only make things worse, Dillon."

She'd finally called him by his first name, yet it brought him no joy. Her eyes were a deep, liquid green with tears she was trying valiantly to blink away—tears that confirmed his suspicions: Charity would go to desperate lengths to avoid her father's wrath, and as long as Noah Scott was pulling her strings, she'd never again be the carefree, high-spirited creature he'd kissed last night. And every moment he spent at her side was likely to incite more anger, which Scott would vent on her when he wasn't around to protect her.

Dillon glanced toward the black-coated clergyman and his flock, then stood up. "There's a craps game in progress downstairs. That's where I'll be if your father wants me."

But what if I want you? she thought as she watched

him disappear in the crowd. Couldn't he see how miserable she was and spend an hour of this tedious trip with her? It wasn't as though he could make any advances—Papa *couldn't* object to his sitting beside her while all these passengers looked on. Yet if the roguish blond found rolling the dice more pleasurable than her company, perhaps Papa was right. Mr. Devereau was first and foremost a gambler, and two kisses—or two hundred—wouldn't change that.

Charity suddenly felt very foolish. After skittering in the rain like an idiot, she'd all but thrown herself at Dillon. He'd stopped short of taking full advantage of her, but his lips and hands had expressed his desires clearly enough that even an innocent like herself had no trouble understanding his intentions. Her body tingled in the places he'd touched her . . . secret places no *gentleman* would seek out. Recalling the way his fingertips had caressed her breast sent a sunburst of shame into her cheeks.

"You need a hat, dear. Or a parasol," a kindly feminine voice said. "That lovely skin of yours has already gotten too much sun."

Not in the mood for conversation, Charity took the opportunity to leave. "I believe you're right," she said. She stood, smiling tightly at the buxom woman, then found a place on the far side of the steamship's rail to continue her brooding.

Thinking about Devereau only annoyed her, so she mused about Mama . . . Mama, who had suffered such a gruesome death before Charity had a chance to see her again, much less say good-bye . . . Mama, whose courageous, encouraging letters had made life with Papa somewhat bearable. Her selfish thoughts pierced her miserable heart like an ice pick, and Charity realized she'd soon be blubbering and calling attention to herself, so she wondered about Aunt Magnolia instead.

Would she be emaciated by now, racked by a consumptive cough? Each letter Mama had sent from

Leavenworth recounted the trials of an illness the latest medical advances couldn't cure, and gave thanks for the companionship only a sister could provide. Charity had seen two women in the parish back home waste away until there was hardly anything left to put in their coffins, and she hoped she wouldn't stare or say something offensive when she came face to face with Maggie. She would have to be on her most agreeable behavior for this aunt and uncle she'd never met . . . and perhaps Erroll would ask her to stay on in their magnificent home to be the companion Mama had been to his wife. Seven bedrooms and a library!

The moment the Powers estate come into view, Charity knew the arduous journey from Jefferson City had been worth it. Overlooking the river from its scenic green hilltop, the stone mansion commanded awe and respect even as Dillon drove their rented wagon through the iron gates at the road. Two towers flanked the entryway to the three-story structure, with wings extending back on either side of them. Huge evergreens outlined the lawn, and the rosebushes along the front of the porch bloomed in rich reds and golds that matched the stained-glass borders of the windows. As they passed beneath a canopy of stately oaks, Charity breathed in the coolness of the shade and wondered if the castles in Europe were half this grand.

Her father cleared his throat. "Perhaps I should have put on a clean shirt."

Charity felt Devereau stiffen on her left, and with good reason—he'd suggested they stop at the Planters Hotel, where he planned to stay, and freshen up before coming out here. She'd wanted to sponge off her face and pull her hair back, if not change out of her sweat-soaked dress, but Papa had insisted that Dillon drive them directly to Aunt Magnolia's. She was hungry and cross, and instead of making a presentable first impression, they'd be showing up on the doorstep like a couple of destitute relations who had nowhere else to go.

"Whoa, girl," Dillon crooned as he tugged at the mare's reins. The Powers home was as ostentatious as he'd anticipated, and he wished he'd ignored Noah Scott's demands and given Charity a chance to tidy herself. Sweat had trailed down her dusty cheeks, and her hair hung around her face in limp, unruly waves. "I'll wait here while you go to the door," he said gently.

She nodded and allowed her father to help her down from the wagon seat. "I hope they offer us lemonade," she mumbled as they approached the imposing carved doors. "I could drink about a gallon, I think."

"Hush. You're whining like a street urchin." He hesitated, then banged on the brass door knocker.

Charity sighed, longing to lift her hair off her damp neck. After they waited several moments Papa knocked again, and finally she heard muffled footsteps. She held her breath as the door swung open to reveal a plump Negro woman in a black uniform and starched white apron.

The maid eyed them cautiously. "Y'all lost?"

Papa smiled and smoothed his hair back. "We must look frightful after riding the steamer all day, but Magnolia and Erroll are expecting us. I'm the Reverend Noah Scott, and this is my daughter, Charity."

The woman's face showed no sign of recognition, and Charity felt a queer knot forming in the pit of her stomach. "We wrote to her—to say we were on our way," she stammered. "When we read Aunt Maggie's letter about Mama, we came as soon as we could."

Scowling slightly, the maid turned and began thumbing through a stack of unopened letters on a mirrored étagère. She held one up, moving her lips silently. Then her eyes widened and she looked at them as though they were long-lost kin. "You be *the* Rev'rend Scott from Jeff'son City?" she asked excitedly. "I'd have knowed you from your posters, 'cept for that nasty eye."

Papa smiled. "Yes, I am. We've come to—"

"Well, glory hallelujah! And to think Mr. Erroll and Miss Maggie knows *you!*" The maid grinned, showing a wide mouthful of uneven teeth—until she sobered. "But they ain't here. Left nearly a week befo' this letter come, to see to Mr. Erroll's business with the railroad."

Charity felt her insides prickle. "But we thought—"

"Mrs. Powers is strong enough to travel?" Papa interrupted.

The maid rolled her chocolate-brown eyes. "Miss Maggie got a mind stronger than any man's body, Reverend, and when she makes it up, there ain't no changin' it."

"I see." Her father's face registered a nervous bewilderment that looked rather gruesome because of his purplish-green bruise. For the first time Charity could remember, he seemed at a loss for words.

"You see," she began uncertainly, "we were planning to visit for several days, and—"

"Lordy, child, you cain't stay *here!*" the maid said with a shrill laugh. "I mean—myself, I'd be happy to have y'all, but the other servants is on leave for the month—"

"We don't require assistance, Sister—"

"—and Mr. Erroll, he'd have my hide if I let anybody in while he's away." The maid stepped closer and lowered her voice. "He don't trust *no*body. Thinks they's all snoopin' into his affairs. I's real sorry, Rev'rend Scott, but I's under strict orders not to let a soul—not President Grant nor Jesus Christ hisself—through these doors."

Charity glanced back toward the wagon with a long sigh. "I . . . I guess we'll register at the hotel, then."

"I suppose we'll have to." Her father shook his head as though he were dazed. "I wouldn't want to endanger your position, sister, so we'll be going back into town. Could you direct us to the cemetery where Mrs. Scott's laid to rest? We—we've come all this way to pay our respects."

She looked confused, but the woman pointed toward the river. "It's over yonder, on the far side of town, sir."

"Thank you. And God bless you, sister." He took Charity's elbow, his expression taut and unreadable. "It's a good thing Devereau didn't unload our luggage and leave us," he said tersely. "If we hurry, we can check into a room and clean up before it's too dark to find the grave. I—I wouldn't think of visiting your mother in this—"

"Reverend Scott, sir?" the maid called after them.

They both turned to see her broad, white smile.

"I s'pose it wouldn't do no harm to pour y'all some lemonade, hot as it is," she said in a hopeful voice. "Won't take me a minute to fetch it."

Charity grinned and looked at her father, but she could tell he was in no mood to dawdle over refreshments. "Thanks, but we'll go on," she replied reluctantly. "You take care now."

Dillon helped her up to the wagon seat, and when she dropped down beside him, the weight of her disappointment made her look older than her eighteen years. "I'm sorry," he said quietly. "I know you were looking forward to—"

"Gone," Charity mumbled as she shook her head.

"Who would've thought she could travel? Especially when she sounded so overcome by Mama's death in her letter."

"And if the servants are away for a month, it's a sure thing Maggie and Erroll won't return any sooner," her father grumbled. "I can't leave my pulpit for *that* long."

Hearing the finality of his tone, Charity sighed. They'd come all this way up the river and would be returning within a day or two, and she hadn't gotten even a glimpse inside her aunt's luxurious home. As she glanced over her shoulder at it, she tried to recall every glorious detail Mama had told her about it in her letters. As adamant as the maid was about keeping them out—and as set as Papa sounded about visiting the grave tonight and getting home—she knew she'd spend the rest of her life wondering what it was like to live so royally.

Leavenworth bustled around them as they approached the Planters Hotel. Shops of every kind lined both sides of Delaware Street—the Western Candy Factory, Flescher Dry Goods, a dentist, a tailor's shop, and dozens of other businesses kept her busy reading their signs. "Quite a place," she said as she watched people striding along the plank sidewalks. "As busy as Jefferson City."

"It's a fitting-out town for wagon trains and people headed west to homestead," Devereau explained. He nodded to a comely woman who was watching him from the bookstore, and then smiled over at his bedraggled companion. "Leavenworth's the last town where you can buy all the necessities for a new life on the plains. Thousands of people make their down payments on a dream here."

Exhausted as she was, Charity still thought the life Dillon described sounded terribly exciting. When they arrived at the Planters, however, there wasn't time for daydreaming. Papa hurried her along after he got them a room for the night.

"Devereau had his nerve, insisting we stay *here,*" he groused as he hefted their suitcases to the landing. "I should've known that dandy would choose the most expensive—"

"Hush! He's probably right behind us," Charity hissed. She turned the key in their door, then couldn't help gaping at the lovely room. The twin bedsteads were carved walnut, as were the marble-topped dresser and washstand. The brass light fixture gleamed above a round table with two chairs, and the striped rug had the same colors as the Japanese screen and the pictures on the walls, which were hung with fancy tassled ropes.

"It's only for one night, so don't take on any airs, daughter," Papa warned her. He swung the luggage onto the nearest bed, scowling at the furniture. "It's ludicrous to spend so much for a night's sleep, when—"

"And ungrateful to keep harping about it, when Mr. Devereau can probably hear every word you're saying." Charity fully expected him to deliver a sermon about children respecting their parents, but she was too hot and hungry to care. She took her blue gingham dress from her suitcase and shook it, then arranged the tall folding screen so she could have some privacy at the washstand.

Except for her splashing and the street noises drifting in through the open window, the room was quiet. She heard the door to the next room open and close, and it occurred to her that after tomorrow, she would never see Dillon Devereau again. He hadn't spoken of his own reasons for coming to Leavenworth, and telling him good-bye seemed as disappointing as not seeing Aunt Maggie and her house, even though she hardly knew him. Charity recalled his kisses wistfully, and she had to button her gingham dress a second time.

There was a knock at the door and her father answered it. "I know you're wanting to get to the cemetery, so I brought you these sandwiches," she heard Dillon say. "You can take the wagon, and if I'm not in when you get back tonight, I'll see you at breakfast."

Charity was pulling her hair back into a ribbon, and she stepped out from behind the screen. "How thoughtful—and lemonade!" she exclaimed. She gave him a grateful smile, wishing she hadn't been so angry with him this morning. "I—I'm sorry you've come all this way with us for nothing. Or do you have business here?"

Dillon smiled slyly. "Yes, but it has to wait until tomorrow when the stores are open again."

His gaze was so devilish Charity didn't ask how he planned to spend the evening. She took a big bite out of one of the roast pork sandwiches. "This is delicious. Thank you again, Mr. Devereau."

With another smile and a nod to her father, he returned to his room. Papa finished buttoning his shirt and then glanced out the window. "We'll have to take the sandwiches along, if we're to read the names on the headstones before dark. I suppose Devereau charged this food to our bill."

"Papa, really!" Charity took a long drink from a glass of the freshest, coolest lemonade she'd ever tasted, and then glared at him. "So far Mr. Devereau has clothed the naked, fed the hungry, and given us his own bed. If you criticize him for helping us this way, aren't you criticizing Christ himself?"

Papa looked ready to lash out at her, but then his bruised grimace relaxed. "I suppose you have a point," he said glumly. "I should be in a more charitable mood as we prepare to visit your mother. But it's so *frustrating* to know . . . let's go, daughter. The light's fading even as we speak."

The ride to the cemetery was quiet. Charity knew her father felt as forlorn as she did about this whole wasted trip, yet as they approached the arched stone gateway, other thoughts crowded out her disappointment. The moment had come, the moment she'd dreaded since the arrival of Aunt Maggie's letter, and she had to accept her mother's death . . . had to look at the rectangular patch of earth, and read the final words inscribed over her remains. She'd sung at dozens of funerals and had never been comfortable watching the agony that always accompanied the ecstasy over another soul going home to God. This was *Mama,* sorely missed and always, always loved despite the distance in miles and years between them.

Papa's face was somber as he helped her from the wagon. They paused to survey the rows of white and gray monuments casting long, slender shadows in the sunset. "Seems we should look for a fresh mound," her father murmured. "We'll have to go stone by stone. She'll probably be near a marker that says Powers."

Charity nodded, shading her eyes with her hand. They walked along, moving slowly enough to read the tombstones. A breeze riffled the cedar trees, creating a whisper that made her think souls and spirits were flying around them in the dusk.

Up one row and down the next, they mumbled the names but said nothing more. Despite her satisfying sandwich, she felt queasy as they came to the last two rows. "You don't suppose she'd be in that mausoleum? The only recent graves we've seen belong to two old men."

Papa glanced toward the small marble building and shook his head. "The carving over the door says Zimmerman, and I never heard her mention that name in her letters. I don't recall that Erroll has any family in town either."

When they resumed their search, Charity found herself holding her breath and walking faster past the headstones. Mama had to be along here . . . her heart pounded as they started up the final row, going almost at a trot in the fading light. But all the names were carved quite clearly, and none of them were Marcella Scott.

The lines around Papa's eyes deepened visibly. He shaded his brow with his hand and surveyed the rest of the cemetery property, and when his gaze came to rest on a few simple crosses in the far corner, he said, "There's the potter's field, but surely they wouldn't have . . ."

Without a word Charity took his hand and they walked quickly toward the only remaining gravestones. Some were initialed and some were only smooth, round rocks—graves of drifters and vagrants, she was guessing—and she knew that Mama wasn't among them. "Let's go," she whispered. "There must be an explanation."

"We'll find the sexton first thing in the morning," Papa declared.

His voice rang with purpose, yet the hand he placed on her back was trembling as they walked toward the wagon. Charity was too stunned to speak during the ride to town, and rather than be alone in the hotel room she stayed with her father while he drove the wagon to the livery stable. *Where was Mama?* She'd heard Aunt Maggie's letter a dozen times, and the colored maid had directed them to the only cemetery she'd seen in Leavenworth, so why was everything going wrong? Instead of having answers to these heart- wrenching questions, Charity had only a sense of deep, aching emptiness.

After they climbed the hotel stairs, she heard a mournful tune being played on some sort of primitive flute in Dillon's room, and she went to the balcony to let the music soothe her. Once outside, she sat on a wicker settee and felt the evening air settling around her as the flute sang to her very soul. Devereau's plans must have fallen through, yet Charity doubted the cavalier gambler would be so desperate for entertainment that *he'd* be playing such a sad song. Curious, she stood up to peek through his open window.

By the light from his chandelier, she saw Dillon and three other men playing cards at a table. They were in their shirtsleeves, and as one of the men poured whiskey into their glasses, Papa stepped out onto the balcony. Charity moved away quickly, but catching sight of the flute player scared her more than any lecture about eavesdropping her father could deliver. He was the biggest, darkest Indian she'd ever seen, and hanging from the belt of his buckskins was a tomahawk with a buffalo head carved into the handle.

Chapter 5

"Charity, I told you this infatuation with Devereau can only lead to—"

"Papa, it's him!" she rasped. "It's the Indian who killed Mama!"

Her father scowled, then he joined her at staring into Dillon's room. As he put a hand on her shoulder, Charity felt a jolt of angry recognition go through his body. "Didn't I tell you Devereau was in league with the devil? That savage—"

Charity sucked in her breath when the Indian stopped playing his flute and gazed haughtily at them. "Papa, no! Surely Dillon can explain—"

But her father was striding into the hotel to confront the redskin, so all she could do was hurry after him. Papa barged into Devereau's room by throwing open the door so hard it slammed against the wall. The poker players jumped in their seats and then glared, until Dillon laid his cards facedown on the table and stood up. "Reverend Scott, I'm pleased you're here, because I've—"

"You've *lied* to us, that's what you've done!" Noah shouted. "You've known this murderer all along, yet you didn't have the *decency* to tell us about—"

"This man's no killer," Dillon stated firmly. "He's my friend Jackson Blue, and I was as surprised as you are to find him in town. And these are my friends Enos Rumley, Sol Goldstein, and B. C. Clark," he continued, gesturing toward each man at the table. "Men, meet the Reverend Noah Scott and his daughter, Charity."

The poker players nodded curtly while Jackson Blue stepped over to extend a huge, dark hand to Papa. He gave Charity a sly once-over and winked, but she was too frightened to do anything except stare at him. Mr. Blue reminded her of a tall, solid tree. His skin was a color she'd never seen—almost ebony, with a brick-red sheen. And rather than being braided, his hair was a tight mass of blue-black curls. He was smiling at her, yet a scar stretching from his temple to the base of his neck gave him a sinister air Charity disliked immediately.

"I'm pleased to meet you both," he said. His voice was deep and resonant, and when he saw that her father wasn't going to shake his hand, he lowered it. "Dillon tells me you've come to Leavenworth looking for your wife, Mr. Scott, but I'm afraid I can't be much—"

"Don't give me that, you lying heathen," Noah barked. "Your very soul is soaked with her innocent blood—"

"Noah, please," Dillon interrupted. "I think we're all civil enough to settle this misunderstanding without getting ourselves thrown out of the hotel. When I told Jackson about your letter, he recalled galloping down the street with a woman named Maggie, but that was years ago, and—"

"How can you cover for this murdering savage when—"

Charity gasped as Jackson Blue grabbed her father by the shoulders and lifted him at least a foot from the floor. "I've never so much as *met* a Marcella Scott," he said as he brought Papa's face within inches of his own. "And I resent being called a savage and a heathen when I'm a baptized Methodist. You'd do well to listen to Mr. Devereau's explanation instead of spouting off like a damn teakettle,

Mr. Scott. Unless you'd like me to shut that other eye for you."

The sight of her father dangling helplessly in the Indian's grasp made her knees go weak, and Charity was relieved that Papa had enough sense to be quiet. She, and the men at the table, breathed considerably easier when the buckskinned scout set his victim on the floor again.

"As Dillon was saying," Mr. Blue continued calmly, "I've just gotten back from escorting a wagon train west, and I was having a drink with our friends here when Devereau happened along. If I could see that letter, perhaps we can solve this mystery. I can understand how frustrated you and your daughter must feel, but I refuse to be called a killer without the chance to refute your ridiculous accusations."

That this rugged, intimidating man could speak with such educated fluency amazed Charity somewhat. Apparently Papa was surprised, too, yet as he reached into his shirt pocket for the tattered page, he was watching Mr. Blue warily. "Get the photograph from your suitcase, Charity. It's best we settle this while we have witnesses."

He unfolded the letter and read the salutation aloud, until Jackson's hand closed around the page. "I can read, thank you," he said stiffly.

Papa surrendered the page, and when he saw that she was still watching from the doorway, he jerked his head toward their room. As Charity returned with the photograph, Mr. Blue was leaning against the marble-topped dresser, reading the last of her aunt's letter to himself. He shook his head as he refolded the paper. "Maggie's got her faults, but lack of imagination certainly isn't one of them," he said with a secretive grin.

"You *know* Magnolia Powers?" her father demanded.

Jackson laughed. "Yes, but her name's Wallace. And with your daughter present, I don't think we should discuss the nature of my acquaintance with her."

Charity nearly dropped the photograph in her disgust. "Aunt Maggie's been married to Uncle Erroll for more than—"

"Erroll Powers? He's a crooked lawyer for the Kansas Pacific Railroad. Has his hand in the till," the Indian replied matter-of-factly, "and he's definitely not the marrying kind. Sort of like Devereau here."

Dillon was following the conversation as closely as his poker partners were, but he sensed things would get ugly if he allowed Blue's baiting to continue. From what he and Jackson could piece together before the Scotts rushed in, there was something terribly amiss—and more decadent than he cared to imagine—going on with Charity's mother, and he didn't want her to be needlessly humiliated. She looked pitifully vulnerable standing in his doorway, clutching the photograph as though one more lash from Jackson's brash tongue might knock her over.

"Let's stick to the subject of Marcella Scott," Devereau said pointedly. "And let's remember that her daughter and husband have spent several days on the river, anticipating a visit with a consumptive Aunt Maggie and preparing themselves to visit Marcella's grave."

Charity's throat tightened as Dillon approached her. "We didn't find it," she said in a hoarse whisper.

Devereau's heart went out to her, and all he could think of to say was, "Perhaps if we show Jackson the picture, there's a simple explanation for all this."

She handed him the photograph and moved closer to Papa, because Jackson Blue's expression hinted at a situation too scandalous to think about. The colored maid had told them Maggie and Erroll were traveling, despite what Mama's letters had described as her aunt's imminent death from tuberculosis, and now this giant Indian was saying Maggie went by her maiden name, and that she wasn't married to Powers at all. And Charity still didn't know where her mother was.

"That's Powers, all right," Jackson said as he nodded at the picture. "And that's Maggie—twice, unless this whiskey's making me see double."

"They're twins," Papa explained, although his voice lacked its usual conviction. "Marcella is seated, and Maggie is at her husband's side."

Mr. Blue continued to study the photograph, his dusky eyes sparkling. "Maggie Wallace is *not* a married woman, and she spends her days relieving Erroll of his wealth—if you know what I mean. And if she had a twin sister . . . Lord, what a time we would've had—"

"That's enough!" Dillon interrupted. "The Scotts are trying to—"

"If you think I'll let you insult my wife's memory—or her sister," Noah began angrily, "then I'll have you arrested for—"

"I'm telling you she's not your wife, or anybody else's. She's a—"

"Gentlemen, please," Dillon insisted as he stepped between Scott and Blue. He was about to motion to his partners to grab them, but a flying fist sent him sprawling onto the rug, clutching his nose. Blood spurted between his fingers, and he rolled out of the way before five sets of feet caught him up in the fray. If Scott was too stupid to know Jackson Blue could overpower him, Dillon wasn't about to defend him again. Especially since he suspected it was Noah's misguided fist that had struck him.

Charity rushed to Dillon's side and snatched his

handkerchief from his pocket. As she held the square of linen to his nose, she glanced nervously at the men who were trying to subdue her father and Jackson Blue. "What should I do? The manager'll kick us out—or Papa could get killed!"

Devereau winced when Jackson freed himself of Rumley and Clark by banging them against the wall. Then the Indian brandished his tomahawk with a leer. "That thick head of hair would look mighty fine in my collection, Mr. Preacher Man," he said in a menacing voice.

Dillon groaned, grabbing Charity before she bolted. "Just stay out of their way, and I'll pay for the damages. Your father's only letting off steam, and Blue has yet to use that hatchet on anybody, so—"

There was a smashing of glass beside them that made Charity whimper. The photograph had landed facedown on the floor, and she snatched it out of the scuffle just before her father broke away from Sol Goldstein and overturned the poker table onto Jackson's moccasined feet. The wooden picture frame fell into two pieces, revealing the photographer's engraving in the bottom corner. She glanced at Dillon, who was wiping the last of the blood from his face. "It says E. E. Henry of Leavenworth took this picture. Is he still in business?"

Dillon thought for a moment, looking away when he saw Jackson lunging toward Noah Scott. "I believe he is. We passed his studio on Delaware."

Gripping the photograph, Charity stood up to speak above the ruckus. "All right, that's *enough,*" she declared as she glowered at the panting men. She braced herself when the ceramic pitcher from the washstand crashed against the doorway, narrowly missing Jackson Blue's head. Mr. Rumley managed to pin Papa's arms behind him, and the other two men were doggedly clutching at the laughing Indian. "We'll let the photographer settle this first thing tomorrow morning," she continued loudly. "*He* can tell us how many women posed with Mr. Powers."

Papa scowled. "How can you even *think* your mother would've lied about—"

"And how can *you* start swinging at the least provocation?" she countered. "You're behaving like a bully behind a schoolhouse—*all* of you are. And we haven't settled a thing."

The men stopped their struggling to glance sheepishly at her, gasping for their breath.

Charity's remark made Dillon chuckle to himself as he got to his feet. "I think Miss Scott makes an excellent point," he said as he looked at Noah and the other men. "Jackson's impression of the woman in question is so far removed from the Reverend's that a third party should be consulted." Glancing at the slender redhead beside him, he asked, "Didn't you tell me that night at the Queen that you've never met your Aunt Magnolia?"

Charity nodded, feeling very uneasy at the direction Dillon's questions were taking.

"And Noah, how many times have *you* seen your wife's twin? Was she at your wedding, perhaps?"

Reverend Scott straightened the earpiece of his spectacles before putting them on again. "I've never actually seen Magnolia," he mumbled, "because she was attending a private finishing school when Marcella and I married. My wife talked about her constantly, though—cherished a photograph that was taken on their sixteenth birthday—so there's no doubt in my—"

"Your wife's twin sister wasn't at your wedding?" Jackson Blue interrupted with a sneer. "Seems to me—"

"We eloped," Noah said in a low, pointed voice,

"and none of this changes the fact that Marcella is *missing.*"

Aware of a strange tightness in the preacher's responses, which he suspected came from stretching the truth over some widening holes in his story, Dillon quickly changed the subject. "I certainly hope Mr. Henry can shed new light on this situation," he said with a shake of his head. He looked at the shattered glass and cards and money scattered all over the floor and cleared his throat. "Well gentlemen, shall we claim what we each chipped into the kitty and start a fresh game, say, tomorrow afternoon?"

Clark, Goldstein, and Rumley glanced at each other as though they didn't like the suggestion, but they picked up their money, and after nodding at Charity and her father, they left the room. Jackson hung his tomahawk at his side, and with a sly wink at her, he said, "I haven't had this much fun with church people in years. I hope Mr. Henry tells you what you came to hear, sweetheart, but I wouldn't bet any money on it."

Papa stepped toward him with a disgusted grunt, so Charity took his arm until the Indian had disappeared down the stairway. "Let's help Mr. Devereau clean up this mess and then get some sleep," she suggested, although she knew the questions raised these past few minutes would keep her awake long into the night.

Her father glanced at the shambles around them and unbuttoned his shirt collar. "I'm having a tub and some hot water brought up. Why don't you and Mr. Devereau relax out on the balcony until I'm finished bathing? It's right outside our window, you know," he added pointedly.

Charity resented the way he'd ignored her suggestion and so openly distrusted Dillon, but she didn't feel up to arguing. When she was outside, seated next to Dillon on the wicker settee, she was so confused and exhausted she let out a sigh that sounded completely overwhelmed. Why did she sense everyone else knew something she didn't, unless . . .

Noting that Scott was giving directions to the boy who was carrying the bathtub, Dillon wrapped her hand in his. "I'm sorry things have taken such a nasty turn," he murmured. "When I brought Jackson over, I intended for him to help rather than to start a brawl."

"Papa took the first swing," she replied quietly. Dillon's hand felt warm and comforting, and his moonlit smile was so sincere she decided to air her doubts politely rather than challenge him with them. "You know Erroll Powers, don't you?"

It was unfair—and senseless—to deceive her any longer. "Yes, Charity, I knew him a good many years ago. But I had no idea he's settled in Leavenworth, until you showed me that picture."

Nodding, Charity laid the photograph on the wicker table beside them. "Is he the scoundrel Mr. Blue claims he is?"

"Sounds to me like he hasn't changed a bit." Seeing her worried expression, he gently lifted her chin. "That's one reason I want to see this thing to its conclusion, Charity. Hopefully without your father getting himself killed."

Looking into his deep golden eyes, Charity cleared her throat. "There must be more to it, Mr. Devereau. You can't stand Papa, and you can't be all that interested in *me.*"

"Ah, but I am," he replied with a tweak of her nose. "Let's just say I have a score to settle with Mr. Powers. And after the way you and your father came bursting in on my poker game, I owe you for the favor."

"*What?* How could tearing up your room be a favor?" She searched his shadowy face for signs that he was teasing her, but saw only an earnest expression and hair that glowed like a halo in the moonlight.

"Those men—Rumley and Goldstein and Clark? They heard I was in town, and they were hoping to win back several thousand dollars they lost to me last time we played," he explained with a grin. "They were cheating me blind—all three of them—so by disrupting the game, you actually saved me from going temporarily bankrupt."

Charity's mouth dropped open. "That's disgusting! How could you *not* lose, with three men ganging up on you?"

Devereau chuckled and hoped she would respect his next confession for the confidence it was. "Well, I wasn't doing so badly, really—thanks to Jackson. He could see their hands as he walked around with his flute, and he signaled what cards they held by playing certain rhythms and songs. It's a system we haven't used for years, but it still works quite nicely."

"*You* were cheating, too?" Dillon, that's the most—"

Laughing, he placed his hands on Charity's shoulders to keep her from springing out of the settee. Her face radiated shock, yet she looked vibrant and far prettier than she had all day. "I never cheat except in self-defense, honey. These days, a square game is so hard to come by we professionals have to rely on a few tricks to stay in business."

"You're not *smart* enough to win fairly?"

"It takes brains and luck and hours of practice to win consistently, Charity. Not to mention a pair of very sensitive hands," Dillon replied. "I take pride in my gaming skills—you can ask Abe Littleton how honest I am. I won the Crystal Queen from him a few years ago, in a poker game where I could've had his house and other properties as well. But I insisted he quit."

"You could've had Voletta beating you over the head with her parasol, too." The image made Charity laugh, and as Dillon's words sank in, she believed there could indeed be honor among card sharps. And there was no arguing about his sensitive hands . . . his touch was wonderfully soothing as he massaged her tired shoulders. He was gazing steadily at her, and for all she knew the Planters Hotel and Leavenworth and everything but the starry night around them had disappeared. "Dillon," she whispered, "I never intended to be such a bother to you. But what if it's *Mama* who went with Mr.—"

"Shhh . . . we'll deal with that situation tomorrow." Her hair was gloriously soft between his fingers, and as Charity looked into his eyes, he regretted wasting so much moonlight on conversation. He lowered his lips to hers, gently at first, until he felt her returning the ardent kiss he'd wanted to share with her all day.

Charity slipped her arms around his neck, oblivious to everything except the sweet warmth of Dillon Devereau's mouth. For all she knew, the photographer would answer the questions that burned inside her heart and thereby take away this handsome gambler's reason for staying with her. His tongue danced with hers, deepening until she heard herself giggling low in her throat, and heard Dillon's subtle laughter in reply.

"I'm finished bathing, daughter. You should come to bed now."

Charity jumped away from Dillon's embrace just as her father's face appeared at the window. She stood up, and with an apologetic smile at Dillon she hurried toward the balcony door. "Yes, Papa. I'm coming."

Chapter 6

When Dillon saw that they were only two doors away from E. E. Henry's studio, he motioned Charity and her father aside, out of the way of the shoppers who were strolling along the sidewalks. It was a beautiful June morning, and he was determined not to let Noah Scott's temper ruin what might be his final hours with the redhead beside him.

"Let's go over the plan once more," Devereau said in a low voice. "I'll do the talking, so Mr. Henry won't mince words. And no matter what we learn about Marcella, there won't be any outbursts. I refuse to pay for any more damaged property. Understood?"

Charity nodded and glanced at her father. Despite the fact that his blackened eye was now open and losing its ghoulish coloring, he looked tired and irritable. And he was clearly reluctant to let Dillon Devereau handle a matter he considered personal.

"All right, all right," Scott muttered. "Let's get this over with."

With what he hoped was an encouraging smile, Dillon took Charity's elbow and escorted them to the studio's door. She seemed a little nervous, yet he sensed she'd analyzed the contradictory facts about her mother's disappearance and had prepared herself for whatever story Mr. Henry might tell them.

A bell tinkled when he swung the door open, and a stout, congenial-looking man came out of the back room. "How may I help you folks this morning?" he asked in a deep voice.

Charity liked him immediately and wished they were here on more pleasant business. Mr. Henry had numerous photographs displayed upon his walls, and she decided they'd be a good diversion if the conversation became too embarrassing.

Dillon pulled the photograph of Marcella, Magnolia, and Powers from inside his coat and handed it to Mr. Henry. "We were hoping you could help us identify the women in this picture," he said, "and if possible, we'd like to know their whereabouts."

The photographer stroked his dark beard and chuckled softly. "I remember this one, all right. A rather unusual request—a prank, in fact." He glanced up, his expression still friendly yet warier. "What would you like to know?"

Sensing the man was protecting Erroll Powers's reputation when he had three strangers in his studio, Dillon shrugged. "They—or she—seem to have disappeared. It's rather urgent that we find her, and we'd appreciate any help you can offer."

Charity saw Mr. Henry's eyes widen slightly when he got a good look at her, so she turned toward the gallery on the wall. Back at the hotel, they'd agreed it was best for Dillon not to mention her relationship to the women in the picture, but her resemblance to Mama was too obvious to be ignored. Papa was wiping his spectacles furiously with his handkerchief, and she hoped a lens wouldn't pop out from the pressure he was applying to them.

Mr. Henry cleared his throat. "As you seem to have guessed, Mr.—?"

"Devereau. Dillon Devereau, from Kansas City."

The photographer nodded, pointing to Erroll and the woman standing next to him. "This was the original photograph, of Mr. Powers and Maggie. Shortly after it was taken, she came back and requested this particular printing using two negatives at once. For a practical joke, she said."

Noting that Charity was directing her father's attention to a large portrait across the room, Dillon continued. "So these women are one and the same? Maggie Powers?"

"Maggie Wallace," Henry corrected with a quick wink. "A fetching woman—quite photogenic, don't you think? But Mr. Powers isn't easily snared."

Dillon nearly choked on the irony of that statement, but he put aside his personal interests to finish his questioning before Mr. Henry grew suspicious. "So when was this taken? Do you recall?"

Pursing his lips, Mr. Henry thought for a moment. "It's been a number of years. Let me check my files."

The photographer disappeared into the back room, whistling under his breath. One look at Charity's pale face told Devereau she'd heard every word and was already piecing the puzzle together. The way Noah clenched and unclenched his fists was a sure sign this inquiry should be finished quickly. Dillon was about to ask if they'd rather wait outside, when Mr. Henry returned to the front counter carrying two square glass negatives.

"This shot of Maggie and Erroll is dated 1869," he said, pointing to the numerals etched near the bottom of the plate.

"Nine years ago. How about this one where she's sitting down?"

"The year before, as I recall. Yes," he said as he tapped the date on the glass. "And when she asked if the two images could be printed without looking patched together, and I explained how I would blend the background and soften any obvious lines as I printed it, she was delighted. Always demands the best and pays well for it, Maggie does."

That explained his suspicions about the pose

when Charity had first shown it to him. Devereau had heard more than enough, and he knew Noah was about to explode, but as he retrieved the photograph from the counter, Charity came up beside him. She seemed amazingly calm as she studied first one negative then the other.

"Do you remember if this earlier likeness was taken for any particular reason?" she asked in a tight voice. She could feel Mr. Henry studying her, so she looked him straight in the eye.

"As I recall, she originally came to Leavenworth hoping to hitch in with a wagon train," he replied carefully. "She put this picture in the store windows around town, hoping to find a sponsor, and Mr. Powers took her under his wing. You certainly resemble—"

"She's my aunt," Charity replied quickly. She was too hurt and confused to consider all the possible reasons for Mama's deception right now, but she was determined to learn all Mr. Henry could tell her.

"Maggie's an adventurous lady," the photographer continued with an admiring chuckle. "And judging from the difference in her clothing from the first photo to the next, I'd say she did very well for herself by keeping Erroll company rather than heading west. Couldn't rightly say where she'd be now, though. Sorry."

Charity let out a long sigh. She was only nine when Mama had sent her the photograph; she'd cherished it because she remembered Mama's simple dark skirt and white blouse, and had gazed wistfully at Aunt Maggie's fashionable gown. And now it seemed the two women were one and the same . . . a practical joke, indeed. She steeled herself for the answer to one last question. Pointing to a large photograph of a buckskinned Indian who held a rifle in one hand and a shaggy buffalo head under his other arm, she asked, "Is there any truth to the story about that man carrying Maggie off on his horse?"

Mr. Henry laughed out loud. "I introduced her to Jackson Blue because he escorted wagon trains when he wasn't hunting buffalo, and the next thing I knew they were galloping down Delaware on Satan—that's his stallion—and he threw her into the river. Maggie must've insulted him somehow, but not so badly that he didn't jump in after her. That escapade made them the talk of the town for weeks, because we all thought Blue was after an auburn scalp for his collection."

"That's quite a story," Dillon said when he saw that Noah Scott's face was turning crimson. "But if you can't tell us where Maggie might be, we'd better not take any more of your time. Thanks for your help, though."

He steered Charity and her father toward the door, and as the bell tinkled, he heard Mr. Henry call out, "Good luck finding her. If she's with Powers, she might be anywhere in the state of Kansas."

The door was barely shut before Reverend Scott cut loose. His face was a contorted red mask with a purple eye, and Dillon hoped he wouldn't kick in Mr. Henry's plate glass window. "Leavenworth must be a town full of *liars,*" he yelled. "If you expect me to believe—"

"Why should Mr. Henry lie?" Charity challenged under her breath. People were staring at them, and she'd suffered all the humiliation she could handle for one day. "It's not like we had to drag the information from him. And he had no way of knowing who we really were."

"Daughter, you know full well that your mother's been convalescing with Maggie and Erroll for the past—"

"That's what her *letters* say," Charity countered with the strongest voice she could muster. "Everyone in town seems to know her, and none of their stories coincide with—"

"Enough of your disrespectful speculations, Charity. Your mother was a devout Christian who would never stoop to such—"

"But Mr. Henry told us—"

"Idle gossip. There must be another woman who resembles Marcella, and I'm not leaving town till I find her," Noah declared. He gripped his lapels and paced in a tight circle. "I'll start at the newspaper office—find an obituary, or the story about that savage riding off with her. Your mother would *never* behave like the jezebel Henry described. She had no reason to."

He stalked across the street, kicking up a dusty wake. Charity watched him until he reached the *Bulletin* office, determined not to cry while Dillon was with her. A few minutes in a photographer's studio had brought her mother back to life, but they had also turned the past ten years into a charade—a deception so cunning Charity couldn't begin to unravel all the minute details Mama had woven into her stories about Aunt Maggie over the years. While she and Papa had assumed Magnolia Powers was the indefatigable nurse described so lovingly in Mama's letters, she was actually the mistress of a wealthy, handsome man—and she was Charity's own mother! What had happened to Mama's twin sister in the meantime? And what sort of scandalous acts had Mama and Jackson Blue engaged in?

"Sweetheart, I'm sure your father didn't mean to call us all liars," Dillon said gently. "Any man would have a hard time accepting his wife's brazen . . ." He stopped when Charity focused eyes like frosty green seas on him. Her face was pale, and he wasn't sure whether she was about to slap him or cry.

"Breaking her marriage vows, and taking on her twin sister's identity, and faking her own death may seem brazen to *you,* Mr. Devereau," she said quietly, "but can you really question *why* she did? *That's* what my father can't accept. And he obviously knows some things he's not telling us."

Dillon was stunned speechless. Was Charity summing up a lifetime of frustration in one singularly astute observation? Or had the truth about her mother sent her into shock? He took her gently by the elbow to escort her back to the Planters, but she began to tremble so badly she couldn't walk. When Charity leaned heavily on him, wracked by sudden, wrenching sobs, he swung her up into his arms and slipped into a nearby alley where she could cry more privately.

"You—you must think I'm a—a terribly ungrateful daughter," she hiccupped. "I—it was wrong to say those things about Papa, and—"

"Shhh. You've heard a lot of unsettling news today. And it's no secret that your father can be . . . rather trying," he murmured near her ear.

"—what Mama did was wr-wrong, too," she continued in a quavery voice. "But I meant it. I . . . was hoping Erroll and Maggie would ask me to stay awhile, so I wouldn't have to go back home. I—I'll probably go straight to hell for even thinking that way."

Despite Charity's blotchy face, red nose, and lashes that were matted with tears, Dillon felt inexplicably drawn to the sniffling waif in his arms. She'd searched out the truth about her mother without flinching, and passed judgments that were blatantly honest about both her parents, yet her innate goodness shone so brightly he was dazzled by it. He knew it made a strange sight, his leaning against the side of a store clutching a gingham-clad redhead to his chest, but he kissed her cheek anyway.

"I—I must look frightful."

"You'll get over it." He kissed the tip of her nose,

smiling when she brightened. "Feel better, now that you've gotten that load off your mind?"

She nodded, loving the intimate melody of his voice. "I really shouldn't have told you such personal—"

"My lips are sealed." The sunlight was dancing in her auburn hair, and Dillon considered taking her for a picnic by the river, or for a horseback ride across the open fields outside of town . . . or just slipping her into his bed, which was where all his fantasies about her led to anyway. But he'd be an inconsiderate fool to seduce her now, after she'd uttered what was undoubtedly the most shameful confession of her entire life. "Shall we walk around town?" he asked softly. "It's a lovely day, and—"

"I'd love to, Dillon, but I should wash out my clothes so they'll be dry by tomorrow. Something tells me we'll be heading home."

"You'll have time for laundry this afternoon," he coaxed. "I'll be playing poker, and perhaps your father will change his mind by then."

"You think he'll go after Mama?" Charity frowned and shook her head. "I doubt his pride would allow that. Now put me down so I can—"

Devereau clutched her to his chest so tightly she couldn't move. "I won't let you go until you say yes, Charity," he teased. "Leavenworth's quite a town, and I'd like to show it to you."

"Dillon, you—put me down!"

"A simple yes is all I need to hear."

Charity tried to push away from him, but he was holding her so firmly—and she was starting to giggle so hard—that all she could say was, "I can wait. You can't hold me this way forever, Mr. Devereau."

"What a tempting challenge," he replied with an arched eyebrow. "But you're right, I'd eventually have to shift you around . . . probably press you against this building and make love to you. Didn't I warn you never to go into alleys, Charity?"

The golden shine in his eyes told her Dillon Devereau wouldn't give in until he had his way with her, in one fashion or another, and her pulse fluttered at the notion that he, too, had thought about lovemaking. Charity kissed him chastely on the cheek. "Papa was right—you're only after my virtue," she said lightly. "So yes, I'll walk around town with you. It's my only decent alternative, isn't it?"

Could she possibly realize how her innocent smiles and sharp wit aroused him? Dillon gazed at her slender face, then deftly lowered her to the ground. "You're right, as usual," he said hoarsely. Then, before his thoughts could stray to the bed in his hotel room, he resolutely tucked her arm around his.

Since shopping was a pastime she seldom got to enjoy, Charity decided to put aside her jumbled thoughts about Mama. She'd have plenty of time to sort things out during the endless, empty weeks after she and Papa returned home. She listened attentively as her handsome escort told her about the shops and businesses they were passing.

"You remember Sol Goldstein? That's his bank across the street."

Charity looked at the impressive brick structure and smiled. "You have friends in high places, Mr. Devereau."

"In my profession, it helps to be on good terms with the money men," he replied with a wink. "Once in a while I come up short—you can't win *all* the time—but my banker friends know I'll make good. It's a matter of honor."

She suspected Devereau was capable of more underhanded schemes than she could count, yet the fact that he could admit to losing—and so graciously—made her admire him all the more. As they passed by a window filled with gilded bird cages, fine china, and other imported luxuries, Charity slowed down to take them all in. Crystal goblets glistened in the sunlight; everything had such a dazzling shine.

Seeing her wide eyes, Dillon reached for the door. "Shall we go in? This is B. C. Clark's china shop, and I'm sure he'd be pleased to see you again."

Charity shook her head. "No use in looking, when I could only *wish* for—"

"Your wish is my command," he said suavely, and he opened the door with a jaunty bow.

"But Papa would never let me keep—"

"You're eighteen, Charity," he murmured. "Accepting a gift from a friend certainly won't ruin your reputation. I'd like you to have at least one pleasant memory of this trip."

As they stepped inside the lavishly appointed shop, Charity's conscience tugged at her. So many fine things—how could she possibly choose a memento Papa wouldn't condemn as impractical or exorbitant? She saw Mr. Clark approaching them and smiled sweetly at Dillon. "I suppose he'd be less inclined to cheat you this afternoon if we at least bought *something,*" she whispered.

Devereau laughed and squeezed her shoulder. "Sounds like the perfect excuse to choose the most expensive item in the store. Get whatever you want, sweetheart."

He let her wander along the aisles while he chatted with Clark. After a moment, the storekeeper went to help another customer and Dillon was free to watch Charity. Her wistful gaze as she lightly touched hand-painted vases, porcelain lamps, and brass candlesticks made him want to buy the whole damn store for her. Most people came to Clark's to add a touch of imported gentility to their homes, pieces the likes of which this preacher's daughter would probably never see again. She paused, fingering a set of tortoiseshell combs.

"Those are perfect. Very becoming," he said as he walked up beside her. "What else would you like?"

Charity gaped at the price tag. "Oh, these are much too—"

"Nonsense. B.C.?" he called to the manager. "The young lady wants these combs. And if you have something else—perhaps a mirror and a hairbrush to match them?"

"Right over here, Mr. Devereau." Clark sauntered to the shelf to pick them up, smiling broadly at Charity. "Will there be anything else, Miss Scott?"

She swallowed and shook her head.

"These combs will look quite fetching in that pretty hair of yours," the shopkeeper commented as he wrapped the parcel. He glanced at Devereau and then back at Charity. "I hope the puzzlement concerning your mother has been satisfactorily solved?"

"Yes, sir. Thank you." She took the package and allowed Dillon to escort her outside before she vented her frustration. "Mr. Devereau, I *can't* let you spend so much—"

"It's my money, and I'll do as I please with it." Her eyes flashed with emerald lightning, warning him of the storm to come, so he gently gripped her shoulders. "Charity, it's impolite to object when a man gives you a gift with the most honorable intentions. Please indulge me," he added in a softer voice. "I rarely meet a woman I truly like."

His tawny eyes were so intense and his tone so earnest, Charity realized his kind words were the greatest gift he could possibly give her. "Thank you," she mumbled. "I like you, too, Dillon."

"Well, then," he whispered as he lifted her chin to give her a brief kiss, "there must be hope for a scoundrel like me after all. Shall we continue?"

She nodded, and as they strolled along the busy sidewalks, Charity felt as though they were floating in a fairyland. He bought her chocolates and lilac-scented soaps, and treated her to a dish of ice cream at a nearby saloon. Dillon was flirting openly with her—even suggesting they sneak into the public bath house together!—and she knew she'd remember every delicious minute of him weeks from now, when her days with Papa became unbearably stifling. They were almost back to the hotel when she noticed a strange movement in the crowd up ahead.

As Charity stared, a clown approached them, doing handsprings. His bright red pants were tucked into his boots, and he wore a huge polka dot shirt and white makeup all over his face. He stopped beside them, his red grin widening as he honked his bulbous nose.

"Afternoon, Miss Scott—Mr. Devereau," he added as he removed his silk hat. "As you can see, ma'am, there's nothing inside—nothing a-tall," the clown crooned while he deftly rolled the hat up one arm and down the other. "But oh—wait a minute . . ."

Charity squealed when he pulled a colorful bouquet of paper flowers from the hat and offered them to her.

"For you, pretty miss," he said as she took the bouquet. "And now, it's back to work. See you later, Dillon."

He sent the black hat spinning above them, and at precisely the right moment he ducked underneath it, grinned, and continued down the sidewalk on his hands.

Dillon chuckled, watching Charity eye the flowers as though they might disintegrate. "That was Enos

Rumley," he explained. "He works at Parker's where they carry circus and carnival supplies. A rather colorful fellow to have around, don't you think?"

She laughed, and when Devereau guided her up the stairs at the Planters, she deliberately slowed their pace. "I—I've had the most wonderful afternoon," she murmured.

"I'm glad." Dillon held her packages so she could unlock her door, then quickly brushed her cheek with a kiss. "I'll see you tonight after my game, all right? I imagine your father'll return anytime now, and he won't want *me* to be here."

He entered his own room and was surprised at how lonely he felt. Was Charity Scott already tugging on his heartstrings? As he changed into fresh clothing, he could hear a boy bringing her hot water . . . then she was bathing, or doing laundry—or both, judging from the constant splashing—and he grinned wickedly. Unless he missed his guess, Noah Scott was still avoiding his daughter's questions and assuaging his wounded pride, and wouldn't be back for hours. Meanwhile, Charity was alone and nude, since all her clothes would need washing. And he had an hour to kill before his card game.

He listened outside her door . . . she was humming in that low, seductive voice that drove him crazy. Dillon smiled and knocked softly.

Chapter 7

Charity froze and pulled her towel tightly around her. Papa wouldn't knock, which was why she'd arranged the Japanese screen around the tub, so who could it be? She stood staring toward the door, dripping, and decided that if she didn't make any noise, the visitor would go away.

"Charity, are you all right? I have a surprise for you."

"I'll *bet* you do," she muttered. Damn that Devereau! He knew she'd have to wash every piece of clothing she owned, so now he was playing tricks on her. Since he might be shameless enough to come in through the balcony window, she stepped quickly out of the tub and grabbed one of Papa's frock coats from the back of a chair. "I can't let you in, Mr. Devereau—as if you didn't know that," she called out.

Dillon swallowed a laugh. "I'd like you to go with me this afternoon, Charity. You'd be—"

"I don't play cards, Mr. Devereau," she replied as she briskly rubbed her wet hair with the towel.

"I don't expect you to. I—" He smiled politely at a man whom he recognized as the hotel's manager, and who was giving him a suspicious looking-over. "Please, sweetheart, let me in," he crooned. "People are staring at me."

Clutching the frock coat around her, Charity opened the door only far enough to glare out at him. "And what do you think *Papa* will do? If you're so concerned about—"

"We'll leave him a note. The game's at Sol Goldstein's, so it's not as though we'll be unchaperoned." Dillon wedged a foot and a hand into the doorway and gently pushed his way inside, noting the wet clothing that was hanging all over the room. Charity's red waves clung limply to the shoulders of a coat that dwarfed her; its sleeves bunched at her elbows and covered her hands, and its hem flapped loosely around her bare knees. He knew better than to laugh or tell her how adorable she looked, so he took an appreciative sniff as he glanced around the cluttered room. "You used your new soap. Lilac suits you."

"One generally uses soap when one bathes," she replied stiffly. The fact that Devereau was nattily dressed in a fresh white shirt and tan plaid trousers only made her feel more foolish and gawky as she stood trembling under his gaze. "Why did you *really* come over, besides to embarrass me to death?"

Dillon chased away thoughts about the fresh, feminine body beneath Noah's coat. "After our pleasant morning, I was hoping to spend some more time with you, Charity," he said with his best smile. "I won't be able to concentrate on my cards, knowing you're here alone, fretting over your mother's disappearance. You can be my good luck charm—my queen of hearts. She's always been my lucky card, you know."

Charity realized his dimpled grin and honeyed words were merely bait—a professional gambler didn't need a castoff like her for luck. But being with Dillon Devereau sounded like much more fun than waiting in this lonely room for Papa to return. "Even if I wanted to go," she pointed out, "I—I certainly can't wear *this.*"

He shrugged. "So don't wear anything. Black's really not your color."

"*Dillon!*" Charity grasped the coat tightly in one hand as she swung the door open. "I knew this was a mistake. Now get out of here before—"

"What if I told you there's a green satin gown hanging in my closet, waiting for just such an emergency?"

Charity's eyes flew open. "But I ruined it."

"Not at all. Katrina saw to it that the fabric dried properly, and it's as good as new." He stepped toward her with a smile. "And think how nicely your new combs will complete the outfit. But we really must hurry."

"Dillon, you're the most arrogant, demanding—" She gasped as he gripped her lapels and pulled her close, wearing a grin as devilish as any she'd ever seen.

"Kiss me, or you'll have to fetch that dress yourself," he teased in a low voice.

Her heart was pounding as his gaze wandered freely along her jaw and down the gaping neckline of the frock coat. "But I—I don't have any . . ."

Devereau kissed her hungrily, until she stopped struggling and returned his affection.

". . . underwear," she breathed when he finally let her go.

Dillon clung to her, laughing uncontrollably for several moments. "I won't tell a soul. I promise."

"But I *can't* go without any—"

"Had I thought about taking you to Sol's while we were shopping, I would've bought you some lingerie, sweetheart," he said as he fought a roguish grin. "Something silky and frilly—much more stylish than . . ."

Charity was ready to demand how he knew so much about her underthings, until she realized the plain muslin garments were openly displayed around the room. "Dillon," she whispered sheepishly, "it wouldn't be proper to go somewhere without—"

"Who'll *know?*" He searched her huge green eyes to keep from gazing at the delicate breast that was peeking out of Noah's coat. "The dress is dark, with several layers of fabric and trim. And the men'll be too engrossed in cheating me to notice anything's missing. Honest, honey. Why, if I thought a lack of lingerie would be obvious, I'd cancel the game rather than *think* of embarrassing you in public."

He was stringing her along again, and he sounded so willing to forgo poker that Charity had no doubt as to how he'd rather spend the afternoon. Dillon brushed her damp hair back with fingertips that trailed as softly as angel tracks along her neckline. When his lips followed the same path, making a bold new desire rush through her veins, Charity sucked in her breath. "You'd better hurry and get that dress, Dillon," she said in a strained voice. "If we arrive at Mr. Goldstein's late, your friends are bound to speculate about *why.*"

That she'd used his own words to avoid being seduced didn't surprise him; that she was actually going to Sol's took nerve few ladies possessed. Dillon quickly brought her the green satin gown and waited outside her door until she'd put it on. This was crazy. Why he thought he could play a respectable game of poker with her in the same room—even fully clothed, as he'd originally intended—was beyond him.

It was even more foolish to help her arrange her hair, but when he saw the breeze and sunlight playing in her waves as she brushed them by the open window, he couldn't keep his hands to himself. He secured her auburn tresses at the crown with the new combs, and then lovingly stroked them with the tortoiseshell brush until they were shiny and dry.

Charity smelled sweet and clean, and her smile of thanks nearly drove him to ravishing her right there on the floor.

During the buggy ride across town, Charity sensed that Dillon had gotten quiet because he, too, was on the brink of giving in to the greatest of all temptations. She tried to think of a topic of conversation that wouldn't sound suggestive, but what could she say? The man sitting beside her knew exactly what she wasn't wearing, and she had the feeling everyone they passed on the street knew, too. She flushed furiously.

"Are you all right?" Dillon asked. "This sun's awfully hot. I should've bought you a parasol this morning."

"It wouldn't make me feel any less . . . naked."

Pleased that she wasn't demanding they return to the hotel, Devereau took her hand. "Underneath their clothing, everyone's naked, honey," he quipped.

"But I feel so *depraved.*"

He chuckled and slowed the horse to a walk. "Most people are that way, too," he said. It was obvious she'd fidget the whole time she was at Goldstein's, thereby calling more attention to herself, unless he gave her something else to concentrate on. "I've got an idea—a way you can help me play better poker."

Charity glanced doubtfully at him.

Dillon considered his plan as he studied her expressive face. She'd never looked lovelier; Charity Scott was the picture of girlish innocence to which the fashionable green gown lent an air of sophisticated grace. But would she be too obvious? "We'll be playing in Sol's parlor," he began in a thoughtful tone, "and there's a sofa you can sit on. It's close enough for you to observe our play yet far enough away that we won't be distracted by your presence. At least not much."

His sly chuckle made a grin spread slowly over Charity's face. "And?"

"I want you to wait until the third or fourth hand and then drop something—one of your combs, perhaps—and lean down to pick it up."

She frowned. "And?"

Dillon laughed, because he could see she was as intrigued by his idea as he was. "Without being obvious about it, look at the underside of our table. If you see anything unusual, *don't let on,*" he added emphatically. "Simply ask Sol if you may play the piano. It's a beautiful thing—a baby grand."

Charity sighed and tugged her dress up by its shoulder. "What am I looking under the table for? I don't know a thing about gambling."

"If you see a spike sticking under there—or two or three of them—play . . . 'The Old Rugged Cross,' a verse for every nail you see," he said with a grin. "Sol's Jewish. He'll never make the connection."

She crinkled her nose. "Why would Mr. Goldstein have nails sticking under his table?"

"They're called holdouts, and they have slits large enough to hold a card or two until the player needs them."

"He'd cheat you in his own home? That's—"

"Those fellows are probably stacking the deck and planning their strategy this very minute," he replied. "I don't come to Leavenworth often, so they'll want to get even today. And when they see *you,* they'll assume I'm too enamored to pay close attention to the cards, and they'll get sloppy. It should be a short afternoon, actually."

His smug laugh confirmed her suspicions, and she withdrew her hand from his. "That's the real reason you brought me, isn't it?" she asked in a tiny voice. "To help you cheat."

Dillon saw the Goldstein home just ahead and thought quickly. "I won't be cheating, sweetheart—I won't *need* to. Once I figure out their game plan, I'll make them bid against themselves," he said with an earnest gaze into her eyes. She looked fragile and almost childlike, and he knew he'd better speak carefully or he'd lose her trust forever. "And I *do* want to be with you, Charity, because I think you'll enjoy this little caper—and because you'll pull it off splendidly. I've never let a woman help me play, and if I didn't feel completely confident in you, I'd have left you at the hotel. Please say you believe that."

Not sure just how much of his speech was sheer flattery, Charity nodded nonetheless. "May I ask you something, Dillon?"

"Certainly, sweetheart. Anything at all."

She gazed at the stately home they were approaching rather than at the devious rake beside her. "*Are* you enamored?"

Once again she'd twisted his own words with her innocence. Since he'd probably never see her after tomorrow, he was tempted to humor her with the line so many women fell for. But when Charity focused her deep green eyes on him, Devereau knew she'd see through any fabrication. "Honey," he began with all the honesty he could muster, "there are some cards a gambler never shows."

As Charity watched the four men lay down their cards at the close of the third hand, she gripped the book of poetry she was pretending to read. Despite the fact that Devereau had lost to each of his three opponents now, he seemed to be the only player who was enjoying himself. Clark, Goldstein, and Enos Rumley wore classic poker-faced expressions as they puffed on their cigars. Dillon shook his head good-naturedly when Mr. Clark collected all the chips from the center of the table, then he flashed her a wink, which the other men caught. When they glanced from her to Devereau, Charity returned her gaze to the poetry.

It was time: Sol was shuffling, and the men were exchanging small talk before the next hand. Charity laid the little volume in her lap to stretch, pointing her toes while she languidly lifted her arms above her head. As she'd hoped, the book slid down her satin skirt and thumped onto the parquet floor between her feet.

"I—excuse me," she mumbled when the card players looked her way. Her cheeks prickled with anticipation and she leaned over to retrieve the book, straightening a bent page until she thought the men had returned their attention to the game. A glance at the table's underside made her pulse pound: not one, but *three* spikes were wedged into it!

Charity sat upright, feigning interest in another poem until she felt a stare so strong she couldn't ignore it. B. C. Clark and Mr. Goldstein were looking fixedly at her bodice, and when she realized they'd seen something far more revealing than she had, her first impulse was to dash out the parlor door. Instead, she managed a demure smile. "Would—would you mind if I played your piano, Mr. Goldstein?" she asked in a low voice. "I rarely see such a fine instrument, and—"

"Certainly, Miss Scott. Please do," her host replied with an agitated smile. "Devereau's told us you put on quite a show—I mean . . ."

Clark and Rumley let out guffaws that they quickly muffled, but not before Charity blushed furiously. Glaring at Dillon, she crossed the richly decorated parlor and seated herself at the baby grand. She felt exposed and ashamed, as though she were parading before these strangers wearing absolutely nothing. As she positioned her hands on the keyboard, she realized she could best avenge her betrayal by giving Devereau the wrong cue. She'd play something loud and raucous, like the O'Leary girls performed at the Crystal Queen.

"Gentlemen, I resent your implications about Miss Scott's character, and the way you've misrepresented my comments about her as well." Devereau rose from his chair, looking sternly at each of his opponents until their snickers and grins disappeared. "Regardless of what you've heard about her mother, I assure you Charity is a proper young lady and a superb musician. If you continue to make lewd remarks, we'll leave. Because the way this game's going, I suspect my companion's not the only one who's being compromised here."

The parlor got extremely quiet. Sol Goldstein glanced at his partners, nervously clearing his throat. "It was a regretable slip of the tongue. I never meant to imply that Miss Scott—"

"We'll get on with our game now." Dillon looked over at Charity with an expression she couldn't read—amusement perhaps, masked by a gaze so intense she wondered if he'd guessed she was about to mislead him. When he sat down again, she began a quiet rendition of "The Old Rugged Cross." It was the polite thing to do, after he'd defended her honor before he could win his money back.

She was at the end of the second verse when the maid opened the parlor door to admit Jackson Blue. The fringe on his buckskins quivered when he came to a sudden halt, staring at her as she played. With a slight smirk, he strolled behind the poker players on his way toward the sofa, as though waiting for the hand to end before he spoke to them. Charity continued the hymn, and when she reached the final refrain his flute joined her, rising into an eerie descant that bobbed in triplets and odd rhythms she assumed were Indian harmonies. His instrument was primitive and it sounded flat with the piano, creating a discord that grated at her nerves. When she finished playing, she folded her hands in her lap and tried to ignore him.

"That was lovely, Miss Scott," the Indian said with a mocking bow. "What shall we try next?"

"Don't humor him," Dillon replied tersely. "He's half deaf from firing that buffalo gun for so many years, or he'd know how terrible he sounded."

Arching a dark eyebrow, the redskin studied Clark, Rumley, and Goldstein, and was met with icy smiles that nearly made Charity giggle. Then he focused on Devereau. "What a congenial group," he remarked. "About as fun-loving as a bunch of undertakers—and as passionate as a marriage of convenience. But let me clarify that, Miss Scott," Blue added with a sly smile. "Devereau's said time and again that marriage is *never* convenient for a man. Right, Dillon?"

Charity watched the suave blond add two more red chips to the kitty with a decisive flick of his wrist. "Did you come here expressly to distract us with your chatter?" he demanded of Jackson. "Or are you passing clues about my cards to these other gentlemen?"

The Indian's dark face froze over. "Excuse me. I must've come to the wrong house." He turned on his heel and strode out of the parlor without a backward glance, slamming the door behind him.

Charity winced, wondering what song she could play to lighten the oppressive silence in the parlor. Then Enos Rumley cleared his throat ceremoniously and fanned his cards out on the table. "If anybody can beat this full house, I'll eat my clown hat," he said with a chuckle.

Clark and Goldstein tossed their cards down with resigned sighs, but Dillon gripped his tightly. "I'm thoroughly disappointed," he said in a low voice. "I was telling Charity during our ride over here that you men were out for revenge, but I can't believe the amateurish way you've gone after it."

The three partners assumed cautious expressions and Clark spoke up. "What's wrong with Rumley's hand?" he asked. "Two queens and three eights. I suppose you've got something higher?"

Dillon stacked his cards facedown on the table. "I won't embarrass you by checking your vests or your sleeves—or the underside of the table," he added with a wry grin, "but I've got a queen of hearts identical to Mr. Rumley's in my hand. Call my bluff and it's worth five hundred dollars apiece—if I'm lying."

"And if you're not?" Goldstein challenged.

"I collect five hundred from each of you for every infraction of the rules I've seen in this game. Or you can cut your losses by cashing in your chips to me without any further discussion, and we'll call it even."

The men shifted in their chairs. After studying his stack of chips for a moment, Mr. Clark let out a short laugh. "How do we know that extra queen's not *yours,* Devereau? Wouldn't be the first time you slipped her in."

"I never mark my decks with a card pricker," he replied coolly. "And I think you'll find that both of these queens have rather pocky complexions."

Charity had no idea what they were talking about, but from the high stakes he'd set, she sensed Dillon had caught the men at a scam even worse than he'd predicted. After a moment Mr. Goldstein sighed and reached for his wallet.

"Count the chips," he muttered. "There's no sense in getting ugly at each other over a card game. But I wish to hell we'd *finish* one."

The other men reluctantly followed suit, and

after Dillon collected his winnings, he bid them all a cordial goodbye. He was whistling as he escorted Charity to the wagon, and after he vaulted up onto the seat beside her, he grinned broadly. "Not a bad day's pay for two hours' work. I'll split it with you, because without your help I couldn't have called them on their cheating so soon."

"Oh, I couldn't accept—"

"Then I'll buy you the best dinner in town—and one for your father, too, since he'll probably be waiting for us," he said as he clapped the reins across the horse's back. While they rode to the end of Sol's driveway, he noticed that she was fidgeting with the shoulder of her dress again. He knew better than to tease her about distracting the men with her cleavage, so he lowered his voice. "Sweetheart, I'm sorry my friends behaved so crudely today. I think Sol's remark really was inadvertant, but there was no excuse for Jackson's baiting you. It's to your credit that you remained a lady in spite of it all, and frankly, I think you make one helluva partner. That book was an ingenious prop—less obvious than your comb would've been."

Charity smiled, tempted to believe his compliments now that he was captivating her with his soulful brown eyes. "You really didn't need me, though," she pointed out. "Spotting the duplicate queen won your game, regardless of how many spikes I found for you."

"You're very perceptive for someone who's never played cards, Charity," he said with a chuckle. "But it was your piano playing that clinched it for me. I set them up in a bet I couldn't lose, yet left them a dignified way out after I caught them."

Charity shook her head, glancing at the tall brick buildings and the shoppers walking along Delaware Street. "One would hardly guess the four of you are friends," she mumbled. Then she looked at Dillon, wondering again how much he could hide behind the handsome, mustached mask she'd observed during the game. "*Did* you have a duplicate queen in your hand, Devereau?"

"Yes, I did."

"Did you plant it there?"

Dillon laughed out loud and hugged her to his side. "No, I did not," he said firmly. "I'm guessing Enos had the other one stashed in his holdout until he played his full house, thinking no one would realize he'd used cards from a second deck. A trick only a tinhorn would try."

Scowling, Charity was sure she'd never figure out the complexities of Dillon Devereau's profession. "But Enos seemed like such a nice man when he was in his clown costume this morning."

"None nicer. Has a wife and three little girls he gets downright gushy about," he replied. "But he's not as proficient a gambler as Clark or Goldstein. The fellows who try the most desperate tricks are usually the ones who can least afford to lose."

She nodded, feeling honored that Dillon was sharing his secrets as though he considered her intelligent and trustworthy—an equal. They were enveloped by the shadows of the livery stable, and Charity became very aware of his nearness as he guided the horse into an empty stall at the rear of the building. She longed to look into the future, to know if their paths would ever cross again after she and Papa boarded the steamer for Jefferson City tomorrow.

As though reading her thoughts, Dillon fastened the reins and turned to her. "I'm glad the poker game ran short," he murmured. "I'm looking forward to having dinner with you—to being seen with such a pretty young woman, even if her father's sharing the table with us. Please say you'll join me,

Charity. It'll make up for the unpleasant afternoon I put you through."

Charity lowered her eyes, too enthralled by the husky timbre of his voice to trust her emotions. "Actually, it was rather interesting to watch you play," she admitted softly. "Mr. Goldstein and the others *looked* ready to lose, from the dealing of the first cards."

"I have a reputation for being merciless," he said with a rakish grin. "I should've warned you, but it's too late now."

He claimed her lips, holding her so tightly she could feel the warmth of his hands through the satin gown. It was an intimacy she'd never experienced, and as his palms roamed over her back and shoulders, Charity let go of her inhibitions and kissed him as boldly as she knew how.

Dillon felt her offering up her heart and soul—her trust—and even though he'd be taking more than Charity really wanted to give, he couldn't resist the last chance he'd have to taste her sweet surrender. Slipping a finger beneath the neckline of her dress, he caressed her shoulder and let his hand drift lower, following it with hungry, urgent kisses. When he cradled the curve of her breast in his palm and then nuzzled its tender pink bud, he felt her tighten with apprehension. But instead of pushing him away, she ran her fingers through the hair at his nape and let out a tentative sigh.

Charity's heart was hammering so hard she thought it might burst. It was wrong to let Devereau touch her this way, yet even as his moist tongue teased her breast into a firm, aching peak she knew he'd stop—if she had the strength to ask him. She glanced nervously around the dusky stable but saw only horses and wagons. Dillon was fondling her other breast now, still caressing the first one while he took her into his wet, warm mouth. Charity giggled loudly before she could stop herself.

He glanced up, kneading her delicate roundness with inquisitive hands. "What's so funny?"

"Your mustache. It tickles."

Chuckling low in his throat, Dillon kissed her again and again, savoring her eager lips as he held her close. She kindled a need inside him, an undeniable desire that surpassed any he'd ever felt for women who'd lured him to bed with their practiced charms. "Charity," he breathed, "honey, the straw's much softer than this seat. Or the back of the wagon—we'd stay cleaner there, and no one'll see us. Your father will never suspect anything. I promise."

Even as he uttered the words, Devereau knew he'd said too much. The young woman in his arms stiffened as though the black-coated preacher were standing beside them, and her breathing became a rapid pant.

"Dillon, we shouldn't—Papa will *know,* even though we don't—"

"Shhh." He silenced her fears with a gentle kiss until he felt her relax. Then he looked into her wide eyes, disgusted with himself for calling up her father's image. "I've told you before I won't force you, sweetheart. But my God, knowing you were on that sofa at Sol's, wearing nothing under your dress, and now finally touching you, well it's . . ."

He turned her loose, raking his burning fingers through his hair to get control of himself. Then he gently tucked her breasts back into the bodice of her gown. "You're a very enticing young lady, Charity Scott. It's good I don't require much sleep, because I won't be getting any tonight."

Charity looked away, torn between feeling like a guilty little girl and a desirable, desired young woman. Dillon Devereau was quick with a compliment, yet his wonderful words rang with a conviction her heart heard very clearly. "Thank you—I think," she mumbled.

"You're quite welcome." He let out a long sigh, realizing that the heat of their embrace had left him smelling of her lilac soap—only slightly, but enough that it would drive him crazy all during dinner.

Chapter 8

"Thinking about your mother?"

Charity looked up from her dinner into Dillon's compassionate eyes and nodded. "The chicken and new potatoes are delicious," she mumbled. "I'm sorry I'm not being very good company."

"Nonsense. You can't help but feel bewildered after what you learned this morning." Devereau reached across the table for her hand. "I won't be the least bit offended if you don't want to talk. But if you need an ear, I'll be glad to listen."

Laying her fork at the side of her half-empty plate, Charity sighed. Now that the truth about Mama had sunk in, she felt more alone and confused than ever. And where was Papa? Surely he knew by now that there was no Marcella Scott look-alike; he'd had all day to face the fact that Mama had duped them. As she saw the shadows stretching across the sidewalk outside, Charity was haunted by the uneasy feeling that he, too, had abandoned her. It was a childish fear, one she couldn't admit to the handsome man whose lean, elegant hand was holding hers.

"I . . . I thought Mama and I were close," she said in a tiny voice. "She always encouraged me when my letters hinted that Papa had been in one of his moods. I could tell her how worthless and homely he made me feel, and she wouldn't write me a sermon about not respecting him."

Dillon didn't know who disgusted him more, Marcella or Noah, as he gripped her trembling fingers. "Charity, you are *not* worthless or homely," he insisted. "I know living with your father won't be easy, but you're old enough—resourceful enough—to strike out on your own and—"

"Why didn't she take me with her, Dillon? I wouldn't have told Papa what she was really doing."

Devereau's throat clamped shut. Once her initial shock had passed, Charity would realize why a cunning, beautiful woman like Marcella chose to run off with Erroll Powers alone, so he gave her a sympathetic smile. "Only your mother can answer that, sweetheart."

"And she *should* answer it—to my *face,*" she blurted. Then she turned away, embarrassed by her outburst. "I'm ruining this nice dinner. I'm sorry."

Even as she blinked back tears, Dillon found her extremely attractive. The candles brought out honey-colored highlights in her cinnamon hair, accentuating fragile features that made him want to protect her from sorrow and disappointment forever. It was a damn shame their last hours together would be spoiled by two parents who . . . he suddenly realized how he could make Charity's wishes—and his own—come true. "What would you think if I—"

"Mr. Devereau? Mr. Devereau, you'd better come quick!"

Dillon looked up to see a husky boy rushing gingerly between the linen-draped tables, a lad who did odd jobs for B. C. Clark and other shopkeepers. "What is it, Billy? Miss Scott and I are . . ."

The boy glanced nervously at Charity and then cupped his hand to Devereau's ear to whisper his message. She recognized Dillon's card-playing face immediately, and sensed she was being excluded because something horrible was happening.

"What's going on?" she demanded in a frantic whisper. "Is it Papa? Did they find him?"

Standing, Dillon gave her hand a firm squeeze. "Your father's fine, and I'm going to see that he stays that way. Wait here, in case he gets back before I do."

Charity was too stunned to argue. Dillon's commanding voice and piercing gaze left no doubt about the urgency of his errand—or that she'd suffer the consequences if she was foolish enough to follow him.

Devereau strode through the hotel's dining room and out onto the sidewalk, forcing himself to maintain the cool demeanor of his profession. Of all the idiotic, careless ways for Noah Scott to work off his anger—yet what the young messenger had whispered didn't really surprise him. As they came to a saloon halfway down the block, he clapped the boy on the shoulder and handed him a tip. "Thanks, Billy. I appreciate your help."

The boy's eyes lit up like Christmas, but Dillon had no time for chitchat. He stepped inside the crowded saloon and found that the situation Billy described earlier had deteriorated dangerously. In the back corner, Jackson Blue was dealing three-card monte, a game only swindlers and suckers engaged in, and Noah Scott had succumbed. The reverend's shirt clung damply to his back and his silver-streaked hair shook each time he jabbed his finger toward Jackson.

"You palmed the ace and switched it for that blasted deuce!" the clergyman accused loudly. He appealed to the crowd around him with outstretched hands. "You *all* saw it! The savage *cheated,* yet he won't return my money!"

Blue let out a derisive laugh. "If you knew I pulled a switch, why'd you bet a thousand dollars you don't have?"

"Because I'm on to your system! I caught you—"

"Mr. Scott, I'll give you one last round to redeem yourself," the buckskinned Indian said as he deftly shuffled the deck. "Three new cards—we've got a king, a four, and a jack, so the king's the baby," he sang out as he laid the cards on the table. "All new, all unmarked, but watch the baby closely because my hands *are* quicker than your eye, sir."

Dillon let out an irritated sigh and eased between the customers who were watching the contest with avid glee. Jackson had flipped the cards facedown and was slipping them over and around each other with the adroitness of a carnival huckster, while Scott leaned on the table to follow the movement closely. "Noah, three-card monte was designed to relieve fools of their money," he said as he came up beside the preacher. "And fools who can't pay—"

"Shut up," Noah snapped. "You're distracting me so this piece of red filth can switch the cards when I'm not watching."

Violence wasn't a tactic Devereau resorted to often, but he was ready to strangle both Scott and Jackson. Charity had been fretting about her father all evening, and here he'd been throwing their money away in an attempt to regain his self-esteem—and Blue was taking advantage of him. Dillon struck like a snake, grabbing the Indian's wrist so forcefully he dropped the cards. "Enough!"

"This isn't your concern, Devereau," Jackson snarled as he shook himself from Dillon's grasp. "I've given Scott every chance to break even—and he did about an hour ago—but he just wouldn't quit. Which card's the king, Preacher Man?" he jeered at Noah. "If you're as good at bending God's ear as you claim to be, you could transform all *three* cards to kings!"

"That's trifling with the Lord's—"

"And you're trifling with my patience—*both* of

you!" Devereau said as he snatched the cards off the table. "I'll settle with you later, Jackson. And Mr. Scott, you're coming with me. Your daughter's worried sick, and I intend to return you to her in one piece, so you can explain your absence yourself. Let's go."

Noah Scott paled slightly and adjusted his spectacles. "You wouldn't dare tell her I've been—this is the first time I've ever—"

"People go to hell for lying, Reverend," Dillon muttered as he prodded the clergyman through the snickering crowd. "You were gambling the night you got your eye blacked, too—*weren't* you? Didn't need your glasses to read the cards, so when you'd lost all the donations you collected and couldn't pay your wages, the bouncer slugged you to get rid of you. How far off am I?"

Scott grabbed his coat from the back of a chair on his way through the saloon door. "Men of the cloth often gamble," he stated defensively. "Why, a friend of mine once won enough at poker to build a new church after a fire destroyed the old one."

"That may be true, but he obviously had sense enough to quit a winner. How will you explain to Charity that you don't have steamer fare?" Dillon demanded. "She won't believe you were mugged twice in the same week."

Noah Scott gripped his lapels, widening his dark eyes ominously. "If you breathe a word of this to her, you'll shatter her ideals—tear her sheltered world and our poor little family apart. Do you want that on your conscience, Brother Devereau?"

He was about to ask how the hypocritical clergyman lived with his own conscience when Jackson Blue stalked out of the saloon, scowling. "We're settling up. I'm not letting this sleazy preacher slip out of town before I've got my money."

Devereau looked from the angry Indian to the

man beside him and knew they'd be bickering all night unless he dealt with them separately. "Go back to the hotel, Noah," he instructed as he reached for his wallet. "Wait for me in the lobby—and don't let Charity see you, because we've got things to discuss that you won't want her to hear. Such as how you're going to reimburse me for getting Blue off your back."

The clergyman stalked away, leaving him to deal with the towering scout who'd been known to lift grown men from the sidewalk and heave them through plate glass windows—with one hand. "How much did you stick him for?" Dillon demanded.

"Two thousand."

"*What?* How'd you plan on getting blood from that turnip, Jackson? That man—"

"Which doesn't include the round you interrupted," Blue added as he crossed his arms. "All sport went out of it when I knew he was broke, but he kept coming at me for one more play to win it all back."

Devereau didn't doubt what his buckskinned friend was saying, but his motives irritated the hell out of him. "Here's a thousand—no more," he said in a low voice. "Next time keep your damn deck in your pocket."

"But I won it fair and—"

"The only time you pitch monte is when you find a sucker so rank he sweats money," Dillon pointed out. "And today you went after Scott to get even with *me,* after you made an ass of yourself at Goldstein's."

Jackson grinned slyly. "What the hell was that about, anyway? Those men don't have the slightest suspicion that you and my flute and I are partners."

"But having *two* spotters gets a bit obvious—and I was already on to them when you arrived."

"Are you telling me . . ." The Indian narrowed his piercing black eyes and leaned against the corner of the saloon building. "Since when do you let a *woman* in on your game? She would've given you away the first time Sol Goldstein looked at her cross-eyed."

"Charity's sharper than you think," he replied proudly. "She spotted the holdouts under the table, and followed our plan without batting an eye. And without being insulting and obnoxious."

"What was I supposed to do?" Blue retorted. "I came to offer my assistance, *knowing* those three jokers planned to clean you out, and—"

"And you made a nuisance of yourself. Had to dig pretty deep for that comment about marriage not being convenient, didn't you?" Devereau saw the anger smoldering in his friend's dark face and suddenly realized what was behind this entire argument. "You're jealous! Of a *preacher's* girl!"

"Well, you're in *love* with her," Jackson jeered, "and that's a helluva lot more dangerous, Devereau. You bailed her old man out to protect her from what he really is—came to Leavenworth to be with *her,* because you couldn't possibly give a damn about finding her mother. Am I right?"

Dillon saw no reason to dignify his friend's accusations with a reply when he needed to be talking to Noah Scott. "What about Marcella—or Maggie, as you know her?" he asked. "Where would she and Powers have gone? I'm guessing they're both up to no good."

Blue laughed wickedly. "Why should I tell *you?* You owe me a thousand bucks, pal." He straightened to his full height and looked smugly down at Dillon. "If Charity's anything like her mother, you might not be man enough to handle her, Devereau. And I've got better things to do than speculate about where some preacher's whore might chase off to next. Good luck. You'll need it."

It wasn't the first time Jackson Blue had dismissed him with a cocky remark, and Dillon sensed the scout had not only cost him precious time but would also interfere with the plan he'd been considering at dinner. He watched until the Indian's tall form disappeared around a corner, and then hurried through the twilight to find Noah Scott. His conversation with the reverend would determine his future—if he had one—with Charity, and he'd probably have to toy with the truth a bit to arrange things the way he wanted them.

To his relief, he saw Scott sitting in a wing chair in the Planters lobby, alone. Devereau wondered how such a worldly, intelligent man had remained unaware of his wife's brazen affair for ten years—had presumedly financed her stay at the Powers estate, but had never gone to visit her. Or was ignorance merely another of the complex clergyman's acts? Dillon wasn't surprised to see the preacher raise a whiskey glass to his lips, but he decided to forgo a drink himself until he could afford to relax. He slipped into the chair beside Scott, reminding himself to keep his aversion to the man under control. "I took care of Blue," he said quietly. "He won't bother you again."

Noah glanced at him sullenly.

Devereau decided there was no point in skirting the issue when Charity might happen upon them at any moment. "What do you plan to do now? I'm sure it was a shock to learn that your wife—"

"I'm returning to my pulpit, where I belong. The woman's made her bed and she'll lie in it."

Scott's insufferable attitude had Devereau ready to black his other eye. "I just paid Blue a thousand dollars not to beat you to a pulp," he said in a tight voice. "I'm considering it a loan, not a gift, so how do you propose to pay for your passage home? Or were you smart enough to keep some money in reserve for steamer fare?"

The preacher tossed the last of his whiskey down his throat. "Charity still has the money you paid her for singing—your idea, I believe," he added with vinegar in his voice. "If that's not enough, I'll set up a revival. I can count on—"

"Your letter about Marcella's murder won't work any more, Scott," Dillon stated coolly. "You don't have enough female followers here to fill the tent, and even if you did, their husbands will hear about today's escapades and keep them at home. Your credibility's shot."

Noah scowled. "Are you implying I don't have the wherewithal to support myself, just because my wife's been hoodwinked by some scoundrel in a fancy suit? I'll have you know that for twenty years—"

It was useless to correct the preacher's assessment of Marcella's affair, so Devereau cast his first line. "I'm offering you a chance to reunite your family, Noah," he began in a low voice. "I'm willing to help you locate Marcella, and I'll finance the trip."

The preacher let out a mirthless laugh. "Why would I want to find her? My parishioners assume she's dead, and it's just as well."

It was obvious that Scott would never admit to his flock that he'd been cuckolded, so Dillon attacked his pride on another front. "I'd think you'd see it as your Christian duty to go after your wife—rescue her from Erroll's wicked influence. Charity's bound to wonder why you aren't trying to save your marriage, since your whole ministry's based upon the sanctity of the family."

"You keep my daughter out of this. I don't have to answer to her—or to you."

In his mind's eye he saw Charity's forlorn, tear-filled eyes and could tolerate no more. Devereau leaned forward until his face was nearly touching Noah Scott's, his voice a harsh whisper. "You are the most selfish, conceited—*poorest* excuse for a father I've ever seen," he began, "and as though forbidding her *my* company wasn't enough, you *abandoned* her this morning, because you were too damn proud to admit Marcella had *plenty* of reasons to run off with another man. Never mind that Charity felt betrayed and deserted when she found out about her mother's—"

"She's an obedient daughter. She went to our room to pray about it—unless *you* led her astray," he added accusingly.

"That's not the point," Dillon spat. "When she needed you most, you left her. And because of you, her mother left her, too. Charity deserves better from both of you, and I intend to see that you at least *try* to bring Marcella back. I'll pay for the trip, no matter how far we have to go, but unless you speak with your wife, the interest on that thousand-dollar debt's going to add up pretty damn fast."

Reverend Scott's eyes rolled theatrically. "This is none of your business, Devereau," he said as he stood up, "so Charity and I will be on our way tomorrow. I have no reason to accept your ridiculous offer. I didn't *ask* you to pay that savage off."

Dillon rose and looked him squarely in the eye. "Fine. By the time you've boarded the boat, I can telegraph everyone I know along the Missouri River—plus some influential statesmen in Jefferson City. And when your congregation hears that your gambling drove Marcella to adultery, they'll shun you like you were Satan's twin. Is that how you want your illustrious career to end, Reverend Scott?" he asked pointedly. "And how will you explain it to Charity?"

The preacher glared at him for several seconds,

but Devereau could see the argument was over.
"Why are you doing this?" Scott demanded.

"I have my reasons. Go console your daughter—she's been worried about you all day."

With a final scowl, the preacher walked slowly toward the hotel's stairs. Dillon watched him until he felt the surge of disgust ebbing and rational thought returned. Why *had* he launched such a crusade, entangling himself in the private affairs of a couple he neither liked nor respected? When Charity answered her father's knock, throwing her arms around his waist, he had part of his answer.

But the rest of his motives had nothing to do with the willowy redhead who'd so quickly captured his fancy. As he headed for the livery stable, he considered the bizarre facts that had presented themselves today. Any woman who would patch two photographs together to deceive her family, and then fake her own death, had undoubtedly hoodwinked Erroll Powers as well.

Hoodwinked . . . Dillon chuckled at the Reverend's term. Marcella Scott was as slippery a character as he'd ever encountered, and she probably had designs on Erroll's fortune—perhaps planned to kill him for it and continue west, where she'd never be traced. And now that Powers had surfaced again, Devereau had no intention of letting a preacher's wife prevent him from getting the revenge he'd wanted for half his life.

A pair like Erroll and Marcella would be hard to track: they could be anywhere in Kansas, as the photographer had said, or they could be amassing another crooked fortune along the Transcontinental Railroad. His only advantages were that Marcella wasn't expecting her husband and daughter to be on her trail, and that Powers couldn't resist a beautiful woman or the chance to swindle somebody.

Charity's unstudied loveliness came to mind, and as Dillon saddled a horse and cantered along the moonlit streets, he knew his mission would be an adventure if not a success, as long as she was beside him.

Charity sighed as she slipped into her gingham dress. The first glow of dawn was lighting the edges of the curtains and she hadn't gotten much sleep. Papa had shaken her awake and was shaving hurriedly. He'd said little when he returned last night, except that they were leaving this morning. He'd prayed long and loudly for Mama's soul and God's guidance, and then he'd gone to bed.

Her heart sagged, because she'd seen the last of Dillon Devereau. He'd returned only a few minutes ago, and she could hear him splashing over his basin. Then he crossed his room several times—packing, probably—and she wondered how he moved so quickly on so little sleep . . . or perhaps he'd slept elsewhere. He had several friends in Leavenworth, and she'd be foolish to think some of them weren't women.

Sighing again, Charity glanced at the green dress, which was hanging on the bronze door hook. She'd had some of the happiest times of her life in that gown, but it was probably best to let the dapper rogue who gave it to her fade into a pleasant memory. Dillon Devereau was long on flattery and short on answers—the way he'd evaded her question about love and Jackson Blue's comment about marriage proved that plainly enough.

It was senseless to mope about a man who was so far out of her league anyway. Since Papa had no patience for packing, she began to fold their clean clothes into the suitcases, so she wouldn't annoy him by not being ready on time. She had the feeling she'd spend the next several weeks avoiding his moods.

As a single, sorrowful tear dripped down her cheek, someone pounded so loudly on the door that Papa cursed when he cut himself. Charity answered it, and saw Dillon's dimpled grin.

"Pack your bags, sweetheart," he said with a mischievous chuckle. "Our train to Abilene leaves in an hour."

Chapter 9

The train was nearly a mile from the station before Charity stopped studying her surroundings to flash Dillon a smile full of wonder. She was seated across from him, her jade eyes asparkle as she gazed at the car's stylishly papered walls and padded seats. It was obviously her first ride on the rails, and Devereau enjoyed watching her peer at the passengers across the aisle, and smile shyly at a man in a tattersall suit who was glancing her way. Beside her, Noah glowered. It was obvious he was aboard only because his reputation and career were at stake.

"Isn't this *fun?*" Charity breathed as she looked out the window. She was fascinated by the rapid passing of amber wheat fields and telegraph poles as the train hurtled along the tracks.

"Ridiculous," her father muttered. "We're chasing across Kansas after a—"

"Well at least Mama's not *dead!* We have a chance to straighten things out and bring her back home."

Charity's voice pulsed with a mixture of shock and hope and duty, and Dillon's heart went out to her. She was trying to make sense of a situation that defied every moral and spiritual principle she'd been raised with, a task Reverend Scott had already deemed useless.

"Your mother's been pulling the wool over our eyes for many, many years, daughter," he replied with a pointed look in Dillon's direction. "She won't be found if she doesn't want to be. And who's to say she'll be in Abilene?"

Both of the Scotts looked at Dillon, their faces expectant, as he decided which details of his answer to leave out. The passenger car was nearly full, and if Noah became irritated, every person on board would bear the brunt of his rantings. "I went back to the Powers estate last night," he began quietly, "because I figured the maid might let something slip, even if she wouldn't tell me Erroll's itinerary straight out."

"And she asked you in?" the preacher demanded.

Recalling how the barrel of the colored woman's rifle had glistened in the moonlight, Devereau smiled. "Not exactly. It was late, and rather than answer the door in her nightgown, she leaned out the window above me," he said. "I told her how urgently we wanted to talk to Maggie—that you were *family*, and needed to find her immediately."

"What did she say?" Charity whispered earnestly.

"*Even if I knowed where she was, nobody—not President Grant nor Jesus Christ hisself—could drag that from me at this hour*" were her exact words, but he couldn't admit that to the Scotts. "You can understand how she'd be afraid of losing her job for divulging such information," he replied with a shrug. "But she did mention that Mr. Powers intended to conduct some Kansas Pacific business at each major station along its route. Which means Abilene is the first logical place to start tracing them."

"It's unlikely they'll still be there, and you *know* it," Scott muttered. His voice was rising with his color as he glared at Devereau. "Marcella's long gone, and it's a waste of my—"

"Where do *you* think she is?" Dillon challenged. "We don't have to stop in Abilene. We'll keep right on going to wherever you'd care to look for her."

Up to this point, Charity had been too fascinated

by the passing countryside to think about anything else, but the animosity between Papa and the gambler sitting across from them was now too heated to ignore. Once again her duty to her father pulled her in one direction while her infatuation for Dillon Devereau tugged her in another. "It sounds like a boring trip, traveling between dusty old cowtowns to conduct railroad business," she said, her voice barely audible above the clackety-clack of the train. "Not the sort of excitement Maggie Wallace must be accustomed to. Not worth leaving her home and family for."

Could she possible suspect the truth? Dillon studied her sorrowful expression, but saw only the pain of being abandoned in her glistening eyes. He vowed that when they caught up with Marcella, she would answer to her daughter—a vow he hoped they wouldn't arrive too late to keep. For Charity's sake, and because Noah Scott would call off the journey in a rage, Dillon couldn't tell them the one piece of new information Erroll's maid had revealed in their midnight conversation. With a white-toothed grin, she'd exclaimed, *"I cain't rightly say when they's to be back, Mr. Devereau. I's just pleased that Miss Maggie and Mr. Erroll's finally gonna quit their carryin's on—and on HIS money, they might be honeymoonin' for a long, long time."*

"I can't imagine why she'd leave you either," Devereau replied gently. "But you wanted to hear her reasons for yourself, and I've agreed to help you find her. That's a promise I'll keep for as long as you want me to."

"You've been very generous, what with leaving your casino and now buying our tickets," she mumbled. "We'll never be able to repay you, Mr. Devereau." A sharp elbow in her side made her look at Papa, whose fierce glare appalled her. She tried to think of an appropriate response, but all she could gasp was, "What's the matter? Don't you *want* Mama back?"

Her father scowled and looked away. "You've no right to ask such an impertinent question, daughter. This is neither the time nor the place to discuss it."

In the twinkling it took for Noah Scott to formulate his rebuff, Dillon's suspicions were confirmed: the Reverend had already known that Marcella wasn't the invalid she pretended to be. But why would a man—especially a man of the cloth—allow such a lie to tear his family apart? And how could a stern, self-righteous husband tolerate a wife who strayed so flamboyantly?

Devereau realized now that he'd seen the answers to these questions when Noah's eye was blacked in Kansas City, and last night when he'd rescued the preacher from Jackson Blue: compulsive gambling. The circumstances didn't dovetail perfectly—Scott had been genuinely shocked at the details of his wife's charade, and humiliated by her legendary antics—yet Dillon sensed the preacher's own secret vice had driven Marcella away years ago. That Charity was the victim of *both* her parents' self-serving obsessions only made Devereau more determined to see that she got the explanations she deserved, and to protect her when Noah and Marcella finally confronted each other.

For several minutes the three of them sat in oppressive silence. The train's rhythmic clatter seemed to intensify the strain between Papa and the dapper blond across from them, and his silent indignation gnawed at Charity, too. Her father had sent Mama to live at her sister's—claimed it was Maggie's Christian duty to care for her, and that they would make do at home without her—yet now that Mama had assumed the identity of Maggie Wallace, Papa seemed all too ready to let Erroll Powers have her. Her mother's behavior was inexcusable, even though Charity understood why she wanted to escape Papa's domineering ways. But why was Papa just letting her go? Was he too proud to face a woman who'd gotten the best of him, or did his grudging acceptance of the situation point to problems she didn't know about—problems Papa didn't *want* her to know about?

Charity was glad when a uniformed conductor came by. "Morning, folks," he said as he punched their tickets. "Everything all right here? There's a newspaper or two and some magazines at the front of the car, if you're interested."

"We're fine," Noah answered stiffly.

Charity smiled at the man, and couldn't help noticing how he gave Dillon a quick, appraising glance and then reached into his jacket pocket. When he returned their punched tickets, there was a slip of paper on top of them. Curious, Charity leaned closer to Papa to read the note as he unfolded it: BEWARE OF PROFESSIONAL GAMBLERS AND CARD SHARPS ON THE TRAIN. She giggled quietly, despite Papa's obvious annoyance.

Dillon tucked his punched ticket inside his coat, pleased to see her smiling again. "Let me guess," he said. "The conductor just warned you about unscrupulous characters and their cards. I suppose since we're riding with so many cowpokes and farmers, my clothes were a dead giveaway."

Charity had been admiring the gambler's deep green frock coat all morning; his ruffled shirt and tapestry vest, crisscrossed with an elaborate gold watch fob, did indeed set him apart from the rest of the passengers. "But why—"

"Once the railroad started transporting people who used to ride the riverboats, gamblers began traveling by train as well," Devereau explained. "I used to earn my keep on the river, and even dealt a few hands along the Transcontinental Railroad.

But I was too honest—got hustled myself, by bloodthirsty sharps with bigger bankrolls than mine. So when I won the Crystal Queen from Abe Littleton, I knew I'd be foolish not to stay put for a while."

Charity's eyes widened. The fact that he'd been crossing the country by water and rail as a professional card sharp, probably when he was her age, made the handsome man across from her seem even more exotic.

Her father grunted. "Hardly a past to be proud of, Devereau. You've been cheating people for more than half your life."

With a chuckle, Dillon reached inside his vest pocket. "Not quite. I left home when I was sixteen, and I'm now twenty-eight," he replied as he riffled a deck of cards between his nimble fingers.

Her father let out a snort, yet he was as mesmerized by Dillon Devereau's quick, dextrous movements as Charity was. The whole deck was in constant motion, slender sections turning in opposite directions between his hands before suddenly falling into place with a shiffling sound that brought them into a single pack again. "Did you meet Mr. Clark and the others during your travels?" she asked quietly.

"I first met Sol Goldstein on the Mississippi. Rumley and Clark wandered into the saloon where I was dealing faro, in Abilene," Dillon replied.

"And left without their money?"

"Precisely," he said, wishing the adoring grin she now wore would grace her face forever. "And we've been trading small fortunes ever since."

Charity laughed, and she couldn't resist asking a few more questions, even though Papa might interrogate her about where she'd spent yesterday afternoon. "I . . . I think I understand how they were using those holdouts to gang up on you," she began cautiously, "but what was it you said about the duplicate queen Enos slipped into the deck?"

Seeing that the Reverend was interested enough not to chastise Charity for such a query, Devereau reached over to the wall and pulled a narrow wooden table down between himself and the Scotts. They immediately scooted closer to it, so he used the situation to his advantage. "If you recall, I mentioned that the queen in question had a pocky complexion," he explained with a smile. "She was marked with a card pricker, which is a small metal device that embosses the surface with however many dots you care to make, according to your marking system."

"I suppose you own such an instrument," Noah commented dourly.

"Every professional has his box of tools," Dillon replied. "Most of them contain prickers, corner shavers, loaded dice, a holdout or two—devices that aid Lady Luck when one's opponents are cheating. I'd be happy to show you my collection of gadgets, but it's packed away."

"So I'm to conclude that you're too *honest* to use such devices?" the preacher asked sardonically.

Devereau laughed. "They're not something I pull out in public, sir. And unless I'm playing other professionals, I don't need them. Plenty of ways to play a square game and come out ahead of a tinhorn."

Charity watched him slide three cards from the deck and flip them faceup in front of her.

"One game, called three-card monte, is particularly lucrative," Devereau was saying, "and as long as you have agile hands, you win every time. For this round, we have a queen, a ten, and a deuce, so we'll call the queen the baby, because she's high. Watch carefully, so you can pick her out when I tell you to."

She felt Papa stiffening beside her, but Charity

was too intrigued to look away from what Dillon was doing. Could this possibly be gambling? He'd flipped the cards facedown, and was doing a flat juggling act, moving each card around the others in a pattern that made keeping track of the queen very easy indeed. When he stopped, she pointed to the center card. "That one."

"Absolutely correct." Devereau grinned at her as he showed the red queen's angular face. "Had you bet money on it, you would've won."

"That was too simple. There must be more to it."

With a furtive glance at Noah, whose face registered an ill-concealed loathing, Dillon shuffled the three cards back into the deck and dealt new ones. "Monte dealers usually let their customers win the first round or two, and they sometimes act clumsy or simple-minded, so people believe they're incapable of any sophisticated trickery. Ace of clubs, jack of hearts, and a four. Which one's the baby, Charity?"

"The ace."

"You're quick," he said with a grin. "But not as quick as the dealer. Never forget that."

The gambler followed a slightly different juggling pattern with the three cards, but at a speed that astounded Charity. She quickly lost track of the ace and gaped at his fingers, which were moving so fast they seemed to blurr before her eyes. When the cards came to rest, she shook her head. "I've no idea. The left one?"

Devereau smiled craftily. "Would you care to hazard a guess, Reverend Scott?"

Papa shifted, making a disgusted noise in his throat. "I've been told that dealers resort to sleight-of-hand, so the ace probably isn't even on the table. Trickery of the lowest sort."

Stifling a laugh, Dillon turned over the card on

Charity's left. "Once again, your daughter's instinct has served her well. Here's your ace, Charity."

Her low laugh made him wish he had no more serious pursuit in the days ahead than entertaining Charity Scott. She tilted her head, her auburn waves brushing her shoulders as she gave him a teasing grin. "You can't really switch cards that way, can you? Nobody could shuffle them around *that* fast."

His response was a dimpled grin that told her he'd pulled such a magician's trick many, many times. In awe she watched hands that were too quick to be human flick the cards into the deck, shuffle three more onto the table top, and stop, poised around the deck they held.

"Where's the baby?"

Charity hesitated. "Is it that little man?"

"The joker," Dillon said with a nod, "which we high rollers call the cuter. Watch him closely—he's about to disappear."

The man across the table repeated his quick manipulations on the table top, making the cards whisper seductively. When he coughed, Charity noted his utterly expressionless face, which seemed not to belong on the same body with the hands that defied watching.

"Did I switch a card?"

"I—I couldn't tell," Charity admitted.

"He did it when he coughed," Noah said darkly. His eyes were hard and resentful, and he stood up. "Rather than waste my time in such useless pursuits, I prefer to read the paper. You should consider doing the same, daughter."

As the preacher approached the front of the car with a cautious, rhythmic shuffle, Dillon saw Charity's face tighten. She nibbled her lower lip—a lip he found extremely erotic, even with dozens of passengers sitting around them—and he reached for her hand. "It was never my intent to corrupt you, sweetheart. Shall I put my cards away?"

She blinked. "No, of course not. You were only helping us pass the time."

Devereau kept a grin in check. He'd shown her three-card monte to irritate her father, and to win some time alone with her. He tightened his hold on Charity's childlike hand. "Do you want to call off the search? We could turn around in Abilene—as your father pointed out, I can't guarantee we'll ever catch up with your mother. I have a feeling the two of you haven't talked much about it."

Charity laughed ruefully. "There's no talking to Papa when things aren't going his way. He was all set to take the steamer home, so I'm surprised he even got on the train this morning."

He couldn't tell her Noah was aboard only because he'd threatened the preacher's ministry. Their search for Marcella Scott and Erroll Powers would probably take weeks, and he wanted to be certain Charity was as committed to the journey—no matter where it might lead or what they might find—as he was. "Is there something else you'd like to talk about?" he asked gently. "You seem preoccupied, perhaps about a subject you can't discuss with your father."

The warmth from his hand was already working its spell, and when Charity looked into Dillon Devereau's tawny eyes, she realized that he could read people as easily as he read a deck of cards. "Now that I've had a chance to think about Mama's lies, something's puzzling me," she began hesitantly. "You see, there's another photograph in Papa's bedroom—a likeness of Mama and Maggie, taken when they were very young, and it couldn't have been faked."

Dillon considered this carefully. "So she does have a twin? When your father admitted he'd never seen Maggie, I thought perhaps your mother had been . . . well, lying to him ever since he met her."

"Not about that," Charity replied with a shake of her head. "She used to tell how Maggie was always the favorite, so ladylike and well behaved—at least when their parents were watching—so they sent her out East to a fashionable finishing school. Meanwhile, Mama had attended some of Papa's revivals and married him. How she met Mr. Powers, I don't know, but I remember she went to visit her sister a few times when I was very young, and I wanted more than anything in the world to travel along with her." She sighed under the sheer weight of Mama's lies and looked at Dillon again. "Now that we know what Mama's really been doing, what do you suppose has happened to my aunt?"

Devereau enfolded her fragile hand between both of his and gave Charity his most sympathetic smile. As a man who'd won fortunes on the strength of a bluff, he knew the best lies were spun from the truth. Marcella Scott had fashioned her secret life into such a finely woven tapestry he wondered if she herself could differentiate between fact and falsehood by now. "Maggie's just one more thing we'll have to find out about when we locate your mother," he replied gently. And silently he added, *I hope to God we find her in time.*

Charity nodded, soothed by the long, supple fingers that were kneading hers. They were never still, those gambler's hands, and a glance at the table reminded her of the monte demonstration that had been interrupted when Papa left. She turned the three cards over, one by one. "You didn't switch these at all, Mr. Devereau. The cuter's right here, whether you coughed or not."

Dillon laughed and picked up his deck, eager to entertain her again. "Monte dealers have endless ways to divert their customers' attention, but I prefer something less conspicuous than a cough or a sneezing fit. I can usually palm a card fast enough that only a skilled observer will spot the switch."

Once again Charity watched him juggle the three cards on the table top while still gripping the deck. When his hands came to rest, she turned the cards to discover he'd switched *two* of them. "How'd you—"

"I won't corrupt you with my tricks, sweetheart," he said while he quickly flipped all the cards into his hand. "Your father won't let me have a another moment alone with you if I do."

Charity peered around the back of her seat and saw that Papa was sitting near the front of the car, scowling at a newspaper. When she faced Dillon again, she was overwhelmed by the golden shine of his eyes, and as he took her hand again, streaks of excitement coursed through her because other passengers could see them clearly. "Uh . . . what else do you do with cards?" she stammered. "If I pick some out, can you guess what they are, like a magician outside a circus tent does?"

He was trying not to laugh: Charity had picked up the deck, and was dealing four cards onto the table with the awkward determination of a child. Devereau stared at the cards with the exaggerated concentration of a carnival huckster, as though he could see through them. Starting with the card on his right, he pointed. "A black queen . . . something less than a nine . . . a red jack . . . the ace of hearts," he intoned.

Gaping, Charity turned the cards over. "These are marked!"

"Yes, they are," he admitted with a pleased grin. "Study the backs of them and try to figure out my system."

Her outburst attracted the attention of several nearby passengers, so Charity did as Devereau suggested to avoid their curious gazes. The deck design was a tight interweaving of black scrolls and curlicues and small marks that resembled the numeral seven. She was so engrossed she didn't realize someone had come to stand beside her.

"Is everything all right here, miss?" a business-like voice asked.

Charity looked up to see the conductor, and flushed. "Yes—I mean—he's only showing me—"

"Don't I remember you from a few years back?" the uniformed man demanded of Dillon. "It was on the run between Omaha and Salt Lake City. Had to put you off the train, as I recall."

Devereau's mustache lifted in an unflustered smile. "I believe it was," he said with a suave nod. "But my circumstances have improved a great deal since then, and so has the company I keep. Miss Scott here is a minister's daughter, and I'm accompanying her to Abilene. Wouldn't dream of leading such a lovely young woman astray—especially since her father's with us."

Glancing toward Noah, the conductor grunted. "An alibi for every occasion. Let me know if he makes a nuisance of himself, ma'am."

He continued down the aisle, and Charity stared after him. Then she studied the elegant man across from her, noting the appearance of his dimple. "Did he really put you off the train once, Dillon?"

Devereau chuckled. "Arthur Chapman takes his job very seriously. Back when I was young and impertinent, I accused a man of securing some choice cards in a holdout he wore inside his vest. I tore the vest off him to prove it, and he didn't take it too well. Started quite a scuffle."

Her eyes widened. "Was he wearing the hold-out?"

"Absolutely. We were locked into separate compartments until the next stop, and since the other fellow jumped out his window as the train was slowing down, I got stuck paying for the damages." She was more awestruck than appalled by his story, so Devereau pointed to the cards in front of her. "Have you figured out my system?"

Charity studied the cards very closely. Here was a man who'd started such memorable fights that he'd achieved notoriety on the Union Pacific, yet he was sharing his trade secrets with her as though she were perfectly capable of comprehending them! "Does it have something to do with this seven-looking mark? The other squiggles don't seem to change positions."

A bolt of pure pleasure made him grab her hands. Beneath her unruly waves and dowdy calico dress, Charity Scott was proving to be one of the most astute women he'd ever met. "Those sevens tell me which cards are tens or higher, while the directions they point tell me which cards they are," he explained. "The red royalty and the four aces have their corners shaved slightly. You don't see it so much as you feel it, when you're dealing them out."

Charity ran her fingers around the jack of diamonds and the ace of hearts. "I don't know how you can tell—"

"When you've marked as many decks as I have, you can pick out the high cards in the dark," he said with a shrug. "I was blessed with nimble fingers and I've spent half my life avoiding manual labor to keep them soft. Not an entirely admirable trait, but the men who accuse me of being less than masculine lose the most money to me."

For the first time, Charity really *looked* at Dillon's hands. She turned his palms up, studying the lean, elegant cut of his fingers . . . the rounded, pink tips appeared as pampered and free of callouses as a wealthy woman's. Yet when he suddenly gripped her again, gazing intently at her, his utter maleness made her ache with the same wild desire he'd evoked in the Leavenworth stable. Recalling the way he'd kissed forbidden places, luring her to the brink of madness, she knew she'd lose herself to Dillon Devereau in every possible way during this journey. Besides wanting to confront Mama, the wanton excitement she felt when he was near was the very reason she'd come along. Startled by this revelation, Charity withdrew her hand from the gambler's and looked out the window.

"Are you ashamed to be seen with me, Charity?"

His voice was quieter than the train's constant rumble; it held no apology and demanded an honest answer. The idea that she'd be ashamed of such a striking, wealthy man—she, who wore calico and whose entire world had been Jefferson City until a few days ago—struck her as absurdly funny. But she couldn't laugh when Dillon again captured her in his golden-eyed gaze. "I'm anything but embarrassed, Mr. Devereau," she replied firmly. "I'm just not used to men asking me such direct questions, or paying me so much attention."

Satisfied that she spoke from the heart, Dillon placed the table back between its brackets and slid onto the seat beside her. "Well, you'd better *get* used to it," he quipped, "because I don't intend to let you out of my sight, for your own protection and because, well—I like the looks of you, Charity. And I like the feel of you, and the smell of you . . . and the taste of you."

The heat that rose into her cheeks wasn't caused by the noonday sun. The hours to Abilene passed swiftly, and even when Papa returned, sitting sternly across from them and making no effort at conversation, Charity felt supremely happy. Dillon told her stories of his misadventures as a young gambler, candidly stating that he'd had moments he wasn't proud of, but that all told, his life and business affairs compared favorably to those of the most upstanding men he knew.

"We make our own successes and failures," he concluded with a serious smile, "and while I had my share of misfortune as a young man, I usually came up lucky when I needed to. And I've learned not to question Lady Luck when she pays me a call."

Charity smiled, well aware that she must seem terribly backward to this eloquent, worldly man. Yet his smile and gaze never wavered. Something in his voice told her he'd suffered a great loss—perhaps a tragedy that forced him to leave home before he was ready—but she didn't feel it was proper to ask him about it in such a public place. She noticed that Papa's head was nodding against his shoulder, and then she felt Dillon's hand wrapping around hers. Giddily contented, she turned her attention to the window, where lush, amber wheatfields rippled in the breeze, a constant delight to her eye. Then she stiffened.

Dillon followed her gaze to where a man on horseback was rapidly gaining on the train. They were slowing down for the Abilene station; men were scrambling along the roof to tighten the brakes of each car, so he knew the dark rider would arrive about the same time the train did.

"Why would Jackson Blue follow us all the way from Leavenworth?" Charity asked in a tense whisper. "Why didn't he ride the train? How could his horse have made the trip as fast as—"

"Whoa, sweetheart. You're jumping to some conclusions," Dillon said gently. "He had to start earlier than we did and ride cross-country to be arriving now. His horse probably knows the way blindfolded, because he often brings his wagon trains along this route."

"But *why*? You can't tell me this is a coincidence, Dillon," she replied in a voice sharpened by suspicion. "Did *you* tell him about our trip, knowing how he and Papa despise each other?"

Her change of mood took him by surprise, yet he understood her apprehension and shared it. "Sweetheart, believe me, I said nothing about it. Jackson undoubtedly figured that if we went after Marcella, we'd start looking in Abilene, because it's the logical place. It wouldn't surprise me if he could tell us exactly where your mother is. Not that he would."

Charity felt her distrust growing as the huge ebony stallion carried Blue close enough that she could distinguish the fringe on his buckskins. "If he's not going to help us find Mama, then why'd he come?"

Devereau could think of several answers, none of them encouraging. "It could be that he has legitimate business here," he replied in a tone that didn't sound terribly convincing. He noticed that Noah was waking up, and fervently hoped he could prevent the Indian scout and the preacher from catching sight of each other at the train station. "And it could be that he's tired of Leavenworth—he has as many friends here as he does there. But I suspect," he added as he watched clouds of resentment darken Charity's face, "that he's come to Abilene to collect a debt."

Chapter 10

As he helped Charity down onto the platform at the train station, Dillon glanced at the people around them. Jackson Blue had made himself scarce—probably until he could cause the most trouble—but Devereau was taking no chances. "I recommend the Drover's Cottage on Texas Street," he said when Noah stepped off the train. "If you'll go on ahead and arrange for our rooms, I'll see to the luggage."

He caught the suspicious glint in the preacher's eye and ignored it, for Charity's sake. Smiling at her, Dillon excused himself and started toward the rear of the train, where the porters would be unloading the trunks and suitcases of the Abilene passengers. The late-afternoon sun was relentless, and he sensed the day would grow even hotter when he quizzed Blue about his purpose here. He saw that the Scotts were on their way toward Texas Street, so he strode across the platform and found the dark scout tying Satan to the hitching post behind the station.

"Even Charity's figured out that you're following us," Dillon said sharply. "Surely you could find suckers enough in Leavenworth, without scalping Scott for money he doesn't have."

The Indian regarded him with cool obsidian eyes. Then, with a low chuckle, he lifted something from the shoulder of Devereau's coat—a long auburn hair. "Methinks the lady hath addled your brains, my friend. It's you I'm following."

"Why?"

"You've got something I want—a thousand of them, in fact." Jackson slapped his stallion's rump affectionately, still wearing his arrogance like a chieftain's headdress. "Man of integrity that you are, I'm surprised you left town without honoring your obligations, Devereau."

"I don't owe you a cent, dammit! What do you know about Marcella Scott and Powers?" he demanded. "You've only come to badger Noah and to watch Charity squirm as she discovers the truth about her mother."

Blue shrugged. "*I* didn't set them on her trail, and I'm not sure why *you* did. But I can guarantee you that if squirming is all Miss Scott does, she's a tougher young woman than I imagined. Maggie's a bitch of the highest order, and she'll be rabid when she learns you're on to her."

"And just how do you know so much about her?" Dillon watched the scout's sneer relax into a knowing smile as he motioned him toward a tavern down the block. He had to walk briskly to keep up with Blue's saunter, a circumstance the dark giant was playing to the hilt as they crossed the dusty street.

"Maggie and I are two of a kind," Jackson replied in a sly voice. "Powers can get a bit high-toned at times, and when she needs a sympathetic ear, she confides in me."

The image of Jackson Blue as a wily, beautiful woman's confidant nearly made Dillon choke on a laugh. He entered the shadowy saloon and leaned against the carved bar while the bartender drew their beers. "Rumor has it she plans to marry Erroll on this trip. Is that true?"

Blue raised his eyebrows. "I don't know how you came by that bit of hearsay, but there'll be a blizzard in hell before Erroll Powers gives *any* woman access to his millions. Maggie's more enterprising than most, though. That's why he keeps stringing her along—besides the fact that she's the most delectable piece of tail west of the Mississippi."

Sipping his frothy beer, Dillon paused to let the Indian's information sink in. Blue's personal involvement with Marcella was coloring his testimony, and he was known to manufacture his own version of the truth, but the haughty scout was the only source Devereau had. "So where would they be by now?"

Jackson grunted while he drank deeply from his tankard. "Depends on how long Maggie can detain him in any one hotel. The way she tells it, he can't get enough of—"

"Cut the crap, Jackson. Where are they?"

The Indian studied him while he polished off his beer, laughing low in his throat until the fringe across his buckskins shimmied. "My, my but we're testy today. Must be from keeping company with a Bible thumper and a vestal virgin. Has she let you kiss her yet?"

Devereau lowered his glass to the bar with a heavy thunk. "That's none of your concern. Now tell me what you know about Powers and Marcella—such as why they're planning to be away from Leavenworth for so long."

"Railroad business, they say," he answered breezily, "although Maggie hinted that this time Erroll was going to cash in big at each station and keep riding the rails into the sunset. Talk around Leavenworth says he's on the fly because K.P. officials caught him misappropriating funds, and that he won't be showing his face around town again without being arrested."

Dillon shook his head when the barkeep gestured toward his glass again, and thought for a moment. He knew better than to believe Powers would abandon his Leavenworth estate . . . and if he was running from the law, why would he tell Marcella they would marry and take a honeymoon, which would slow them down and give Kansas Pacific officials a chance to catch up with him? It didn't add up.

"You know, if it weren't for that thousand dollars that's come between us," the scout continued slyly, "I might be persuaded to ride ahead and detain the illustrious Miss Wallace and her consort. You could bide your time here, cozying up to the Scotts, until I telegraph Maggie's whereabouts to you. Think of the time and effort you'd save."

"You know where they are, don't you? If you were any kind of a friend, you'd forget about that damn money and—"

"It's because I'm your friend I'm telling you to go home. Powers and Wallace are out of your league, Dillon, and you're leading the Scotts straight to Hades if you insist on following those two shysters." Jackson Blue's eyes took on a mischievous glint as he leaned against the bar and sipped his second beer. "When you figure out that it's cheaper to retire Scott's gambling debt than to keep spending your money on that little piano pounder, let me know. Maggie Wallace has a penchant for pleasing two lovers at once, and with the contrast in our coloring and tastes, we could show that woman a time she'll—"

"Will you never cease to disgust me?" Dillon turned from the bar, and he was halfway to the batwing doors before he remembered the other reason he'd wanted to confront the foul-mouthed Indian. He cleared his throat loudly as he addressed Blue's backside, waiting for the scout to acknowledge him. "If you so much as show your face to Noah Scott," his coiled voice echoed in the nearly empty saloon, "consider yourself arrested."

* * *

"This is just another example of how Devereau's not to be trusted," Papa said with a grunt. He looked around the small, tidy room with its twin beds and then glowered at Charity again. "What sort of man would direct us to a hotel that doesn't even exist? It's probably best we chose this boardinghouse anyway. Undoubtedly more economical than the lodgings our escort had in mind."

Lifting her hair off her sweaty neck, Charity sighed tiredly. "Please, Papa, can't we freshen up for dinner without bickering about Mr. Devereau? I'm sure it was an honest mistake," she said as she poured water into the bowl on the washstand.

"Honest! Now *there's* a word we'll always associate with our fine-feathered friend," her father continued. "Why, for all we know he abandoned us—got back on the train and took our paltry possessions with him! Or at the very least, he stayed behind to tip the conductor for allowing him to remain aboard. Gamblers pay for the privilege of fleecing railroad customers, and I would imagine such bribery costs him—"

"If you despise Dillon so much, why did you agree to come on this trip?" Charity demanded. After watching him scowl and mutter all day, her fear of Papa's punishment was suddenly overridden by a fierce anger that had been smoldering since they'd left Kansas City. She knew why Dillon had lingered at the station, and the strain of keeping yet another secret to appease her father was more than she could bear. "I don't understand you, Papa. You're always claiming poverty as your excuse, yet when someone pays your way to find your wife, you act as though—as though you don't give a damn about what's happened to her! I want to know *why*."

Her vehemence shocked Papa as much as it surprised her. He raked his fingers through the silvery sunburst in his hair, his face contorting with rage.

"How dare you address me in such a presumptuous fashion? I won't tolerate your—"

"I'm *tired* of hearing that my questions are out of line, Papa. I'm eighteen. It's no secret to *me* why Mama would leave you, but I can't understand why you're so willing to let her get away."

Even as the words escaped her, Charity knew she'd overstepped her bounds. Papa's nostrils flared and he clutched his lapels as he stared at her, yet he made no move to slap her. Instead he backed toward the door, pointing an accusing finger.

"By the God that made me, I swear I'll tear Devereau limb from limb for filling your head with such insolence," he said in a terse whisper. "And then we're getting back on that train and going home. You'd better be here when I return, daughter, or you'll be eternally sorry."

The door shuddered on its hinges for several moments after the slamming noise died away. Charity stared at it, her legs going rubbery as the consequences of her outburst sank in. Because she couldn't keep her suspicions to herself, her father was returning her to the limited world of home and church—an existence that would be even more stifling because Papa wouldn't let her out of his sight . . . and because she'd never see Dillon or her mother again. She was shaking so violently she had to sit down on the narrow fainting couch beside the door.

After several minutes she regained control over her trembling arms and legs, yet she didn't answer the soft rapping on the wooden jamb. Charity heard her visitor slip into the room. She assumed it was Mrs. Yancy, the beaky, inquisitive woman who managed Hathaway House, come to inquire about raised voices and slamming doors, so she kept staring mournfully at her calico lap. Only when two arms in white shirt sleeves wrapped around her did she realize that Dillon had somehow escaped her father's wrath. She opened her mouth, but he laid a gentle finger across it.

"A thousand apologies, Charity," he said as he studied her anxious expression. "I knew the Drover's Cottage closed up and moved west with the cattle trade, but it slipped my mind. Abilene's nothing like I remember it from my days at the faro tables."

She was so happy to see him that her words tumbled out before she could think about them. "I suppose you were booted out of town for the same reason you were put off the train?"

"Well, yes I was, honey," he replied with a laugh. Her puckish tone proved her resilience once again, and he gave her a quick hug. "Only instead of enraging a customer, I made the mistake of falling for a lady of . . . questionable repute, shall we say? Another of her admirers showed me what a foolish move that was, and since his name was Hickok and his motto was 'Shoot straight and shoot first,' I never returned."

"Hickok? You knew Wild Bill Hickok?" she gasped.

Dillon grinned. "Well enough to clean him out nearly every time he sat down at a faro table. He could've been my twin, except he had blue eyes and wore his hair to his shoulders. We both dressed to the nines and had a taste for wild women," he continued with a wistful chuckle. "Spent our days at the Alamo Saloon, the finest hall in town—used to be right down the street from here. But most of those establishments closed up or moved to Ellsworth when the cattle started going there. That's history, though, and I'm boring you with it."

Completely awestruck, Charity gazed at the blond man whose virile smile was only inches from her own. She smelled beer and the day's heat on him, and saw the beginnings of stubble along his lean jawline, yet these details made him all the more appealing. That he'd cavorted with whores and found disfavor with a legendary lawman made her wonder again why he was here, with *her.* Fighting the urge to kiss him, she forced her thoughts along a safer line. "Did you speak with Mr. Blue?"

Devereau grunted. "And got nothing but one vague come-on strung to another. I think he knows where your mother is, and because of his dealings with her, I don't trust a word he says."

"He's your gambling partner, yet he plays you false? Why do you still consider him your friend, Dillon?"

Charity's upturned face, so innocent yet so wise, made his insides tighten. Now that she'd forgotten whatever she and Noah had been arguing about, the last thing Dillon wanted to discuss was the other man who was making their lives difficult. She'd asked a valid question, though, and she deserved an answer.

"Jackson and I have known each other since we were first on our own, back when he was a buffalo hunter and I was a greenhorn gambler," he replied in a thoughtful tone. "The adventures we shared, and the fact that I once saved his life, bind us together, honey. Blue sometimes repulses me and he makes me angry faster than any man I know, yet I understand him. He's stringing me along now because he's enthralled by a beautiful woman—and my behavior baffles *him* for the very same reason."

Several questions popped into her mind as Dillon spoke, but when his final words sank in, she was too tongue-tied to ask them. He was holding her closely enough that their shared warmth brought out the spicy fragrance of his cologne as well as the earthier smells of liquor and light sweat. Tentatively, she raised her lips to his.

Devereau closed his eyes to savor the taste of her,

despite the naggings that told him her father could walk in at any moment. Her mouth opened sweetly at his slightest coaxing, and he was lost in the silken wetness of her tongue and inner lips as he pressed her body against his. "Charity," he whispered, "each time I hold you this way, it gets harder to stop with just a kiss."

She knew what he wanted as surely as she knew she couldn't give it to him, but rather than pull away she considered her options. "Mama used to write me that if a girl kept all her clothes on and put both feet on the floor, she couldn't get into any trouble," she murmured as she stroked his mustache with her finger. "Is that true, Dillon?"

Her naive challenge sent desire flooding through his loins. "Depends on your definition of trouble," he whispered against her ear.

Charity giggled, aware of how sultry she sounded and of the effect it was having upon the man who held her. It was too late not to trust him—his kiss swept away all of her father's dire warnings. She wrapped her arms around him and scooted lower on the couch until her feet were planted firmly on the rug, and then returned every nuance his gentle, insistent mouth was teaching hers.

Devereau wasn't about to tell her how her change of position had only made her more accessible—just as he wouldn't spoil the moment by breaking her rules. As he shifted to fit against her, Charity sighed and sounded blissfully content. Her eager lips yielded to him, and with her slender body partway beneath his, he could no more stop fondling her than he could stop time itself.

Charity felt his fingers on her breast and held her breath. When the heat of his hand penetrated her dress and camisole, she nestled against him; his hypnotic touch told her he was now in complete control of her, and yet she anticipated something more—something beyond her present understanding.

Her response made him strain against trousers that threatened to emasculate him. Since it was too much to hope that she would give him the satisfaction he craved, Dillon concentrated on showing her the realm of sensations her body could experience, given the restrictions of her clothing. He imagined her pert pink breasts, and skin that would be fresh and fragrant with lilac soap even after the day's journey . . . except for places rendered intoxicatingly female by her awakening passions. With renewed purpose, Devereau kissed her firmly while lifting the hem of her dress above her knees.

Charity froze for only a moment. He was still honoring her request—her clothing was secure and her feet touched the floor—but the first silken caress of his fingertips on her inner thigh made her realize how artificial such limitations were to a man of Dillon's experience. His touch called up a vaguely exquisite memory, and she felt her temperature rising with his hand. When his palm came to rest below her abdomen, her eyes flew open.

Her expression was a mixture of fascination and fear, along with a yearning that brightened her irises to a brilliant shade of green. The flush on her cheeks made her sprinkling of freckles disappear, and Charity Scott was as lovely a woman as Dillon had ever beheld. He lightly kissed the bridge of her nose, then rose up again to watch the play of emotions on her face.

His fingertips were sure and thorough, using the barrier of her underwear to their own advantage. Charity parted her legs without realizing it, already engulfed by the subtle flames he was kindling inside her—flames that seemed to spiral and intensify at his slightest bidding. He was pushing her beyond sanity, beyond the point where she should either resist or lose her very soul, and just when she was ready to push him away, Dillon's hand suddenly stopped moving.

"Charity?"

His whisper was a final submission to her will, his consideration a heady aphrodisiac that urged her across the threshold of a passion from which she could never turn back. "Dillon . . . please don't stop."

He resumed his urgently tender massage, unable to resist slipping a finger through a gap in the seam of her pantaloons. When his skin met hers and found a frenzied knot of femininity she never dreamed existed, Charity writhed, gasping until her dizzying pain became a pleasure so wild she had to muffle a cry against his shoulder.

Dillon knew if he gave himself even a heartbeat to think about it, he'd be thrusting inside her despite her innocent trust in him. He sat up to take a ragged breath, enjoying the dazed sweetness on her face despite his discomfort. "Honey, I want you desperately. Next time I'll have to take more."

Still woozy, Charity managed a grin and bent his head down for a kiss. She was struggling to sit up against the wall, formulating a reply that would sound coy yet encouraging, when the door opened and her father stepped into the room.

"I daresay you can have all you want of her, Devereau," Noah said in a mocking voice, "because any man who takes such liberties with my daughter is going to marry her. Tonight."

Chapter 11

Too stunned even to gasp, Charity stared at her father and then hastily sat straight up. Dillon had been thoughtful enough to drape her skirts over her legs again after he proved how much trouble one finger could cause, but she might as well have been stripped naked. Her face was aflame. Even if her father had only been guessing at what they'd done, she knew her expression confirmed his worst assumptions. She'd always been a poor liar, because it seemed the man in black could look into her soul and know how much she'd reveled in whatever sin she committed—and this one was certainly her worst.

Dillon stiffened, sensing another of Noah Scott's devious ploys. "Apparently you didn't have your ear pressed to the wall quite firmly enough," Dillon said in a biting whisper. "Had you really listened, you'd know that I've done nothing to disgrace your daughter."

Scott let out a short, sarcastic laugh. "The fact that you even talk to Charity disgraces her, Mr. Devereau. I've expressly forbidden the two of you to see each other when I'm not present, and since you've ignored my wishes repeatedly, marriage is the only recourse. I'll not allow Charity to spit in our Lord's face the way her mother has."

"Your daughter is still a virgin—a fact any doctor can verify," Dillon asserted as he rose from the fainting couch. He approached the preacher slowly, hoping a devil's-advocate strategy would force Scott to back down. "So why would you sentence her to life with a man whose profession defies everything you've taught her? You've done nothing but condemn me since we met."

The preacher gripped the lapels of his black frock coat, as though lifting himself to Devereau's height. "Those who have lusted in their hearts have *fornicated* in the eyes of the Lord. Marriage and children are sure cures for those wandering thoughts of yours, Brother Devereau. And they're Charity's chance to reclaim her salvation."

"You don't love your daughter much, do you?"

The tiny room became so airless Charity thought she'd suffocate. Dillon and her father were poised to spring at each other, and her first impulse was to run—to flee the shame she'd associated with sexuality since she was a child, and to escape the consequences of not bending to Papa's will. But where would she go in this town full of strangers? How could she leave Abilene, when her earnings from the Crystal Queen were in the suitcase Dillon hadn't brought in yet?

"Get out of our room, Devereau. We'll see you in an hour, when we're ready to walk to the church."

Dillon grunted. "If you think for one minute I'll go along with this farce of a—"

"I think you'll do what's best for Charity," Scott said coldly. "Now *leave,* so my daughter and I can prepare ourselves for the ceremony."

Clenching his fists at his sides, Dillon looked at the young girl who was cowering on the couch and knew Noah Scott would have his way. Charity was miserable, pale-faced and pinched with fear, but she would look even less like a bride if her father resorted to physical punishment—"Spare the rod and spoil the child" was undoubtedly his favorite line of Scripture. With an impatient sigh, he backed toward the doorway. "You know you're wrong, Scott. You can't force two adults to—"

"Charity's my daughter and she'll see the wisdom of my ways. Get out, before I have Mrs. Yancy summon the sheriff."

The preacher's eyes were as dark and unforgiving as his stiff black frock coat. With an apologetic glance at Charity, Devereau closed the door on a harrowing dilemma: he was the wrong man for a fine girl like Charity Scott and they all knew it, but he was responsible for the mess she was in. And he was condemning her to eternal damnation if he refused to marry her. Rather than go down the hall to his own room, Dillon lingered near the doorway and tried to think of a way to prevent this absurd shotgun wedding.

He heard Charity sniffling, trying to find her voice. "Papa, please . . . I—I'll forget all about finding Mama, if you'll only—"

"You can't bargain for your soul, daughter, with me or with the Lord either. Now wipe your face and—"

"But we didn't do what you're thinking," she pleaded. "I—I don't *love* Dillon so why—"

Devereau flinched, yet he admired the spunk it took to stand up to a father who heeded no voice but his own. He heard quick, heavy footsteps. Charity gasped and the couch thudded against the wall.

"Love is not the issue here—it seldom is in a marriage—but you're too starry-eyed and silly about Devereau to think straight," Scott replied brusquely. "We're talking about duty and respect for your—"

"And since Mama stopped believing in those things, you're taking your anger out on *me!*"

At the sound of Noah Scott's slap, Devereau threw open the door. Charity was reeling from the force of her father's blow, holding the left side of her face, and he barely caught her before she stumbled backward onto the couch. That Scott had orchestrated this nasty scene just so he would rescue the girl didn't matter now: Charity's life was in his hands.

"You snake-tongued son of a bitch!" He spat the words out, glaring at the preacher's malicious little grin. "This is your revenge for having to come to Kansas, isn't it? And you know damn well I'll marry Charity rather than subject her to your heavy-handedness—which means you'll be completely free to indulge in your *own* little sins. Let's go, Charity, before I forget your father's a clergyman and flatten him."

Charity had been stunned by her father's forceful slap, but now she became fully alert again. "We're not going anywhere, Dillon," she protested, struggling against the grip he had on her shoulders. "Papa has always *told* me what to do, and this is where it stops. I'm not going to marry you!"

Ordinarily he admired feistiness in a woman, but Devereau sensed that Charity didn't realize the gravity of her situation. He held her close so he could talk softly into her ear. "If you stay with your father, you'll live to regret every day of your life—the man has no concern for anyone but himself," he murmured. "And if you run off, then what? When your money's gone, you'll have to hire on at a brothel like so many other decent girls who've come west. You're too good for that, Charity."

"What do *you* care?" she retorted. "The last thing you want is a wife, so it seems I'd only be settling for a different sort of hell if I married you."

Her vehemence shocked him. She was squirming, twisting her head so she could bite the hand that held her left shoulder, and her father was enjoying the spectacle immensely. Before Charity's teeth met his knuckles, he dipped and swung her into his arms, then slung her over his shoulder to carry her to the privacy of his room. She struggled and kicked until she nearly knocked him off balance in the hallway; he closed his door with his foot and dropped her unceremoniously onto the bed. "You have every reason to be angry—"

"You're damn *right* I do!"

"—but let's consider our choices, Charity," he continued in the most controlled voice he could manage. "You're right—I don't want a wife. Until a few years ago I was a nomad, wandering to the next cowtown for the highest stakes, and I couldn't ask a woman to share that existence. And you deserve better than a gambling man, even if he owns the most prestigious parlor in Kansas City. But you're wrong about one thing, sweetheart. Very wrong."

Charity gazed up at him from the bed, in awe of the powerful restraint he was displaying as he leaned over her. "Wh-what's that?"

"I *do* care about you. That's why I'm prepared to strike a deal—a bargain your father doesn't need to know about." She was still sprawled on his bed, her clothes and hair in wild disarray, but he had her undivided attention now. He sat down beside her, trying not to feel disappointed when she refused to hold his hand. "Charity, for your own safety, I think you should marry me. It's not the head-over-heels romance every girl dreams of, and I'm certainly not ideal husband material, but once we've cornered your mother, you and I can quietly get an annulment. I'll set you up—in a music shop or a studio where you can teach, or whatever you like—and we'll be free to go our own ways again. No strings."

Her eyes widened as she thought about his unorthodox proposal. "I . . . you've already done too much," she said with a shake of her head. "I can't accept any more—"

Dillon silenced her with his finger. "Here's your chance to pay me back in full, just by becoming my wife for a few weeks. Interested?"

Frowning, Charity took his hand from her mouth and held on to it. "What are you talking about?"

He sensed she would accept his offer now, yet he was very careful about the way he worded it. "I'm chasing after Powers for my own reasons, you know," Devereau reminded her. "Even though the gambling trade left Abilene and other cowtowns years ago, I won't be welcomed back with open arms because I usually departed . . . under a cloud, shall we say?"

Charity felt the beginnings of a grin. "Because of wild women and crooked cards?"

"And barroom brawls and a few unpaid debts," he continued, nodding. "Having a wife would lend me a certain respectability. The men who ran me out would not only accept repayment if they thought I'd changed my ways, but they might provide the information we need about your mother and Powers. It beats getting booted out before we can ask any questions, doesn't it?"

She crossed her arms over her stomach, studying the handsome man who was returning her gaze with a disarmingly boyish grin. "So I'd get out from under Papa's thumb and you'd become a pillar of society, and then we'd part company? Sounds like a deal with the devil."

"It probably is," Devereau said with a chuckle. "But as long as we enter into this union of our own free will, for purposes we understand and agree to, we're really no different from any other partners in marriage. What do you say?"

She felt foolish even hesitating—what woman wouldn't jump at the chance to marry a debonair, wealthy man like Dillon Devereau? Yet marriage ranked with birth and death as a milestone to be celebrated with sacraments . . . an event to be entered into seriously, rather than out of spite or for other reasons. "It—it's still a big decision," Charity mumbled. "I can't ignore the teachings I've grown up with, and yet . . ."

"I can't expect you to throw aside your past or ignore your conscience, honey—any more than I can," he replied quietly. "But your father's waiting for an answer, right outside the door, for all we know."

She glanced nervously toward the entryway and lowered her voice. "It seems that once again I really don't have a choice," she replied, "so I guess I'll accept your offer. It's more than generous."

Dillon sighed to himself, wishing she'd shown more enthusiasm. "All right then, it's settled. We'll go tell your father, before he sends the sheriff in here to arrest me for kidnapping or some other trumped-up crime. Shall we seal the deal with a kiss?"

Charity watched his lips part in anticipation, yet she held back, suppressing a giggle. "I—I would, but Papa might suspect we're working around him. I don't want him to think I'm one bit happy, and a kiss would show all over my face."

Chuckling, he helped her up and straightened the folds of her brown calico dress. "That's the spirit. I'll act as though I finally forced some sense into your head, and you can be the submissive daughter—though we both know what an act *that* is."

She laughed, muffling the sound with her hand as he closed the door behind them. Then, when they reached the room where her father was waiting, Charity turned to look up at Dillon. "Those things I said about you when Papa and I were fighting?" she ventured hesitantly. "Well, they weren't entirely true. I think you're a decent, trustworthy man despite your occupation. And even though you talk me into things I know aren't proper, I still like you a lot, Dillon."

It was the most he could hope for, given their awkward situation, and Devereau felt his pulse speeding up. "I like you, too, Charity. I don't know much about marriage, but I intend to do you justice as a husband, even if it's only for a few weeks."

She nodded, her heart skipping happily, and then grasped the doorknob while trying to muster a suitably resigned expression for Papa. Suddenly something occurred to her; she bumped backward into Dillon with a beseeching look. "It's not that important, really," she faltered, "but . . . I don't have a dress good enough to . . ."

Even a girl of modest means expected certain niceties at her wedding, and Devereau hugged her fiercely. "You will, sweetheart," he vowed. "I'll take care of everything. While you're mine, you'll have the best."

Charity bit back a smile and prepared to submit to her father. Wearing what she hoped was a doleful expression, she opened the door and saw Papa pacing before the window. His gaze went from her face to Dillon's and then lingered on hers again, gauging their moods.

"Do I perceive penitence and a newfound sense of responsibility?" he asked in a domineering tone. "I was beginning to think you'd run off and left me."

She stifled a laugh by clearing her throat. "We—we'll do as you say, Papa. It's for the best."

"Excellent." Her father adjusted his glasses as though trying to see through any mockery or pretense. "I suggest we look for a church, so I can perform the ceremony before any evening services might be—"

"We're waiting until tomorrow." Devereau placed a hand on Charity's slender shoulder and looked her father in the eye. "You may locate a clergyman tonight, if you wish, since you'll be giving the bride away. Tomorrow I'll take care of the other details to make our wedding the memorable event it should be. Your haste lends an essence of gunpowder I find totally inappropriate, Reverend Scott—especially since Charity and I have done nothing wrong."

The preacher bristled. "All that's required is the repetition of vows before witnesses—"

"Your daughter deserves better," Dillon replied firmly. "Since she hasn't enjoyed any sort of engagement, or had a chance to plan the biggest day of her life, the least we can do is find her a suitable dress and—"

"Who's paying for such wastefulness?"

"It'll be my pleasure to provide the bride's trappings," Devereau replied smoothly. "Despite your opinion of me, I do appreciate an attractive, virtuous woman—a rare combination these days—and I'll be proud to call her my wife."

Before Scott could object any further, Dillon turned Charity so she faced him. Her jade eyes were huge, as though she just now realized that they really were getting married. "Rest tonight, and leave everything to me," he said with a smile. "It's bad luck for a man to see his bride the day of the wedding, so have your father tell me what time he's set the ceremony for, and I'll see you at the church."

She nodded, dumbstruck. And as the tall, virile gambler—her fiancé!—left the room, Charity felt the first pangs of regret that such a wonderful man wouldn't be hers forever.

Chapter 12

There was no mirror in the small storage room where Charity was dressing, but as excited as she felt, she knew she must *look* like a different person, too. As she'd anticipated, Dillon had brought along the cream-colored gown she'd worn on the Crystal Queen's stage; it had been laundered and delivered to her room at the boardinghouse that afternoon. What she hadn't expected were the large white boxes from Bright's Ladies' Shoppe, which contained a crinolette with a built-in bustle to wear under the gown, as well as seven sets of pastel camisoles and pantaloons, and two nightgowns of the sheerest fabric she'd ever seen.

"One for every day of the week," she'd marveled as she lifted the delicate undergarments from their box.

Papa had muttered something about it being the least Devereau could do after dishonoring her, and left their rented room with a disapproving glance at the lingerie she was scattering over the bed. He hadn't returned by the time Charity thought they should be leaving for the church, so she'd carried the awkward boxes of clothing down the dusty street herself. Without Dillon's smile, it had been a long, lonely day—nothing like the giddy prenuptial excitement she'd dreamed of while she was growing up.

But when she stepped inside the church, its cool shadows soothed her. The fragrance of fresh flowers made her peek into the sanctuary, where she saw ribboned bouquets adorning each of the pew ends along the center aisle. The organist stopped practicing for a moment to wave and smile at her.

"I imagine you'll want to dress in this room behind me," the young woman said, pointing to a doorway. "Mr. Devereau told me the service was at seven. I'm going home to change now."

"Yes . . . thank you," Charity murmured. She hurried down the aisle to where the organist had directed her, wondering if she could possibly hope for the miracle it would take to transform herself into the lovely bride she'd always wanted to be—the bride Dillon deserved.

Exchanging her muslin underthings for a set of lacy white ones, she felt a shiver of goosebumps when the silk caressed her skin. Next came the crinolette, with its cagelike contraption that made her feel extremely conspicuous from the rear. She slipped into the embroidered gown as quickly as she could without wrinkling its voluminous silk skirts, hoping no one walked in on her. Surely it was almost seven, yet the silence inside the church was deep and undisturbed.

As she fastened the last of what seemed like dozens of contrary pearl buttons on her bodice, a door at the far end of the building opened and there was a steady creak of floorboards—Dillon, perhaps? Was her dress hanging correctly over the bustle? Did she have the front buttoned right, nervous as she was? And how could she possibly make her hair presentable without a mirror?

"What a lovely gown," a voice behind her said. "Devereau told me you might want some help, but it looks like you've managed just fine. I was so fidgety on my own wedding day I broke out in hives and was ashamed to show my face—which must've struck everybody as a fine joke indeed."

Charity turned to see a petite woman a few years older than herself coming through the doorway, a woman so stunning she found the hive story hard to believe. Her ebony hair was swept up in a graceful topknot with tiny ringlets at the temples, and her scarlet dress accentuated a glowing opalescent complexion. Dark eyes studied Charity with a catlike gaze until she finally found her tongue. "I—I could use some help with my hair," she stammered. "There's no mirror."

"Of course you could," the woman answered with a coy smile. "We'll pin it all on top and then attach this veil Devereau had me make up," she continued, setting a round box on a table beside the door. "Have a seat, dear."

Confused yet curious, Charity perched carefully on the room's only chair. Her dark-haired visitor began to brush her long, wavy tresses with hands that were surprisingly cool on this warm summer's evening. That she knew Dillon was apparent, but her tone suggested an acquaintance that went far beyond asking her to fashion a veil. "I—I don't mean to seem distant or rude," Charity said quietly, "but Dillon didn't tell me to expect anyone."

Her hairdresser let out a giggle that sounded out of place in church. "No, I don't suppose he would," she replied in a spritely voice. "I'm Phoebe—Phoebe Thomas. My husband owns the general store, and we knew Devereau back when the streets were so splotched with cow pods a decent lady couldn't cross 'em except in a wagon. Not that it stopped *me.* There—let's have a look at you."

Phoebe stepped daintily around her cream-colored skirts, appraising her with a satisfied nod. Then she lifted Charity's chin, her expression wry. "And where might Devereau have met such a tender thing as you, dear?"

Charity cleared her throat nervously. "At his casino. The Crystal Queen in Kansas City."

Mrs. Thomas raised an eyebrow, and then went to open the box she'd carried in. "The music's starting," she said. "We'll have you all prettied up in no time. Now stop looking so worried and *smile,* Charity. You've lassoed the heartthrob of Abilene, you know."

Charity felt a hairpin going into either side of her upsweep, and then the gossamer folds of a veil edged in tiny pearls fell gracefully around her face. She stood, allowing Phoebe to adjust her bustle and skirts, trying to keep her knees from knocking as the organ music suddenly swelled behind them. "Do—do I look all right?" she breathed.

"Like an angel come down from the pearly gates," Phoebe replied as she stepped toward the door. "No tears now—promise? As I recall, Devereau can't stomach a woman who cries."

Charity gaped after her, remembering several times when Dillon had shown the utmost compassion for her tears. The woman in scarlet was a baffling creature—who did she think she was, feigning such familiarity with Dillon Devereau's preferences?

When Papa stuck his head in through the hallway door, however, she forgot all thoughts of Phoebe Thomas. A wedding march was playing, and he was here to escort her down the aisle . . . she really was getting married, instead of having another schoolgirlish fantasy about it. At that moment, Charity desperately wanted her father's approval—some sign that he loved her. An acknowledgment that she was more than just a duty life had thrust upon him.

His eyes widened briefly behind his spectacles as he looked her up and down. "Well, daughter, they're waiting on us."

"Yes, Papa," she mumbled, vowing to forget that

servile phrase once she was Mrs. Dillon Devereau. The sound of her new name brought a smile to her lips as they hurried down the narrow hallway that led to the back of the sanctuary.

When she saw the small gathering of people watching expectantly from the front pews of the little church, she nearly lost her nerve. They were Dillon's friends, of course—he wouldn't want her walking through an empty sanctuary. Phoebe stood on the left near the organ, and to the right of the aisle a large, blocky man awaited them, fidgeting with a starched collar that looked a size too tight beneath his beefy face.

And then Dillon stepped into place along with the stout little preacher, looking regally tall and dapper in a black pin-striped suit. His cravat was studded with a huge ruby that winked at her as he shifted his weight. But it was Devereau's face that kept Charity stepping steadily to the music, oblivious to all else. His cool card-playing mask was now alight with awe. His lips parted, hinting at nervousness until he flashed her a grin of unabashed, almost devilish delight.

And then she was beside him, slipping her arm from Papa's and under his, repeating vows she knew by heart yet was barely aware of as she mouthed them, all the while gazing up into his golden eyes and basking in the glow she saw there.

The preacher paused, and Dillon was slipping a diamond the size of an organ's stop knob onto her finger. "With this ring I thee wed," he murmured in a husky voice.

"And by the authority vested in me, I pronounce you man and wife," the clergyman droned. "You may kiss the bride."

"You better believe I will."

Charity held her breath as he gently lifted the veil up and over her head, all the while beaming down at her with a smile that rivaled those in her fondest fantasies. Lightly he touched her cheek, and then lowered his lips to hers with a subtle sigh. For a moment she froze, remembering their audience, but the raw hunger in Dillon's kiss consumed her. Clinging to him, Charity returned his ardent affection until her knees were ready to buckle and she heard a twittering from the audience. She broke away with a gasp, clutching his lapel to keep her balance.

The organ burst forth with a flourish and the small congregation was on its feet, coming to greet them. Phoebe was first with a congratulatory pat on Charity's back and a loud kiss for Dillon. She was joined by the large man who'd stood beside them.

"You've met Phoebe," Devereau was saying, "and this is Will Thomas, her husband, who owns the general store."

Charity nodded mutely, thinking the awkward, jowled storekeeper an odd match for the petite Mrs. Thomas. Dillon was introducing her all around, saying names that were forgotten before they were drowned out by the loud music. Her heart was hammering rapidly and she felt her head spinning in dangerous, light-headed spirals, and then, as though he sensed her discomfort, Dillon held up his hand.

The organ went silent. The handsome blond slipped an arm around her and gave his friends a suave grin.

"Charity and I are pleased you could share this occasion with us," he said smoothly, "and I've reserved a table at the restaurant across the street, hoping you'll all be my guests this evening. I trust you won't be offended if my bride and I don't join you."

The admiring little crowd parted and Dillon walked her quickly up the aisle. "My God but you're beautiful, Charity," he whispered, "and all I could think as you came toward me was how damned *happy* I am that you're mine."

Her mouth dropped open. To hear such a rush of unguarded emotion from Dillon—the man who'd suggested this wedding as a convenient deal rather than an event with any heart in it—suddenly had her blinking back tears. "I—I think we'd better leave before I start blubbering," she replied in a quavery voice.

Chuckling, Dillon kissed her before swinging the church door open for her. "As you wish, sweetheart," he said with a bow.

Charity smiled and then something made her pause to glance back at the people clustered near the organ. Papa was standing apart, looking over the pews at her, wearing an expression that needed no explanation. It was the smug smile of a man who'd gotten exactly what he wanted.

Dillon removed his coat and cravat, watching his bride wander about the suite as though she were in a dream. She'd taken off her veil and the back sections of her hair had come undone; her fingers trailed lightly across the mahogany furnishings, and when she stopped before the bouquet of roses on the highboy, her smile was tremulous. She turned, looking like a priceless figurine from a china shop.

"Thank you for the wonderful wedding, Dillon," she said quietly. "You went to a lot of trouble, making all those arrangements in one day. Everything was so . . . perfect."

He smiled and unfastened his heavy gold cuff links. "It was a good way to renew old acquaintances and pay off a couple of long-standing debts," he remarked casually. "But besides restoring my reputation, it was a chance to treat you to the finery you deserve, Charity. You were radiant, honey, and you're still taking my breath away."

She glanced nervously at her feet. "Oh, Dillon, you needn't go on so just to make me feel—"

"This is not a gambler's bluff, Mrs. Devereau," he said, quickly crossing the room to take her in his arms. "My proposal wasn't very romantic, but it was sincere—just as my compliments are. You're as fine a bride as ever graced any aisle, and even though our lives have been forced around an unexpected corner, I'm certainly not complaining. In fact, I can't remember the last time I felt this happy."

Charity looked deeply into his tawny eyes and saw the same open delight he'd displayed in church. His face felt virile and smooth beneath her inquisitive fingers, except for the thick mustache which curled around his lips. "It seems Papa changed his mind about us, too. As though he'd been playing the matchmaker all along but didn't want us to know."

Reverend Scott's parting smile hadn't escaped Devereau's notice. He sensed that Charity had also seen through her father's gloating but didn't want to think of herself as his pawn right now. His own impression was that the preacher had resembled a tomcat who, after whetting his appetite with a small mouse, was looking forward to hunting bigger prey. "Do you mind if we don't talk about him?" he asked gently. "Holding you this close reminds me of what I was wanting when I kissed you after the ceremony, honey."

Dillon's fingers began a slow journey down the front of her dress, freeing each pearl button from its slender loop. His shirt was open to the center of his chest, revealing swirls of golden hair Charity longed to touch, yet she refrained, wanting to savor every moment of this passing from maidenhood to the mysteries of becoming a man's woman. She swallowed a moan when Dillon's fingers slipped beneath her bodice to cup her breast. "There's something we should discuss before things get . . . out of hand," she began with a coy glance at her bosom.

"What's that?" he whispered. "I have no intention of letting any part of you out of my hands, now that we're finally alone, Charity."

She fought the urge to nuzzle his chest, to inhale the essence of cloves and cleanness that rose from inside his shirt. "It's about the annulment part," she replied in a weakening voice. "The way I understand it, once a marriage has been . . . consummated, you can't act as though it just never existed."

As Devereau read the playfulness in her sparkling green eyes, he also realized that what she said was true: regardless of how the law read, he knew damn well that once he'd made love to the alluring young woman he was holding, there would be no pretending it had never happened—no forgetting the infinite ways Charity pleased him, come time to follow their separate paths.

Dillon sensed she didn't want to think about their parting any more than he did, so he indulged her stall tactic. "Are you saying you don't want me?" he asked in a wounded whisper. He forced his hands from around the firm globe of her breast and backed away, all the while fighting a smile. "Perhaps I'm conceited, but I'm not aware that any other woman has found me lacking, Charity."

He turned abruptly, striding to the table where the hotel's manager had provided a decanter of whiskey and a bottle of champagne. Pouring half a glass of the amber liquor, he waited for her to rush up behind him.

Charity stared at his back, speechless. Dillon must think her a heartless prude indeed—and so ungrateful, after his generous wedding arrangements, and compliments that made her feel wanted for the first time in her life. Perhaps she'd chosen a poor time to play games, yet if Devereau was too damn sensitive to . . . she pressed her lips together, determined not to beg his forgiveness.

Halfway through his drink, Devereau was still facing the wall and trying not to snicker. Charity's teasing surprised him and made him want her all the more keenly. Behind him, he heard a secretive silken rustling . . . she was calling his bluff now, pretending to pack her things into the Bright's boxes so he'd beg her not to abandon him on their wedding night! He made himself swallow the last of the whiskey, carefully composing a remark that would make her laugh and run into his arms.

When he turned, Charity was standing beside the fourposter bed wearing only the delicate white camisole he'd bought her this morning. One hand was tugging at a lacy strap and the other flew down to cover a patch of auburn curls above her long, slender thighs. Undressing had mussed her hair, and her face was frozen in an expression of determination mixed with a wantonness he'd never dreamed her capable of. "Honey, I was only—"

"It was you—your *lust* that forced me into this marriage," Charity said with a boldness she was unaware she possessed. "So by God, Devereau, you *will* make love to me."

A hairpin fell, sending a cascade of red waves over her bare shoulder, and Dillon lost his tenuous hold on self-control. The most experienced temptress couldn't have coaxed him across the room this quickly, and when his hands found Charity's silk-covered back and the firm, warm flesh of her behind, he kissed her with an insistence that left no doubt about how he intended to spend their first night together.

Charity felt herself being carried to the edge of the high bed, which Dillon turned down with an impetuous yank of one hand. His lips never left hers while he lowered her onto the fresh sheets, and his urgent hands were driving her beyond the point where she could play games anymore. Easing his tongue between her teeth, he gently pushed her backward until he was on top of her, supporting his weight on his elbows.

He kissed her again, and the feel of her body beneath him sent his imagination soaring. How could he best initiate her into womanhood? She deserved his utmost tenderness this first time—and every time—yet he knew his immediate need for her would override his good intentions the moment her body yielded to his. Dillon gazed down at her rapt, angelic face and his decision was made. With a soft chuckle, he let his mouth drift along the finely carved line of her jaw until he was nuzzling her ear. "Charity," he murmured, "there are many ways to kiss a woman. If you find any of them unpleasant, just kick me."

His dimple made her wonder what he could possibly be hinting at. What sort of woman *kicked* her husband the first time they made love? When his tongue traced lazy circles around each of her aching nipples she drew in her breath; his mustache tickled her stomach through the silk lingerie as his mouth descended with agonizing slowness. Indeed, the muscles in her legs were tensing, as was every fiber of her being, because Dillon's nibbling sent bolts of pure pleasure into the very core of her.

Devereau sampled each inch of his willowy partner only briefly, because her responses made it clear she was as eager for release as he was. Charity moaned when he brushed the hollow of her abdomen with his lips; she tensed, but allowed him to continue kissing her along the top of her thigh. Her delectable essence was driving him mad, yet he held back, touching the deep pink bud displayed so temptingly before him with only the tip of his tongue.

Gasping, Charity clamped her legs together. The warm roughness of Dillon's cheeks became even more intimate now, as did the stroking of his agile tongue, and a white-hot desire surged within her until she had no choice to but offer herself completely to him. Instinctively she raised her knees, amazed that her hips were quivering as though possessed. She dug her heels into Dillon's shoulders and wadded the sheets in her fists as the first waves of passion crested within her.

Dillon caressed her more deeply, grasping her slender hips to keep her arousal under control for the longest time possible. When he realized her ankles were hovering near his ears, he rose up. "You're not really going to kick me, are you?" he teased softly.

Her mouth fell open, but all she could breathe was, "Don't . . . please don't stop."

His mouth overtook her again with a merciless kneading that made her feel as though she might burst into flame. Charity cried out, and then stifled the noise with the back of her hand. When the intense waves of giddiness subsided and she could open her eyes, she found Dillon's face directly above her as he studied her with obvious pleasure.

"Such a passionate outburst," he said with a chuckle. "I like a woman who expresses herself."

Charity grimaced. "Everyone must've heard—"

"So what?" Devereau pulled himself away from his bride and finished unbuttoning his shirt. "This is the honeymoon suite. We've every right to sound like lovers, sweetheart."

"I . . . it wasn't like I thought it would be," she mumbled. His shirt fell to the floor and he reached for the buttons on his trousers, his face glowing with a solemn desire that made her wonder what could possibly follow. Her limbs were still rubbery and weak, yet he apparently expected more from her.

"I like to give my woman some pleasure before I take my own," he explained in a husky voice. "I wanted you to enjoy at least a part of our first love-making as much as I will."

The sight of Dillon's unclothed body gave Charity pause. He was firmly muscled, lithe as a tiger, and he displayed a powerful grace as he stepped out of his pants. Broad shoulders tapered to a narrow waist; swirls of golden-brown hair funneled down into a peak that seemed to point to his arousal. Charity had a general idea about how that particular part of him was supposed to fit inside her, yet she couldn't imagine having *room* for it.

Sensing her hesitation, Devereau kept his own desires in check by trying to rekindle hers. "Come here," he whispered as he helped her up. "Let's take off your camisole so it won't come between us. Nothing compares to the luxury of skin upon skin."

Charity stood, leaning into him as he lifted the light silk over her head. He was right: the warmth of his body, the subtle caress of the hair on his chest, created a stirring within her. She smiled up at him and was greeted with a ravenous kiss, which followed the hollow of her throat until Dillon was burying his face between her breasts. With a moan that echoed her own yearning, he lifted her onto the rumpled bed and stretched out alongside her, his hands in constant, urgent motion.

The light, lilac scent of her . . . the skin of creamiest velvet . . . the taste of innocence and the wide-eyed wonder which never left her face as her breathing became as shallow and rapid as his own: Dillon couldn't remember the last time a woman had ignited his senses to such a fever pitch. Charity's lips parted as she drew a teasing toe up his calf, and he was undone. He took her swiftly, hoping she would understand.

After a brief, piercing pain made her suck in her breath, Charity followed the lead of her lover's rhythmic hips, rocking, rocking, until a frenzy overtook him and he siezed her in a frantic grip. When his warmth shot through her, she leaned into his final shudders and was rewarded with an internal sunburst that was mellower yet every bit as sweet as her first.

He clung to her, and when her calling out died away, Dillon knew that no matter how many songs she sang in her sultry contralto, Charity's ecstatic moaning of his name would be the sweetest music he would ever hear.

She felt a film of perspiration form where their bodies were pressed together; Charity heard his heartbeat, felt his breathing ruffle her hair, and wondered if lovemaking was always this grand or if Dillon Devereau simply had the knack for it, as he did for so many things. She toyed with a tuft of his chest hair. "I—I hope I wasn't too big a disappointment, after the other ladies you've—"

"Disappointment?" He lifted her chin so he could search her lightly freckled face. Her jade eyes shone up at him without wavering. "Honey, it was an honor to be your first, and all I can think about is spending the rest of the night—and many nights to come—showing you a dozen kinds of affection."

They both stiffened when someone pounded on the door. "Your dinner, Mr. Devereau," a male voice announced. "Compliments of the management."

Dillon rose up on his elbows, glowering as he tugged the sheet over his wife's trembling body. "We don't *want* dinner, Mr. Blue."

Chapter 13

Charity huddled under the skimpy covering the sheet provided. Dillon was bristling beside her, sliding the lower half of his body beneath the bedclothes as he faced the door. Jackson Blue was already entering their room, his dark eyes mocking them while he carried a tray laden with shiny silver domes to a table near the bed.

"I stopped by the inn for dinner and an old friend of ours invited me to join the wedding party," the Indian said. He crossed his arms over his buckskinned chest, studying them with a derisive smile. "Imagine my disappointment when I learned my best friend had gotten married without telling me, let alone inviting me. To show there are no hard feelings, I brought you the best steak in town, cooked to the pink as you prefer it, Devereau. Figured it was the least I could do, since you bought my meal tonight."

"You insufferable *bastard!*" Dillon muttered. "You knew damn well what Charity and I would be—"

"And I came to apologize," Blue continued, as though unaware he was interrupting anything. "I once implied that your beloved here was too virtuous to succumb to your wolfish intentions, and I was wrong. Can you blame me for being stunned? You're the *last* fellow I figured would end up with powder burns on his privates."

Charity flushed furiously. She gripped the edge

of the sheet more tightly above her breasts and was about to demand that Blue leave, when her husband swung out of bed and hit the floor with a hard thump.

"You and I will settle this, so my wife won't have to endure any more of your obnoxious behavior," Devereau ordered. He pointed angrily toward the doorway that led to their sitting room, but Jackson didn't budge.

"I hear she made a beautiful bride, and that the Reverend even acted the part of the proud papa, rather than admitting his little girl—"

"Get out!" Charity blurted. "You of all people have no right to judge what we've done—especially since we've done nothing wrong."

The treelike Indian regarded her coolly and then looked Dillon up and down. "I can see my wedding present is unappreciated, so why should I bother sharing what I learned about Charity's mother? I'll just do the gentlemanly thing and go."

"What'd you find out?" Devereau snapped.

Jackson's smile was foxlike. "Ask Phoebe. She sends her love, by the way."

"Does she know where Mama is?" Charity leaned forward, trying to ignore the scout's leer. "If you don't tell us—"

"I was just leaving," he said with a shrug. "In fact, Abilene's so tame now that all my old cohorts have moved on, and I see no point in wasting my time here. Happy trails, Devereau." As stealthily as he came in, Blue disappeared through the doorway on moccasined feet, his snide laughter trailing him down the corridor.

"That's the best wedding present of all," Dillon muttered. "Any *friend* would've waited until morning." He stopped his ranting to look at Charity with a resigned sigh. "I'm truly sorry, honey. I never dreamed he'd—"

"I'm not surprised," she answered with a shrug. "Papa will always act sanctimonious, Mama will get what she wants with her smile, and Jackson Blue will behave as though he's still out among the buffalo. It's their nature, Dillon."

Once again her poise caught him off guard. Instead of cowering when Blue had barged in, she'd confronted him; instead of bemoaning yet another mishap on her wedding day, Charity displayed an insightful tolerance beyond her years. Dillon smiled at her. "You're right. I hadn't thought of it that way."

"Of course I'm right," she quipped, letting her gaze follow the length of his body. "What were we going to do—chase him down the hall, both of us naked, if he didn't leave?"

The thought struck him as so ridiculous that he shook with laughter. Charity was studying him with the solemn interest of an Eve who was anything but ashamed of her nudity, her gaze so provocative he felt himself hardening again. "It's a good thing you're not like the average preacher's daughter," he said as he approached the bed. "We'll probably run up against many an embarrassing situation between now and . . . what's the matter, honey? What're you staring at?

"You." Devereau probably didn't enjoy being scrutinized, yet now that he stood before her, with the last rays of the sunset casting a golden spell on his body, Charity couldn't pretend to be embarrassed by the sheer physical beauty of him. "You look like the famous statues I saw in a book once," she continued softly. "Except you're not wearing a leaf."

He stroked the tendrils of hair from her forehead, wondering how his life had taken such a turn in the few days he'd known this disarming young woman. When he reached for the sheet, Charity sat stockstill, letting him gaze at her pert breasts as the bedclothes fell away from her. She opened her arms, and with a reverence akin to prayer, Dillon made love to her until the room grew dark around them and the evening breeze cooled their sated bodies.

Charity shuddered, caught between dreaming and wakefulness, and inhaled the warm, spicy scent that could only be Dillon's. He was propped against the pillow-padded headboard, sipping whiskey, his arm loosely cradling her.

"Welcome back," he murmured. "Your timing's perfect, because our dinner just returned. The cook was none too pleased about warming it at this hour, though."

She stretched langidly and gave him a lazy grin. "What time is it?"

"What does it matter? Appetites are allowed their own schedule on a wedding night."

He kissed her forehead and rose to fetch the supper tray. Charity sat up, suddenly ravenous when the aromas of warm beef and bread reached her nose. The room's furnishings seemed to sleep in the shadows created by the small lamp Dillon had lit. He twisted a bottle carefully between his hands as he braced it against a firm thigh, and then a loud *pop* made her jump.

"Champagne," he explained as he held the streaming bottle over two goblets on the night stand. "I thought you might like to taste it even if you don't finish the glass."

Charity took the fizzing goblet he offered, smiling at the tiny bubbles that were spraying her hand. He slid onto the bed beside her and clinked their glasses together. "To you, my dear Charity," he said with an intimate grin, "and to the laughter and loving we'll share along the way."

She smiled and sipped lightly from the delicate

stemware. A tiny, bittersweet explosion occurred in her mouth, making her cough and laugh as she looked at Dillon. "Tickles all the way down," she gasped.

"Careful there. We can't have you turning into a lush—not when we have business to tend to later today." He went to get the supper tray, removing the silver domes from the two plates before bringing it to the bed. "Perhaps we can sit cross-legged, facing each other with this between us for a table," he suggested.

Eagerly she scooted around into the position he'd described, bumping her knees and shins to his. Their plates were laden with succulent steak and soft slices of bread, and carrots that smelled tangy with orange sauce. "Jackson Blue may be crude, but you can't argue with his taste in dinner."

Dillon laughed. "I can remember plenty of times when I was down on my luck at the tables, and he'd rustle me up some buffalo or whatever else he had. He's not always the inconsiderate lout you've seen."

Charity nodded and washed a bite of meat down with more of her champagne. "I figured he had some redeeming qualities or you wouldn't have saved his life."

Dillon watched her eyes meet his, requesting the story, and he was again amazed at how she seemed to recall the tiniest details from everything he'd ever told her. He struggled to keep his gaze on her face rather than on the two lamplit peaks swaying above her side of the tray. "We met here in Abilene, back when we were both starting out," he began quietly. "He didn't come into town often—preferred keeping company with those shaggy herds to rubbing elbows with drovers and merchants and sporting types."

Scowling, Charity chewed for a moment. "If he liked the buffalo, why'd he slaughter them? I thought Indians believed in the sanctity of the land and killing only to meet their needs."

"True enough. But for Jackson, killing buffalo was a way to earn a good living and get revenge on his mother's people at the same time." She was listening so intently she'd forgotten about her dinner, so he raised a forkful of carrots to her lips. "You see, Blue's only half Indian—Northern Cheyenne. His father was a colored man who abandoned his mother to go to the gold fields shortly after Blue was born, and even though the tribe took her back, they made their disapproval quite plain. Which is why he ran off."

"So that explains his odd coloring," she replied thoughtfully. Charity sipped from her goblet again, recalling the times she'd observed the overbearing scout. "But why's his English so perfect? He's obviously an educated man."

"Also true," Devereau replied, pleased that her dislike for Blue hadn't clouded her perception of him. "He attended a small mission school for a few years—long enough to learn to read and get baptized, before the freedom of the plains called him away. Blue studies every book he can get his hands on, and he can do a damned impressive recitation of Shakespeare when the mood strikes him."

"So how'd he end up at death's door? My guess is that an irrate husband went after him."

Devereau laughed loudly. "A logical assumption, but his paramours were too loyal and he was too slippery to get caught in the act. No pun intended."

A curious lightness was working its way up into Charity's head, and she grinned at her husband's joke. "So he cheated at cards, and the other players tried to scalp him with his own tomahawk. That's how he got the scar down the side of his face, right?"

He glanced at her goblet and realized the champagne was talking, because Charity wasn't a woman who took pleasure from someone else's pain. "Close as we can figure," he said quietly, "something spooked his horse, and the crazy animal charged into the herd they'd been stalking. Blue lost his seat . . . got gored by at least one buffalo, and should've been dead when I found him outside his cabin. His foot was still stuck in the stirrup."

She suddenly felt sick. "What'd you do?"

"I kept him drunk enough that the town doctor could patch him up," he replied as he squeezed her hand. "He was a surly patient. The first day he could hold a pistol, he asked me to lead his horse to the cabin door, without telling me he was going to shoot it."

"Oh, Dillon . . ."

"I think he harbors some resentment toward me to this day," Devereau finished with a wistful smile. "Had he died, he wouldn't have to admit to losing control of his mount—to himself or anyone who asks about his scar. Proud to a fault, Blue is."

The image of Jackson Blue's bloodsoaked body dangling from a horse still wasn't setting well. Charity laid her fork down. "Why doesn't he make up another story then? He's certainly capable."

"I'm sure he does when the occasion calls for it." Devereau sensed that the remains of their meal would go untouched, so he laid the tray on the night stand and coaxed Charity to snuggle up beside him. "That wasn't a fitting tale for a wedding night, honey, and I'm sorry I spoiled your supper."

His warmth accelerated the effect the alcohol was having on her. She shook her head, wearing a smile that felt lopsided. "You only told it because I asked. No harm done."

Charity's wooziness made her eyes wobble and she let her head flop endearingly against his shoulder. He pulled her close, tucking the sheet around them. She had every right to be exhausted, and she was giggly with her first liquor, and Devereau fully intended to let her sleep . . . if only she weren't running her fingers lightly across his chest, in a rhythmic pattern that occasionally grazed his nipples. He sucked in sharply when her ring snagged a tuft of hair.

Charity bolted upright. "Dillon, I didn't mean to hurt you. I—"

"No harm done," he echoed. He kissed her hand, noting the way the gold band twisted loosely on her finger. "I should've had the goldsmith make it a little smaller. It was nearly twice this size when I took it into the shop this morning."

Vague questions ran through her mind, questions she wasn't sure she should ask. "You had this ring before?" she mumbled, studying the diamond's wide, flat face for the hundredth time. The stone was so large she saw her own miniature image in its glistening surface.

"I bought it with my first big winnings, after a spectacular night aboard the *Delta Queen,*" he replied with a grin. "Do you like it, Charity? I can get you another one if you'd prefer a different shape or setting, but I didn't see one I liked at the jeweler's today."

"Oh no, it—it's lovely." She hesitated to quiz him about this rather sensitive subject, yet her tongue was loose enough to let the question slip out. "Was this ring originally for another woman, Devereau?"

Charity's doleful face made him hug her close. "No, but it does have a shady past, I'm afraid." He smiled, doubting she'd feel offended by the truth. "That was my first shiner. It's a genuine diamond, the kind gamblers wear when the stakes are high. By slipping the stone to the underside of your hand," he explained as he demonstrated on Charity's slender finger, "you can read the cards as you deal them out to your opponents. It takes a lot of skill to pull it off without being detected, but it's one more way to defend yourself against unscrupulous sharps."

Suddenly she was giggling, a victim of the champagne. Then she wiggled the massive diamond in the light from the lamp, delighted with the rainbows that flashed on the white sheet in front of her. "And how do I defend myself against *you,* Mr. Devereau?" she asked in a husky whisper.

"You don't." He gave in to the urge to kiss her upturned lips, knowing it would lead to anything but the rest his adorable new wife deserved. "You entrust your heart and soul to me, dear Charity, as I've entrusted mine to you."

The afternoon sun blazed down, and squinting made Charity's head pound harder. Why did people drink, if this awful, sick throbbing was the result? Or did they become drunkards by drowning the pain with more and more alcohol? Her stomach rumbled queasily and she forced herself to keep pace with Dillon, who was reminiscing about his previous days in Abilene.

"The Drover's Cottage I originally directed you to used to be right over there," he said as he escorted her along Texas Street. "It stood three stories high and had a hundred and twenty rooms. The Gores ran it—served imported liquor and food as good as you find in St. Louis—but they dismantled the place and moved on to Ellsworth, where the cattle business was still flourishing."

A blind man could tell that the girl beside him had a first-rate hangover, but she'd refused to rest in the hotel room. Devereau kept up his patter as they went to visit with Phoebe Thomas, hoping to make her feel better. "And over there was the Lone

Star, a dance hall where the girls wore knee-length skirts and Mexican camisoles. The Texas cowpokes liked that sort of thing, I suppose."

"And you didn't?"

Dillon bit back a laugh, because Charity sounded as though even her voice was in a great deal of pain. "Some of them weren't too comely, as I recall, but when the longhorns were in town there was such a demand for female companionship that looks didn't matter much. Lots of those ladies wore white kid boots with derringers tucked inside them, because when hell was in season—that's what we called it when the trigger-happy Texans showed up—everybody feared for his life."

It didn't sound like such a fine place to be, and yet he spoke in a tone that glorified all the chaos that must have reigned in Abilene back then. Charity held her tongue as they kept walking, knowing her headache would sour any comments she made. They passed in front of a school building, and she couldn't help noticing a neat yellow house across the street. "It's not often you see such a high board fence around a place in town," she remarked. "Was that to keep the rowdy element in, or to keep it out?"

Devereau wondered if his bride had a sixth sense about such things. "Actually, that was the classiest bordello in town—and maybe it still is," he replied with a chuckle. "Mattie Silks served only the finest champagne, and her girls were the prettiest things this side of Kansas City."

From the corner of her eye, Charity saw his dimple appear. "And how would you know that?"

Devereau cleared his throat, still laughing. "That's where Hickok and I had our shoot-out, when Mattie's choicest dove couldn't decide which of us deserved the pleasure of her company," he replied lightly. "Here we are, sweetheart. Are you sure you want to go in? I can ask Mrs. Thomas a few questions while you rest on that bench, if you'd rather."

The worn wooden seat outside Thomas's Dry Goods Emporium looked terribly inviting, shaded as it was by the store's porch roof, but Charity declined. Phoebe Thomas was her best chance to hear about Mama—anyone passing through Abilene was likely to visit the general store—and it was up to her to gather information Dillon might miss. He was normally as observant as any man, but returning here had put him in a nostalgic mood and Phoebe Thomas was a friend from those early years . . . a very pretty friend.

The moment they stepped through the door, Mrs. Thomas flashed a beguiling smile, as though she'd been expecting them. "Surely you newlyweds aren't so bored that you've come to *shop,*" she teased.

Charity suddenly wished she'd worn Voletta Littleton's deep green gown. Not only was Phoebe radiant in a rose blouse and a flowing skirt of a slightly deeper hue, but a glance around the tidy store made her feel even frumpier: the curtains were made from the same blue gingham she was wearing. The storekeeper's spritely wife had noticed this, too, and dismissed her with a bat of her long lashes.

"What can I show you today?" she asked with a smile intended only for Dillon.

"Two things, actually," Devereau replied. "We'd like to look at your yard goods first. I doubt we'll have time to get any dresses made before we leave, but I thought we'd check your stock."

"And?" the raven-haired proprietress asked as she led them toward the fabric bolts stacked along the wall.

"We've come for some information. Jackson Blue thought you might be able to help us."

Charity preceded him down the aisle behind Phoebe, feeling more mortified by the minute. Ordinarily the prospect of new clothes overjoyed her, but buying yard goods from a woman who was so fashionably dressed—and who was openly flirting with her husband—was the ultimate embarrassment.

"We have some lovely new linens and silks," Phoebe was saying. She waved a graceful hand toward bolts of summery pastels, and then glanced at Charity's dress. "Or perhaps Mrs. Devereau prefers the simplicity of cotton prints."

"Mrs. Devereau wants only your best," he replied, running folds of the elegant silks through his fingers. "What would you choose for yourself, Phoebe? You've always dressed to perfection."

Mrs. Thomas lowered her eyes coquettishly. "Linen and broadcloth make the nicest skirts. For dresses you can't do better than silk or organza. What colors?"

A glance at Charity told him she was still in her hangover's nasty grip, so he draped an arm loosely around her shoulders. "Enough for a dress out of the lavender silk, and one from the green-striped bolt," he said in a thoughtful tone, "and while you're cutting, we'll ask you a few questions. Wouldn't want Will to think we were wasting your time on idle gossip."

Charity looked toward the store's front counter, where Mr. Thomas was trying to wait on a well-heeled gentleman without being obvious about watching them. He was large and bulky, with indistinct features, as though a sculptor had carved him from a block of pale granite and became bored before he finished. She recognized his expression, though: he, too, had the feeling that Phoebe and Dillon were oblivious to the presence of anyone else.

"Will's not a sharp enough storekeeper to complain about how *I* do business," Phoebe was saying in a low voice. Her scissors flew swiftly across the width of the lavender silk. "But then, Abilene doesn't need the sort of store Jake Karatofsky used to keep when the cowboys overran us each summer. After you and the cattle left, the place really died back, Devereau. But I guess you've noticed."

Dillon chuckled. "I can't take all the blame. The town lost a lot of its luster when Wild Bill was ushered out."

Phoebe waved him off with a girlish laugh that made her dark eyes sparkle, and then began unrolling the striped silk onto her wide wooden cutting table. "William Butler Hickok was so full of 'imself I'm not sure he realized why they fired 'im. Married some widow named Agnes—when she came through with the *circus,* mind you—and headed west to where the gamblin' was greener." With a coy shake of her head she glanced surreptitiously toward the front of the store. "You boys didn't leave me many choices. Wasn't gettin' any younger, so I settled for Will a few years back. A decent man—though decency never cut much butter with me, you know."

Charity's head was throbbing harder, and she found Phoebe's chatter both annoying and inappropriate. She gave Dillon's ribcage a purposeful nudge with her elbow. "Perhaps you should show her the photograph now."

Devereau gave her an indulgent smile and reached for the inside pocket of his coat, but not before Phoebe could continue her prattle.

"I see you haven't lost the Devereau charm. Still keeps the ladies pawin' over you, doesn't it?"

Charity felt her color rising with her temperature. How *dare* this woman behave like such a hussy, making suggestive statements as though she weren't even there? She snatched the wooden frame from Dillon's hand and shoved it toward Phoebe Thomas. "Have you seen these people lately?" she demanded. "We thought they might've come through town, or we wouldn't have stopped here ourselves."

The woman's eyes narrowed slightly; her manner became catlike as she compared the woman in the picture to Charity. "So Blue wasn't just shootin' the breeze," she said with a knowing grin. "Maggie and Mr. Powers passed through several days ago—it's been like old home week in Abilene lately. Or was she a legend before your time, Devereau?"

Dillon shrugged, a bit confused. "I don't recall ever meeting—"

"Oh, you'd remember her," Phoebe replied. She nipped her lush lower lip, as though deciding which sordid details to reveal. "Must've been when the Kansas Pacific was bein' completed, because Powers was here to oversee it—and no woman alive would forget *him* either. Which was why Mattie catered to 'im herself."

Devereau glanced at Charity, who was looking decidedly peaked, and thought he'd better speed the conversation along. "Any ideas where they were going? It's important that we find them before—"

"West!" she replied with a dramatic flip of her wrist. "It's where they *all* go. Probably to Wichita or Dodge, because Ellsworth and Newton are pretty small potatoes to an operator like Erroll."

Charity was ready to thank the petite actress and head for the train station to buy tickets, but Dillon was apparently too enthralled by Phoebe's performance to budge. She gritted her teeth, knowing that whatever else this jezebel revealed about Mama would be aimed right at her heart, to puncture what little pride she had left.

"Powers was a wise one all right," Mrs. Thomas

continued in a low, animated voice. "Only brought Maggie to Abilene once, because he had trouble keepin' track of 'er. Seems she had a hankerin' for cowboys—liked their whips and spurs, I heard—so he checked 'er in at Mattie's, with firm instructions that Miss Silks was to keep a close eye on 'er. Next thing we knew, the law got called in."

Obviously pleased with herself, Mrs. Thomas folded the two pieces of silk into a neat pile. Charity lost all patience when she saw that the woman intended to leave her story unfinished while she took her sweet time replacing the bolts on the shelf. "Well?" she demanded. "Just what did this Maggie *do?*"

Wearing a smile that was both devious and delighted, Phoebe turned toward them. "She sneaked out of Mattie's private quarters and took on a little business for herself—a cattle baron, as I remember it. Got to playin' 'im a little rough, and all but bit the poor man's ear off. Made a terrible mess, and—"

Devereau, seeing Charity's face pale as though someone had sucked the life out of her, quickly steered his wife toward the door. "Have that parcel delivered to Hathaway House," he instructed over his shoulder. "I'll send the money back with your errand boy."

Anger like she'd never experienced churned within Charity, and by the time she and Dillon were outside she was ready to explode. She shook herself out of his grasp, glaring at him. "Did you enjoy that little *visit,* Mr. Devereau? If you intended to shame me all to pieces, you did a damn fine job of it."

"*Me?*" he replied in a purposeful voice. "Honey, we went there because Blue said she—"

"Don't play games with me!" she shrieked. "Phoebe's your old flame—the whore you and

Hickok shot it out over. And now you've made me feel poor and wretched and homely and—and—"

Her face became splotchy and tears suddenly drenched her cheeks. Devereau knew he deserved every bitter accusation she could hurl at him, because he should have remembered how vindictive Phoebe could be in the presence of female competition. He hadn't approved of the way Mrs. Thomas belittled her husband or spoke so suggestively, but it was too late to explain that to Charity now. She was devastated—never mind the jealous streak as green as her overflowing eyes—and she would probably never trust him again. And even though he hadn't been responsible for Phoebe's barbs or Maggie's disreputable behavior, he was sorry Charity had been hurt by them.

She blustered at him a few moments more, oblivious to the stares of people passing by, and then she wound down like a top about to topple. She rubbed her forehead gingerly, still feeling the champagne's vengeance. Dillon waited until all her anger had evaporated, and then spoke very gently to her.

"Charity, I regret what's happened," he said, imploring her to meet his gaze with her own. "I'll understand if you want to stop searching for your mother, honey. We'll buy our tickets for Kansas City and head home first thing in the morning."

She considered his suggestion only briefly before shaking her head. "Forget it, Devereau. A deal's a deal, and I'm not letting you out of it," she replied bitterly. "After all, I entrusted my heart and soul to you. Remember?"

Chapter 14

Her words still stung the next morning as Devereau settled beside Charity on the train seat. She'd remained distant since their quarrel on Texas Street; not cold—her red-rimmed eyes and pale face proclaimed her misery to all who saw her—but certainly not the loving bride he'd looked forward to entertaining during the ride to Wichita.

Dillon reached over to steady her when the train lurched away from the station, only to have her shrink from his touch. He could feel her father studying them from the opposite seat, but he didn't acknowledge the preacher's presence. He'd traveled hundreds of miles in contented silence when he was a railroad sharp, yet these few moments of his wife's stifled anguish were already tearing at him. "I—I sent Abe a telegraph this morning. Told him we'd be out awhile longer," he mumbled.

Charity nodded and continued gazing out her window. The outskirts of Abilene were giving way to sparse farmsteads and pastureland, which didn't inspire a reply.

Dillon shifted to allow her more room. She was leaning against the papered wall of the car, all but pressing her face to the window to avoid looking at him. When the conductor came by and asked for their tickets, he was glad for the intrusion. Had his married friends told him about the wrath of a wife scorned, he would've scoffed at their inability to charm their women into talking again. But Charity's heartache separated the two of them from the other passengers, actors in a painful little drama he was forced to share and understand.

And he did understand it: Charity, in her sheltered innocence, had romanticized his profession, a freewheeling life that included a few sporting women along the way—until one of those women stepped out of his past and flaunted herself. Not even a seasoned, secure wife would welcome Phoebe Thomas's flirtatious presence or her advice about clothing. He'd been a fool not to anticipate that. With a sorrowful glance at Charity's calico dress, he resigned himself to the monotony of a long, silent ride.

Charity ached all over from avoiding Dillon's attention, but her physical pain was nothing compared to her frustration. She stared out the window, vaguely aware of the train's steady rocking as the pastureland and rippling wheat fields passed by, seeing only Phoebe Thomas. The storekeeper's wife embodied all the graces she could never possess: coquettish charm, flawless beauty, a nimble wit . . . exactly the sort of woman Dillon Devereau should have married. She almost smiled—he *did* deserve the haughty shrew beneath Phoebe's opalescent facade, after the way he treated her in the dry goods store!

Glancing at the nattily dressed man beside her, Charity was surprised to see his brow puckered with uncharacteristic remorse. Gone was the boyish dimple and the smooth, emotionless face he wore to play cards; his eyes belonged to a sad old hound who'd lost his mistress, and she quickly looked away. Perhaps he wanted to explain or apologize, but since Papa and the other passengers were within earshot, there was little chance of that. She excused herself to the front of the car to choose two magazines, and spent the remainder of her ride studying pictures of the latest fashions and hats.

The sky was overcast when the three of them stepped down onto the platform at the Wichita station. Dillon directed a young boy to see that their luggage got to the Occidental Hotel, and then guided her toward the main part of town with his hand on her elbow. He felt stiffly formal walking beside her. Papa followed a few paces behind them, his footsteps light and jaunty.

"Certainly looks like rain," he commented cheerfully. "By tomorrow these streets will undoubtedly resemble a hog wallow."

Devereau wondered how the subject of hogs had occurred to the preacher, yet he was glad to be part of a conversation. "A few years back, summer showers were the bane of every merchant and saloonkeeper in town—made for such messy floors, when all the cowboys tromped in, you know," he added over his shoulder. "But as you can see, a lot of the halls here have also closed and the owners have probably moved on to Caldwell or Dodge."

Sighing, he glanced at the young woman who walked so quietly beside him. What could he say to draw her out of her disappointment? How could he erase the shadows that lurked around her woeful green eyes? "I think you'll enjoy staying at the Occidental," he offered in a voice that sounded inept even to his own ears. "It's one of Wichita's finest lodgings."

Charity cleared her throat. "Of course. I—I think I'd like to rest for a while."

"Train rides can be tiring," Dillon agreed as they entered the Occidental's main parlor. He secured two rooms at the front desk while Charity and her father watched out the window for their luggage. As he escorted them up the hotel's elegant staircase, he wondered at how he'd changed since he last rented a room here: the bold young Romeo who'd lavished his winnings on many a willing lady was now desperately trying to woo his wife with talk of train rides. Handing Reverend Scott's key to him, he guided Charity to the next room down the hall.

She glanced joylessly at the elegant furnishings, avoiding an ornate gilt-edged mirror for fear of what she'd see there. Why did she feel as though they were attending a wake instead of continuing their honeymoon? The room's window let in the eerie light that preceded an afternoon rainstorm, but looking out to the street below seemed better than lingering awkwardly in the gloom with Dillon, so she went to stand in front of it.

Charity's forlorn silhouette made Devereau clench his fists, annoyed with himself. Only two days ago he would have tossed his pretty wife upon the bed and kissed her playfully until she laughed or made love to him. Now her posture signaled that she wished to remain untouched, alone with the agony he'd caused her. "I . . . I'll check around town to see if the locals recognize Powers or your mother from the photograph," he said quietly. "After you've rested, we'll go downstairs for dinner."

"Perhaps," she mumbled. The door closed behind her, and Charity's shoulders sagged. Holding Dillon's past against him was a foolish waste of their time together, yet she couldn't forget Phoebe's indiscreet chatter and sparkling eyes. That Mrs. Thomas had been a prostitute wasn't nearly as unsettling as the knowledge that she'd inspired Devereau to fight for her company. Would he challenge another man for *her?* As Charity watched his slender form cross the street, she knew the answer didn't really matter. Once they found Mama, it would be as though she and Dillon Devereau had never met.

The door behind her opened to admit Papa and

the errand boy, who set her suitcase beside the bed and returned to the hallway for a large trunk. Her father reached into his pocket for a coin, and then closed the door behind the boy.

"I should've guessed a dandy like Devereau would travel with such sizable luggage," he said, all the while studying the pressed-metal pattern on the trunk's top. "But covering a tip's the least I can do for my new son-in-law."

She was surprised to hear Papa refer to Dillon as part of the family, and more surprised that he sounded pleased about it. Charity sensed he was leading into a lecture, so she gave him a weak smile. "I was hoping to take a nap—"

"Which is precisely why I can't understand the way you've shoved Dillon out the door with your cold shoulder," Papa interrupted. "When your mother and I were newlyweds, you couldn't have pried us apart with a—that is, we . . . we couldn't bear to leave each other's sight."

In light of what they'd learned about Mama this past week, Charity could only glance curiously at her father for admitting such a thing. "He wanted to see if anyone recognized Mr. Powers and—"

"He was acting extremely patient, considering how little experience he's had at being turned away by a woman." Papa studied her face as though it were a passage of Scripture whose deeper meaning eluded him. "No matter what we may think of Devereau's profession, he's proven himself a kind, thoughtful man who's obviously attached to you. What crime has he committed, that you've cast him away so soon?"

Charity stared, unable to answer him. She could recall instances where her father had scorned the handsome gambler to his face, not to mention the ultimatum that led to a marriage for her honor's sake. "I—I don't understand how you can defend Dillon all of a sudden, when you used to—"

"You're not a little girl anymore, Charity. I realized that when I was ushering you to the altar," he replied wistfully. He brushed her hair away from her face, a gesture of utmost tenderness from a man who'd bruised her on occasion. "I admit that my means weren't the noblest, but the end certainly justified them. Which of the hapless lads back home would make you a suitable husband? Devereau can give you everything you'll ever want, and he respects your intelligence and talent."

Charity gazed steadily at her father as tears rose to her eyes. He was being the gentle, concerned parent she vaguely recalled from her childhood—but he didn't know the truth about Phoebe Thomas, or what she'd revealed. She looked at the floor, knowing that if she mentioned Devereau's former flame she must also tell what she'd learned about Mama, which would be easier to discuss if Papa weren't suddenly acting so sympathetic.

"A bridegroom can inadvertantly hurt his new wife in an . . . impassioned moment," her father suggested gently.

She blushed, unaccustomed to talking about such an intimate topic. "No, he—everything's *fine*, Papa," Charity stammered. He wouldn't leave her alone until she explained the way she was treating the husband he'd chosen for her, so she took a deep breath. "We talked with a lady friend of Dillon's yesterday. Someone he knew from when he lived in Abilene."

"Ah. I imagine she was a fetching sort," he said as he adjusted his spectacles. "Devereau wouldn't be seen with any other kind."

"Papa, how *can* you—"

Her father grasped her arms gently. "He certainly has eyes for *you,* daughter. Don't sell yourself short, just because you married him under unusual circumstances."

Confused by Papa's tenderness, Charity could only utter, "She was a who—prostitute, Papa. It was Phoebe Thomas, from the wedding."

His eyes widened, and then he sighed. "Such women flourish where cowboys and gamblers have cash to burn. Devereau has apparently outgrown his penchant for her type, though, or he'd house a few at the Crystal Queen. We should give a man who's mended his ways—and a woman who's married out of that profession—the benefit of the doubt, don't you think?"

Papa's gaze remained calm as he awaited her response. And he had a point: Dillon's gambling establishment was no brothel. Forgiving his past was the Christian thing to do, but dammit, Phoebe Thomas would've dropped her dress the moment she found a way to get Dillon alone! It was then that Charity realized the hussy's inclinations weren't her husband's fault, and she let out her anger in a long, sheepish breath.

"Now then," Papa continued with a smile, "tell me why your husband would expose you to this relationship from his past, unless the benefits outweighed the risks. He's not the sort who'd be cruel to you on purpose."

Where had Papa hidden this compassion all these years? Charity wished that her answer was less likely to hurt his feelings, now that he was in such an understanding mood. "Dillon thought Phoebe might've seen Mama and Erroll Powers," she began quietly. "She knew them, all right. She was the one who suggested we look for them here in Wichita."

"Ah." Papa cleared his throat expectantly. "Did she say anything else? Perhaps tell how long ago—"

"Mrs. Thomas has a talent for storytelling, it

NEW YORK TIMES BESTSELLING AUTHOR
JANELLE TAYLOR
DESTINY MINE
SHANNON DRAKE
BLUE HEAVEN, BLACK NIGHT
BESTSELLING, AWARD-WINNING AUTHOR
GEORGINA GENTRY
SONG OF THE WARRIOR
BETINA KRAHN
MIDNIGHT MAGIC

seems, and her information wasn't very complimentary."

"I see." Her father looked around the lavishly furnished room as though he felt embarrassed for showing her a sensitive side he'd kept hidden for most of her life. "No sense delving into things beyond our control—that's for God and your mother to settle between themselves. I'll leave now, so you'll be rested when Dillon returns . . . probably find us a church, so we can attend services tomorrow."

She watched Papa until he shut the door, wondering if their conversation had actually taken place. Charity had seen her father sort through parishioners' problems with the same level-headed patience he'd just shown her, but being the recipient of such wisdom was a new, immensely comforting experience. Like being soothed by the hand of the Lord.

Charity felt her resentment melt away, along with the tension that had kept her rigidly distant from Dillon for twenty-four hours now . . . twenty-four lonely, aching hours of holding the wrong grudge. Sleep was suddenly the last thing she needed, and the urge to see her husband made her hurry to the mirror. Her eyes were bright, her cheeks flushed with anticipation, and before common sense could slow her down she stepped out of the room and descended the stairs.

Douglas Avenue stretched before her in either direction, thronged with people doing their Saturday shopping. To the west she could see a vast maze of wooden corrals and gates, reminders of when cattle and cowboys clogged these streets only a few years ago. The Douglas Avenue Hotel and the Texas House dominated the shops that stood shoulder-to-shoulder beside them, their plate glass windows bright with sunshine that pierced the ominous clouds rolling in from the prairie. Charity walked east along the avenue, guessing she was more likely to spot Dillon at that end of town.

The people she passed were plainly dressed and industrious-looking—wheat farmers, she was guessing, because of the supplies the men were hoisting into wagons and the leathery faces that spoke of days spent in the heat and the wind. Most of the women wore calico, although a few sported fashionable hats and dresses, their parasols tilted toward the unrelenting sun. It could have been a street in Jefferson City, and Charity strolled contentedly along, window-shopping when she wasn't searching for her husband's familiar form.

She spotted a white steeple, probably the church where Papa was inquiring about services. Then she stopped, directly across from a building called the New York Store. Two Indians were standing beside the large window, staring fixedly at her.

A man jostled her, but Charity scarcely noticed. The brick-red faces across the avenue were expressionless, with somber, dark eyes that seemed riveted upon her. One of the Indians wore his shoulder-length ebony hair loose, held in place by a leather band that bisected his forehead; his companion's hair was pulled back in a braid. Both were dressed in shabby white men's clothing. They were a breed apart from aggressive, arrogant Jackson Blue, projecting the pathetic image of a beaten people. Yet their gaze never wavered.

Determined not to appear frightened, Charity turned to study the window display behind her and was seized by two hands that locked upon her shoulders.

"Do you see why I've told you never to walk strange streets alone?" Devereau demanded in an urgent whisper. "I could've been *anyone*, Charity, and you could've been whisked away before your father or I knew to come looking for you." Still grasping her tightly, he glanced across the street to where she'd been staring. The Indians were gone. "And where *is* your father?"

"He—he went to see about attending services tomorrow," she stammered. Her heart was hammering from the shock of being accosted. "I was looking for you, because I wanted to . . ." Charity stopped explaining, all desire to make amends replaced by resentment.

"Well, it's a good thing you found me," he muttered, turning her toward the hotel as he took her elbow. "We'll discuss this in the room. I don't want to repeat the public argument we had in Abilene, if you don't mind."

Hurrying to keep pace with Dillon's long strides, Charity *did* mind being ushered along as though she were an errant child caught in her misdeeds. She pressed her lips together, holding her temper until they'd marched into the Occidental and past a desk clerk who smirked knowingly at her.

The door to their room was barely closed behind her before Charity wrenched herself from Dillon's grasp. "You can't just herd me down the street like some little *heifer!*" she blurted. "I'm a married woman, perfectly capable of—"

"I know," he said with a chuckle. Dillon crossed his arms and leaned against the door, watching her vent her frustration as only Charity knew how.

"I was looking for *you,* Dillon, because after talking to Papa I realized how silly I was to—oh, never mind! You're not worth it!" She turned away, blinking back tears that only infuriated her more.

"You're absolutely right." Noting her jutting chin and clenched fists, Devereau grinned openly. His sulking child-bride was now the vibrant woman he preferred, and he didn't care what caused the transformation so long as she didn't shut him out with her awful silence again. "Perhaps I was a bit overbearing—"

"Damn right you were."

"—but watching two redskins ogle you while you returned the favor would make any new husband jealous of—"

"What?" Charity could see enough of his face in the gilt-edged mirror to catch the flicker of his dimple, and she wheeled around to confront him. "You're laughing at me! This is all a joke to—you know I wasn't *ogling* those—"

"I know what I saw," he replied with a teasing shrug, "and if you'd rather feel the arms of some savage around you, holding you the way I—"

"You're the most despicable—obnoxious . . ." Charity fully intended to leave the room, but Devereau moved to block the door. When she reached up to shove him aside, he pulled her against his rigid body. Her next protest was stifled by a kiss so powerful it rocked her head back, the kiss she'd been longing for but had wanted to bestow herself.

When Dillon realized she wasn't responding, he gently released her. "I didn't intend to corral you like a—heifer—out there, honey," he whispered, "but you do need to watch out for yourself. Wichita's close to Indian territory, and I'd never forgive myself if . . . why are you staring at my vest, sweetheart?"

Charity sighed. "I was coming to tell you . . . I thought you'd be glad to see me, and instead you staged a big act like—like Papa does."

He winced, wishing he'd handled the incident differently. "I *was* glad to see you, Charity—glad to see the sunshine of your smile again," he murmured against her ear. "And I was in such a hurry to get you back here because, well—I didn't want to kiss and make up out there on the street. It could lead to behavior that gets me kicked out of town again."

His grin teased her until she couldn't help looking into his playful eyes. "Lewd and lascivious behavior, Mr. Devereau?" she asked quietly.

"Pure, unadulterated lust," he replied, relieved to see her sense of humor returning. "The kind that pops a man's pants buttons. The kind Phoebe Thomas is too hardened to share or understand. The kind I feel when I see your hair floating around your shoulders and your eyes snapping with laughter . . . the kind I missed so damned badly last night, honey."

Charity's mouth fell open at Dillon's eloquence. His gaze was warm and direct, all signs of teasing gone as he mesmerized her with a smile full of passion's promise. "I missed you, too, Dillon."

"Show me how much."

His whispered challenge sent a bolt of summer lightning through her body. Was that distant thunder she heard, or the roar of her own pulse? Charity wasn't sure how to begin—she didn't know how to lead a man in the intimate, physical way Dillon was asking for. In a sudden burst of inspiration, she tried to think of how Phoebe might have taken matters in hand.

When her fingers closed firmly around his manhood, Devereau rejoiced. It was an effort not to tear her clothes off, and the only control he had over his burgeoning need for her was the thought that her hesitant, unschooled advances would fuel his ardor by forcing him to wait for release.

Yet Charity was already unbuttoning his shirt, nuzzling his chest with eager lips as she bared him above the waist. Her fingers were surprisingly nimble, and his buckle and buttons gave way without causing her a moment's frustration. Before he could whisper his approval, his wife's hands were spanning his bare hip, shoving his trousers and underwear down past his thighs. Dillon grabbed at both sides of the door jamb to keep his balance, the blood rushing through his head. Surely she wouldn't be so bold as to . . .

With Devereau's shaft pointing directly at her, her next move seemed obvious yet unsettling—until Charity recalled how much he had enjoyed pleasing *her* with his mouth, and the unexpected rapture she'd experienced because of it. She knelt to kiss the rounded pink tip of him, inhaling the earthy scent of his secret parts, and then lowered her mouth very slowly. His groan and gentle thrusting were all the encouragement she needed.

Dillon felt himself being carried away on a tide of urgency. Taking deep, gulping breaths, he gently pushed Charity away. "Lie down on the floor," he breathed. "I don't want to hurt you, or offend you."

Scowling, Charity felt herself being rolled backward. She doubted that anything her handsome husband could do would seem offensive; his smile tightened with desire as he slipped his hands beneath her dress to lower her underwear. "Dillon, I—"

"Shhh, I want you to enjoy this, too," he murmured before kissing her firmly on the mouth.

Charity felt her silken pantaloons slither over her shoetops and then Dillon was lowering himself onto her, his eyes half-closed. They became one quickly and forcefully, his breathing as agitated as hers, yet her mind refused to go along with it. She bucked beneath him, shoving at his chest. "I was showing you how much I missed you last night, remember? Roll over and let me finish, Devereau."

Dillon felt himself being pushed sideways onto the rug. Charity was scrambling on top of him, never losing the tight, intimate grip she had on him even though their clothing made the maneuver tricky. The determined glint in her eye made him chuckle. Then he sucked in his breath as she sat up and slid down the length of him again and again. "Charity, I—"

"Promise me you'll never make me feel small in front of another woman," she ordered in a husky voice.

"I—I promise." His hoarse laughter nearly choked off his reply. It took all his restraint not to rush ahead of her deep, purposeful thrusts, but he wanted Charity to discover her own needs and responses, things he couldn't teach her with words.

"And promise me we'll never waste another night being angry at each other," she continued, although her desire threatened to destroy even her command of the simplest language.

Dillon hadn't been angry at *her* after their meeting with Phoebe Thomas, but he was in no position to quibble. "Y-yes ma'am," he replied in a strained voice. He saw her eyes closing and her jaw going slack as the fire of their lovemaking consumed her. "Mrs. Devereau?" he whispered.

Charity braced herself, her hands flat on the floor. With great effort she raised her hips and opened her eyes, suspended above him. "What?" she rasped.

Dillon grinned devilishly. "Don't stop until you *can't* stop. And don't let me quit before then either."

"You . . ." Charity instinctively sought the places and pressures that would bring them both release, but Dillon grasped her hips and held her above him again. "Now what?" she panted. "Dammit, Devereau, I—"

"Never, never fake your own pleasure with me, my love," he said with deliberate emphasis. "It's highly insulting. And Phoebe wasn't nearly as good at it as she thought she was."

Why anyone would want to shortchange herself with a lover like Dillon Devereau was beyond her, but Charity didn't have the strength to contemplate such pretenses. Whimpering, she lunged toward him again, finding the exquisite fit that would send them both to the heights of this new glory she'd found with him. Wondrous shudders overtook her and she clung desperately to his neck, too incoherent with joy to reply with words.

Devereau heard all he needed to. He wrapped her in his arms and spent himself until he was drained of the resentment and boredom and loneliness other women had left him feeling at this moment. Charity filled him with her unstudied warmth—spontaneous combustion was another of her finest talents, he decided. He rested on the floor, her sweet weight so perfectly fitted against him, until both of them could breathe normally again.

"Let's undress and get into bed," he murmured. "Until my card game tomorrow afternoon, I've nothing better to do than make love to you, Charity. In fact, there *is* nothing better than making love to you."

The tenderness in his golden eyes made her gulp against a rush of happy tears, and she didn't remind him that Papa would expect them to attend church. For now, all that existed was this man who could turn her soul inside out with a single smile—a husband who offered his past as a source of the most pleasurable enlightenment, if she would accept it as such. Charity kissed the tip of his nose, slowly stood up, and offered him her hand.

As they explored each other's senses and preferences, Charity felt like a graceful dove soaring above the things of this earth on the luxurious currents of Dillon's affection. Her leg muscles grew limp, her lips ached from what must have been a million kisses, and she was unaware that her husband was in the middle of another anecdote about his cowtown acquaintances when she drifted off to sleep, nestled against the comforting length of him.

Chapter 15

When she awoke, the room was lit by a single lamp and Dillon was watching her emerge from her dreams, appearing dreamlike himself as he smiled at her. He scooted onto the edge of the bed and reached for her hand. "Are you all right, sweetheart? You've been asleep so long, I was ready to wake you."

"What time is it?" Charity rose up on her elbows, shaking away her drowsiness as she took in Dillon's earnest expression. He was dressed in a clean white shirt and gray striped trousers, looking freshly shaved and rested.

"It's nearly eight. I brought us up some breakfast, but if you're not hungry—"

"I'm starved," she insisted, sitting up to emphasize her reply. Languid sensations lingered in her body, reminding her of how they had spent the previous evening. She recalled their exchanged promises, which, though centered upon carnal matters, were somehow every bit as sacred as the marriage vows they'd taken. And to think Phoebe Thomas had only pretended to be satisfied when she was with Dillon . . .

Charity then realized it was Sunday morning, time to prepare for worship, and she didn't want to enter God's house with unexpressed apologies on her conscience. "Yesterday after you went into town, I finally realized how stupid I was to blame you for Phoebe's slatternly behavior," she said quietly. "That's why I went out alone to look for you. I'm sorry for the way I assumed—"

"The apologies are all mine, sweetheart." He reached over to knead her lovely bare shoulders, gazing directly into her eyes. "Phoebe hasn't changed a bit since our Abilene days, and I should've found someone else to ask about your mother's whereabouts. I can't blame you for being furious with me, although I certainly don't regret the way we made up. Do you?"

Charity grinned coyly, recalling each intimate nuance of their lovemaking. "I was more jealous than angry. She's very . . . fetching—that was the word Papa used."

"You told your father about our visit to her store?"

"Only because he quizzed me about why I wasn't speaking to you. And I left out the stories about Mama being at Mattie Silks's place." She glanced toward the tray of food Dillon had left on the bedside table and lifted the linen cloth from it. Hunger stabbed her empty stomach when she smelled the warm bread, and she took a generous slice. She was pleased they wouldn't have to rush downstairs to eat, because these quiet times talking to her husband were moments to savor.

The lamp cast a golden aura around his hair and shoulders; the rain-cooled breeze from the window brought out his vital, masculine scent—another reason Charity preferred to remain in their room just now. "We had quite a talk about you, Mr. Devereau," she continued in a soft voice. "Papa's very happy to have you for his son-in-law, and he convinced me how unfair I was being, holding you accountable for Mrs. Thomas's wicked ways."

Dillon chuckled, biting into the bread she was holding in front of his mouth. "You're sure there wasn't more to it? He's not exactly enthused about this trip, you know."

Charity looked deep into Devereau's earnest eyes and knew that forgiving him was one of Papa's finest ideas. "He admitted we didn't marry under ideal circumstances, but he was concerned about us being at odds so soon. I don't recall such a time myself, but he told me he and Mama were inseparable the first few years they were together."

"Back before she met Powers, I imagine," he replied with a short laugh. He studied her for a moment, and decided she would be sympathetic to a secret he'd been keeping, now that she understood other parts of his past. "My parents were very close, too, until my father died in a fire. Mama's injuries were relatively minor, but she was gone less than a month later. Victim of a broken heart, I think."

"Oh, Dillon, I'm sorry." Charity reached for him, sensing he'd shared his pain with very few people. "Is that why you left home when you were so young, and became a gambler?"

"Partly." He wished he hadn't burdened her with the tragedy that shaped several years of his life, yet he knew she was curious about his family—and as his wife and traveling companion, she had a right to know more of the story. "It was my father's casino in San Francisco that went up in flames, so gambling was the natural profession for me to follow. And it financed my traveling while I tracked down the man who murderd him."

Charity's eyes widened. "Someone *set* the fire?"

"Indirectly. And I spent nearly eight years chasing the killer's shadow, unable to corner him because he was always a few days or a few states ahead of me." He gave her a wry smile, smoothing the glossy red waves that sleep had mussed. "When I won the Crystal Queen, I decided it was time to stop wasting my life and my money on a manhunt that wouldn't bring my parents back. Until the night *you* showed up."

"Me?"

Her confused expression made Devereau scoot closer so he could enfold her in his arms. "When you sang 'In the Sweet By And By' up on the Queen's stage, you reminded me so much of my mother I couldn't take my eyes off you," he explained. "And when you showed me the photograph you thought was your mother and her twin with Powers—"

"Powers!" Charity pulled away to look closely at him. "You didn't admit you knew him until we got to Leavenworth, and now you're saying he killed your father, aren't you?"

"You don't miss a trick," he whispered in a voice muted with awe. Charity was fully awake now, her jade eyes wide with shock, and he hoped the woman in his arms would listen carefully. "Now you know why I was so eager to go to Leavenworth with you, and why I've agreed to finance the search for your mother. If you don't want to become further involved in the chase, I'll understand. The fact that your mother's in league with a cold-blooded killer ups the ante quite a lot, as far as the danger's concerned."

She considered his story, caught between demanding the full truth about his tragedy and remaining ignorant of her husband's darker motives. "What did Powers do, Dillon?" she asked quietly. "Why would he kill your father?"

"For spite," Devereau replied with a snort. "He was there to bankrupt our business, which competed with his own, and when my father ordered him out, Powers cried foul play. Shot down a chandelier, which knocked my father to the floor and set his clothes on fire. In the panic that followed, Powers somehow escaped."

Charity gazed sorrowfully at her husband, whose eyes had lost their usual luster. "And you think Powers will try to kill *you* if he learns you're on his trail again?"

"I'm guessing he already knows," Dillon sighed. "A man of his means undoubtedly has spies on his payroll." He toyed with a lock of her hair, wishing he could bury his face in her softly rounded breasts rather than broach this uncomfortable subject again. "Erroll Powers's greed knows no rules or limits, sweetheart. If he can't get to me, he'll retaliate by hurting you or your father, which is why you're free to go back home if you don't want to risk your life because of me. I'll certainly understand."

Charity felt a sinking sensation in the pit of her stomach. "Don't you want me to stay with you, Dillon?" she asked softly.

If he answered yes, he would be responsible for her life, because he knew damn well Powers would put Charity in jeopardy as a means to derail his search. And he sensed Marcella Scott would turn against Noah—and probably her daughter—without a second thought. Yet if he told Charity to go home, especially after the physical and emotional intimacies they'd shared these past few days, she'd be devastated. He was pleased that her father had finally shown her some consideration, but he took Brother Scott at face value: life in Jefferson City would be an eternal funeral for the sensitive, talented woman he now held at arm's length. "I want you to have a long, happy life, honey—a chance to pursue your music, and have a family, and—"

"I don't recall expecting any of those things of you," she interrupted quietly.

Devereau suddenly wished she *did,* so they could either make the break or commit to each other forever. "You deserve more than I can give you, Charity. And if you were to get hurt—or get killed, for Chrissakes—I'd never forgive myself."

Her half-eaten slice of bread was no longer appealing; her appetite had disappeared along with the glowing warmth she'd again begun to feel for this man, who was now searching her face with his gambler's eyes—eyes she could no longer read. "A deal's a deal, Devereau," she replied dryly. "I'm giving you the respectability you need and you're providing a free ride so I can find my mother. Maybe you should've told me up front that Erroll Powers killed your father, but it probably wouldn't have affected my decision. I think I'd better get dressed for church."

Devereau would have preferred a resounding slap to her quiet reminder of his *deal.* Why the hell had he worded his proposal in such a way? He got no pleasure from watching Charity don pale green lingerie he'd bought to complement her eyes, because her halfhearted manner showed exactly how disappointed she was with him. The forest green dress reminded him of the evening they'd dashed through a downpour and shared a first kiss, and although his fingers itched to arrange her auburn waves with the tortoiseshell combs, Dillon knew she would refuse his help.

Papa was waiting for them downstairs in the hotel's parlor, his eyes following their moves and moods. Charity tucked her arm through Dillon's and smiled sweetly. "Good morning, Papa. Did you rest well?"

"Not badly, considering how many strange beds we've slept in of late." He patted the breast of his black frock coat, which rattled slightly. "After meeting Brother Hayes yesterday, I had some handbills printed to distribute after this morning's worship. A fine man, Hayes—has heard of the crowds I've drawn to my tent meetings, and is pleased to host one for us. Of course, that means we have to share the take with him, but at least I'll earn enough to cover my expenses for the remainder of our journey."

Devereau held the door open, wondering if Scott had scheduled the revival to postpone the confrontation with his wife. But he was pleased the preacher was once again full of himself: it meant he'd be too busy saving souls to go looking for a monte game, and perhaps too preoccupied to notice his daughter's crestfallen mood. "That certainly speaks well of your reputation, Reverend," he commented as they walked along the avenue. "My offer still stands, though. I'm even happier to pay your way now that Charity's my wife."

Charity forced herself to return her husband's smile, wishing with all her heart she understood the man who could show her dizzying delights one moment and then plunge her into despair only a few words later.

"You're most kind, Brother Devereau, but I don't want to wear out your generosity. I may need it again someday." The preacher gave him a polite nod then looked at Charity, who walked quietly between them. "I'm assuming you'll be available to accompany our hymns, daughter, but if you and your husband have made other plans—"

"I'll be happy to play, Papa," she mumbled.

"Good. And would you help take up the collection, Devereau?" Scott asked. "It would give me great pleasure to introduce you to the congregation, with testimony as to how you've seen the evil of your previous—"

"Perhaps another time," Dillon interrupted. "I'm playing poker with some old friends this afternoon."

The Reverend's brow furrowed. "It's the Sabbath, Mr. Devereau, and—"

"I earn my living at cards, sir. And after the expenses I've incurred these past few days—"

"—I can't imagine where you'll play. The gaming rooms here in Wichita all seem to be closed."

"—I need to replenish my pockets." Dillon almost laughed: the preacher *had* looked for a game! "And I think these fellows might point us toward our next destination, since one of them works for the Kansas Pacific and the others own businesses on Douglas Avenue." He opened the door of the white frame church they'd arrived at, smiling at his father-in-law. "Ordinarily I'd be pleased to spend Sunday with my new family, but time's of the essence when it comes to finding your wife. Don't you agree?"

Charity saw a look pass between them, an exchange she sensed she wasn't supposed to understand. Men of the congregation were approaching them with outstretched hands, and their wives were smiling at her, so it was no time to appear lost in her own confusing little world. Judging from the enthusiastic greetings they were receiving, Reverend Hayes had spread word of Papa's presence, and the start of the service had to be delayed so all the introductions could be completed.

But once the opening hymns were sung and Brother Hayes read from the Scriptures, Charity's mind wandered. She focused on the gaunt, balding preacher so no one would suspect she wasn't listening—a skill she'd honed to perfection over the years—and pondered what had passed between herself and Dillon. Why had he waited until this morning to inform her that Mama was in cohoots with the man who killed his father? And how could he take her into his confidence one minute, arousing her sympathy over the loss of his parents, only to suggest with his next breath that he thought she and Papa should return to Missouri? Surely a man who made love so tenderly felt *some* sort of affection for her, and yet . . .

"—but before I deliver the day's message, I'm pleased to make one final announcement," the preacher said in his reedy voice. He smiled directly at them, so Charity responded with a nod, as Papa did.

"We have as our guest the renowned theologian, the Reverend Noah Scott," Hayes continued. His smile was almost sappy as he surveyed the murmuring congregation. "He and his lovely daughter Charity are passing through en route from Jefferson City, Missouri, and have offered to hold a revival here at two this afternoon. Mildred McCurdle has informed me that the Women's Christian Temperance Union will provide refreshments afterward, so I encourage each of you to attend this event, which will undoubtedly enlighten and uplift us all."

Devereau smiled to himself while he watched people turning around for a better look at Noah. The WCTU was the main reason the Reverend couldn't find a gambling house open these days, and the most compelling reason for Fred McCurdle to host a private game while his wife served refreshments at the revival. The winnings wouldn't be as impressive as in the days when he and Fred and Gabriel Iverson and Ollie Zumwalt drove up the stakes at the local gaming establishments, but he hoped to collect enough that he wouldn't have to telegraph Abe for a bank draft. Littleton would be flabbergasted if he knew how much he'd spent on Charity this week. The thought made Dillon chuckle a little too loudly as the sermon began.

It was the only laughter Charity heard for the rest of the day. After church they passed out handbills and accepted Hayes's offer to buy their noon meal, since he had no wife to cook one for them. The men carried on dinner conversation with only an occasional remark addressed to her, which gave her ample time to wonder yet again how Dillon really felt about her. He patted her hand and smiled at appropriate times, keeping up appearances as a new husband, but when they left the restaurant he seemed eager to be on his way.

Dillon took Charity's elbow and gave her father a pointed look so he would allow them a few moments alone. "I'm sorry I won't hear you sing this afternoon, sweetheart," he said quietly. She was so withdrawn, obviously hurt by the way he'd treated her—again—and he wasn't sure how to win her back. "Had I known your father was planning a revival, I would've—"

"It's all right, Dillon," she mumbled. "You're the only one of us who knows where to get information about Mama and Powers. And I *have* cost you a lot of money."

He let out an exasperated sigh. "Honey, I would gladly have spent *twice* what I—the money's not the issue at all." Devereau held her by the shoulders, beseeching her with his gaze. "Wealth can't warm my bed or sing to me in the morning or make me the least bit happy, yet *you* can do all those things without even trying. Charity, I want you to stay with me. This whole trip's meaningless without you, and if you want go home, I'll be on the eastbound train with you."

She studied him solemnly, watching a shadow fall across his face when a cloud covered the sun. "Do you really mean that?"

"Absolutely." Devereau gave her a grin, hoping she'd return it. "We make a good team, you and I. Nothing I'd like better than to have you spotting holdouts for me this afternoon, but you have obligations to meet, just as I have."

Nodding, she glanced toward Papa's retreating figure and then smiled timidly at Dillon. "I'd love to watch you play. And I—I'd like you to teach me more about the cards sometime."

"We'll start tonight," he replied, squeezing her shoulders. "Strip poker's the perfect game for newlyweds, don't you think?"

"But I won't stand a *chance!* I'll surely lose—"

"That's the whole point, my love," he said with a chuckle. He leaned down and kissed her, hoping to restore the confidence and trust his badly phrased words had eroded earlier.

His lips were firm and warm, and Charity wound her arms around him, forgetting that they were standing on Douglas Avenue amid people who were strolling to Sunday afternoon engagements. When he finally released her, she looked cautiously into his golden eyes. "Dillon, may I ask you something?"

"Certainly, sweetheart."

She gripped the hands he'd wrapped around hers, hoping to keep him from evading an honest answer this time. "Am . . . am I really your love?"

He'd used the endearment often, so it deserved to be more than a casual phrase. And his wife's expression said she wanted very much to believe it. "Yes. Yes, you are my love, Charity," he murmured as he raised her delicate hands to his lips. "And tonight when we're alone together, I intend to prove it. Again and again."

Dillon's suggestive tone filled her with a giddy warmth that rose straight to her cheeks. He kissed her quickly on the mouth and gave her bustle a playful swat.

"Better put all your new underthings on before our game tonight, Mrs. Devereau," he said with a teasing wink, "because your husband can't wait to take them off you."

Charity watched him walk down the street, waving when he turned toward a residential section of large, impressive homes. But at one-thirty, as she was coming out of the privy behind the church, a broad hand covered her mouth and she was roughly hoisted onto a painted pony, into the arms of the Indian wearing the headband. His partner let out a low, triumphant whoop and swung onto his own horse, and they went galloping down Douglas Avenue.

Chapter 16

"So what brings you to Wichita, Devereau? Last I heard, you was makin' millions in a Kansas City gamblin' house."

Dillon smiled at Ollie Zumwalt while keeping a careful eye on the poker preparations. The four of them were seated around a table in Fred McCurdle's parlor; Ollie and Gabe Iverson arrived several minutes earlier than he had. "We're here on my wife's behalf," he replied as Gabe dealt the first hand. "Looking for her mother, actually."

"Don Juan Devereau got married?" Iverson said with a laugh. "You must have a ring through your nose, to be hunting your mother-in-law."

"Or else the wife's a sweet young thing who's got him wrapped around her finger," Fred teased. His face lit up, as though a smile felt good. "But then, Dillon could never refuse a lady anything her heart desired."

He expected their ribbing, after the way he'd behaved on his last visit, and he sensed these men had also settled into a life that was much less exciting than the days when Wichita teemed with whores and gunslingers. "Man can't live by money alone," he said with a shrug.

"I'd sure like to try it," their host replied. He laid a pair of cards on the table. "I'll take two, Gabe."

"Yeah, and gimme a couple while you're at it," Ollie chimed in.

They studied their hands silently. On his left,

Fred McCurdle gripped his cards in fingers that were as pale as the royalty Devereau held. Fred was an accountant whose clients had once included cattle barons and madames, a man forced to adjust his standard of living when the money moved on to Dodge. Across from him, Gabe Iverson's mustache fluttered as he exhaled cigar smoke. When Zumwalt pulled a pair of blue-tinted spectacles from his pocket, Devereau's hunch was confirmed: the deck was marked with ink only Ollie could see, a method Zumwalt had used when he was the dealer in Bessie Earp's whorehouse. Though less educated, he was the shrewdest among them, so Iverson and McCurdle would be depending on him to carry their game.

"How's the smithing business?" he asked Ollie as he placed ten dollars in the center of the table.

"Well, I'd ruther be shooin' whores than shoein' horses, ya know," Zumwalt replied with a guffaw, "but it's a livin'. Lotsa plows and farm wagons to fix, now that the wheat's nearly in."

Dillon nodded, watching the others put in their ante. He detested chatty games, but with three men vying for the fortune they falsely assumed he'd brought along, he planned to use talk of bygone times to his advantage. After the bet went around, he raised it by twenty dollars. "You're not still holding a grudge about that *last* wager I talked you into, are you, Zumwalt?"

The smithy chortled and threw in his money. "Hell, no! Got y'outta town so's the rest of us could afford to play cards, didn't I?" He glanced at Gabe, adjusting the tinted spectacles. "Was you around for that, Iverson? That time him and the Injun conned us into bettin' whether the ant or the louse would run offa hot plate faster?"

Iverson's lips pursed. "Sounds like a contest only a rube would fall for."

"Rubes, hell! Wyatt Earp hisself was there. It was a slow night at Bessie's, as I recall," Zumwalt continued with a nostalgic chuckle, "when in walks the biggest damn Injun y'ever saw—this was before we knew it was Blue, y'see—and he was askin' if there's any cockfights or such around. And when a big'n like *that's* got questions, ya damn well better answer 'em."

Devereau kept his grin carefully controlled as Ollie Zumwalt brought the memory back. The blacksmith's eyes shone with the telling, and even Gabe looked more interested in the past than the present, so he slipped another twenty into the jackpot. The others followed his lead without paying much attention, as he'd hoped they would.

"Well, the Injun and Devereau got to talkin' about racin' ants against lice, of all things," Ollie continued, "and we shoulda knowed it was a setup, seein's how Blondie here wouldn't have no truck with *lice,* for Chrissakes, but we didn't know they's friends at the time. Well anyway, Devereau bet the Injun that a ant would have sense enough to git offa hot plate faster'n a dumb ole louse would. And while Blue went to find 'im a louse—prob'ly one of 'is own—Dillon stepped outside for a ant, and Bessie herself was heatin' up a china plate to run the race on. Me and Wyatt and th'other boys was arguin' pretty hot, and of course we plunked our money down for Devereau."

Iverson rolled his eyes behind his veil of cigar smoke as Fred McCurdle looked from one man to another, awaiting the story's outcome. Dillon tossed another bill into the kitty. "Still in," he said quietly.

Gabe glanced briefly at his cards and went along; McCurdle followed without a moment's consideration.

"Me, too," Ollie said as he tossed in his money.

"So I s'pose by the time Devereau and Blue come back there was a thousand dollars or more—"

"Fifteen hundred," Dillon corrected.

"—ridin' on a damn ant and a louse. Bessie got that plate good 'n hot, and when the two critters was dropped in the center of it there was hollerin' like you wouldn't believe. Fellas was shovin' each other aside so's they could see the race, and before ya know it, the whole thing was over. Damndest con I ever saw. 'Bout sliced Devereau's head off, throwin' that plate at 'im."

McCurdle scowled. "Why? What happened?"

Ollie let out a grunt. "That damned ant got to th'edge of the plate and kept circlin' like a brainless idjit, and the louse, he waddled to the edge and *fell off!* So a Injun who we first saw only ten minutes before walked out with fifteen hundred of our dollars and a helluva smile, I can tell ya. Bessie offered drinks on the house—didn't want her fancy place smashed up, ya know. And it woulda worked, 'cept Devereau excused hisself real quiet-like insteada actin' as upset as the rest of us. He didn't spend another night in Wichita, becuz we run 'im out on a rail!"

Fred cleared his throat uncertainly, but rather than ask the obvious question, he studied his cards.

"I went out back of Bessie's to split the take with Blue," Dillon explained. "Not one of my smoothest moves."

Their host's eyes widened with comprehension while Gabe stubbed his cigar in his ashtray. "I repeat," the railway overseer muttered, "that only a rube would fall for such an unlikely contest. Who's still in, gentlemen? The pot's up to two hundred fifty dollars."

"How the—" Zumwalt covertly eyed his hand and his pile of money. "I'll fold."

"Me, too," said Fred in a bewildered voice.

Gabe's hooded expression told Devereau the portly dealer was aware of how the stakes had gone so high, and he wasn't surprised to see Iverson toss in another twenty dollars.

They were silent as Dillon pretended to ponder his hand. Iverson could afford to lose, because his Kansas Pacific salary allowed for mistakes at the game table; his bushy beard concealed any bluff that didn't show in his deep brown eyes. And for all Dillon knew, the three men had stacked the deck so the hand would come to just such an early showdown. Clearing his throat, he said, "I'll see your twenty and raise it fifty."

"Got you this time, Mr. Devereau," Gabe replied, fanning out his cards to reveal three queens.

"Never knew ya to be such a ladies' man, Gabriel," Zumwalt quipped. "Can ya beat that, Dillon?"

Suppressing a grin, Devereau laid out his hand without flourish and began picking up the kitty.

"Three kings? How the hell—" McCurdle stared pointedly at Dillon. "You wearing one of those holdout gadgets underneath that fancy vest, Devereau? Seems to me the only way—"

"I'll remove my vest if everyone else will," he said with a shrug. He returned each man's gaze, and when none of them reached for their front buttons, he tossed a ten-dollar ante into the kitty again. "I didn't come to start any fights, gentlemen. Just wanted a friendly game and a little information. Your deal, Fred."

McCurdle nodded nervously and began shuffling the deck. Gabe and Ollie put in their ante, and then Gabe clasped his hands over the front of his fashionable tweed suit. "Would this information be about your mother-in-law, perhaps?" the railroad overseer asked. "Most men would be *pleased* if theirs disappeared."

Glad to see his companions relaxing, Dillon pulled the photograph from his coat pocket and slid it toward Zumwalt. "Have you seen this woman? Her name's Marcella Scott but she also goes by Maggie Wallace. She and her escort—"

"Had I seen the likes of *her,* I wouldn't forget it," Ollie replied with a shake of his head. "Her sister lookin' for a man? I'm still available, ya know."

"That's a separate likeness of herself, blended in from a different negative." Devereau was watching Iverson's reaction, which was encouraging. "Recognize that man, do you?"

"Every agent of the Kansas Pacific knows Erroll Powers," Gabe replied dryly. "Just yesterday I learned the government is on his trail—finally waking up to the way he's been double-dealing. Why on earth do *you* want to find him?"

He didn't want to go into all the details, because he suspected this hand would be decisive where Zumwalt and McCurdle were concerned. "Let's just say I have a personal score to settle," he commented, "and when my wife learned what sort of man her mother was associating with, we thought we'd better talk some sense into her."

Iverson raised an eyebrow as though he didn't quite swallow this explanation. Fred finished dealing and laid the deck down before gazing thoughtfully at the photograph. "You know," he said slowly, "I recall seeing this woman just a day or so ago. Matter of fact . . . yep, I'm sure it was her I saw talking to that Indian friend of yours."

Devereau masked his surprise. "Blue's in town?"

"He drops in every now and again," Ollie spoke up. "Last time he had me shoe that damn stallion, I told 'im the price was double. 'Bout lost both my feet that day."

Nodding absently, Dillon wondered if the scout was keeping track of Marcella or of him. "You wouldn't know what they were discussing, would you?"

"Nope, I was clear across the street," his host answered. "But I've seen him with another gal—the whore who stuck around after the houses in Delano closed down."

"He's still lookin' after Lula?" Ollie asked. "Damn! Don't know how he could give her the time of day if he's got the likes of this Marcella woman interested in 'im."

"It's the scar," Fred answered matter-of-factly. "Draws women like a magnet. Mildred says so herself."

The thought of McCurdle's hefty wife—a pillar of the Women's Christian Temperance Union, who spoke out against every habit Jackson Blue held dear—made all of them except Fred fight a smirk. The bets went around the table twice and Dillon folded, allowing Zumwalt to claim a smaller pot this time. Then Devereau picked up the cards to shuffle. "Any idea where Powers went when he left Wichita?"

"Dodge," Gabe answered. "I doubt he'd venture south to Caldwell again, after the stunt he pulled during his last visit. That's in Indian Territory, and rumor has it he and the government agent there sold off the cattle and commodities shipments. Told the Indians it never arrived. Powers barely escaped with his life, so I hear."

"Yep, them tribes is pretty hungry and damn restless," Ollie said with an emphatic shake of his head. "Seen more aimless redskins hangin' around than I care to lately. What sort of trash did you deal me here, Devereau?"

Letting the blacksmith's last remark pass, Dillon gave two cards to McCurdle and two to Iverson. His own hand was as well populated as he'd planned. "Can't blame them for being angry," he said when his strategy was intact. "I don't recall a single promise the government has kept since they herded the Indians onto reservations. Red men resent being dependents, just as you and I would."

"Which is why the Cheyennes' chief, Dull Knife, wants to lead his people back north, to their original territory," Iverson commented as he unwrapped a fresh cigar. "No doubt in my mind things'll flare up. Too many hungry braves'll raise hell if the government won't let them go."

"Saw two of 'em hangin' around town just yesterday," Zumwalt added. "And you can bet I told the sheriff 'bout 'em, too."

Dillon considered this information as the bets were seen and raised around the table. He recalled the redskins Zumwalt referred to, the hapless desperadoes who'd stared openly at Charity, and he was glad his wife was at the revival. The unsavory pair wouldn't dare approach her with so many people around.

Gabe cleared his throat and didn't bat an eye as he tossed a hundred dollars into the kitty. "Looks like it's between you and me again, Mr. Devereau. Make it worth my while. Double or nothing."

Dillon lowered his cards to his vest. "No, thank you. I have a wife to support now."

Iverson snickered, triumphantly revealing his hand. "Full house—tens and jacks. You can't beat *that!*"

Devereau smiled politely. "I believe I have. Royal flush."

"What the—"

"How the hell did you—"

"Cheated!" Iverson yelled, standing so suddenly his chair clattered backwards onto the floor. "By God, Devereau, there's no way you could've—"

"Mildred!"

The parlor rang with McCurdle's stunned exclamation and then became uncomfortably silent. Fred's wife was framed in the doorway, surveying the gathering with small, glittering eyes and fists on her ample hips. "I—I thought the revival would last much longer, so—"

"Obviously." Mildred McCurdle peeled the white gloves from her pudgy hands and looked at each man in turn. "But without a piano player, even the Reverend Scott can only hold an audience for so long. So how do you explain—"

Devereau's heart constricted. "But she *had* to be there. When Noah asked her to—"

"The Reverend Scott excused his daughter by saying she was spending the afternoon with her new husband," Mrs. McCurdle replied archly. She flicked a crumb from her cushiony bosom, looking sourly at Fred. "She'll learn soon enough what a waste of time *that* is."

Dillon stood up and hurriedly scraped his winnings together. "Excuse me, but I really must go—"

"Like hell you will!" Gabe barked. "If you think we're going to let you run like some damned rabbit—"

His heart was indeed fluttering like a frightened animal's as he stuffed the money into his vest pocket. "We'll have to finish this game another time, gentlemen. Mrs. McCurdle," he added with a nod, "it was a pleasure to see you again, and I hope—"

"Sit down, Devereau!" Zumwalt ordered. "You ain't leavin' till we get the chance to—"

"I'm leaving *now*—and I'm probably too late," he muttered. Then it struck him, why his friends were staring at him so heatedly. "*I* am Charity Scott's new husband," he explained, "and I have a feeling she's been kidnapped."

It took utmost control not to dash through the McCurdles' home, and when Dillon reached the street, he broke into a run. Rain splashed his face, and he dodged people carrying umbrellas. If those two savages had abducted Charity, he'd stop at nothing short of war until she was safely recovered.

Devereau threw open the Occidental's front door and bounded up the stairway to pound on Noah's door. "Scott, open up! Charity—are you in there, honey?"

The Reverend answered with a puzzled frown. "Whatever's the matter? I just got back from—"

"When McCurdle's wife said you had no pianist, I—*where is Charity?*" Dillon gazed earnestly at the minister, his worst fears confirmed when Noah's eyebrows furrowed above his spectacles.

"I thought she was with *you.* When I saw the clinch you had her in after dinner, I assumed the two of you—"

"She's gone," Devereau interrupted, "and she's probably the hostage of a couple worthless Indians I saw watching her yesterday." Dillon removed his dripping hat to rake his hair back. "Pack your things—and ours—while I try to find Jackson Blue. I'll be back within the hour."

"You're saying Indians kidnapped my daughter, and you're trusting *that* savage to find her?"

"Do you have a better plan? Chief Dull Knife is preparing to take his tribe north," Devereau exclaimed. "If you want to see Charity again, we have to move quickly. Be ready when I return!"

Without waiting for any further objections, Dillon rushed out onto Douglas Avenue. The search for his wife made a horse a necessity; he selected one and also paid the stable man handsomely for his boot-length duster. Dillon then cantered west toward the suburb known as the Delano district, where the bawdy houses were clustered a few years back. Lula Ralls hadn't improved her standard of living, if she still allowed the likes of Blue to come and go, and he prayed the scout was with her now.

Wheeling his mount to a stop before her tawdry little shack, Dillon crinkled his nose. Even the pouring rain couldn't wash away the stench of chamber pots emptied too close to the house. He took the unpainted stairs two at a time and pounded on the door.

After several minutes he was greeted by a sloe-eyed blonde wearing only a rumpled chemise. She looked him up and down with a distracted glance. "And what can I do for you?" she slurred.

Dillon searched the dim, smoke-filled room behind her. "Where's Blue? It's urgent that I see him."

"He left town," the Indian replied sarcastically from the shadows. "In search of friends who honor their debts and possess enough integrity to—"

"You damn—they've kidnapped Charity!" Dillon snapped. "She'll be some drunken Cheyenne's whore if we don't find her in time."

He heard the stealthy creak of floorboards, and then Jackson Blue appeared behind the bedraggled woman, holding a long, carved pipe. "Language like that won't win you any favors, Devereau," he said with a smirk. "Come in out of the rain and renew the ties that bind. Lula says my pipe makes the earth move and she sees God. Does your woman ever tell *you* that, Dillon?"

The sharp, sweet peyote smoke made him turn away in disgust. "This is no time for games, Jackson. My wife's in danger, and I need your help. I'll give you that damn money as soon as I have it, if you'll—"

"Is Scott going?"

Dillon blinked. "Of course. He's packing our things so we can be on our way."

The dark scout slipped a hand into Lula's chemise and eased her against his bare chest with a chuckle. "You swore you'd have me arrested if I saw the Reverend again. So you're on your own, Mr. Devereau."

Chapter 17

Hell can't possibly be any worse than this, Charity thought, and as her body went numb from the endless hours she'd spent on horseback, she welcomed the lack of feeling. Now there were only the relentless sun, the viselike arm around her midsection, and the ceaseless pounding of the ponies' hooves on the plain beneath them.

When she realized she was being kidnapped, Charity had fought and struggled—clawing her captor's cheek had earned her the binding around her wrists, and her outcries got her gagged. Both constraints were torn from the hem of her green gown, which was now clinging to every perspiring inch of her. Why couldn't she have been wearing the calico dress? Dillon had taken such pains to outfit her fashionably.

The thought of her debonair husband made her squeeze her eyes shut against tears. Neither he nor Papa knew where she was. She would probably never see them again.

The two Indians rode in silence toward the sunset, across a prairie scattered with buffalo bones and past an occasional caved-in sod house. The horizon remained unchanged from one hour to the next—only her captors knew what lay beyond this vast, treeless range—and Charity wondered if their tongues felt as thick as hers did. It was good she'd used the privy when she did, but even so . . .

The headbanded brave who held her raised an

arm, signaling. His companion broke into a gallop, his braid flying behind him, and left Charity and her escort in a cloud of dust that made her eyes sting. Their pony snorted as though he, too, desperately needed a rest. Then he strained forward, as though anticipating an oasis, and when she squinted at the painfully bright sky, Charity thought she could make out a low, square building. It looked miles away in the shimmering heat, yet it held the glimmer of a promise: perhaps a place to spend the night?

She noticed shadows circling the ground a short distance in front of them: vultures. Charity's stomach lurched when she saw the advance rider dismount to inspect the birds' dinner. The dead animal's condition apparently suited him, because by the time they reached him, he'd dispatched the carcass. She couldn't tell what sort of meat it was and didn't care. Only the knowledge that they'd have to rest while it cooked gave her any hope.

The structure she'd spotted turned out to be an abandoned soddie. Charity gasped when her prickling, rubbery legs would barely support her as she slid off the pony. Both braves snickered as she tottered around; she entreated them with grunts and wide eyes to unbind her wrists and remove the gag that cut her face in two. They sensed the source of her most urgent discomfort, though, and kicked at the shredded hem of her dress to make her dance between them.

Disgusted, Charity suddenly sat down. The braves taunted her with Indian jibes, but they soon tired of their sport and went to build a fire. As she'd hoped, the brave with the braid then came over to untie her bindings. Charity gave him a grateful half-smile before staggering to her feet, and as she rounded the corner of the sod shack, his halting English stopped her:

"Don't run far, Hair of Flame. Got you this time."

Turning to stare at him, Charity caught a glimmer in his obsidian eyes that made her insides shrivel. What did he mean, *this time?* And where on God's earth did he expect her to run?

When she'd relieved herself, she leaned against the crumbling soddie to collect her thoughts. The aroma of cooking meat wafted her way, but the thought of eating a scavenger's leftovers sickened her. She made a face when the headbanded warrior offered her a greasy leg joint; he shrugged and walked back to the fire, tearing into the meat himself. Charity longingly recalled the steak she'd shared with Dillon . . . tender bread and loving golden eyes and the clove scent of him were memories so sharp she nearly cried out—until her kidnappers grabbed her roughly between them. They were breaking camp to ride on into the dusk.

She was once again hoisted up in front of the taller, black-haired brave with the beaded headband. Did they never rest their poor horses? How did they expect to travel in the dark? Her stomach rumbled; she licked her parched lips and stared ahead at the nothingness as night's shadows fell around them. Her eyes grew heavy in spite of her intentions to remain alert, and lulled by the steady rolling of the pony's back, Charity's thoughts lingered on Dillon before she drifted off. He was nuzzling her hair, whispering against her temple with the tightness in his voice that betrayed his desire. . . .

But the hand pinching her breast was *not* her husband's, and Charity awoke with a cry. It was daybreak, and they were surrounded by a ragtag assortment of Indians who eyed her sullenly, as though they recognized her. Most were dressed in a combination of white men's clothing and Indian garb, which gave the impression that they belonged to neither race. Her captor's arm tightened possessively beneath her bosom, and as he made a triumphant announcement to the crowd, the listless red faces took on more life. The men studied her with calculating expressions, while the women threw her contemptuous glares before tending their morning chores.

Charity then realized they were in a camp, where underdressed children scampered between the lodge tents with wolflike dogs. "Wh-what's happening? Why did you bring me here?" she demanded in a raspy voice.

The brave with the braid caught her as his friend pushed her off the pony. "You become Cheyenne!" he crowed. "When sun dance across sky, you be Soaring Eagle's squaw!"

Her mouth dropped open and the Indian wearing the headband—Soaring Eagle, she now realized—leered down at her from atop his horse. "But I'm already married! I can't—"

"Not married to Soaring Eagle. Not yet," the brave who held her replied. His grip tightened and he steered her toward the tall, pale tents. "You make him promise—you *keep* now. No more run away."

"But I never even *saw* him before—"

"Do not anger gods with forked tongue, Hair of Flame," her captor warned. He lifted the flap of a tent that was separated from the others. "Eat. Rest. spirit must be clean. We *wait* . . . for Hair of Flame to be ready."

"Then you'll wait till hell freezes over, you—" The muscular Indian shoved her into the dim tent and secured its flap from the outside. Charity scrambled clumsily toward the opening, her muscles in agony after the long hours on horseback, but the flap was tight. She heard low male voices outside. She was trapped, under guard until she became ready. Whatever *that* meant.

The only object in the tent was a pallet of worn blankets, which lay crumpled beside the circle of ashes in the center of the dirt floor. Charity flopped onto it, too exhausted to try to escape. She bunched one end of the dusty blanket under her head and was just sinking into sleep when daylight fell across her face. Bolt upright, she watched the wizened old woman who was entering the tent.

The ancient squaw returned her distrustful gaze with eyes that were as dark as a moonless night. Then she set a battered tin plate of corn cakes on the floor. A piece of buckskin was folded over her arm, and she tossed it toward Charity with a grunt. It was a beaded, fringed dress that looked too detailed to be worn for everyday. Charity scowled. "I suppose that's some sort of ceremonial gown, and you expect me to—"

"Shut up. White slut to be dressed when Soaring Eagle come," the old woman said in a guttural voice. "You and raven-haired snake deserve to die. When Soaring Eagle make you slave, you *wish* for death."

Raven-haired snake. Charity was struggling to comprehend what the wrinkled squaw meant when the tent flap was raised again to admit Soaring Eagle himself.

"Rise, Hair of Flame. Woman who keep Cheyennes waiting dishonors bridegroom," he stated curtly.

"You are *not* my bridegroom, and I refuse—" Charity yelped when the muscular redskin jerked her to her feet. "Why are you *doing* this to me?"

The warrior's laughter sounded like a snarl. "Soaring Eagle keep you here so dark partner come for you," he grunted. "Then, when two-faced bastard dead by my hand, *you* pay for lying and starving my people."

Charity's mouth dropped open as she realized who this brutal redskin had to be referring to. "But—but I'm *not* the woman who—"

"You *dress* now, for marriage ceremony," Soaring Eagle commanded with a shake that made her teeth rattle. "Then you eat, so—"

But Charity wasn't listening. She glared up into his haughty brick-colored face and said, "If you think for one minute the United States government or my husband will let you—"

"Government—hah!" Soaring Eagle grabbed the front of her green gown and tore it with a force that sent her reeling backward. "White man's government care nothing for Cheyenne and nothing for *you.* Only out to cheat and grow fat while Indian nation die off."

She had to appeal to his sympathies—had to prove she wasn't the woman who'd betrayed his people—but his flaring nostrils told Charity to consider her own safety first. Despite her dust-smudged face and bedraggled hair, he was leering at the gap in her clothing, ogling the pale green camisole Dillon had purchased when she became *his* bride. "Please, Mr. Eagle," she pleaded. "If you'll let me explain . . ."

She landed in a heap on the pallet, and Soaring Eagle gave the old woman a command in Cheyenne. The squaw retrieved the plate of corn cakes and turned to go, but then wheeled around and spat vehemently in Charity's face.

Charity was still gaping, spittle running down her cheek, when the Indian tore her dress until it was hanging in two ragged halves. He dropped a canteen beside her and straightened to his full height. "When Hair of Flame see reason, I return with food and prepare her for marriage."

Bright daylight blinded her for a moment, and then she was alone in the dusky tent. Charity grasped the edges of the green satin gown, shaking with silent sobs. It was the nicest dress she'd ever worn, a token of a husband who couldn't possibly save her from a fate too frightening to think about.

And Mama was to blame for all this. Charity thought back to when she'd first seen the two Indians staring at her in Wichita. They obviously thought she was Maggie Wallace, and that her raven-haired snake of a partner had used her in a conspiracy that led to great suffering here on the reservation. How had Erroll Powers cheated these people, to make the two redskins bold enough to kidnap a white woman in broad daylight? If she ever got out of here, she vowed to find out.

Wiping the spit from her cheek, Charity sighed. Her backside and legs ached from hours on horseback; her hair was dirty and tangled, and her face felt scorched. She was trembling with hunger, and her head was throbbing. Escape was out of the question right now.

Perhaps if Soaring Eagle thought she intended to marry him, he would allow her to recover from their grueling ride. What man would want his family and friends to see his bride looking so miserable? Slowly she stood up, every stiff muscle in her body rebelling, and replaced the ruined satin gown with the dress of beaded buckskin. Then she eased down onto the pallet again, to rest and plan her strategy. A sip from the canteen was so refreshing she had to refrain from gulping the water.

Charity was nearly asleep before she realized something was desperately, dangerously wrong. Her thoughts jumbled. Images of Soaring Eagle and the bitter squaw floated in her mind, yet she couldn't remember where she'd seen them. Dillon's face haunted her—he was trying to warn her about something, his garbled voice fading in and out. Charity tried to sit up, hoping to clear her head, but the tent whirled madly around her and she collapsed again.

In her more lucid moments she suspected her water was drugged. She was vaguely aware of the old squaw peering at her and of Soaring Eagle's occasional visits. How many days and nights had she been his prisoner?

Her sense of smell was heightened: aromas from cooking food tormented her, and Charity knew the moment her arrogant captor entered the tent because his body odor was nauseating. Perhaps it was this reflex that kept her mind alert enough to refuse his demands. Each time he left the tent he hurled insults at her as he carried away the corn cakes he'd tempted her with. All she had was the canteen of water—water that held her hostage, yet kept her alive.

Then came the day when Soaring Eagle yanked her to her feet. "We marry," he announced brusquely. "No more wait for Hair of Flame."

Charity felt her body swaying as she blinked to keep the savage's face in focus. He was wearing a feathered headdress and buckskin breeches—and the grin of a victor. "Broken Willow braid your hair now. We marry and then eat, so you be strong for Soaring Eagle's mating."

Every pore of Charity's body revolted at the thought of coupling with this crude warrior, yet she was powerless to prevent such a fate. Broken Willow, the hag who spat on her, was now dragging a gap-toothed comb through her matted hair. Charity whimpered when it bit her scalp; she tasted blood and then realized she was biting her lip to keep from crying. All these sensations were hopelessly disjointed as she was escorted from the dim tent into dazzling sunlight. Dozens of dark eyes mocked her, while from somewhere behind her a primitive flute and drum began to play.

Then, from a distance, came a shout—two voices, hollering above the discordant music, until the crowd turned to see who was causing the commotion. Charity heard thundering hooves and saw four riders approaching at a gallop: two were clad in black, flanked by two crowing Cheyenne braves. Soaring Eagle raised his hand for the ceremony to stop.

Before his escorts could grab him, one of the white men dismounted and scrambled toward her, his golden hair flashing in the sun. "Charity! Charity!" he called out.

She gazed at the man's handsome, mustached face but he remained a stranger. He grabbed her hands, talking rapidly in words she recognized as English but which held no meaning. Had she passed on to the next world, to be ushered to God's throne by this golden angel who radiated compassion and the essence of . . .

Cloves. Just as Charity identified his familiar scent, just as her drugged mind was searching for the name that seemed a step beyond her reach, Soaring Eagle's friends seized the intruder.

"You not belong here!" the warrior declared. "White man no watch sacred ceremony of the Cheyennes."

"This is my wife!" the blond protested, struggling against the braves who were grabbing his arms and legs. "She's not Maggie Wallace! And she's never even *met* Erroll Powers!"

Soaring Eagle raised an eyebrow. "Her name Hair of Flame now. She trick me—betray my people—and now she become squaw."

"I can prove you're wrong! I have a *picture* of the woman you're after, and it's not Charity!"

Somehow the man broke free and pulled a photograph from inside his black duster, and the likeness he flashed at Soaring Eagle tripped a switch in her memory. She knew this blond man, and she recognized the three people in the photograph as—

"Hair of Flame! And Black Weasel!" the warrior beside her exclaimed. He grabbed the photograph from his challenger's hand and held it up beside Charity's face. "Who this? Only saw one Hair of Flame on reservation."

The word finally came to her, and Charity gasped, "Mama!"

Soaring Eagle scowled. "Then who *you?*"

"She's Charity Scott Devereau," a voice boomed through the crowd, "and if you don't unhand her this minute, the United States Army will send every last one of you heathens to your happy hunting grounds."

Her heart beat faster. "Papa!"

"He's right," the golden-haired man chimed in. "We alerted the authorities in Wichita that my wife was abducted by you and your friend here. Turn her loose, and we'll cause you no further trouble."

Charity was nearly choked by the possessive arm that snaked around her shoulders. "Hair of Flame to be my squaw," her captor challenged. "White man want her, white man must win her from Soaring Eagle."

Devereau knew he had to proceed with utmost caution: Scott's insults could ruin any chance for escape, and Charity was obviously unable to assist him. Her glassy eyes and trembling, rail-thin body scared the hell out him, because he suspected she didn't know who he was. He'd attracted the attention of some braves hunting near the reservation's boundary, to keep the men in the camp from opening fire when two uninvited palefaces demanded their hostage. And now it was up to him to prevent all three of them from becoming the Cheyennes' prisoners.

He reached into his vest pocket for the money he'd won at Fred McCurdle's. "You play cards?" he asked, knowing most redskins were eager gamblers. "If you win, you keep Hair of Flame and have enough money for guns or whiskey or whatever you want. If *I* win, the woman is mine . . . and maybe I'll be grateful enough to give you some of the cash. A goodwill gift from a white man to the Cheyenne."

Noah opened his mouth to object, but Dillon silenced him with a nudge. "Either way, you can't lose, Soaring Eagle," he continued in a low voice. "But just so you won't be misled, I'll warn you that I'm very, very good at poker. Takes a helluva man to beat me."

The powerful brave gave him a cocky grin. "We play with my cards. But only one game. Soaring Eagle hot to bed red-haired squaw."

Charity looked on as though from behind a glass curtain: the blond man and her kidnapper set up to play with cards that were decorated with primitive hatchets and horses. She heard them clarifying the rules of the single game that would determine her fate, but she felt oddly removed from these events. She was seated on the ground between two of Soaring Eagle's friends, across the low table from the man she recognized as Papa. He was mouthing words she couldn't understand, so she turned her attention to the arresting blond instead. The entire camp looked on, silent, as the slender white man shrugged out of his duster and prepared to play.

His agile fingers arranged the cards Soaring Eagle dealt; his face assumed a calm expression that was achingly familiar . . . if only she could remember where she'd seen this amber-eyed gambler! His dusty clothes complemented his lean physique—he was obviously wealthy, with that gold watch fob draped across his vest, yet he was playing for *her*. Charity brushed at the ill-fitting buckskin dress, too ashamed to meet his eye.

Dillon struggled to concentrate on poker, but the waif seated a few feet away tugged at his heartstrings. Soaring Eagle bluffed an amateurish, too-confident game, and even though Devereau had drawn cards that completed a full house, he sensed the Cheyenne would declare himself the winner no matter what cards he held.

When the betting ended with all of Devereau's cash on the rough table, Soaring Eagle laid out his hand. "Three chiefs! Hair of Flame belong to *me!*"

Dillon carefully displayed his own cards. "But we agreed beforehand that a full house beat anything except a royal flush. So I'm the winner."

The redskin rose suddenly, as though he suspected trickery. Then he pounded the table with an exuberant fist. "Squaw like Hair of Flame no ordinary prize. Must also win *red* man's contest to claim her."

Dillon wasn't surprised that his host had changed the rules, but his temper was rising—until he saw Charity's forlorn, empty eyes fastened upon him. Outnumbered as they were, this was no time to risk their safety. "What sort of contest did you have in mind?" he asked in the most gracious tone he could muster.

"Horse race!" Soaring Eagle declared. "*Real* man need stallion's power to do justice to red-haired filly."

The thought of this foul-smelling Indian riding his wife gave him the strength to curb his protests. It would be a sign of weakness to suggest a tamer sport, since he had named the first game himself. "Two out of three," he countered. "If I lose this contest, I name the final one."

The redskin let out a haughty laugh, sneering at Devereau's uncalloused hands. "If you survive, *berdache,* we play any game you can manage."

Jackson Blue had often slighted his masculinity with that insult, but anger was his worst enemy right now. Soaring Eagle would win this contest and they both knew it, because Dillon was obviously not a skilled equestrian.

Even worse, the camp had come to life. The women were stealing covert glances at him while the men exchanged personal objects and coins . . . betting, not on whether he'd win, but on how long he would last. The crowd was now walking eagerly toward a large open area beyond the lodge tents, where the Indians held their sporting events. Soaring Eagle directed some younger braves to set long poles between two pairs of forked branches that stood at the far end of the field.

Devereau pulled Noah aside. "If something happens to me, wait for the Army to—"

"You fool!" Scott blurted. "These savages will let you ride across the field and then shoot you full of poisoned arrows!"

He forced an indulgent smile, for Charity's sake. "It's a race, Reverend. Each rider gallops full speed toward his crossbar, and the one who stops his mount closest to the pole without touching it—and without flying off his horse—wins. Simple as that."

"How in God's name do you expect to—"

"I can't win," Dillon admitted, "but when my wife's life is at stake, I can't back down either. Now if you were to create some sort of diversion . . ."

Devereau could see the workings of the devious minister's mind, but before Noah came up with an idea, Soaring Eagle clapped his hands to silence the crowd. "We begin," he called to Dillon from atop his sturdy pony. "Kiss your woman good-bye."

It was the best idea he'd heard all day, and as the

Cheyennes took their places along the sidelines, he was left standing with Charity and her father. He stroked her sunburnt cheek, his throat going dry when he saw confusion clouding her emerald eyes. She still didn't know him, didn't know why he was about to kiss her.

Dillon gazed at her, memorizing the wisps of auburn hair that defied her unnatural braids, and the sprinkling of freckles on her red nose, and the green, green eyes that seemed to belong to someone else . . . perhaps to a woman who would never recall his name, if the Cheyennes had addled her brains with their potions. And all because he hadn't kept close enough watch on her.

He leaned toward her and gently, gently pressed his lips to hers. She didn't retreat, nor did she respond. She simply accepted his kiss with open eyes and a vacant expression on her face. Devereau wanted to grab the small pistols secreted beneath his waistband and shoot Soaring Eagle off his horse. Instead, he whispered, "I love you, Charity. If you remember nothing else, remember that." Then he turned toward the mount a chuckling Cheyenne brave was holding for him.

Charity watched him, her heart beating faster now. He swung onto the horse with a familiar grace, this lithe gentleman with the golden eyes. He tasted kind and sweet, like someone she once knew. . . .

He was approaching the starting line now, exchanging words with Soaring Eagle. The crack of a pistol sent the two racers into a gallop, kicking up a thick fog of red-brown dust. Charity saw the crossbars they were speeding toward and her breath caught in her throat: surely the horses couldn't *jump* that high, so why were they charging straight toward the poles? The crowd was yelling, some of them pushing and straining to see—

But all she knew was that the scent of him lingered. Charity touched her fingertips to her lips, recalling his firm, tender mouth and the tickle of his mustache. He smelled clean and virile . . . *like clove soap,* a thought from deep inside her surfaced.

She gasped, struggling to clear her dazed mind. The riders were heading hell-bent toward those awful crossbars, yet to Charity it suddenly seemed as though their motions had become slow and exaggerated as she watched them . . . inches away now, veiled in thick red dust . . . yanking back on their reins, first Soaring Eagle and then—then—

"Dillon!" she cried out, her voice echoing inside her head like church bells in a steeple.

But something was wrong. The crowd of Indians was now deathly quiet, inching back toward the lodge tents, no longer caring about the bone-splitting climax of this gruesome race. Dillon's mount screamed and reared, and Charity reached for the protection of Papa's arms.

Then she saw the apparition approaching the field, astride a tall black stallion decked out in tack that glistened red and silver in the afternoon sun. The rider sat serenely, unaware of the contestants whose mounts had thrown them. He was arrayed in a magnificent red satin robe that shimmered in the breeze, its silver-sequined edging sparkling like a band of diamonds.

Charity looked at his face and gasped: it was a huge, horned buffalo head. "Papa," she breathed, "it's him, it's—"

But the agitated crowd closed in around them, jostling her from her father's arms. Too weak to catch herself, Charity stumbled over his shoes and got lost in a sea of feet.

Chapter 18

Charity hovered on the brink of awareness, mentally taking stock of her situation. She was lying on some sort of mattress, with a cool dampness across her forehead. Her stomach growled as a wonderful aroma drifted over her . . . bacon! Men were talking nearby, their familiar voices bringing her closer to consciousness.

"Not so tight, dammit! You wouldn't be wrapping my ribs if you'd just ridden onto the reservation, instead of arriving like a damn carnival act!"

"I saved your three sunburnt necks, didn't I?" came the lower-pitched reply.

"You could have saved me busting my *butt,* had you just put some speed on. I'll be hobbling around like an old woman for weeks!"

Charity awoke with a quiet gasp. It was Dillon who was being bandaged—he'd survived that awful fall from his horse!—and Jackson Blue was gloating over his triumphal entry into the Cheyenne camp. As her eyes adjusted to the dim light, she saw strips of muslin draped beneath the rafters above her, heavy with clods and stones the rains had washed loose. They were in a sod shack, she realized. Somewhere on the plains of Kansas. Charity hoped that bacon didn't burn while the men argued, because its tantalizing smell was making her hungrier than she'd ever been in her life.

"And had I come galloping in, they'd have fired on me," Blue replied matter-of-factly. "As it was, they thought I was some sort of god, and I got you out of there while the element of surprise was ours. We'll be damned lucky if Soaring Eagle and his cohorts didn't follow us here."

Cringing at the warrior's name, Charity turned her head to watch Jackson Blue tuck the end of the bandage into the white wrapping around Dillon's bare torso. Her husband had nasty bruises on his shoulders and back, but his protests told her that he was otherwise all right. Papa leaned against the open doorway, fidgeting with the barrel of the rifle that paralleled his leg.

"What made you change your mind about helping me?" Dillon asked. He gritted his teeth against the pain as he gingerly checked the bandage around his midsection.

The dark Indian shrugged. "I've got my reasons." He rose to tend the skillet that was crackling in the fireplace, as though the subject was now closed.

But Charity, too, wondered about the boastful scout's motives. "Why *did* you rescue us?" she asked in a dry, croaking voice. "As often as you've told us to go home, I'd think you'd be glad to get rid of us."

Three heads swiveled at once, and Papa rushed toward her bed. "Charity, you're awake!"

"How do you feel, sweetheart?" Dillon asked. He limped across the small room, gazing at the precious, reddened face that was half covered with a wet rag. She'd been following their conversation—she remembered where she'd been and knew who was with her now!

Jackson Blue lifted the cloth from her forehead. "Hair of Flame return from netherworld," he teased, his touch surprisingly tender as he checked her face for fever. "Don't talk until you've had some water. You're badly dehydrated."

Charity eyed his tin cup warily. "What's in it besides water? I've had enough Indian trickery, thank you."

Blue laughed, his ebony eyes hinting at admiration. "Shall we let Devereau sample it first? He'll be praying for pain killer soon enough, after the fall he took."

"Give me that," Dillon muttered. He gently slid an arm beneath Charity's shoulders, watching her sip as though every swallow of the water refreshed him as well. "When I realized you were out of your head, I was afraid you'd never remember who I was, or—"

"I saw your horse rear up, and wondered why on earth you were running straight at a pole." Charity gripped the cup, letting her fingers fill in the gaps between Dillon's long, slender ones. "I thought I'd never see you again."

They shared an intense silence, each experiencing the other's agony and vowing to erase it as only lovers knew how. For Charity, it was enough that they were together again. Dillon wondered if she recalled the words he whispered before he galloped off toward certain defeat, but this was no time to ask her.

Noah cleared his throat. "Well, that bacon certainly is calling *me* to the table."

"You preachers hear any call that promises a profit," the scout beside him scoffed. "These newlyweds are ruining my appetite. Let's put on the plates."

Chuckling, Dillon eased himself cautiously down to the edge of the mattress. "Some things never change," he murmured, assisting her as she took another sip. He glanced briefly at the sacklike buckskin dress, which accentuated her bones and hollows, and then looked into her shining green eyes. "Can you sit at the table, honey, or shall I bring your dinner over here?"

"I'll try to make it. Thank you." Charity sat up slowly, adjusting to this position while she looked around the small soddie and then at her dirty dress. "I don't suppose there's any way I could take a bath," she said as she wrinkled her nose.

Dillon grinned provocatively. "There's a stream running out back. It should be wonderfully cool, and we could do more than bathe, if you'd like."

Charity glanced at the two men beside the fireplace and then looked into her husband's glowing eyes. "But your bandage shouldn't get wet, and—"

"To hell with it," he whispered as he nuzzled her cheek. "Your arms will be all the medicine I need."

"—they'll see us—"

"I doubt they'll have enough gall to watch. They're embarrassed even now." He looked behind him, to where Scott and Blue were making awkward small talk despite their previous animosities. His heart pounding within his chest, Devereau pulled Charity as close as his bruises would allow and kissed her fervently on the mouth.

She answered the invitation of his tongue, savoring the sweetness of an embrace she once thought she'd never share again. His lips taunted her; Charity felt fully alive for the first time in days, and her heart swelled with the knowledge that he'd saved her life. "Dillon, I—"

"By the time you two patients get to the table, the food will be on," Jackson's voice interrupted.

Dillon sighed. "That's our cue to behave ourselves—for now. Everything's going to be fine, Charity. We can stay until we're both recovered enough to travel, thanks to Blue's hospitality."

She glanced at the tall Indian, who looked odd performing such a wifely task as carrying a pan of mush to the table. "This is your house, Jackson?"

"I borrow it occasionally," he replied. "The original homesteaders were killed in a tornado, and since I gave them a decent burial, I've taken the liberty of stashing some supplies in their root cellar."

She nodded and rose slowly to her feet, spurred on by the heaping platter of bacon and the fragrant steam rising from the mush. Papa was holding a chair, and after Dillon helped her take a few awkward steps, she landed in it. Her plate was chipped, and the enamel coffeepot their host was pouring from had only half its lid, but Charity didn't care. She was eating civilized food again with the people she loved.

After Papa offered up grace, Charity looked at Jackson Blue until he focused his midnight eyes on her. "We have our differences," she began hesitantly, "but Papa and Dillon and I are truly grateful for your help, Mr. Blue."

The scout seemed surprised, and he busied himself with ladling mush onto their plates. "You're quite welcome, Mrs. Devereau," he said with the slightest hint of a smile. "Some of my motives were purely personal. If your husband thinks about it, he'll realize why I chose to prevent a crisis on Chief Dull Knife's reservation."

Dillon's brow puckered while he passed her the bacon platter. "You've always said conditions deteriorate every time the government gets involved with Indian affairs," he answered. "Perhaps you wanted to do your people a favor—spirit us away yourself, rather than calling in the Army—and meanwhile come out the hero."

Their host let out a short laugh. "I don't consider the Cheyenne my people. But they're my mother's people, and she's refused my support. Seems to feel she deserves winters of starvation and miserable, hot summers away from the lands farther north, which once belonged to the tribe."

As she listened to Jackson Blue, Charity saw another side to the normally hostile redskin and respected his concern for his mother. "The women there were little more than slaves," she commented quietly.

"Yes, and because she fell from grace, my mother attracts more than her share of abuse—from men and women alike. Perhaps you saw her. Broken Willow, they call her."

Charity's eyes widened at the memory of the wrinkled woman who spat in her face. She nodded, taking a bite of mush rather than expounding about his mother's rudeness.

"You see, she married a Negro, who abandoned her for the call of California the day I was born," Blue continued. "She had no choice but to return to the Cheyenne. They scorned her and made my childhood pure hell, despite my inability to change my pedigree . . . or my color."

Jackson's dusky face registered deep emotion, as though the resentment of bygone years still stung him. "Indian children acquire new names as they accomplish deeds that display prowess and maturity. While other boys were called Flying Arrow and Little Wolf, my name remained Turtle . . . Droppings. I was barred from the rites of manhood and forced into the role of *berdache.*"

Charity felt a horrified sympathy for the man seated across from her. Sensing he didn't want to define the Indian insult, she glanced at Dillon and resumed eating.

Her husband cleared his throat, wondering how to explain the term without offending Charity or her father, who looked equally appalled by Blue's life story. "A *berdache,*" he began quietly, "lives his life as a woman. Prepares the meat brought home from the hunt rather than going with the other men to kill it, for instance."

Charity's eye's grew wide. How could *anyone* question Jackson Blue's maleness, unless . . . Her cheeks burned with embarrassment and ignorance of such matters.

"I'm a man in every way, Charity—make no mistake," the scout replied. "I was the first of my peers to drop a buffalo unassisted, a boy who sneaked girls into the trees to explore their . . . peaks and valleys. You can imagine my anger when those girls' fathers forced me to wear a dress and called me queer to my face. That's why I left the Northern Cheyenne and abandoned my mother, when she refused to come along."

"And you became a buffalo hunter, to get revenge by killing the Indian's food?" she asked quietly.

Blue chuckled. "So I thought. But it took more than one man to massacre those awesome herds." He tapped her plate with his fork. "Better eat, Hair of Flame. Golden Peacock grows anxious for the attentions of his woman."

"Golden Peacock?" Charity snickered, and then she was giggling so hard she couldn't stop. The mush slid from her spoon down the front of the buckskin dress, which only made her—and everyone except Dillon—laugh harder.

"What's so funny?" he asked with mock resentment. "A peacock is a stately bird—"

"Who struts around impressing the women with his plumage," Noah finished, nearly choking on his laughter. "It's the perfect name for you, Devereau. No offense intended, you understand."

"Of course not." Dillon glanced from his father-in-law to Blue, who seemed to be in a much lighter mood now. "I'd be interested in hearing Jackson's Indian name for *you*, Reverend."

"Me?" Scott dabbed moisture from his eye, still chuckling. "How could anyone possibly ridicule *me?*"

The shack grew silent while Jackson, Charity, and

Devereau considered answers to that question, each of them wearing a secretive grin.

Scott laid his utensils down with an indignant sniff. "You young people are impossibly rude," he said, but Charity could tell her father secretly enjoyed being the object of their mischief. The rest of the meal passed pleasantly—a miracle, considering all they'd endured these past several days.

It was then that the reason for their journey came back to her, and the thought of how Mama's misadventures with Erroll Powers had complicated so many lives made Charity feel suddenly tired again. "I . . . I'd like to bathe and change out of this awful dress," she said quietly.

Devereau rose to help with her chair, but it was Jackson who spoke. "Weak as you are, the undertow will drag you down, young lady. I'll heat you some water—"

"Dillon's going with me," Charity stated, knowing her husband had more than her personal hygiene in mind.

The Indian's lips twitched. "Devereau's in no better shape than you are. I'm going along, to keep you both from drowning."

"I'm perfectly capable of watching out for my wife," Dillon insisted. "Get your dress and soap from your suitcase, sweetheart."

But Blue was already at the door, gun in hand, wearing his usual arrogant grin. "I couldn't in good conscience let my friends bathe unprotected, while heathen savages are undoubtedly waiting for the chance to attack them. Scott, if you'd be so kind as to clean up . . ." He stooped, and was out the soddie's doorway.

Charity looked helplessly at her father, who waved her on. "You two attend to your bathing. I suppose cleaning up is the least I can do."

Nodding, she preceded Dillon outside. The sun

hovered on the horizon, basking in its own red-orange spendor, and the only sound was the *chirrip chirrip* of locusts in the distance. Charity could see the stream now, a ribbon of glistening water bounded by the only tall green grass in sight. It wound around a slight rise in the earth, and Jackson had already stationed himself at this vantage point. He chuckled at her hesitant expression.

"Never fear, Mrs. Devereau. Your husband and I have shared plenty of whiskey and women in our day, but your emaciated condition will keep my back turned tonight."

What had happened to the gracious host who'd shared his food and his history, as if pleading for her to understand his antisocial facade? Charity turned in disgust and stalked toward the tallest rushes she could find.

"Men exaggerate their exploits," Devereau said softly. "Blue and I shared a lot of things, but a woman was never one of them. He complained that my companions were too demure to suit him."

His tender massage around her shoulders relaxed her, and she chuckled. "I suppose I fit that description well enough," she said softly. "But I'm still not comfortable, knowing he can watch our every move and hear us talking."

"So we won't talk," he murmured. Dillon led her behind the rushes and silently knelt with her on the grassy banks of the stream. He pulled Charity to him, ignoring his sore muscles to clutch her close for the kiss he'd been wanting for days now.

Deftly he peeled the fringed dress up over her hips, past her concave stomach and her breasts, all the while plying her lips hungrily with his. He could feel her passion rising, somewhat subdued because she was so weak, and he pulled away reluctantly. "Blue made a valid point about the undertow. I couldn't swim strongly enough to—"

"So we'll just wash each other, where the current's not so strong."

He kissed the tip of her sunburned nose. "I probably shouldn't wet my bandage, since—"

"So I'll take it off you. We'll wrap your ribs again when we get back to the house." As her hands wandered over his bruised shoulders, Charity felt a familiar flame licking inside her. She found the end of the wide, white strip of linen and uncoiled it quickly. "You're not one to sleep in your own dirt, Dillon," she added in a husky voice. "You'll thank me for this, truly you will."

Devereau couldn't bear to disappoint her, and he prayed that the fall from his horse hadn't made him too sore—or temporarily unable—to respond to the invitation in her glimmering eyes. They removed the rest of their clothing as quickly as their aching limbs would allow and slipped into the water.

Charity shuddered, grabbing for her husband. "Why didn't you warn me how *cold*—"

"Because I hoped you'd cling to me this way," he murmured as he coaxed her legs around him. "You've become quite the hoyden, Charity."

"Don't tell Jackson, or he'll join us." She nibbled his ear and then playfully rubbed against him, delighting in her power to arouse his desire. His skin felt warm and slick beneath the water, and the light stubble on his chin rubbed her seductively as he kissed the ridge of her jaw and the hollows of her collarbone. Charity let her head loll back, luxuriating in the tenderness of a tongue that caressed first one breast and then the other.

Despite their buoyancy in the chest-deep water, Dillon's legs trembled and he thought better of sliding her down onto his manhood. He loosened his grip, allowing her to skim against him until her breasts bobbed in the water again. "We'd better save it for bed," he whispered. "If I slip in this mud, we're both goners."

Realizing how valiantly he was hiding his pain, Charity nipped her lip. "I'm sorry, Dillon. I forgot—"

"You are not! You're taking advantage of my weakened state, and you know it."

She smiled coyly. "Well, there's *one* part of you that feels plenty strong—Golden Peacock!"

"You little . . ." Dillon lowered his eyelids, chuckling. "I think it's time we douse this Hair of Flame—don't you?"

Charity shrieked as her husband tossed her toward the center of the stream. He dove after her, pushing her under the water until they tussled beneath the surface, rolling over each other with a playfulness that heightened their desire. When Dillon found her nipples with his lips she retaliated by gripping him between the legs.

He surfaced with a raucous hoot. Charity popped up close behind him, shaking her wet hair so it would slap him on the back. They turned to each other, laughing as they shared another hug.

"We'd better bathe," Dillon whispered against her ear. "Jackson won't sit idly by while we're having so much fun."

"You're right. And it's getting dark." She fetched the bar of lilac soap from her pile of clean clothing, and lovingly stroked Dillon's shoulders with it. "Mmm . . . Golden Peacock smell pretty," she teased.

"Golden Peacock get his revenge come bedtime, woman." He took his turn with the soap, gently caressing her breasts, her back . . . her slender thighs and the soft coils between them. Charity's wet skin radiated heat and desire; her heart throbbed against his own as he held her for a lingering kiss.

Their escort was silent as he walked them back

to the sod house, staying a few steps behind. Dillon didn't care—he felt too invigorated to humor Blue's disapproval or jealousy or whatever was making him glower. At the door he kissed his wife and then swatted her behind. "Tell your father to join us out here while you get ready for bed," he suggested.

Charity nodded, still radiant from their foreplay and anticipating a more satisfying embrace. After Papa stepped outside, she pulled one of her new nightgowns from her suitcase, aware that in a one-room shack there was no way to make love without the other occupants knowing it. She stepped into the far shadows, contemplating this problem as she removed the gingham dress.

Male voices drifted inside, Jackson Blue's sounding as crass as ever. "You're stronger than I thought, if you can throw your woman across the stream."

"You were spying on us?"

"She screamed. I thought she was drowning."

Charity rammed her arms into the sleeves of her nightie. How dare he *watch*, when he knew damn well—

"My point is," the Indian's deep voice went on, "that I suspect you'll be on your way soon. I'm telling you again to leave well enough alone, Devereau. After Powers pulls his heist in Dodge, he plans to disappear to San Francisco—by this time he and Maggie are probably on the train. Why waste your time and money chasing after a woman who'll make you *extremely* sorry if you catch her?"

Papa coughed. "What did Powers do to the Cheyenne that prompted them to kidnap Charity? They obviously mistook her for Marcella."

"Part of it was cocksure stupidity," the Indian replied, "but they had good reason to be after that pair. The tribe nearly starved last winter because Powers and the government agent sold the beef and commodities meant to supply the Cheyenne for several months. He told Dull Knife the cattle never made it to the railhead. Maggie apparently let the truth slip when she was distracting Soaring Eagle and the tribal elders, while Powers was playing the sympathetic railroad representative. You're married to one slippery bitch, Reverend."

Papa's response was indignant, yet it sounded as though he agreed with Blue and planned to let Mama slip away. *THEY weren't held prisoner with only drugged water to keep them alive—THEY didn't feel Broken Willow's spit on their faces,* Charity fumed. She crossed her arms tightly, debating whether to march outside and remind them about what she'd suffered because of Mama and Powers, but she crawled onto the bed instead. It was just like a bunch of men to decide what was best for her without asking her opinion!

Outside, Dillon's battered body ached and all thoughts of taking delight in his wife vanished while he listened to Blue's arguments. The scout looked expectantly at him, for the answer to a question he hadn't been paying attention to. "I'll consider your advice," he hedged, "but I have my own reasons for confronting Powers. And I doubt Charity's ready to give up either."

"You're a fool to let her wheedle you into this," Blue retorted. "Haven't you taken enough abuse because of her wild-ass ideas?"

He was suddenly too exhausted to fight back. "I've been called worse than a fool for listening to a woman, gentlemen," he said wearily, "and I'm going to bed."

The cabin was dark except for the red glow of embers in the fireplace, and it took his eyes a moment to pick out the few pieces of furniture. Charity was stretched out next to the wall, looking as pathetic as an undernourished kitten beneath the folds of her nightgown. Again he chided himself for getting involved in the Scotts' personal business—for encouraging them on a journey that had nearly cost Charity her life.

But a deal was a deal, and his feisty wife would remind him of that if he told her they weren't traveling any farther. Dillon let his pants drop, trying to recall the feel of her wet, satiny skin and the grip of her legs wrapped around him, and the wild abandon she'd driven him to when they frolicked in the stream. He knew ways to keep her on the verge of exploding until Blue and her father were asleep, ways to love her that wouldn't wake them up . . . unless she moaned in that alley-cat way she had.

As he stretched out beside her, he caught the warm scent of lilacs, and his manhood snapped to attention. If he could keep his strength up—and keep her quiet . . .

But she was already asleep.

Once again Charity awoke to the rich aromas of bacon and coffee and cornmeal mush. All traces of the drug had left her body and she felt alert and refreshed. Glancing around the small shack, she realized the men had gone outside so she could dress.

She quickly donned the blue gingham gown and tried to tame hair that was unruly from being slept on wet. When she stepped outside, her husband and his companions were seated on inverted wooden crates, drinking coffee. "Breakfast smells wonderful," she said, managing a smile for their host.

Three unshaven faces looked at her over tin cups, only Dillon's hinting at any enthusiasm. "You slept well, I trust?" Blue asked.

It occurred to Charity that he and her father had spent the night on bedrolls, which accounted for

Papa's sullen expression. "Yes, thank you," she replied pertly, "and if Dillon feels up to traveling, we won't bother you any longer."

The Indian stood, as if to establish his authority. "And where will you go, Mrs. Devereau?"

Charity saw no purpose in pussyfooting around her reply. A wagon was parked off to the side of the soddie—they'd needed it to carry the luggage here, of course—and Satan and a pair of horses were grazing the sparse grass in the shade of the house. "I overheard your conversation last night," she replied staunchly, "and Dodge City is our logical destination. If we leave after breakfast, we might catch Mama and Powers before they hightail it to California."

Jackson rolled his eyes and Papa quickly stood up. "Haven't you witnessed enough of your mother's brazen behavior?" he demanded. "What can we possibly gain by confronting her, daughter? What's left to say?"

Charity caught Dillon's amused smile and thought, *He's learning.* Then she looked each of them straight in the eye. "Satisfaction," she stated. "The satisfaction of hearing Mama admit to all the terrible cons she's pulled, and the chance to ask why she left us in the first place. *That's* what you're afraid to hear, isn't it?"

Her father reached up to grip his lapels, preparing for a lecture, but he lost steam when he realized he wasn't wearing his coat. He had secrets he wasn't telling her, yet Charity felt sorry for him out here, so far removed from the domain of his pulpit. She sighed and smiled at him. "You've got to go to Dodge to catch the train home anyway, Papa. You might as well go with us."

Chapter 19

Charity could only gape as they entered Dodge City, too amazed to notice the blazing sun or the way her dress clung to her sweaty body. Dillon was driving them along the widest main street she'd ever seen—with railroad tracks down its center!—yet their path was too clogged with excited people for the horses to make much headway. "What's going on?" she murmured, unable to take her eyes from the mass of humanity that surrounded them.

Papa shifted beside her on the cramped wagon seat. "They say Dodge City's the Babylon of the frontier, and I believe it! One saloon after the other! Don't any of these people *work* for a living?"

Chuckling, Dillon reined in the horses to avoid running over a gaggle of giggling ladies. "It's the Fourth of July," he reminded them. "There's a banner up ahead. What's it say?"

Charity squinted at the sign. "Independence Day parade, two o'clock. It must be nearly—"

"One-thirty," her father declared as he snapped his pocket watch shut. "Why do I have the feeling we'll get our pockets picked, or at the very least be stranded without a hotel room? I *knew* we shouldn't have come here!"

Devereau kept his grin to himself. Noah Scott had complained for the entire trip, clearly hoping Marcella and Erroll were long gone. "Horse thieving's the most prevalent crime here," he reassured his riders. "However, I've heard rumors that a man could break all ten commandments in one night, die with his boots on, and be buried in Boot Hill the next morning. Sounds like a town that needs divine guidance, Reverend."

Her father let out a snort, unimpressed, while Charity read the saloon signs they were passing . . . the Alamo, the Alhambra, the Long Branch. They stopped in front of Wright and Beverly's mercantile, where two white, mounted buffalo flanked the doorway.

"I'll check the Dodge House first," her husband was saying, "and if it's full I'll ask the saloon keepers about lodgings. No doubt some of them remember me."

Charity watched him swing down a little stiffly from the wagon seat. "I suppose you've been kicked out of *this* town, too?"

Dillon laughed, holding his sides to keep his ribs from aching. "No, sweetheart, I've never been to Dodge. Some of these establishments were hauled here on flatcars from Abilene and Wichita. You'll be perfectly safe until I return—these people are too excited about the parade to get nasty."

As he headed for the boardwalk, he was swallowed up by the crowd, and Charity's insides twinged. What if there were no rooms available? What if Mama and Erroll Powers were already on the train—or if not, how could she *hope* to locate them in a town so full of boisterous people?

The sun suddenly beat hotter on the back of her neck and she scooted away from Papa to cool off. If they didn't start looking soon, they'd miss Mama for sure . . . all these days wasted, and her father would never let her forget it. She couldn't expect Dillon to escort them all the way to California, so perhaps Dodge City was the end of the line for their marriage, as well as their search.

Her throat tightened at the thought of losing him.

A band was tuning up, and people were finding places to stand along Front Street, but none of Dodge City's gaiety touched her. She hadn't allowed herself to think about what life would be like without Dillon, and the bustle of activity around them made the odds seem overwhelmingly stacked against remaining his wife. Their unorthodox deal had seemed like the only alternative at the time, yet now—

"That husband of yours is taking his sweet time about coming back," her father muttered as he tugged at his shirt collar. "We'll be swept up into the parade if we don't move this wagon soon. Perhaps I should trade places with you and drive us—"

"Sit down!" she snapped, and was immediately sorry. She was as apprehensive about confronting her mother as Papa was, and her nerves were shot after listening to him yammer all morning. Maybe Dillon knew they wouldn't find Mama and he'd already abandoned them, to avoid a bitter good-bye. Maybe another of his former flames had come to Dodge . . . such a town offered dozens of opportunities to a man in his profession. Maybe he thought Soaring Eagle had coupled with her while she was drugged . . . he hadn't made the slightest move toward her during the night.

And then he was looking up into her face, his smile framed by a mustache that shone with golden highlights. "We're set," he said, and he pulled himself slowly up to the seat. "Two of the fanciest rooms in town are waiting for us, and the first person to protest can spend the night in the Elephant Barn with the cowpokes and the vagrants."

Charity glanced at Papa's furrowed brow, and then at Dillon, whose expression remained unruffled. "Where are we staying?" she murmured as the wagon jerked to a start.

"With a friend."

The band down the street struck a few opening chords and then piped a jaunty rendition of "Yankee Doodle," which sent pedestrians scurrying to the boardwalks to watch the parade's beginning. A few in the crowd applauded their wagon, and Dillon gave them a ceremonious wave, as though he were the lead entry. Charity chuckled, and as he steered the horses down a side alley, he hoped she would retain her sense of humor. He halted the wagon behind a frame building, glancing at their reactions as the back door was swung open by a scantily clad young woman with a come-hither smile.

"Where *are* we?" Charity murmured. Their greeter's lacy camisole gaped over an ample bosom and was tucked into pantalets that displayed lush hips and calves. She felt Papa's temperature rise with his indignation.

Devereau leaned in front of his wife to speak to Scott. "Reverend, I got us the only rooms I could find—and only because two of Miss Silks's ladies were nice enough to accommodate us. A show of appreciation is in order here, or there's the Elephant Barn down the way."

His tone was friendly but firm, and Charity felt her father holding his breath while the fetching brunette kept smiling at them. Finally, he relaxed and tore his eyes from her. "I never thought I'd see the night I slept in a bordello," Papa said in a tight voice, "but I can't very well have my suit smelling like a stable either."

Dillon coughed to keep from laughing, because Noah was enjoying the scenery more than he would admit. "Well then, let's unload our luggage and get settled. From our windows we should have an excellent view of the festivities."

As they stepped inside, Charity doubted that Erroll Powers' mansion could be any more lavish. The flocked wallpaper, fringed lampshades, and gleaming mahogany woodwork were rivaled only by the exquisite gowns or underthings on the boarders, who eyed them as they carried their belongings to the second floor. The upstairs hallway had a large, lace-curtained window at its end, from which three silk fannies blossomed. The ladies were waving gaily at the parade, unaware that a preacher and his family were passing behind them.

"What a convenient way to advertise," Charity mumbled. "Are you sure we won't be overrun by customers?"

Dillon laughed and opened the door closest to them. "No one comes to this floor except by invitation," he assured her, "and Mattie promised we'll be undisturbed. We have adjoining rooms," he added, gesturing toward the door Noah was to use, "so unless we're leaving the building, we have no need to venture into the hallway to see each other."

"Lead us not into temptation," the Reverend intoned with a roll of his eyes. He lowered his end of Devereau's trunk and then carried his own suitcase into the next room.

Charity gazed around, grinning. It was a corner room, and the curtains were a gaudy print that complemented the fuschia bedspread. A gold plaster cupid dangled from each corner of the four-poster. The picture above the washstand was a nude reclining on a couch, her hand draped suggestively between her legs. Her coy smile reminded Charity of Phoebe Thomas. "I could never feel at home in a room like this," she said in a low voice.

"I'll see that you never have to." She looked hot and tired from the long wagon ride, and Dillon enfolded her gently in his arms. Would the next hours bind them together or tear them apart? He should have warned them that Marcella might be married to Powers—that bigamy was another of Maggie Wallace's many sins—before they came so far to confront her. Noah would probably accept such a situation, heinous as it was. But Charity would have good reason to demand a divorce when she found out how long he'd known about her mother.

He held her close, gathering his courage. "Sweetheart, there are a few things about your mama . . ."

"Have you looked outside?" Noah exclaimed as he entered their room. "The parade's over, and there are more contests than Satan has sinners!"

Dillon sighed and released his wife so she could view the spectacles below them. He sensed again that the Reverend had a trump hidden up his sleeve and that he was stalling for time—which wasn't such a bad idea. Searching for Powers and Maggie was impossible, crowded as the streets were, so they'd be better off watching the day's events from the room. It might be the last time he saw Charity smile.

Devereau opened his trunk and brought out a pair of binoculars. "Try these. Lean out the window and tell me what all you see."

She gave him a delighted smile as he raised the sash. "You won't let me fall out?"

"Of course not. How would it look if my wife tumbled out a whorehouse window?"

Charity giggled and flashed her husband an exaggerated wink. "Hold tight, now. We wouldn't want to embarrass Papa."

When she stuck her head out the window, Devereau got an inviting view of her blue gingham bottom, pointed flirtatiously at him. She'd come a long way since she'd first gaped at him at the Crystal Queen; she remained girlishly demure, yet was wise to her own womanly power over him. He glanced at Noah, who was engrossed in watching the contests himself, and then grasped Charity by her hips. The crowd below roared its approval, and he couldn't help chuckling. "What do you see, honey?"

"Firemen in red union suits, having a tug-of-war," she chirped. "And beyond that's the greased pig contest and a pie-eating race. Oh, Dillon—so many *people!*"

Positioned against her as he was, Devereau could think of only one person and the havoc she was wreaking while she wiggled against him. He kneaded her waist, wishing her father would watch the festivities from his own window. He longed to hold her close in this exotic bed, to strip away her clothes and pleasure her until they both cried out, before too much truth brought their tenderness to an end.

She swiveled, making him grit his teeth against a bolt of desire. Charity was aiming the binoculars above the crowd now, past the storefronts to the residential section. "Such grand houses," she murmured, "and people celebrating on their lawns. Too bad they can't see the games, like we can."

Trying not to sound wolfish, Dillon said, "Perhaps your father would enjoy using the binoculars, honey. From his room he could see—" His words were cut off when Charity stiffened abruptly. She was trembling as she stared fixedly at something he couldn't distinguish from this distance. If he hadn't anticipated her, she would have whacked her head when she jerked back through the window.

Charity's heart was beating wildly and she nearly dropped the binoculars. It couldn't be, yet she'd seen it with her own eyes!

"Honey, what's wrong?" Devereau grasped her hands and was shocked at how cold they felt. "Did you see a burglary, or a shooting? You're pale as a ghost."

Indeed, she felt as though she'd *seen* a ghost, a spirit swathed in white with a smile that was at once alluring yet frightening beyond comprehension.

Charity tried to speak, but all she could utter was, "Mama."

"Daughter, you must be mistaken!"

"Let me see those," Devereau said as he grasped the binoculars. While Scott was repeating his litany of reasons they'd never find Charity's mother, he adjusted the focus. He found the lawn party his wife had been observing: long refreshment tables draped in linen . . . a gathering of guests, fashionably dressed, as though for a . . . *oh Jesus, they just got married!*

Dillon's thoughts raced. Marcella was wearing an elegant white gown and stood beside a dark, dapper man in a dove-gray suit, and Charity had reached the only logical conclusion. How the hell could he explain? What could he possibly say to prevent Charity and Noah from rushing into this powderkeg situation with their fuses lit?

He gazed earnestly at his wife. Her eyes were glazed and she offered only feeble responses to her father's suggestions that she'd seen a woman who merely resembled Marcella Scott. "After all, daughter, you were only eight when your mother succumbed to—"

"Stop it, Papa," she said bitterly. "You knew all along she didn't have consumption. I-it's Mama and Erroll Powers at that . . . reception, isn't it, Dillon?"

He'd never directly lied to her and this was no time to start. "Yes, I believe it is." He gripped her trembling fingers, praying for the right words. "Charity, we should think carefully before we—"

But Charity's thoughts were years away. Goosebumps prickled up her spine. Her mouth dried out, and the words of the awful letter that started them on this journey sped through her mind, read by Mama's own voice. A rush of emotion rendered her speechless: despite all her lies and tricks and sins, this woman in a wedding gown was her *mother*—the mother she'd presumed dead and had mourned, the mother she'd longed for while she was growing up. The mother whose letters couldn't replace the smiles and hugs Charity had ached to share.

He'd read the faces of men in desperate straits, and Dillon saw his wife's attitude change within a heartbeat. Where she'd once stood strong, demanding explanations, Charity now quavered vulnerably. He should have listened to Jackson Blue and never brought her here. "Honey, I know you've missed her a lot—"

"*Missed* her?" Charity gasped. "I thought she was *dead,* and now we have a chance to make up for all the—"

"She'll rip your heart out," Dillon insisted, gripping her slender shoulders. "This is the worst possible time to barge in—"

"God deliver us," Noah muttered, and Devereau knew without looking that the preacher had spied his wife. Scott came back into the room looking as bleached as his shirt. His eyes were wide behind his spectacles; he raked his fingers through his hair, looking as though he, too, were shaken to the core.

Then the Reverend composed himself, and with a beseeching gaze he said, "Charity, I know how you've needed a woman's love—how lacking I've been as a parent. But before you go running to that . . . *party,* full of questions, I have most of the answers you need. I—I should have explained about your mother long ago, but I—"

"Yes, you should have!" Charity snapped, "and all you're doing now is stalling me again! You can't preach another revival, or tell me to wait a day and recover my strength, because when that party's over, Mama will be gone! I'm going to *see* her, and *touch* her, and by God she'll know I'm on to her tricks! Stay here and soak in your own sweat if you want to, but I'm leaving."

Dillon caught her arm as she whirled toward the door. "Charity, you can't go alone."

"So come with me! This is your big day, too, as I recall." Her pulse was thundering through her head, and as she rushed down the stairs, she was too worked up to think straight. She had no idea how to get to the party, where she'd undoubtedly be thrown out, but Dillon's footsteps behind her—and Papa's!—were the insurance she needed. Elegant Mr. Devereau and the imposing Reverend Scott were never refused admittance, so once they found the right house . . .

"This way, Charity," Dillon directed. "We'll never get through the crowds out front."

Walking rapidly past the back sides of saloons and stores, Charity forced her two companions to stride along at a breathless pace. "When's the west-bound train leave?" she gasped.

"I don't know, but we could ask at one of these—"

"Forget it! We'll get there in time—we have to!" She recalled at least two blocks of houses before the lawn where the party was going on; she'd recognize it by the border of honeysuckle bushes, and then they'd slip in. . . .

"Charity, whoa!" Devereau gripped her arm, keeping his voice low. Noah looked ready to pop, he was so bug-eyed, and his wife apparently planned to make a grand entrance that would get them all thrown out. "That's the yard, right ahead of us," he said with a nod. "We should sidle in behind the refreshment tables, as though we've been here all along. You two sip some punch while I—"

"But she's *my* mother, and I—"

"—make my way through the reception line," he finished firmly. "Your mother doesn't know me, and Powers won't cause any commotion in front of all these guests. I'll ask her to step inside, before she spots you. You're the *last* people she expects to see, you know."

Charity's heart was pounding so hard she thought her ribs would shatter. Papa was fidgeting with his collar, looking utterly foreign to her in his agitated state. "All right, we'll wait," she replied in a strained whisper. "But what if someone asks who we are?"

"Tell them you're friends of the bride," he suggested with a rueful grin, "and exclaim over the lavish refreshments. Just don't give yourselves away."

Papa looked absolutely mortified, and food was the farthest thing from Charity's mind, but he'd given them a logical answer. They walked slowly toward the honeysuckle hedge, Dillon first, and let him lead the way to the deserted buffet nearest them. "I'll dip out some punch and make my way to the porch. Sit here until I give you a nod."

Before she could reply, he was mingling with the other well-dressed guests, cup in hand, and she was left with Papa. They were fools to come here. She stuck out like an urchin at a grand ball, and her hair fluttered uncontrollably in the hot breeze. Charity accepted the punch Papa handed her and sat down at a small table in the back of the yard, avoiding the eyes of the other guests.

"Charity, I hope you'll understand about—"

"Please don't talk, Papa," she pleaded. "Let's just watch for Dillon's signal. We've come too far to mess things up now."

She panicked when she lost sight of her husband's stylish checked jacket. But there he was, almost up to the veranda where Mama and Erroll Powers smiled gaily at their guests. Charity thumped the ground with a nervous foot; she felt like a watch wound so tightly that its works would explode. Dillon had only a few places in line to go. What would she say to a mother who'd faked her own death, cavorted with Indians and whores, and had now married another man? What *could* she say to Mama, who looked as beautiful as her fondest memories from a childhood cut short?

Devereau struggled for an appropriate opening line. Marcella was standing on this side of Powers; he hoped he could lure her into the house before Erroll recognized him. Some men nearby congratulated the host for throwing this last-minute reception—for the surprise visit of a Kansas Pacific attorney, they said—and they speculated over the promotion that was undoubtedly coming his way.

Powers, you raven-haired snake, he thought as he stared at Erroll's dapper face. Sixteen years had passed since the bastard's gunfire burned his father's gambling hall to the ground, but time had been kind to the con artist. His wavy hair was still coal black, his eyes a blue that sparkled like ice above a thick mustache and a mouthful of even, white teeth. He touched Marcella's arm as though he *were* her husband, yet Dillon sensed a coldness that precluded any chance of matrimony. Erroll's maid and Maggie had their fantasies about this long-standing relationship, it seemed, but Devereau knew at a glance that the women were just two more victims of the shyster's magnetism.

Or was Marcella smart enough to latch on to Erroll's wealth another way? Dillon studied the woman who so closely resembled his wife: her upswept hair was darker than Charity's, with the help of henna dye, he suspected. Her lithe body appeared youthful in the maidenlike dress, but the lines around her eyes and mouth betrayed her upon closer inspection. It was a hard mouth, lacking warmth. Her face was made up, destroying the innocent beauty he'd come to love about Charity, and her eyes glimmered a pale, catlike green.

But when Marcella flashed him a flirtatious grin,

Devereau knew why Scott had fallen for her, and how she'd duped an entire tribe of Indians. How many Kansas Pacific employees would be caught with their pants down when it was discovered that she'd distracted them so Powers could raid the company coffers?

"Hello," she purred, her voice perfectly suited to a Magnolia. "I don't believe we've met—and I'm so glad you could come today."

He immediately forgot the list of this woman's sins—nearly forgot how to talk, he was so taken by her. "Dillon Devereau," he managed, kissing her hand to regain control of himself. Everything he'd endured with the Scotts these past weeks had culminated in this moment, and only the smoothest of maneuvers would get Marcella into the house without causing a stir. "I—I was wondering if we could discuss some business," he said suggestively. "It will require but a moment, and I hate to take Mr. Powers from his guests."

Marcella's glance flickered over him, as though she assumed him to be another kowtowing railroad executive. Yet when the wary moment passed, she was all sunshine . . . sultry, languorous sunshine. "I'm sure I'll find your business highly refreshing," she replied, running her tongue along her upper lip. "Some of these things get so . . . long."

Her last words tugged at Dillon's fly buttons. "Shall we step inside?" he suggested, glancing at Powers as though he shared Marcella's devious intentions. "Your fair skin will take a beating in this merciless sun."

Marcella chuckled coquettishly and turned from Erroll's side. When Dillon reached the door, he pulled his gaze from her swaying, white hips long enough to jerk his head at Charity and Noah. The sight of his wife's anxious face reminded him that

Marcella was Charity's *mother,* for God's sake, and he had no business flirting with—

"Are you all right, Mr. Devereau?" she asked in a honeyed voice. "Perhaps a neck spasm I can ease away while we discuss our . . . business?"

"Probably just my collar buttoned too tightly," he replied as he reached around her for the doorknob. But when she froze beside him, staring toward the far end of the lawn, Devereau knew he was in trouble. "Perhaps we can find a cozy alcove—"

"What the hell are *they* doing here?" She glared wickedly at Dillon, all resemblance to magnolias gone. "This business of yours *stinks,* Mr. Devereau, and whatever it is, you *damn* well better not get Erroll involved. I refuse to—"

"Is this gentleman bothering you, Maggie?" Powers inquired behind them. His voice was as rich and deep and deadly as Dillon recalled from his youth, and he had no answer for the jet-haired man whose expression demanded one.

Erroll's deeply tanned face reflected annoyance and then startled recognition when he came face to face with Devereau. He glanced at Marcella, quickly following her gaze to the two figures who were hurrying through the crowd. In the blink of an eye Dillon's scheme had collapsed. Powers's scowl told him he didn't know Scott or Charity, but he certainly realized they were connected to Maggie.

Rather than ask questions, the con artist retreated, wary of being exposed in front of railway officials. Reverend Scott and Charity were only a few steps away, their faces taut, and Marcella was growing paler by the second.

"Erroll, please, I can explain," she pleaded, but her consort was descending the porch stairs, staring at Charity as though she were a ghost.

Dillon sensed they were about to witness a fireworks display like no Fourth of July had ever seen.

He opened the door and slipped a firm arm around Marcella's waist.

"I'm not going inside with any of you god-damned, scheming—"

But Charity stepped onto the porch, blocking Marcella's escape. Her hair was an untidy mass of waves and sweat trickled down her dusty cheeks, yet Dillon recognized the strength in those jade eyes as daughter faced mother for the the first time in ten years. "We have to talk, Mama," she stated quietly.

Marcella stared at Scott for a moment, but it was Charity who held her attention. After an endless silence, during which Devereau felt Powers and the entire gathering watching them, she relaxed against his arm. She preceded him into the house, but he sensed Marcella would turn like a trapped tiger the moment the door was closed.

Chapter 20

Charity followed Dillon and Mama past the curious kitchen help, who were preparing more trays of sandwiches and cakes, into the unoccupied dining room. It was an elegant, airy salon with stately furnishings and a glittering chandelier above the table, a room like the ones her mother was undoubtedly accustomed to entertaining in. Except now Mama was standing before the pink marble fireplace with her arms crossed tightly beneath her breasts, facing the mantel.

She pulled a gold case from her skirt pocket, selected a cigarette, and struck a match. Then she turned to Dillon, glaring. "So what's *your* part in this little charade, Mr. Devereau? Or perhaps that's not really your name."

"Oh, it is," he assured her. "My business with Erroll has waited sixteen years and it'll keep a little longer. It's your daughter and husband who wish to speak with you."

Marcella laughed abruptly. "Poor Charity was deeply distraught over my last letter, I bet. Her father undoubtedly turned my gruesome fate into a text for several sermons and made a tidy buck on them. He has a particular talent for that."

Reverend Scott bristled. "And *your* flair for decadence never ceases to amaze me, woman. It wasn't enough to go galavanting around with *Uncle Erroll,*" he said, pointing a condemning finger. "You had to rub my nose in his wealth with every letter, and send a damn *photograph* to remind me of him."

"That *was* a nice touch, wasn't it?" She blew the smoke from her nostrils in a thin stream. "But you deserved every sleepless night since you got that last letter, for not upholding your end of our bargain."

Charity slipped her hand into Dillon's, seeking his gentle strength. Her parents must have struck a devious agreement years ago, just as she and Devereau had done, and animosity was now whirling between them like a cyclone. "I—I don't understand," she pleaded in a tiny voice.

"Of course you don't. I *knew* your father would shirk his responsibilities with you." Mama inhaled deeply on her cigarette and then gestured toward the parlor with it. "We may as well sit down. This'll take a while."

Her mother led the way and perched in a wing chair by the window. Papa leaned on the mantel, keeping his distance; the armpits of his black coat were dark with perspiration. As Charity settled beside Dillon on an elegant settee, she was only a few steps away from Mama. It was like viewing her own reflection in a plate glass window: the image was distinct, yet her mother looked smaller than she recalled, cool and untouchable. Her catlike eyes lingered for a moment on Charity's large diamond, and then studied her face and figure.

"I met your father at one of his revivals, when he was preaching in Atlanta," she began. She sounded calmer now, yet her eyes smoldered with irritation when she glanced at Papa. "He stole my innocence, promising my salvation with each secret meeting. And when my parents guessed I was pregnant and threatened to send me away, he did the honorable thing and married me. To prevent nasty rumors, we moved to Missouri."

Charity's jaw dropped. She'd been conceived in sin . . . and the revelation left her speechless. Time had obviously erased Mama's guilt, because she continued with a sardonic chuckle.

"But Noah didn't know the *meaning* of honor. Thought his occupation would fool people—thought I'd be eternally grateful because he'd rescued me and removed the stigma of illegitimacy from you," she explained in a chilly voice. "When I asked why the collection plates were full yet there was never any money for clothes or household goods, he looked me straight in the eye. Swore every extra cent went toward the mission of the church. He was a compulsive gambler, Charity, and by the looks of your dress, he hasn't changed one bit."

Charity turned to stare at her father, who appeared to be choking. His eyes were pinched shut and his beet-red face confirmed Mama's accusations, which made a lot of missing pieces fall into place. All his evenings out . . . his moodiness . . . perhaps even the black eye that was now only a shadow behind his spectacles. She looked away from him, humiliated, and felt grateful for the compassionate squeeze of Dillon's hand.

"I see you've found a man yourself," Mama continued, "but I'm surprised you married for the same reason I did. You were such a *pious* little girl."

"No! I . . ." Charity's throat went so dry it squeaked. "Di-Dillon gave me a splendid ceremony and—and we're very happy. And I'm *not* in the family way," she added, hoping she sounded positive rather than desperate.

"But you *are* easily led, dear daughter," her mother replied with a shake of her head. She drew deeply on her cigarette, making its tip glow red while she considered her next words. "For me, marriage and motherhood were a trap—not that I resented *you,* personally—and being divorced sounded heavenly compared to living with a hypocritical cheat. But your father wouldn't hear of a divorce—what a scandal *that* would cause!—until I threatened to expose his gambling habits."

Mama's face creased with a smug, mirthless smile. "Saint that he was, Noah agreed to untie the knot—but only if he could keep you, and only if I swore I'd never come home. I went along with his conditions because he said I could write to you, and because he agreed to tell you all these things when you turned eighteen. We devised the story that I'd contracted consumption and was staying with your Aunt Magnolia so you wouldn't be shunned by your father's parishioners. It was a workable agreement, until I realized he wasn't ever going to tell you the truth."

Too stunned to look at her father again, or to comprehend the *lie* they'd all lived for the past ten years, Charity stared at her lap. Mama's cruel story was shredding her heart into ribbons, but this was no time to retreat into the naive fantasies of her youth. Too many questions remained unanswered, so she forced herself to look at her mother. "Everyone in Leavenworth knows you as Maggie Wallace, Mama. What happened to your sister?"

Dillon held his breath as he watched Charity's face tighten with the courage it took to ask such a question. The situation was even more disgusting than he'd imagined, and there seemed to be no end to the layers of sordid lies that were coming to light.

And Marcella sounded so calm—almost proud—as she responded. "Your Aunt Maggie died of consumption when we were seventeen, right before I met your father. No one in Missouri knew that, of course. And since Maggie was always so saintly and helpless, it gave me great pleasure to assume her identity and give her a whole new reputation. Your father's spent his entire life covering his butt, but when I became free, *I* at least lived honestly. I decided to start a new life out west, so I—"

"Looked for a sponsor on a wagon train and moved in with Erroll Powers instead?" Charity finished bitterly. "So we heard, Mama. And you had that picture made to fool me. Do you know how many times I *prayed* for an invitation to that mansion you described in your letters? But you never *intended* to see me again, did you? Living in that big house with that handsome man, you could forget I even existed."

The parlor rang with a stunned silence. Marcella clenched her jaw; she missed the ashtray by several inches when she rubbed her cigarette out on the marble-topped table beside her. Dillon heard Noah's labored breathing, but it was his wife's face that captivated him. Charity's sunburned cheeks remained dry—he suspected she was too shocked for tears—and her lips were a grim, determined line as she awaited her mother's reply. He cleared his throat and addressed Marcella in the most civilized tone he could manage. "Your daughter deserves an answer to those questions. And you'd damn well better give her one."

Marcella's eyes narrowed and she fumbled in her skirt for the cigarette case. "What choice did I have?" she demanded. "A man like Erroll wouldn't waste a second glance on a woman with a child, and my only other option was whoring. I figured once he married me, I could soften him up about bringing you—"

"And after all this time he *hasn't,*" Charity challenged. She wondered where she'd found the fortitude to speak to her mother this way, but she wasn't about to back down now. "Sounds to me like you took up a different sort of whoring. You could've written me the truth, but *no*—you sent Papa and me on a wild-goose chase with that last letter. Made us suffer the indignities of your adventures with Jackson Blue and Mr. Powers. We thought you were *dead,* Mama!" she blurted. "I cried and cried, thinking I'd never see you again. And here it was all a sham, just like the last ten years of my life!"

Again there was an awkward silence, this time underscored by the *pffffi* of Mama's match and the approaching whistle of a train. Marcella glanced nervously toward the door. "And had I told you the truth earlier, you would've found a way to Erroll's estate—we *both* would've been kicked out," she argued. "I never *dreamed* you'd go to Leavenworth, after the gory details I wrote. I thought your father would know better."

"Papa didn't want to go," she replied quietly. "And now I wish I hadn't threatened to leave without him, but I—I *loved* you, and . . ."

The train's whistle was loud and distinct this time, and the crystal chandelier in the dining room shimmied as the engine roared into town. Mama sprang from her chair, pointing her glowing cigarette at Charity. "Don't snivel at *me,* young lady! Powers was going to marry me in Frisco—till you three chased him off! He thinks you're railroad detectives, trying to catch him—"

"He's known me for years, and my unsettled score has nothing to do with the Kansas Pacific," Dillon interrupted. "And it isn't Charity's fault that Erroll knew who she was the moment he saw her."

"It wasn't my fault I was mistaken for you in Wichita either!" Charity chimed in. She felt bolder, because her mother's explanations sounded no more honest than her letters of the past decade. "You made *quite* an impression on Soaring Eagle and the Cheyenne, Mother. Not that Jackson Blue hadn't warned us about the—the *way* you have with Indians."

Marcella's face hardened, and then she snickered. "Redskins think my hair color makes me a goddess," she replied archly. "And Western men admire a woman who speaks her mind and can cut the noose of traditionalism. Your father never allowed me an opinion—not even about my own clothes, for God's sake! He's hardly the same *sex* as the men I've met since I left him."

Papa drew an outraged breath that seemed to bring him back to life. He strode a few paces closer, gripping his lapel as he pointed at her. "You can't be proud of what you've become, Marcella. Any woman who—"

"And who are *you* to preach?" The auburn curls at Marcella's temple shook with her anger as she blew smoke in his face. "The Reverend Noah Scott probably left a trail of gambling debts from here to Jefferson City. You've lied to your flock and to your daughter about my absence, and you've reveled in the chance it gave you to keep playing cards! Charity never guessed why she was only allowed two dresses, because you told her that *Christians* didn't adorn themselves with material possessions. Nice suit, Noah. Is it new?"

Charity's distraught expression told Dillon the initial shock of all she'd learned was wearing off. He tried to draw the conversation to a close, hoping Marcella could still catch the train and be out of their lives. "Your daughter traveled for days, hoping to visit your grave," he said in a low voice. "And when she learned what you've really been doing, she *still* wanted to see you. No matter how you feel about Noah, you at least owe Charity an apology."

Marcella smirked. "I never apologize, Mr. Devereau. And if you think I'll change now, you're as naive as my daughter."

Mama spat into her palm and then stuck the end of her cigarette in it. Charity's eyes widened, and she couldn't respond when her mother glared at her and said, "So now that you know the truth, you should *go home.* Which is more than *I* can do, now that Powers is probably on that train."

Chapter 21

The front door slammed behind Marcella, and the parlor echoed with silence.

Devereau couldn't remember the last time he'd been too stunned to speak. From Jackson Blue he expected cutthroat betrayals and blatant immorality, but Marcella Scott had just made every whore he knew look like the Virgin Mary! What kind of mother left her child, and then wove a web of lies to protect the life of a well-heeled harlot? What sort of woman assumed her dead twin's identity and then faked her own death to avoid ever seeing her family again?

Only a bitch with the heart of a dragon. And the way she fumed and smoked one cigarette after another, that was precisely the beast Marcella reminded him of.

Reverend Scott was leaning against the mantel, his head resting on his folded arms as though he were praying to the ornate clock that ticked above him. Charity sat limply on the settee, staring at the lace curtains. They were both in shock, and Dillon felt responsible for their anguish.

"Sweetheart, I'm truly, truly sorry for what's happened, and for bringing you here to witness it," he whispered. He brushed her hair back from her face, expecting her to flinch from his touch. "I should've listened to Blue—to your father's objections—and left you in Leavenworth."

With a rueful laugh, she focused her liquid green

eyes on him. "I was on my way to see my mother before I ever met you, Mr. Devereau. If you think Papa and Jackson Blue could keep me away from her, you don't know me very well."

Her uncompromising reply relieved him immensely. Yet her eyes contained a pain no tender word could erase, because no one learned of her untimely conception or her mother's resentment without suffering the deepest sort of agony. There was no excuse for Marcella's selfish behavior, and when the sting of today's revelations wore off, Charity would realize just how callously she'd been rejected.

Dillon wrapped his arms around her, hoping his touch would tell her of his deepening love. Here was a woman who'd gambled on a long shot and lost life's most elemental love, that of a child for her mother, yet Charity had retained her sense of self. "I'm not sure I could remain so . . . unruffled, if my mother had deceived me for most of my life," he said quietly.

Charity nuzzled his chest, soothed by his familiar scent. "I think I suspected something was amiss all along," she replied in a whisper. "Mama was *never* sick—even at eight, I was shocked to learn she had consumption—and by the time she wrote to me about it, she'd been visiting Aunt Maggie for a month. Her letters sounded so cheerful for an invalid's telling about evenings with Maggie and Erroll in their splendid house. Lonely as I was, I ate up every word. Her letters and that faked photograph were all I had," she added in a voice that trailed away.

Loosening herself from his embrace, Charity gave him a quavery smile. "Jackson Blue and Mr. Henry merely supplied the missing pieces by telling us about her escapades in Leavenworth. And when you consider the magnificent life we've cost her, I guess Mama could've done more than shout the truth at us. She had a pistol in the other pocket of her dress."

Dillon, too, had seen the weapon's shadow beneath the folds of Marcella's white skirt, and he sensed Charity's mother had only begun to vent her wrath. He knew their paths would cross again, as surely as the queen of spades brought him bad luck.

Behind them, Noah cleared his throat. Devereau watched him brush the sleeves of his black coat as though he'd been trounced in the street; the preacher's shoulders sagged and the leonine pride that had been his trademark was nowhere to be seen. He looked only at Dillon, and he spoke with quiet resignation. "I suppose we should leave, before our host comes looking for us. He's been quite indulgent, considering the way we interrupted his party."

Devereau nodded and studied Charity, whose face reflected pain and betrayal when she glanced at her father. His parents had never lied to each other and rarely fought, so Dillon felt unqualified to reconcile the silent accusations and anguish that hung between father and daughter.

He couldn't justify the preacher's lies and self-serving behavior over the past decade, yet he ached for Noah Scott. The man had been cuckolded by a jezebel who was even more hypocritical that he was. He'd accepted the responsibility of raising his daughter to be a fine Christian woman, despite his own moral failings. And today, because he'd agreed to a divorce ten long years ago, he'd been humiliated and exposed in front of the child he'd been trying to protect.

Dillon fell into step beside Scott, who gazed at Charity's back as they headed toward town.

"I owe you an apology, Noah," Dillon said in a low voice. His father-in-law's eyes remained fixed on Charity's faded gingham gown, so he continued without expecting any response. "Had I listened to you and minded my own business—had I realized how vindictive Marcella would be—I wouldn't have insisted you come along."

The Reverend let out a wry laugh. "What's the line about hell having no fury like a woman scorned? And I certainly can't cast the first stone."

They walked without talking for a few more blocks. When they turned toward Front Street, they discovered that the crowds had gone to the open fields outside the city limits to watch the fireworks display, leaving the litter of food vendors and paper streamers behind. The only sound was a rumbling like slow thunder, accented by whistles and yips and the bawling of cattle.

Charity looked over her shoulder and then stopped to stare. "Would you look at that! I think that herd's coming right down this street!"

Dillon glanced toward the approaching cloud of dust, chuckling. "It is. And once those longhorns are penned up across town and the drovers are paid, we'll see another sort of fireworks entirely."

His wife's face softened with awe at her first sight of a spectacle he'd seen hundreds of times, and he used the herd's noise to his advantage. "I don't intend to tell Charity how you lost the monte game to Blue, or about the way I coerced you into continuing this trip," he said, leaning toward Noah. "So forget what you owe me."

Scott glanced toward his daughter. "We all have ways of getting what we want, don't we?" he replied with a hint of his usual rancor. "But it's an offer I can't afford to refuse. And since you haven't received your satisfaction from Powers, I assume you'll continue your pursuit?"

He couldn't mention the deal he and Charity struck on the eve of their wedding, and he wasn't going to let on about the quandary he was in because of it. After half a lifetime, Dillon again had the chance to make Powers answer for his father's death, yet he couldn't subject his wife to further abuse from Erroll and Marcella. He *had* fulfilled his part of the bargain by delivering Charity to her mother, yet . . .

"I—I'm not sure it's worth the cost," he hedged. "Perhaps we'll stay in Dodge a few days. Rest up and decide on our next move."

The preacher looked again at the lowing, shuffling herd, which was nearing the first businesses on Front Street. "I'm sure you'll understand if I don't join you. Right now I could use a whiskey, and then I'm buying my train ticket home. If you'll excuse me . . ."

Devereau watched the man in black step off the boardwalk into the dusty street, wondering if he ever intended to apologize to Charity for all his lies. Maybe he'd spend the last hours until his train left getting suckered at monte.

But suddenly there was no time for pondering past wrongs. A raucous female laugh rang out across the street, and a chamber pot came sailing from a window above the Alamo Saloon. The plodding longhorns, startled by the shattering china, bellowed in unison and charged full speed down the street, right toward Noah.

Devereau had seen those murderous hooves trample a man into pulp, and had witnessed the fatal gorings of those pointed horns, so he sprang toward the preacher. There was no turning back—no time to think—as the animals stampeded toward him. He grabbed Noah's shoulders and shoved, not knowing where he got the strength for such a feat, not even aware that he was screaming.

When Charity heard his cry, her heart stopped. All she saw was a roaring mass of mottled, bony bodies armed with wicked horns, and then she herself dove into the nearest doorway to escape the cattle that came crashing down the boardwalk. The noise was deafening, and the dust drifting in under the batwing doors nearly choked her.

Were Dillon and Papa alive? For endless minutes, hooves and legs thundered past the saloon she'd landed in, and she could only wonder.

When the roar receded, followed by the cursings of the helpless cowboys, Charity stood up. Her heart throbbed . . . the dust was so thick and Front Street so wide, it was impossible to tell if the stampede had claimed any lives. She forced herself to step out to the edge of the boardwalk, where the shattered hitching rail lay in a dozen pieces at her feet.

There was still no sign of them. But as the brown cloud settled and the buildings across the way became visible, a movement on a second-story balcony caught her eye. A woman was leaning out to gaze at the street below her—*has to be a mighty drunk whore, to throw a chamber pot out the window,* Charity thought angrily. And then she gaped.

It was Mama.

"Ouch! Are you using Satan's own tweezers, doctor?"

"Hold still, Reverend, or so help me I'll tie your hands behind your back!" came the reply. "Devereau here was the perfect gentleman while I wrapped his ribs."

"He'd sing a different song if you were picking glass out of *his* face."

Charity sat in the doctor's tiny waiting room, listening to the volley of remarks that came through the wall. Papa's spectacles had shattered when Dillon knocked him to safety, and one sleeve of his coat was torn, but they were picking themselves up out of a heap, just inside a dance hall door, when she'd found them.

She'd hugged them fiercely and then marched them straight to the doctor's office. Neither man was a gracious patient during the examination for broken bones, but Charity could understand that, after the ordeal they'd been through. It was a miracle they survived.

The door opened and the grizzled Dr. Wason shook his head at her. "Don't envy you the job of keepin' these two scallawags quiet for a couple days," he said in his gravelly voice. "You got rooms, Miz Devereau?"

"Yes sir, but—"

"*Keep* 'em there. Anybody fool enough to run in front of a stampede won't live long in this town."

"Yes, sir." Charity bit back a grin when her father and Dillon filed into the room, wearing expressions that told her they had no intention of playing patient. "How much rest do they need? And when should Dillon's wrap come off?"

"Two or three days oughtta do. And the longer those ribs stay wrapped, the better they'll feel."

They made a curious sight crossing Front Street, with Papa hobbling ahead and Dillon leaning heavily on her, but there were few people paying attention. The fireworks show was just beginning, lighting the night sky with splashes of red and blue and white. Charity longed to watch for a while, but she knew neither man would stay in the room without her supervision.

When they reached Miss Silks's establishment, Dillon hastened to open the door for Noah, who was about to run into it.

"Thank you, but I'm not helpless," Scott groused. "And if going through the back door of a bordello isn't bad enough, it's unadulterated *shame* to be seen going in the front."

"Papa, hush," Charity warned, smiling politely at the ladies who watched them enter. They looked a fright, the three of them, and she was embarrassed to be tramping across these elegant Persian rugs.

But Papa's complaining grew louder, and Charity was mortified. "Papa, please—they'll think we're not grateful to be—"

"Enough! I just thank God I'll never again have to rely on your husband's choice of lodgings."

Charity felt anger rising into her throat, and she could barely contain herself until the door of their room was closed behind them. "What do you *want?*" she demanded tersely. "My husband saved your wretched *neck* today! Maybe he should've let Mama's stampede take its course."

The words hadn't left her mouth before she realized the seriousness of her remark, and realized how overwrought they still were from the confrontation with Mama. But dammit, he could show her a little decency after all the deceptions he'd kept alive the past ten years. Unless . . .

"Papa," she said with a tight sigh, "were all those things Mama said today true?"

Devereau had been expecting this conversation, just as he'd guessed Marcella started that longhorn charge. Easing onto the bed, he watched the Reverend Noah Scott sag into a chair, like a candle left too long in the sun. The clergyman peeled off what was left of his coat, his face fixed in a grimace of private agony.

"I'm afraid they were, daughter," he said in a subdued voice. "I used to tell myself your mother gave me no choice—repeated a litany of indignities I suffered because she left me. And when she wrote about her life of leisure with another man, only a few weeks after the divorce, it was more than I could bear. You were too young to understand that, of course," he said in a gentler voice, "and I couldn't tell you your mother wasn't really ill. We'd made a deal with the devil and we were both upholding it, but it was *I* who paid for it. And you, Charity. God knows you didn't deserve to live between the lines of our lies."

She'd never heard this miserable timbre in her father's voice; had never considered that despite his fame and fire, Noah Scott was a very lonely man. Charity stood awkwardly before him, feeling humbled and small for all the times she'd laid blame on him. "I—I'm sorry, Papa. I never realized—"

"How could you have known?" he interrupted with a shrug. Her father smoothed his hair back, letting his fingers wander to the jagged line of stitches that curved from his temple to his cheek. "By the time I realized the consequences of our deception, it was too late to back out of it. The parishioners were sympathetic, you were hearing from your mother regularly . . . and she was right. My gambling was an easier habit to hide once she was gone."

Charity wished with all her heart she'd considered her father's feelings before forcing him into this journey. Suspicions about their marriage had nagged at her for years—especially since Papa never visited Mama—yet she'd ignored her intuitions and insisted on traveling to Leavenworth. But what else could she have done? It was unthinkable not to mourn her own mother.

"Don't blame yourself, daughter," Papa said quietly. "I didn't believe your mother had been murdered—who would've written that letter, if she were dead? But I wondered if she was in some sort of trouble and needed my help," he said lamely. "It was my part of the bargain to inform you of these things on your last birthday, and I . . . I couldn't."

She'd been staring at the floor, and looked up to see Papa's face contorting with anguish. Charity went to him immediately, sadly aware that it had been years since she'd embraced him. "Don't worry, Papa," she whispered as she wrapped her arms around his neck. "I understand. I never meant to—"

"Let me finish," he said in a ragged voice. "Confession is my only outlet, Charity, because I've been a poor excuse for a father. I kept you in threadbare dresses, hoping the young men wouldn't notice you were as beautiful as your mother. I deceived you all these years, because I knew that once you learned how truly reprehensible I was, you'd leave me. And I couldn't bear that, Charity. You're all I have."

Tears trickled down her face and she crushed Papa's head to her breast. It was impossible to comprehend the change that had come over the proud, swaggering revivalist she'd resented for most of her life, but Charity had no doubt that his words were sincere. As she stroked his dark hair, she realized the wetness coming through her dress wasn't like the tears Papa often summoned in the pulpit. "Forgive me for all the nasty things I've said and thought," she mumbled.

"Forgive *me,*" came his muffled reply. He hugged her tightly, and then reached for his handkerchief. "You're a woman now—a wife—and Devereau earns a damn sight more at cards than I do," he added with a shaky laugh. "Your affection for him is clearly being returned, so I no longer have such qualms about letting you go, daughter. I'm boarding the train tomorrow, for Jefferson City. It's time to get on with my life."

Charity nodded, wiping her eyes with the back of her hand. "What will you tell everyone about Mama?"

He dabbed at his face and replaced his handkerchief. "They think she's dead, and for all practical purposes the Marcella Wallace I married *is* gone," he said quietly. "I'll let it stand at that. Everyone will miss you, but they'll be ecstatic when I tell them about your marriage to Devereau here."

Papa stood up, and after giving her shoulders a squeeze, he walked over to Dillon with his hand extended. "For all our differences, I think you're a decent, respectable man and I know you'll take care of my girl," he said, his voice returning to its usual strength. "Bring her home to see us now and again, will you?"

"Certainly, I—" He swung his legs to the edge of the bed, but the preacher stopped him.

"Don't get up. We're supposed to be invalids, remember?"

Dillon smiled. "If you're ever in Kansas City, drop in at the Queen."

"Wouldn't miss it." He turned toward the door, nearly bumping into the washstand on his way to his room. Then he faced them again, wearing a myopic scowl. "No need to see me off tomorrow. The train leaves early, and you've plenty of reasons to stay in bed."

Charity's heart rose into her throat, but Papa's pride kept her quiet. He was a different man, standing there with his torn, dusty frock coat draped over his arm and a red cut circling his eye, and tomorrow when he was freshly groomed he'd have no patience for a tearful farewell. Appropriate parting words were hard to come by, given what they'd been through. "Be sure to get new glasses first thing when you're home," she said in a tight voice.

Papa chuckled. "Of course, daughter. Seems I've always been nearsighted."

When the door to the adjoining room closed, Devereau saw his wife's shoulders slump and he slid off the bed to comfort her. Such strength in this slender frame—such *heart,* to bear the burdens her parents had thoughtlessly thrust upon her. Charity turned in his arms and he held her as tightly as his bruised body would allow. Her lips sought his, and he kissed her long and hard, tasting the salt of her tears and the sweetness of the desire he felt rising between them.

But when Charity rested against him, he knew she was drained. "I think we'll turn in early," he murmured against her hair, "and see what comes up in the morning."

She chuckled, and after they'd bathed and were stretched out in bed, she quickly relaxed against her husband's comforting length. "Good night, Dillon," she mumbled.

"Sweet dreams, my love."

She was asleep before he said it, and as Devereau studied her nightgowned figure in the dusk, he recalled the first time he'd watched her in slumber, in his bed at the Crystal Queen. She'd looked helpless and innocent, and his loins ached with the same longing he'd felt for her then, even though neither description fit her now. But it was just as well she slept, he mused, because they both needed their strength for what tomorrow would bring.

Charity reached for her husband, and when she realized how cold his side of the bed was, she awoke with a start. As her eyes adjusted to the pale light coming in around the curtain edges, she saw that he'd propped a note against the dresser mirror—and his trunk was gone!

"Damn you, Devereau!" she said in a hoarse whisper. Why was it that men cowered in the face of good-bye? And what was she supposed to do *now?* Crawling back to Jefferson City with Papa was unthinkable, and Dodge certainly wasn't her sort of town.

She went to the dresser to grab the note, and then noticed the thick white envelope lying beneath it. Charity gasped: it contained more cash than she dared to count.

How often had she bluntly reminded Dillon of their deal, never really expecting it to come to this conclusion? He'd left her enough money to start up a studio or whatever business she desired, and here, in this floozy's room, Charity felt like a whore who'd been overpaid. Not a whole lot different from Mama.

Feeling utterly disgusted with herself, she stared at her reflection in the mirror. Her lacy, low-cut nightgown was rumpled, and her light auburn hair fell unevenly about her shoulders, and her face was a freckled bronze—hardly the portrait of the good Christian girl who'd left home for the first time only a few weeks ago. And there was no turning back, no redemption of innocence lost.

Dillon's neat script appeared blurry as she skimmed his letter: he was leaving her this money, as they'd agreed . . . a Dodge attorney had the divorce papers ready for her to sign . . . he couldn't in good conscience take her to San Francisco to face more of the torture she'd already endured . . . Powers had wired him, threatening him if he didn't stay the hell away—but of course, he'd bought his train ticket . . . Papa was a changed man who'd give her a better life, now that the truth was out. He would miss her laughter and her sweet voice, and because he cared for her more than he'd ever imagined possible, he couldn't risk losing her to whatever traps Erroll would undoubtedly set. It was a private vendetta, avenging his father's death. It was for the best.

Charity choked on these last words. Nobody

wanted to lose her, yet nobody *wanted* her either. Mama had abandoned her ten years ago—the pain she'd inflicted yesterday would take months to heal—and Papa had graciously resigned himself to life without her. And now Dillon Devereau, after claiming her heart and soul and body, was on his way to San Francisco.

For the first time in her life, Charity was totally alone. Once again the people she loved had left her no choice, so she picked up the thick white envelope, tucked Dillon's note into it, and did what she had to do.

Chapter 22

Devereau watched the passing Kansas landscape with a sour taste in this mouth. He'd taken the coward's way out, and by now Charity was calling him worse names than that—and there she was, haunting his thoughts again. He'd never be free of her. Even now he saw her awe-filled face as she'd gazed out the window on her first train ride . . . heard the music in her voice when she teased him, and felt her body's sweet surrender as she murmured his name over and over—

"Stop it!" he ordered. He glanced around his private car and was glad he'd requested one. God knows what the other passengers would think if they heard him swearing at himself this way.

Yet his elegant quarters were merely a polished, upholstered hell, because had Charity not constantly reminded him of their deal—and had he not watched her parents heap degradation on each other and on her—she would have been sharing this hideaway on wheels. They could have been indulging each other's fantasies on a honeymoon trip to wherever they pleased.

But he'd watched Marcella tear two lives apart, and he knew damn well the auburn-haired dragon was also on Erroll Powers's trail. Devereau intended to get his satisfaction from his old nemesis first, before Marcella got to him. There would be ugly scenes—perhaps a killing—and Charity didn't need any more pain heaped upon her.

That's what he told himself, anyway.

And what of poor Noah? Without his elaborate deception to maintain, the man was like a sailboat on a breezeless sea. He was doomed to lose himself either to his ministry or to the monte dealers, and Dillon sensed the latter would claim him if he were left to his own devices.

Charity would know that. She was probably packing at this very moment to start a saner, more comfortable life with her father. Thanks to Mattie Silks's credit, he'd left Charity set up so well she could afford to do nothing but *think* about her bank account for the rest of her days. She'd find a new purpose in her life . . . perhaps remarry and have children.

It sounded good, anyway.

Devereau shifted in his chair, absently reaching into his vest for his deck of cards. He shuffled and reshuffled, without thought of anything but the soothing riffle the cards made as they flitted between his hands. It was best she wasn't here to distract him, because the past few weeks without regular play had left his reflexes in sorry shape. He needed to be in top form when he challenged Erroll Powers; no straying thoughts or letting down of his cool, professional facade.

It was for the best.

Charity was better off without him, but she was too lovestruck to know it.

It really *was* for the best.

That's what he told himself one more time, and then he rose, disgusted with the way her memory taunted him, and with this emptiness of his own making. Dillon headed for the parlor car, hoping some other poor fool was as desperate for entertainment as he was.

* * *

"But Mr. Devereau requested a private car, and I have strict instructions—"

"Mr. Devereau didn't know I was going to join him," Charity insisted quietly. She and the colored porter were being watched by all the passengers in the crowded railroad car, so she concocted a story she hoped would get her out of the limelight.

"I bought a second-class ticket and dressed in this poor old calico gown so no one would spoil my surprise. It—it's our first anniversary!" she added with sudden inspiration. "He has so much on his mind he forgot it, and he'll be so *embarrassed* if you tell him why I'm on board."

The uniformed porter shook his head. "I don't know, Miz Devereau. Mr. Dillon, he looked mighty preoccupied, and he told me that under no circumstances was I to—"

"Then I'll go from car to car until I find the right one," Charity replied. She reached for her suitcase, pleased to see he wasn't going to release it. "Or you could tell me how many cars I'll pass through to get there. I promise I'll tell him I gave you the slip, so you won't get into hot water for helping me—"

"Oh no, Miz Devereau, that won't be necessary." He flashed her a purposeful smile and started toward the rear of the car. "If he thought I wasn't payin' attention, I'd get in hot water for sure. Like tea leaves in a pot, Miz Devereau. Watch your step here, ma'am."

Charity followed the muscular porter and kept her grin to herself. They passed through several passenger cars, an observation car, and a dining car, where the delicious aromas reminded her of the breakfast she hadn't eaten so she could make this train. When they entered a parlor car, she saw her escort stiffen: Dillon sat at a small table playing poker with another gentleman, his back to them. The colored man walked on through, silent as a cat on the prowl, and two cars later he stopped and grinned at her. "We made it, Miz Devereau. Surprise intact."

Charity giggled at his conspiratorial expression and handed him a folded bill. "I owe you a thousand thanks, Mr.—"

"Hollister. George Washington Hollister at your service, ma'am," he replied, "but I couldn't take this much money, just for—"

"And do you have family back home, Mr. Hollister?" She smiled kindly, knowing exactly how put-upon he felt because she'd donated more than was expected.

"Why, yes ma'am, I do. My wife Lettie and four little children."

"Buy Lettie something special for the next time you see her." Charity reached for the door handle and gave him a smile that was warm with a new pleasure—that of being able to afford such a gesture. "I really appreciate your help, and I assure you that Mr. Devereau will, too."

She stepped into Dillon's private car and gaped, taking in the grandness of it. The walls were papered in green and ivory stripes, and wing chairs and a table were arranged near the window on one side. There was a bed, a copper tub, a wash stand, a table for eating on and two chairs . . . Charity blanched, wondering if, since Dillon assumed he was a free man, he'd brought along some female company.

But the only luggage she saw was his. His frock coats and trousers hung neatly near the wash stand and his boots stood at attention beneath them. Everything looked so tidy she felt like an intruder. What would she do if Devereau didn't take her back?

Refusing to accept such a possibility, Charity took the cream-colored gown from her suitcase and shook the wrinkles out of it. She donned a daring set of pink underthings Dillon had bought her, and then pulled the sides of her hair back with the tortoiseshell combs. A look in the mirror confirmed it: a night's rest and a mischievous plan were giving her a fresh radiance. Dillon would *have* to want her. She would leave him no choice.

Charity returned to the parlor, stepping carefully between the train's cars as they clacked along the tracks. Devereau was still engrossed in his poker game, so she slipped over to the organ she'd noted when she was following Mr. Hollister. Nodding to a cluster of curious people, she seated herself, pulled a few stops, and set the volume at its lowest point. Then she began to pump the foot pedals and play softly.

As she'd hoped, a grandmotherly woman nearby asked if she knew any hymns, and Charity sang "Amazing Grace" in a low, reverent voice. Other people requested songs, too, as they gathered around the organ to watch her play. She couldn't see Dillon anymore, but when a swarthy gentleman in a tattersall suit asked if she knew anything a little catchier, she grinned and raised the organ's volume.

" 'You never miss your sainted mother . . . till she's dead and gone to heaven,' " she crooned in her torchiest voice. Her audience chuckled, following her dips and swells, exactly as she'd planned.

Devereau wasn't aware of when his heartbeat had started to accelerate, but he suddenly lost track of which cards he held. That voice . . . like the touch of his mother's hand across the years . . . but it *couldn't* be Charity!

"Well now, lad, d'ye mean to finish this 'and, or shall I just take yer money and be done with it?" the Scot across the table teased. "Per'aps that lass'd give ye a tumble. Or per'aps she'd prefer the likes o' me, rich as I'll be."

Dillon shook himself out of the spell Charity's contralto was casting and stood up. "Take the money, but the lady won't give you a second glance," he said as he collected his deck. "She's got a face like an angel and a tongue as pointed as Satan's tail."

His opponent grunted and picked up the money. "Sounds to me like she's put a mark on *yer* tail, lad."

Dillon didn't respond—didn't care that the man was walking away with a kitty that should have been his. He turned toward Charity with a heart so full of questions he couldn't see straight. He'd said his farewells and put his wife behind him. He'd made his reasons for leaving clear enough that any besotted young woman could comprehend them. Yet here she was.

Devereau eased between her admirers, gazing at red hair that shimmered past silk-covered shoulders. He had to reach an understanding *now,* and get her off this train. Her enthralled listeners might keep her performing for hours, so when she finished the barroom ballad he called out, " 'Beautiful Dreamer.' Key of E flat."

Charity held her breath. Her eyes closed and her fingers found the introductory chords—a monumental feat, because she felt Dillon standing behind her now, and smelled his familiar, masculine scent. She opened her mouth, praying the right words came out. "*Beautiful dreamer . . .*"

"*. . . wake unto me,*" Dillon's tenor joined in, and Charity soared with the sublime joy that comes when souls unite in the heartsong written only for them. The ladies sighed and the men looked on enviously as the simple song ended with Dillon's note ringing clearly above her own. She gazed up at him in sheer happiness, but his golden eyes met hers only for a moment.

"If you'll excuse us," he said to their audience, "this angelic creature and I have a rendezvous—with destiny, if you will." He guided Charity between her adoring observers until they stood on the platform that led to the next car. His grip tightened, and above the racket of the rushing train he said, "And just what the hell are *you* doing here?"

The spell they'd cast in the parlor car was blasted away by the hot Kansas wind, and Charity wondered if her destiny included being shoved off the train. Devereau's face was taut as he waited for her answer. "And just what the hell kind of question is *that,* from a man who sneaked off in the dead of night?" she retorted. "You figured you'd justify your exit by leaving me a ludicrous amount of money—is that it? Well, I *won't* be paid off like some whore!"

He should have realized a woman unaccustomed to having even pin money would feel insulted by his settlement. "You needn't have chased me onto this train to return it," he reasoned. "You could've deposited it—"

"You think that's why I'm here?" she hollered above the clacking of the train. "That hurts, Dillon. You have your faults, but I didn't think being cruel was one of them."

Charity swung open the door to the next car and stalked through it, leaving him more devastated than he wished to admit. He hadn't intended to hurt her, and the unshed tears in her eyes tugged at him until he followed her to his private car. All hopes for a clean break were gone. He couldn't allow her to lay claim on his heart again, yet he couldn't let her go before she understood *why* she shouldn't accompany him to San Francisco.

Charity perched nervously on one of the wing

chairs by the window. She'd been a fool to think Dillon would be hers again for a song! His sweet harmony wrapped around her heart for those few ecstatic moments, but it was all for show: her audience couldn't see how he'd glanced at her with eyes as cold as gold coins. Destiny, he'd told them! He didn't know the meaning of the word, and she'd have to define it in terms he'd understand. She stood up and reached for the top button of her dress.

Devereau entered his car quietly and watched her from the closed door. Her back trembled as she stared out the window, her hand at her throat. It was the hardest thing he'd ever done, but he had to cut this reunion short before they both got hurt. "I thought we had an agreement," he began in a low voice. "We married, temporarily, so you could find your mother and pacify your father. I provided for your independence, upholding my end of the deal—a deal you certainly reminded me of when it was to your advantage. But now—"

"When has anything been to my advantage?" she interrupted in a ragged whisper. "All I wanted was to see my mother, and between you and Papa my course was pretty well mapped out—until you both *left* me! Maybe I'd like to be *asked* what I want, instead of being forced to choose from the same options Mama has as a woman alone."

She was manipulating his emotions, yet Devereau had never considered the consequences of their agreement from her perspective, and her words stung him. He should have settled her in a more likely town than Dodge and gotten her studio started . . . which would have meant a deeper entanglement, and he would have lost Powers's trail. "I assumed you'd return home with your father. He certainly needs you, so why did you follow *me?*"

"What about what *I* need, Dillon?" Charity

turned to face him, allowing the silk dress to float down over her bare shoulders. "All my life I saw to Papa's wants. Then you came along and showed me how to love and be loved, and I can't just walk away from that." Looking into his unreadable gambler's mask, she could only hope she was making an impression rather than making an ass of herself. "And maybe you'll need me more than you think, come time to deal with Erroll Powers."

Devereau couldn't argue with her logic, but damn her! She didn't want to be treated like a whore, yet she stood before him wearing only a lacy pink camisole and pantalets, her motive as transparent as her lingerie. He did need her—a need he had to repress for both their sakes—but her heartfelt voice and lovely body made it difficult to continue a rational conversation.

He shifted, longing to take the combs from her hair. "What about the divorce papers?" he asked in a strained voice. "You're not a woman who ignores the spiritual or legal ramifications of—"

"They're not valid unless I sign them. And I don't intend to."

"But we *agreed!*" he protested lamely. "Charity, we found your mother, and we've parted ways so you could lead a safer, more respectable life. No strings, we said!"

The argument was going nowhere, so Charity stepped out of the silken puddle around her ankles. Having few cards left to play, she grasped the pink ribbon threaded through the neckline of her camisole. "Do you see this, Dillon?" she whispered as she approached him. "*This* is a string."

He let out a tortured sigh, watching her delicate lingerie slither down over the soft, rounded breasts he'd so often caressed. He was an idiot to let Charity continue this seduction, yet she was surprisingly adept at it . . . she removed her combs and then shook her auburn waves until they curved invitingly around her shoulders.

"And do you see *this?*" she continued coyly, offering him the daintily tied bow at the waist of her pantalets.

Dillon nodded and swallowed hard.

"Are you man enough to pull it—to claim me as your lawfully wedded wife?" Charity asked in a purposeful tone. "Or shall I use that money to hire the best attorney in San Francisco, so I can sue you for all you're worth?"

His jaw dropped. "You wouldn't! On what grounds?"

"Desertion!" she blurted. "And I'll find a witness, because whoever loaned you all that cash knows you left like a thief in the night—and so does that Dodge lawyer! And if I tell Papa what you've done, his state government friends will shut down the Crystal Queen before you can say 'ace of spades.' You think about that!"

Devereau was finding it difficult to breathe, much less think, about anything except the half-naked spitfire standing before him, her hands on her hips. Where had this preacher's girl picked up such pluck?

It didn't matter. Charity had outmaneuvered him with her intellect as effectively as she'd trapped him with her innocent beauty, and he closed the distance between them with two strides. Grasping the ribbon she'd taunted him with, Dillon pulled her against him. "This sort of shenanigan's beneath you, sweetheart," he murmured as he slipped a hand behind her head.

"And beneath *you* is exactly where I want to be," Charity quipped. "But only if we remain married. Permanently, without any deals."

"You'll see a side of me you won't like when I tangle with Powers," he insisted against her silky hair. "It'll get nasty. I may not survive."

"My money's still on you, Mr. Devereau." She drew her hand down the front of his crisp white shirt and then grasped him where his arousal was most apparent. "Say yes. It's all or nothing."

Dillon closed his eyes against his rising exasperation and then clutched her lingerie, lifting it until he was sure she suffered the same exquisite torment she was dishing out. He kissed her with all the pent-up hunger of the past several days, not letting up until she squirmed to breathe. "Two can play this game, little lady," he rasped, "and you're at the end of your uh, string. We'll renegotiate in San Francisco. That's my final offer."

Charity knew not to push her luck. She hadn't won, but she'd earned the right to remain Mrs. Dillon Devereau, which was victory enough for the moment. Reaching for his lips, she wrapped her arms around his neck and surrendered to the desires he awoke with each touch of his inquisitive hands.

But instead of kissing her, he pulled away. "I have to hear you say it, honey. We'll renegotiate in Frisco, or I'm setting you out at the next stop," he said in a firm voice. "No wishful thinking or delusions. No complaints that I left you without a choice, or entrapped you before you had a chance to know Dillon Devereau at his worst."

Charity couldn't imagine complaining about the debonair gambler or the life they'd share, so why did his words sound so ominous? Dillon's amber eyes held her gaze, revealing just how seriously he took this change in his plans. "All right," she said quietly, "we'll reevaluate. After you've dealt with Erroll Powers."

"Thank you, sweetheart," he murmured, coaxing her willowy legs around his midsection. "I hope you won't regret it."

Tempered by her playful come-on and his solemn demands, their lovemaking took on a special urgency. Devereau clasped her against his hips, undulating in an embrace that made them both frantic. He buried his face in her soft breasts and pleasured each puckery nipple in turn, rejoicing in her glorious, lilac-scented warmth. In his callower days he'd have sworn that a woman was a woman, regardless of the commitments they shared, but now he knew there was no deeper joy than loving *this* woman for a little while longer.

Charity moaned and allowed his tongue to search out the sensitive areas along her jaw. Even fully clothed, Devereau excited her; their hips meshed in a mating dance that made its own rustling accompaniment. When her husband took a faltering step backward, she realigned her weight against him. "I forgot about your ribs," she whispered. "If you want me to get down . . ."

He tightened his hold on her. "My ribs haven't felt this good since the last time we made love, honey," he replied. "It's that other bone you'd better be thinking about. Get me out of these clothes."

Charity unfastened his buttons as quickly as her trembling hands would allow. When she knelt to remove his boots and pants, his male finger beckoned and she flickered her tongue along its length. He smelled of musk and cloves, and when he tugged her up off her knees, she stepped willingly into his embrace.

Knowing how she loved to be wooed slowly and thoroughly, Dillon kissed her with a deep, smoldering passion. He felt the cloth binding being loosened from around his ribcage, all the while sampling the sweet silk of her inner lips. His tongue dueled with hers, and Charity's throaty giggle sent him over the edge. With one swift movement Dillon lifted her onto the bed and slipped her pantalets off.

"You'd be doing me a big favor if we could skip right to the good part," he said hoarsely. "We'll have whole days to—it's been so long . . ."

Charity arched to meet his advance, her need matching his own. She felt like a glove that was a size too small, yet the intensity of his initial thrust was unlike anything she'd ever experienced. Silently they writhed on the bed, joined in the eternal rhythm of life. A moan started low in her chest and increased until she was clutching and clawing and crying out like an alley cat in heat.

Devereau plunged, lost in the animal abandon of the woman in his arms. She found her release and begged for his, clinging until the last spasms were only a smile that lingered around her closed eyes. He rolled them slowly onto their sides, unable to speak for the sheer ecstasy they'd shared. And to think he'd nearly doomed himself to living without her!

Nuzzling the downy curls on his chest, Charity started to giggle uncontrollably.

"What now, Mrs. Devereau?" She was an armful of cuddly, girlish delight and he prepared himself for another of her unexpected remarks.

Charity opened one eye, still laughing. "Quick—which Bible verse describes what you just did?"

He groaned, thinking back to when he'd sat on a church pew beside his mother. "Uh . . . 'Adam knew his wife.' Something like that."

"Close, but the dealer wins this one," she replied gleefully. "Try the Twenty-third Psalm—'Thy rod and thy staff, they comfort me!' "

"That's disgusting! Only a preacher's daughter would think of it."

As her giggles subsided, Charity rested against Dillon's lean frame and savored the contentment she always felt after they made love. She belonged in this man's arms as surely as she drew breath, yet her hold on him would remain tenuous until a scoundrel named Erroll Powers decided her fate. An unsettling thought.

Charity ran a finger along the brown swirls that met in the center of his chest. "Dillon," she said hesitantly, "did I do the right thing? Are you glad I came after you?"

It was a woman's question spoken in the vulnerable voice of a little girl, and Devereau felt an overwhelming love for her flooding his soul. "Yes, sweetheart," he whispered. "You challenged the hand I dealt you, and you were absolutely right."

Chapter 23

In Denver they switched to the Union Pacific, and the private Pullman car Dillon requested had Charity wide-eyed as they pulled away from the station. The domed ceiling was inlaid with mosaic tiles in deep blue, ivory, and a crimson that matched the damask curtains. The walnut woodwork glistened richly, and again they had a tub and a dining table. "It . . . it's like being in our own home," Charity breathed, although she'd never in her wildest dreams pictured herself living in such luxury.

"A cozy thought. And if we grow tired of gazing at each other," Devereau said softly, "we have the Colorado landscape to enjoy. Dozens of times I've ridden these rails and I never tire of the scenery."

The reverence in his voice sent Charity to the window, where she saw rugged mountain peaks emerging from green forests, and a crystal-blue sky so bright it made her squint. Up ahead, the train snaked around a curve behind a brass-trimmed engine that belched a gray cloud. It looked as picturesque as she'd imagined, until a lithe figure emerged from the vapor trail and leaped onto the roof of the next car. "There's a *man* out there, Dillon! Could it be one of those robbers you read about? Maybe Jesse James?"

Devereau chuckled and came to stand behind her. "You'd better hope it's a brakeman, honey. Those spoked wheels on the roofs keep the cars from careening down the mountains faster than the engine can stay ahead of them."

Embarrassment singed her cheeks. "I knew that," she insisted. "Missouri banks are more Jesse's style anyway."

As he studied her defiant profile and the way she watched the brakeman, Dillon had a devilish idea. He let his tongue trail along her hairline until it tickled her ear. "If it's outlaws you fancy, I know a rogue who'd gladly rob you of your clothes," he murmured. "I'll tie you to the bedposts, naked, and make you my prisoner of love—until we change trains in Utah anyway."

Charity felt a sultry giggle coming on, but it caught in her throat when the train lurched. They were climbing higher, wending their way toward the Continental Divide, and the breathtaking view suddenly left her short of air. "I . . . I feel—"

"Sweetheart, are you all right?" When Devereau saw her rosy complexion pale to a sickly green, he grasped her firmly by the arms.

"—a little funny," she finished weakly. "Better . . . sit down."

"Bed's the place for you, young lady," he teased. He scooped her into his arms and laid her gently atop the large bed, where he began to unbutton her blue gingham dress. "We'll both feel better when you're out of these clothes, and—"

"You *are* a rogue," Charity mumbled. She closed her eyes against a wave of nausea that turned her stomach upside down and dropped it. "Dillon, the last thing I feel like doing is making love, and I'm—"

"I know that, honey," he replied. "I suspect it's mountain sickness, caused by the thinner air at this altitude. A common problem until your body's adjusted."

She managed a quavery smile. "Sorry. That prisoner of love idea sounded interesting."

"We'll keep it in mind for later. You just rest." When her eyes fluttered shut, Devereau removed his own clothes and slipped between the sheets, lending her clammy body his warmth while she napped.

As he watched over her, he pondered his dilemma. Charity's devious reappearance pleased him more than he cared to admit, and he was truly enjoying her company. But wanting her so keenly could pose problems when it came time to confront Erroll Powers: she could unwittingly make herself the con man's target, or distract him when he most needed to concentrate on Powers's next move.

And there was no denying how difficult it would be to end their marriage if Charity ever decided he was too despicable to live with, because he was desperately in love with her. The only logical thing to do was to refrain from touching her, which meant her mountain sickness might be a blessing in disguise.

She looked so pale and pitiful lying in his arms. Dillon stroked her hair back and found himself checking her uneven breathing every few minutes. And despite his intentions about weaning himself from her physical pleasures, he kissed Charity the moment she smiled up at him from the cradle of his embrace. Ever so gently he loved her, showing her ways to accept his affection that wouldn't upset her system. Hours he spent, cuddling and kissing and returning the rapture he saw reflected in her clear jade eyes, until they both drifted off in a sated sleep.

You'd better find a new profession, he warned himself when he awoke to find his limbs entwined with hers. *This marriage could kill you, Devereau.*

But a gambler's heart beat in his chest and Charity's adoration was the sweetest prize he'd ever played for—a risk that made his pulse thunder the way it had when he won the Crystal Queen on the turn of a card. High stakes kept a man alert, gave him a purpose.

"What on God's earth are you thinking about?" Charity asked with a chuckle. "That scowl makes me wonder if you're keeping Satan at bay single-handedly."

Once again her perceptive remark won his admiration. "Perhaps I am," he answered, unable to remain morose in the sunshine of her smile. "And it's time to show you the tools I'll use to conquer him."

Charity watched him open his camel-back trunk, still in awe of his graceful physique even though she knew every golden inch of it by heart. As Dillon leaned over, giving her a provocative view of his firmly muscled backside, he seemed as intriguing as the first time she saw him. Only his expression betrayed his serious mood as he returned to bed with two flat wooden boxes that were inlaid with mother of pearl. "Your cheating gadgets?" she asked.

"My equalizers." Devereau lifted the top of the tallest box and removed his card trimmer, a flat brass square with a ruler along one edge and a steel blade attached to the end. "This trimmer's perfectly legitimate. Cards are only paper, and if their edges get tattered, they don't shuffle or stack properly."

Charity warily ran her finger along the trimmer's cutting edge. Then she watched him lay a card against the ruler, lift the blade, and slice a mere fraction of an inch from the top of the ace of clubs. "So if all these cards aren't exactly the same size, you can feel the difference when you deal them out?"

"Precisely." He flashed her a pleased grin. "You must have been a card sharp in a former life, Charity. And here's the companion piece—a corner rounder. Also legal, and mostly used to mark the high cards, as are all these gadgets."

Studying the small brass stand, she watched Dillon place the ace along its right-angled ridges and then plunge the handle down. The card he handed her appeared no different than it had before. "If all professional gamblers use these, and they all mark the high cards," she began as she turned the ace over in her hand, "then why bother to cheat? You know each other's systems."

"An excellent point, sweetheart." Dillon chuckled and put the two items back in his box. "A gambler knows how much he shaves off his own cards, whereas his opponent's cards feel different—trimmed more at the bottom than at the top, for instance. Here's a card pricker like Enos Rumley used to mark his queens."

The brass tool was small but heavy. It had a handle with a slit to hold the card while a plunger raised a bump on the back of it. "But you caught Mr. Rumley, and it cost those men the game."

"The hazards of being a tinhorn. Any sensitive hand could have felt the dot on his card—and as you've discovered, I have extremely sensitive hands," he added with a dimpled grin. "Why, I can feel your nipples straining against that sheet, and I'm not even touching you."

Charity giggled. "Keep your thoughts about dots to yourself, Mr. Devereau. I'm trying to understand this complicated profession you're so good at."

"And my secret is simple: never use the obvious things, like the blue-tinted spectacles that read phosphorescent ink, or card prickers, or even that shiner you're wearing as a wedding ring," he explained as he reached for the second box. "If the wrong man catches you playing crooked, you could wind up dead."

As though to emphasize his point, he opened the

other box and Charity gasped. The center compartment held a deck of Steamboat playing cards, a pair of dice, and a tiny pistol. One of the other velvet-lined sections housed a sinister set of silver rings with a short blade on one end, and a small dagger with an abalone-shell handle was fitted neatly against the edge of the box.

Charity gazed up at her husband. "Do you . . . *use* these, Dillon?"

He slipped the silver-ringed object over his fingers. "I carried these weapons when I worked the riverboats," he replied in a low voice. "This knuckle-duster belonged to a friend who was accused of cheating aboard the *Delta Queen.* His accuser also wore one, and he was faster with it—punch, stab. Justice in two strokes."

It wasn't so much Dillon's language as his tone that made Charity shiver. He sounded so detached, as though that knuckle-duster would be concealed in his grip the moment he came into the same room with Erroll Powers. Until now she'd refused to believe her husband could be as cutthroat as he'd hinted, but the weapons in his velvet-lined box gave credence to his darker side.

Devereau read her face and removed the knuckle-duster. "I keep these as a precaution, honey. A reminder of how precarious my profession can be," he said softly. Her lower lip was trembling and he ran the tip of his finger over it. "They scare the hell out of me, too. But if unscrupulous types see them when I open my game case, it keeps them honest. Well—relatively honest."

Charity nodded mutely.

Her complexion had gone waxy again, so Dillon took out the deck of cards and closed the lid on his arsenal. "Let's try a few games. Do you remember three-card monte?"

She relaxed against the pillow-padded headboard. "The high card's the baby, and it's the victim's job to find it while the dealer suckers him with some sleight-of-hand."

Devereau laughed as he shuffled and displayed the first three cards. His wife was perking up again, her eyes following the rapid movement of his hands. As he manipulated the cards with increasing speed, he explained how he could deal from the deck's bottom without being detected. She in turn called him when he switched cards, or requested that he name them before he turned them over. It was the nicest afternoon he could remember, alone at last with the fetching young woman who seemed such a contradiction of moods and morés at times.

His thoughts strayed again to her seductive body. "Charity, if I didn't know what a virtuous girl you were," he began in a teasing voice, "I'd say you were purposely distracting the dealer, letting your sheet slip to reveal—"

A knock at the door made them turn their heads. "Don't mean to intrude, Mr. Devereau," a familiar voice said, "but we'll need to detrain soon. Wobbly trestle comin' up."

Dillon pulled his trousers on and went to the door, where George Washington Hollister's white grin greeted him. "What's this about a trestle?"

The porter handed him a paper sack. "Here's some sandwiches for you and the missus. That bridge over the Weber River's seen some flood damage, and we have to unload to take the train across it. Thought I'd better remind you in case—well, just in case, it bein' your first anniversary and all."

Devereau smiled at what must have been Charity's ruse for gaining entry to his car in Dodge. "You're a good man, George. And just in time," he added with a wink. "We'll be ready to step off as soon as the train stops rolling."

He closed the door and turned to Charity. "Your friend Mr. Hollister thought you might want something to eat," he said lightly, "and we need to get dressed for our walk across the Weber. One of the scenic inconveniences on this leg of the ride."

Dillon went on talking about how routine such a precaution was, out here where canyons and mountain passes were spanned by wooden trestles, which took a beating during blizzards and spring thaws. But his patter did nothing to reassure her. If the crossing was so unsafe, why did they take the train over it at all?

Charity dressed quickly and ate half her sandwich to appease her husband, but when they stepped out onto the ground, her worst fears were confirmed. The river canyon *was* scenic, its mountainsides striped with waterfalls. And the process of getting first the flatcars and then the empty passenger cars slowly across the awesome wooden bridge was interesting to watch. But when passengers began stepping from board to board across the trestle, Charity froze.

"I—I can't do this, Dillon." Her stomach was upside down again and she wondered if her lungs held any air at all. "L-look at that! Those spaces between the boards—why, one false step—"

"I'll hold on to you every inch of the way, sweetheart," Devereau promised as he took her elbow. "I've done this a dozen times. It's rather exhilarating as long as you don't look down."

Charity immediately gaped at the river below them, and then she hugged the upright beam at the end of the trestle as though she'd never let it go. "I—I can't—"

"We have to cross, honey," he coaxed quietly. "If the train leaves without us, we're stuck out here." He felt truly sorry for her. The vein in her throat was throbbing and her face had turned that ghastly green again. He gestured for the passengers behind them to proceed.

"Is everything all right, Mr. Dillon?" Hollister's voice came up behind them. "The missus must think that river's quite a sight."

Devereau gave him a perplexed look. "Charity's got altitude sickness, I'm afraid. Swears she's not walking across, and I can't budge her."

The porter patted her shoulder with a kind smile. "You're not the first one who ever got stage fright crossin' the Weber, Miz Devereau, but it'll pass. Ole George'd be happy to carry you across—I've done *that* a time or two, and—"

"But what if you step through? We'll *both* plunge to our deaths!" she squeaked.

Seeing the alarmed looks on the other people's faces, Dillon hastened to calm her. "Honey, we have to get started. I'll go fetch my trunk, and George can help me carry you—"

"How could I *breathe,* worrying about you two—"

"It's either that or swim, Miz Devereau," Hollister teased. "Looky yonder—the first folks are across, safe and sound. We haven't lost one yet."

Her pulse pounded as loudly as the water that was rushing through the canyon below them. They couldn't wait any longer—couldn't be stranded here because of this silly fear that gripped her insides—but what could she do? A final look at the trestle, and then a glance at the river, made her reach for her top button. "Then I guess I'll swim," she mumbled. "It's the only way."

Devereau grabbed her arm. "Honey, that's insane. That's *ice* water—snow melt!—and the current—"

"I was baptized in a river. I'll take my chances." She looked him unflinchingly in the eye and then glanced at the porter's shocked brown face. "If you'll be so good as to stand as my dressing screen, and give me my clothes on the other side, I'd be very grateful, Mr. Hollister."

When he saw that she was serious, Dillon searched frantically for an idea that would frighten her into crossing the trestle instead. "But the canyon's sides are—how'll you get down to the water, much less—"

"The railroad construction workers did it, didn't they?" She handed the porter her gingham dress. "I'll climb down from pillar to pillar, and then swim from one support pole to the next until I'm on the other side. Sounds a damn sight more sensible than stepping between those boards."

Swallowing his urge to drag her across the bridge, Devereau shrugged out of his coat. "I can't believe I'm doing this," he muttered. "You'd better be all prayed up, young lady, because of all the gambles I've ever taken—"

"You *thrive* on risk, Devereau. And think of the adventure—the stories you can tell your children."

The possibility that she might be carrying his child gave him pause, but there was no time to waste. "K-keep your shoes on," he rasped, "because the rocks'll tear your feet to ribbons. And Mr. Hollister, you do your damndest to keep the train from leaving without us."

"Beggin' your pardon, Mr. Dillon, but you're a crazy man to—"

"Don't say it. Don't even *think* it," he said, handing the porter his wadded-up clothes. "We *will* see you on the other side."

Charity held her breath and began clambering down the canyon wall. The footing was rough, with scrubby bushes and rocks to trip over, so she turned sideways to keep from plummeting toward the water. Her idea about going from one pillar to the next was sound, but she slipped in loose dirt and nearly slammed into the first pole before she could stop herself.

Devereau groaned, his heart thundering in his throat. "Maybe I should have told the missus you weren't on this train," George's voice floated down after him, but he was too damn scared to respond. The San Francisco streets he played on as a boy were molehills compared to the sharp grade he was negotiating now. His foot struck a rock and he skittered wildly toward the pillar Charity had just left. *By God, woman, when I get you back on the train I'll—*

But Dillon's opinions of her harebrained idea were the furthest thing from Charity's mind. The rough surface she'd been slip-sliding on was turning into treacherously smooth rock that ran perpendicular to the river, a hazard she hadn't foreseen from the train tracks. Caught between climbing back to be carried across the bridge and plunging off the sheer canyon walls, Charity paused at a pillar to check on Dillon's progress.

When Devereau saw her foot slip and then witnessed the terror on her face, his life passed before him. All thought of chastising her fled; instinct took over where rational thought left off. Her filmy lingerie was billowing around her slender limbs as she fell out from the canyon wall, a stick figure against the flowing river below. When she disappeared with a tiny splash, he was leaping away from the rocky cliff, praying he would surface close enough to grab hold of her . . . praying he would surface.

Charity hit the icy-cold river and gasped, choking on the water that rushed down her throat. Deeper and deeper she plunged, swirling in a silent world that carried her along as though she were a speck of flotsam. When she felt herself rising, she forced her eyes open and began to scissor-kick through the churning water. Her strength was ebbing—she shuddered with the urge to cough and breathe—yet somehow her hands kept reaching for the surface, which eluded her with every faltering stroke. *The Lord is my shepherd, I shall not want . . .*

Devereau surged upward through the freezing water, cursing at the drag his underwear and shoes caused. When his head broke the surface, he gazed desperately around. There she was, approaching a support pillar. He wanted to call out to her, but the water was so damn cold his lungs felt paralyzed. If she didn't grab on to that trestle, she'd drift beyond it, and every fiber in his body was screaming that he'd never be able to tow her against the current, back to the safety of the wooden post. Her head went under—

She shook herself and reached for Dillon, her body vibrating with a burst of life—he was *here!* But he was cold and hard and unyielding . . . it was a trestle post. Charity let herself relax against it, regurgitating water and the sandwich and . . . and she was losing her grip.

Devereau yanked her up by her camisole and grabbed on to the trestle with his other arm. His head was spinning—he'd never been an athlete—and he had no idea what the hell they'd do now, with the river holding them hostage between the canyon walls. He couldn't bear to think about the climb ahead of them. It was all he could do to hang on and catch his breath.

Charity was wondering if God had transformed the trestle pole into an angel who was holding her, alive, gentle, wheezing. . . . When she opened her eyes, she saw that Dillon's hair was plastered to his head and his face was ghostly white and water ran in rivulets from his drippy, droopy mustache. He resembled a half-drowned dog. All because she wasn't sensible enough to walk across a bridge.

It was no time to snivel an apology, so Charity put on the most disarming smile she could manage.

"Didn't I tell you it would work?" she croaked cheerfully. "Why, between our fine diving and the help from the current, we're nearly to the other side."

Both arms were busy or he would have throttled her. Dillon couldn't believe that the lumpy-haired, pale-faced woman who'd wrapped her legs around him was actually laughing. Not two minutes ago she'd been going under, all but dead.

And as her melodious giggle tickled his ear, Devereau realized she was doing this for his benefit. Their situation was absurd—and they *were* only one set of pillars away from safety—and he found himself laughing in spite of his labored breathing. "Charity, you have the most warped sense of humor I ever—when we get back on that train, I'm going to—"

"Don't say it, Dillon. Don't even think it," she mimicked. "Save your creativity for that canyon wall, because damned if I know how we'll get up it."

"Fine time to admit that." He held her shivering body against him while they assessed the remaining distance to shore. "We should be getting over there. The train won't wait forever."

They took a deep breath and shoved off, swimming within an arm's length, certain they couldn't scale the wall that loomed before them. Clambering up out of the water depleted most of their remaining energy, but neither dared admit defeat after coming this far. The breeze was chilling, and Charity tried to forget about how her soaked underthings were clinging to her cold skin. She forced herself to find footholds in the steep cliff, praying she and her husband could keep challenging each other up to the top.

Devereau glanced at her goosebumpy backside and knew she'd never make it. From some unknown reservoir of strength he found the power to pull ahead of her. "Watch where I step," he gasped, "and follow me."

From then on he couldn't look back. He could only listen to her faint wheezing and imagine her agonized expression. Dillon dared himself to gaze higher and took heart: ahead were rocks and roots to grab on to, if they could make it that far. He could still hear his wife struggling close behind him. Charity had more grit than any other woman he knew, and she'd need every ounce of it.

From above them came the strident whistle of the train.

"Jesus God," he muttered, but when he tried to scramble faster, he nearly lost his grip on the rock. And then, as if he hadn't suffered enough, a snake came wriggling down the cliff. There was no time to warn Charity—no place to move without—

"Grab on to that rope, Mr. Dillon," a voice drifted into the canyon. "We're all pullin' for you, sir."

It was a miracle! Charity struggled up the rock wall on sheer willpower, until she was in the crook of Dillon's arm and he was encircling them with the rope. One steady pull after another raised them up, and they let their feet bounce against the cliff to keep from smashing into it. Then they were trotting doggedly onto the shrub-studded hillocks just beneath the bridge.

She could hear excited chatter as they stumbled up over the last ridge, propelling each other forward. There was a cheer and loud applause, along with the train whistle, and George Washington Hollister was rushing toward them. "Miz Devereau, let's wrap you in this coat and—here, sir, I'll pull that rope off you. God Almighty, we thought you were goners!"

Devereau had no strength to respond. He was gasping for air, his entire body was quaking, and his palms smarted from the most grueling physical exertion he'd endured in his entire life. Men were slapping him on the back while their women watched, wide-eyed. He saw the Negro catch Charity up and carry her, all the while urging the crowd to board the train.

"Go on now, folks—the engineer's got her fired up," George exhorted above their chatter. He hurried through the caboose and swung the door to Devereau's compartment open, catching it with his foot so Dillon could enter first.

Charity had apparently passed out, so Devereau gestured toward the bed and fell into the nearest chair. The porter tucked his wife in with infinite tenderness, keeping the rumpled frock coat wrapped around her drenched body.

"I'll be back quick as the kitchen can rustle up some soup," Hollister fretted. "Can you wiggle out of that union suit, sir, or do you need my help?"

Devereau had nearly drifted off out of utter exhaustion, but the prospect of dry clothes and hot food made him struggle to his feet. "I'll be fine, George. You saved our lives, and I'll certainly tell your supervisor about your exemplary service."

The porter beamed. "Why, thank you, sir. I—well, I couldn't just leave you hangin' there, could I?"

He watched the burly colored man reach for the door and then thought of something else. "Hollister?"

"Yessir, Mr. Dillon?"

Devereau let out a bone-weary sigh. "Next time you let a woman into my private car against my orders, I'll see that you're fired. On the spot."

"Yessir, Mr. Dillon."

Chapter 24

Charity was barely aware that they changed trains in Ogden, and she dozed fitfully across Nevada. During her moments of wakefulness, every glance at Dillon sent a dagger of remorse through her heart. Her foolish fears had almost cost them their lives—how *stupid,* to assume she could swim the Weber River! Only the grace of God and the efforts of George Hollister had saved them, and she wondered if her husband would be as compassionate. He had good reason to want her out of his life now.

She pretended to be asleep as he asked the porter for bath water. How ironic, if she were to drown in the tub after surviving the river. Devereau would act appalled enough—"she was so exhausted she must've slipped under the water while I was shaving!" he could claim. It would be a quick solution to his problem.

From beneath her trembling lashes, Charity saw Mr. Hollister fill the tub with hot water. Her body ached for a steamy soak! But when the colored porter left and Dillon approached the bed, Charity wondered if she were watching her executioner draw near.

He sat down beside her and stroked her hair; a nice touch, but she wasn't fooled. "Hollister's brought us some bath water and a menu, sweetheart," he said when she finally looked at him. "I thought you'd enjoy eating in the dining car once before we arrived in California."

As usual, his smile and voice revealed none of his true emotion. "I couldn't eat a thing," she mumbled. "Don't let me keep you from a nice meal, though."

Devereau held a palm to her forehead. Normal. And she hadn't eaten since Hollister rescued them. "You'll be hungry once you're up and around," he said gently. Then he gave her a teasing grin. "The tub's too small to share, but I know ways to make your bath an . . . unforgetable experience."

I'm sure you do, Charity fretted. The steam rising from the copper tub taunted her, and the silence was interrupted by a loud, long rumbling of her stomach. "I . . . why don't you go first, while I finish waking up?"

Had the playful, amorous woman he married been washed away by the river? She was cowering beneath the coverlet, trembling visibly. "Are you afraid of water now, sweetheart? You know I'll—"

"*No!* I—I just—"

"Do you feel sick at your stomach?" He reached for the parchment menu and began reading it. "Boiled California salmon . . . stuffed, roasted quail . . . sweet potato pie . . . coconut pudding with wine sauce . . . Catawba grapes . . . Surely *something* sounds good to you."

Sounds good? She was ready to eat the damn menu! He wasn't going to give up, so she had to appease Dillon without falling prey to him. Any man who carried three weapons in his game box had to be watched. "Perhaps I'll soak a bit," she mumbled. "And I can bathe myself."

For Charity to refuse food was one thing, but when she avoided his touch, Devereau knew something was seriously wrong. Her eyes were too wide, and she was holding her breath without realizing it. "Are you going to tell me why you're suddenly scared to death of me, wife? Or do I have to review my wicked inclinations and figure it out for myself?" he asked softly. "Seems a strange way to treat me, after I followed you into the river without once criticizing your fear of that trestle."

Why did he have to sound like such a damn martyr? And how did he know she felt so terrible about turning him away? Suddenly she was crying, shaking with guilt and fright. "You—you must hate me for what I put you through," she blubbered, and for several moments she couldn't say any more. The words were too painful to think, much less express to the golden-haired man seated beside her. "I . . . I'm sorry for all the trouble I've caused you, Dillon. I can see why you'd want to be rid of me."

Her nervous glance toward the tub told him the rest of the story, and Devereau was stunned. "Honey, if I wanted to drown you, I had the perfect chance in the river," he said in a choked voice. "But had I lost you, Charity, my own life wouldn't be worth living."

She sniffled loudly. "Y-you mean that?"

"With all my heart." He lifted her chin, waiting for her to look at him. "Ducking out on you in Dodge was the most shameful thing I've ever done. A man of honor wouldn't have turned tail on his woman, no matter *how* noble his intentions. Can you forgive me?"

He hadn't said he loved her outright, but his earnest expression spoke volumes. Charity drew a shuddery breath, relieved that her fantasy about being drowned was just another foolish idea. "I can forgive you that, if you can pardon my tendency to jump into the jaws of death."

"Consider it done," he murmured with a chuckle. "And you were right. Our adventure in the river will make a helluva story to tell our children."

As Dillon lifted her out of bed, she felt as though she were floating toward heaven. He not only wanted her, he wanted children! His words painted cozy images in her mind, images of fireside evenings and picnics and a proud blond father with a child riding his shoulders. It was a picture of the permanence and love she longed for, and Charity was so engrossed in the details of her daydream she didn't notice that he'd removed her nightgown until he was lowering her into the tub.

She watched, entranced, while Dillon found her lilac soap and rolled up his shirtsleeves with a knowing smile. How had she attracted such a handsome husband, a man who humored her whims and respected her opinions? His eyes glowed with an amber lovelight as he slowly lathered every inch of her body. His hands cast a languid spell with each wet caress, and when her head fell back against the rim of the tub, Dillon kissed her hungrily. The sweet insistence of his lips made her quiver with wanting him; he slipped his fingers between her legs, and his artful massage made Charity grip the edge of the tub, bucking and gasping, heedless of the water that sloshed out around her.

Her grimace of ecstasy was satisfaction enough—for now. Devereau let her relax, drinking in the loveliness of her sated smile. "While you're soaking, I'll shave," he said softly, "and we'll dress in our best clothes for the elegant sort of dinner I intend to treat you to every night we're in San Francisco."

Charity chuckled, still woozy from his attentions. "You'll get awfully tired of Voletta's ivory dress."

"We'll have your yard goods from Abilene made up first thing, and I'll order you a closetful of colorful gowns," he promised with a jaunty smile. "They'll be the perfect incentive for me to bankrupt Powers quickly, so we can get on with our life together."

Had he forgotten about renegotiating their deal?

His loving looks as he shaved were too precious to risk asking about it. His touch was dreamlike as he helped her dress and then fashioned her hair into an upsweep with her combs.

"Sit pretty, Charity," he murmured as he donned a tobacco-brown frock coat. "I'll reserve us a table and a bottle of champagne, and I'll be right back."

Charity threw her arms around him and shared a kiss that held promises of everlasting passion. As he stepped out the door, she sank into a chair, her fingertips on her lips, her heart beating out a love song only Dillon Devereau would ever hear.

He stepped proudly through the parlor car, smiling at everyone who greeted him. He was a hero in their eyes, and all was right between him and his woman, and Dillon felt a solid satisfaction that financial success alone had never given him. He planned to make quick work of Erroll Powers now, because life was suddenly too damned sweet to waste his energies seeking revenge.

Devereau entered the dining car, with its white linens and gleaming stemware, and stopped short. Marcella Scott was talking to a chef.

Her presence on the train didn't surprise him, but he should have been prepared for her to appear at the least opportune time. She turned, smiling as though she'd been planning this encounter since they met in Dodge City.

"How wonderful to see you again," she said in a husky voice. She swayed toward him in a stylish green gown—*dragon green,* he reminded himself. "You cut a dashing figure diving into the river," she continued. "The picture of virility and strength, an image of sheer manhood the women aboard this train will recall for the rest of their lives. Too bad you were saving such a goose of a girl."

Devereau ignored the jeweled hand she offered him. "Charity's my wife and I love her. Any husband would have done the same."

Marcella let out a jaded laugh. "Save your modesty for a woman who appreciates it, Mr. Devereau. I admire a man of courage and action, and I think we'd make a fine team. Why not work together to snare Erroll and then split his fortune between us? Plenty of it to go around."

He had to give her credit for coming straight to the point, but Dillon had no intention of continuing this conversation. Other diners were filing in around them, so he gestured toward the kitchen. "We'll settle this now and be done with it," he said tersely. "You're a snake in the garden, and Powers knows it as well as I do."

She preceded him to a corner by a stove, waving away a cook who stirred a tall, bubbling pot of oxtail soup. "You sound like Noah," she jeered, but as she turned to him, her face assumed the glazed sweetness of a china doll's. "Why are we quibbling? I know his contacts' names and you know your way around San Francisco. We'll trap him and be sharing what's due us in no time."

"I'm not in this for the money," Devereau insisted in a low voice. "Powers robbed me of my family, when I was too young to get back at him. But I don't suppose you understand my sentiments, having gone to such lengths to destroy your own ties."

The skin around her catlike eyes crinkled with mirth. "Fine! Wreak your revenge, and *I'll* take his money. I'm very easy to deal with when I get my way."

He couldn't ever recall being so disgusted with a woman, and he reached up to take her by the shoulders and march her out of this steamy corner.

But Marcella grabbed his wrists, planting her feet so he couldn't budge her.

"What elegant hands you have," she whispered, "so supple and strong, they surely know how to pleasure a woman beyond mere ecstasy. Charity can't possibly appreciate such a caress," she went on, her voice becoming steely. "And she'll wish she stayed home—you'll regret not minding your own business—"

Before Dillon knew what was happening, she jerked him around and pressed his palms flat against the pot of boiling soup. He saw a white-hot flash of pain and cried out, curling his ravaged hands against his vest as Marcella Scott strode away, chuckling.

From her window, Charity watched the tiny engine puff up another incline in the distance. The hills of California were a lush green, dotted with bright flowers she'd never seen. She'd have to ask Dillon about them at dinner.

But where was he? She had no way of telling the time, but a painful rolling of her stomach convinced her to walk to the dining car. Some of the other passengers had probably detained him, asking for an account of their treacherous swim.

Charity was on the platform outside the parlor car when the train lurched, sending a shock wave rippling through the entire line of cars. Shaken, she hurried inside before the next vibration could knock her off her feet.

Through the window, Charity saw that the engine had topped the ridge; the flatcars were still moving very slowly, as was the back half of the train. She squinted, thinking she saw a movement on the side of one of the cars.

"What on God's earth . . ." She watched the door

of the car slide sideways, and then saw a black horse leap gracefully to the ground, bearing a skirted rider. A black-haired man in buckskins followed them, rolling when he hit the grass, and then he swung himself onto the horse behind the woman.

Charity's heart stopped. The stunt itself seemed incredible, even considering the snail's pace of the train, but how long had Mama and Jackson Blue been aboard? It *had* to be them, riding Satan, and yet—

She let all her breath out at once, struck by a premonition of doom. It wasn't so much their presence as their timing that worried her: why would the two conspirators jump off out here in the foothills, unless they knew something horrible was about to happen?

As though on cue, the whole line of cars shuddered again, sending a roll of thunder along the rails. The train was picking up speed, and now Charity heard men shouting above her, their footfalls clattering along the roof. The brakemen! Their words were unclear, but the panic in their voices was unmistakable.

Charity rushed through the next car and the next, and by the time she entered the dining car, her alarm increased. Beautifully dressed diners sat at the white tables, eating courses that smelled heavenly, but they shrieked when the wine sloshed out of their goblets. George Hollister bustled through the opposite door, his face taut.

"You folks hang on now!" he instructed. "The brakemen're doin' their best, but we've got ourselves a runaway train!"

Charity looked desperately for Dillon, but then the dining car was jolted again and she dove for a safe spot beside a heavy buffet. Vases of flowers were tumbling off the tables, as were the candles, and people stumbled into each other as they scurried to snuff the flames. Food was flying everywhere, because they were now traveling at the dizzying speed of a carnival ride gone crazy.

Charity clutched at the buffet, wondering if Mama and Jackson Blue had tampered with the brakes. It seemed such an elaborate, dangerous scheme, just to get back at her and Dillon, yet—

When a swoop into a valley sent plates and goblets shattering around her, the car rang with frightened shrieks. Charity closed her eyes, praying that if the train jumped the tracks and the cars went careening down the hills, human life would be spared.

After what felt like hours, she relaxed her grip on the buffet. They seemed to be slowing down. When she opened her eyes, other passengers were peering out from under tables, murmuring about whether it was safe to come out yet. Charity watched husbands and wives cling to each other, and she longed for the security of Dillon's arms. Cautiously she stood up, steadying herself against the buffet. "Has anyone seen my husband—Mr. Devereau?" she asked above the whisperings.

The passengers smiled in recognition, but they shook their heads.

The train was traveling swiftly along, but Charity sensed the engineer had regained control of it. She peeked into the kitchen, where white-aproned cooks were mopping up soup and putting empty pots and utensils in place again. There was no sign of Dillon.

She walked carefully to the next car, gripping the door handles as she crossed the platform, and then she stopped to stare. George Hollister knelt in front of her husband, who was seated by one of the large observation windows. Dillon's head rested against the wall; his face was dead white, and he wore a grimace of pain that sent fear racing through Charity's veins.

She rushed to the porter's side. "What happened, Mr. Hollister? I tried to find—"

"He'll be hurtin' bad till the doctor in Sacramento can see him. Goose grease is the best I can do."

When the colored porter looked gravely up at her, Charity realized he'd been wrapping her husband's hands—both of them! Along with the physical torture he was suffering, Dillon was already grappling with the professional implications of such an injury.

Her insides shriveled as she slid onto the seat beside him. "How did this happen?" she whispered. "When you didn't come for me, I thought you were just talking to people."

Dillon blinked rapidly and exchanged a glance with Hollister she couldn't read. The Negro cleared his throat, picking up his cannister of grease. "Your man's hands have been severely burned, Miz Devereau," he said quietly. "It was a kitchen accident, right before the train went out of control. I'll bring some dinner to your car just as soon as I can get there, ma'am."

Kitchen accident? Charity swallowed a lump of confusion that threatened to make her cry. "Shall we go, Dillon? I—I think the train's slowed down to a safe speed now."

Devereau clenched his teeth against the hellish fire that seared his palms. His wife was acting brave and efficient to keep from bursting into tears, so he nodded and stood up slowly. "Lead the way," he rasped.

Charity was only too glad to walk in front of him, because she couldn't look at the mummified fingers sticking out from the sleeves of his brown coat. She held doors and cleared the clutter from his path in the dining car, fearfully aware that he couldn't grab on to anything if the train jolted him. But they made it to their car without incident, the object of hushed, anxious comments from people they passed. Dillon dropped into a chair as though he'd never have the strength to get out of it again.

"Is there something I can do? Anything I can get you?" she asked him.

He shook his head and stared out the window.

Several minutes passed, an awful time when Charity's questions threatened to spill out, yet she feared his answers and didn't want to aggravate his horrendous pain. The look she'd seen pass between Dillon and Hollister haunted her, though, and her husband's pointed silence finally drove her to desperation. "How did this happen? What on earth were you doing in the kitchen?" she asked in a choked voice.

He remained motionless, his bandaged hands lying palms-up in his lap. When at last he spoke, it was in a lifeless monotone. "I met up with Marcella. I refused to help her find Powers. She held my hands against a boiling stock pot."

Charity felt the blood rush from her head. Mama had struck again, wounding Dillon in a manner more odious than any man would have contrived. Were she and Blue sneaking off the train to escape punishment for this crime? What part had her husband's closest friend played in this devastating drama? She sank into the nearest chair, more confused than ever. All she could think about was coming into a strange city where her husband couldn't mount a horse or drive a wagon, or even feed himself.

And Dr. LaMont in Sacramento delivered yet another blow. "These are serious burns, Mr. Devereau. They'll require at least a month of diligent treatment before the skin can replace itself and heal." He handed Charity a bottle of ointment and a box of rolled bandages, adding, "You'll need to change his dressing every day, ma'am. And at the first sign of gangrene, you call a doctor."

Charity nodded numbly. "H-how will I know?"

Dr. LaMont glanced at Dillon, who seemed miles away, and lowered his voice. "He'll smell like he's already dead."

It was a gruesome, tactless statement and it startled her out of her misery. Charity checked them into a hotel, and got them onto a train bound for San Francisco the next morning, painfully aware that her husband was unable to sign the register or buy their tickets or carry their luggage—tasks a man with hands took for granted. He was understandably quiet during the entire ride.

During his silence, Charity drew upon her inner resources. Once the ointment eased his pain, Dillon would rally; his vendetta against Erroll Powers would be his incentive to get well. This recuperation period offered the perfect chance to become better acquainted with the man behind the gambler's mask: while remaining his wife and lover, she would now become his nurse and helpmate, a companion and a friend. It was her chance to repay him for rescuing her from the Cheyenne camp and the river, a time God had given her to honor the sacred promise "in sickness and in health."

It was the ultimate mission of mercy, and when she took Dillon's elbow at the San Francisco station, Charity felt serenely confident that she would have him healed and ready to challenge Erroll Powers in record time.

Chapter 25

The cottage on Winthrop Street was everything the newspaper advertisement promised: cozy, tastefully furnished, close to shops and markets. But when the landlord quoted Charity a price, she paled. "Goodness, Mr. Overby. Where I come from, you could rent the governor's mansion for that."

Overby chortled, smoothing his dark fringe of hair. "You'll find no place prettier for this price. And where you come from, there's no view of San Francisco Bay."

Charity had to agree. The little house sat high enough on a hill to afford a magnificent view of barges and boats and piers, which extended like fingers into the expanse of sparkling water. It was comfortable and private, the perfect place for Dillon to recover. "All right then," she said as she handed him enough for the first month. "We're lucky to find such a place our first day in town—aren't we, Dillon?"

Her husband kept on staring out the parlor window.

Charity gave Mr. Overby an apologetic smile. "He's in terrible pain. I'm sure he'll feel more sociable when his medication starts to work."

Nodding, the landlord studied Dillon's back. "And what'd you say your name was, sir?"

When he remained silent, Charity replied, "We're the Devereaus, Dillon and Charity. Thank you again for your time."

"Used to know some folks named Devereau," Overby commented. "Had a gambling establishment in town, they did. But that's surely a coincidence, after all these years."

"Yes, it is," Dillon snapped. "Now if you don't mind, we'd like to unpack."

Fuming, Charity watched the landlord amble to the street. *She* had found the house, *she* had hired the carriage, and this was the thanks she got! "What is your problem?" she demanded. "Mr. Overby was trying to be friendly, and you practically bit his head off. It's a wonder he let us have the place."

Devereau scowled at her. "He suckered you into paying a ridiculous amount. For a *view.*"

"No more ridiculous than what you left me in Dodge," she countered. "If it were left up to you, we'd still be sitting at the station sulking. Someone had to find us lodgings, Dillon."

His amber eyes flashed and he muttered something as he faced the window again. Charity almost challenged him to repeat it, but she caught herself: he was exhausted and hurting, still upset because Mama had injured him so seriously. He'd resume his affectionate ways when she nursed him back to better health. Anyone who'd lost the use of his hands would be testy, she reasoned.

But two days later Dillon revealed the real reason for his cruel moods. Charity was dressing his wounds, an awkward task that brought her as much pain as it did her husband, when he jerked his hand away so violently the bottle of ointment flew across the parlor.

"Dammit, woman, you don't *dig* at those blisters!" he cried out. "I swear to God you studied medicine under your mother!"

Charity blanched. "But Dr. LaMonte said—"

"LaMonte couldn't have cared less. Didn't bother showing you the *proper* way to dress my wounds."

"I'm doing the best I can," she answered in a quavery voice. "If I don't clean the skin thoroughly, you'll develop gangrene."

"So what? Even if my hands heal, I've lost my feel for the cards and I'll never be able to bankrupt Powers. Can't you see that, Charity?" he demanded bitterly. "Might as well amputate the damn things right now."

Devereau waved his raw, oozing palms in front of her, his face contorted with anguish. His hair needed trimming, and three days' growth of beard added to the wildness of eyes that flashed like a wounded animal's. He'd already lost all resemblance to the genteel gambler she'd fallen in love with. "What do you want me to do?" she mumbled.

He hated the monster he'd become. His wife deserved none of the abuse he'd heaped upon her since Marcella had incapacitated him. But this helplessness ate away at him—the *humiliation,* of having to be fed and dressed and wiped, for Chrissakes! Dillon wished with all his heart she'd stayed in Dodge, because the bright promises he made her aboard the train haunted him day and night.

Charity sat before him, her crestfallen eyes rimmed with red. When he considered the caretaker's role she was now condemned to, there was only one humane answer to her question. "Take your money, ride back to Dodge, and sign those divorce papers," he replied quietly. "Playing nursemaid to a man who's cashed in his chips is no life for a fine woman like you, Charity."

Her heart pounded in a rapid-fire staccato. "But Dillon, you'll *heal!* In a few weeks—"

"Powers will have skipped the country by then," he retorted. "The Kansas Pacific has detectives on his trail. He can't possibly remain anonymous, the way he loves to flash his money."

"So forget about him! It's only a card game!"

Charity blurted. "You still have the Crystal Queen—you still have *me,* Dillon! You'll lead a fulfilling, busy life among your friends, whether or not you gamble."

It was her definition of "fulfilling" that missed the mark, but Charity couldn't be expected to understand how deeply the risks and challenges of high-stakes gambling were ingrained in his soul. Before she came along, it was all he had to live for. "I want you to bandage my hands," he muttered, "and then you're packing your suitcase. Go home, Charity. I've nothing left to offer you."

He might as well have kicked her down the front stairs. With tear-filled eyes she retrieved the ointment and made a clumsy job of wrapping his hands. "H-how will you take care of yourself?"

"I'll hire someone. Whoever has to put up with me deserves to be paid."

Charity turned away, choking on her naive dreams of becoming closer to him, his helpmate and friend. "So pay *me,*" she offered. "You'll see things more clearly when you feel like yourself again."

"But I'll never *be* myself again! My life is *over,* Charity," he snapped. "Marcella has probably found Powers and told him I'm here, maimed and helpless. They'll show up to finish me off someday, like maggots in dead meat, and I won't make you their target again. I'll not subject you to being my servant—or my whore—either. So go home."

Tears were streaming down her face. "I thought a man of honor didn't turn tail on his woman," she said desperately. "And a gentleman wouldn't reneg on our deal."

"Goddammit, I'm not a gentleman!" he hollered, "I'm a useless sonuvabitch who'll have to wear gloves for the rest of his life! I'm *sick* of not being able to drop my own damn drawers, so *leave!* Our deal's off."

Charity shuffled out of the parlor, caught between obeying her husband and defying the self-pitying martyr he'd become. Once again he'd abandoned her without leaving her any options, because neither staying with him nor returning to Missouri without him seemed possible.

Had his pain affected his reasoning? His distasteful allusion to Mama, Powers, and maggots sounded farfetched . . . yet even if Mama *didn't* ally herself with Erroll again, she had Jackson Blue with her—a dangerous situation, because Dillon didn't know about his best friend's betrayal. Only a heartless bitch would abandon Devereau to the three wolves who might be prowling the city now, lying in wait for him.

Yet he'd made himself clear. He was a proud, handsome man whose vanity and pain were stronger than his love for her. It hadn't occurred to him that his hands would return to normal, and that her love for him would remain strong no matter what he looked like.

Charity collapsed on the bed—a bed Dillon didn't share; a bed where she'd lain awake, aching to hold him. There was more to marriage than physical bliss, yet living without his lovemaking was every bit as painful as watching Devereau defeat himself. He'd spoiled her with his affections: she could never take another husband, because all others would fall short when she compared them to Dillon.

Not knowing what else to do, she packed her few belongings. On an impulse, she took the colorful folds of fabric from Dillon's trunk—what use would Devereau have for these exquisite silks? She tried to arrange her hair, but the wretched face in the mirror made the effort seem wasted.

Charity paused at the door to the parlor. Devereau's back was to her, and his shoulders sagged. He was staring out the window as though searching the Bay for the meaning of a life gone wrong.

At least he can't hold his pistol to his head, she thought grimly. Her throat closed up in agony, and against the yearnings of her heart and soul, Charity walked out the door.

She was vaguely aware of the refreshing breeze coming off the water, such a contrast to hot Midwestern winds. The streets were lined with small shops and markets, yet she had no interest in the unusual local wares. Having no idea where she was going, Charity wandered in no particular direction. A strong odor of dead fish assaulted her near the water's edge; strange languages floated in off the piers, yet she felt no curiosity about the foreigners who spoke them. When the sun sent slanting shadows across her path, she stopped in a small café to make plans for the evening. San Francisco streets were no place for a young woman alone.

Charity ordered a seafood chowder and sat at a back table, assessing her situation. She felt terrible leaving Dillon, defenseless as he was. Who had fed him his supper? Who would dress his hands and tend to his other necessary functions? He was too busy wallowing in his losses to call someone in, and that aspect of him had caught her completely by surprise. Never had she imagined the flirtatious, decisive Dillon Devereau as a victim of his own pity.

He seemed so sure Erroll Powers would leave town before he could challenge the con artist at cards—unless he came after Dillon first. He thought Mama would track him down, too, and if either scoundrel found him, he'd be a sitting duck. Charity bit into her bread, trying to make sense of all these contradictions. If only she could convince Devereau to defend himself until his hands healed. . . .

By the time her stomach was filled with the rich chowder and tangy sourdough bread, Charity's outlook had improved. She found a room as the sun was setting over the Bay, making millions of diamonds as the sky deepened from afternoon blue to lavender dusk. Gazing at her own diamond, Charity suddenly knew what she had to do. She went to bed early, praying for guidance and rest—and for the audacity to save Dillon's life.

Devereau gritted his teeth against the pain that still scorched his palms, hugging his salvation against his chest. The fire had died hours ago and he had no way to strike a match, so he was headed for bed. After the agonizing search for accessible food, he'd found something better: a decanter of whiskey, nearly full. He thanked God that the previous tenant had forgotten it, and propped himself against the headboard.

He held the decanter in the crook of his arm, tugged the cork out with his teeth, and balanced the bottle between the most padded parts of his bandaged hands. The first swallow scorched his empty stomach. His hands burned like hell itself when he lifted the liquor to his lips, but he'd soon be too far gone to care.

Again Devereau heard the hateful words he'd hurled at Charity, and he took a long pull on the bottle. Ordering her to leave was the best thing for her, because he would despise himself even more as the pointless days wore on. He recalled her retreat to Winthrop Street—she looked so crushed and pathetic—and he swallowed another mouthful. The whiskey tasted mellower now, and its warmth was spreading from his stomach to his legs.

For the hundredth time he cursed himself for not being wiser to Marcella's wiles. Would the she-dragon sweet-talk her way into Erroll's good graces again, or come at him by herself? One of those fates was inevitable. But just as he imagined Powers laughing maliciously and cornering him, or saw Marcella drawing the pistol from her pocket, Charity's face would float before his mind's eye. A comforting image, yet the most haunting of all because of the shame it brought him.

Devereau also recalled his parents' faces, probably because he hadn't been to San Francisco since shortly after their deaths. They would have liked Charity . . . he heard his mother's voice rendering "In the Sweet By and By," joined by his wife's contralto, and the beauty of their harmony sent tears steaming down his face.

It was the whiskey making him weepy, it was his own goddamned stupidity that had set him up for this fall . . . it was Charity who stood like a beacon in the Bay fog, if he would only follow her light. But he'd sent her away, to strange streets filled with untold dangers—yet the dark alleyways offered more protection than his blackened soul would provide. It was for the best. . . .

Dillon slipped into a stupor where he envisioned his wife keeping watch by the bedside. The damndest part was, even though his whole body felt numb his hands still pulsed with fire—until she took them in her own soothing grasp and held them, smiling in spite of it all.

For the first time in three days, he slept.

When Charity opened the cottage door two days later, a powerful stench nearly knocked her backward. The windows were all shut, yet she shivered as she surveyed the empty bottles strewn between the kitchen and the bedroom. She needed to air the house and build a fire and set the crocks he'd used for chamber pots outside—so many things should be done first that she was glad Devereau was passed out on the bed.

Only when she was lighting the lamps did it occur to her what other odor still pervaded the house. Charity rushed to the bedroom, guilt and fear making her tear at Dillon's bandages. The sickening sweetness of putrified flesh made her gag as she ran to the back door with the soggy bandages. On an impulse, she stuck the wash basin under his hands and poured whiskey over his oozing palms, rubbing them briskly with a cloth, praying gangrene hadn't already started its death march across her husband's hands.

Devereau came to with a disoriented cry, thinking his palms were submerged in molten lava. He swore the phantom who blurred before his eyes was a nightmare, until he realized no imaginary demon could inflict such godawful pain. "What the hell're you doing?" he gasped.

"Saving your sorry life," Charity snapped. She forced the ten fingers to uncurl, scrubbing each one until she was satisfied it was free of rotting skin.

"I sent you home. *Jesus God, that hurts!*"

"Lucky for you I didn't listen. Had you gone through another night with these hands wrapped, you'd have lost them," Charity lectured. "As it looks now, though, the blisters and dead flesh are gone and your palms are healing nicely. You can thank me later."

Could this virago be the dear Charity who'd kept him company in his dreams? Devereau squinted at her through the haze in his head, and then dared to glance at his hands. They were throbbing miserably, yet even to his bleary eyes they appeared to be mending. "I need a drink," he rasped.

"Too bad. I disinfected your hands with it."

"You *what?*" He sat up too suddenly, then fell back with the painful realization that he was hung over. "That was Scotch. Overby has remarkable taste for a landlord."

"Well, I hope you enjoyed it, because you've guzzled your last." Charity carried the empty bottle and the basin to the kitchen, and found a crock of fresh water and some bread Mr. Overby had apparently left for him, too. Damn that Devereau for spoiling her homecoming! Yet when she returned to find him only half-conscious, pale and emaciated beneath the crumpled sheets, her resentment gave way to remorse. She had, after all, left him, knowing he couldn't care for himself.

With utmost tenderness she doctored his hands and let him sleep. The next morning she checked on him, dressed, and went to the market for the day's food.

Devereau drifted into consciousness, smelling bacon and biscuits in his dreams. It was the whiskey, torturing him beyond his limits. A pale blue image swam before his half-open eyes and he could hear the damn *sizzle*—

He jerked, fully awake now. Charity was pulling a chair to the bedside while balancing a tray in her other hand. Where had she come from? He recalled a ghastly dream in which a spiteful vixen had rubbed his hands raw, yet his palms felt only stiff and sore now, a controlled pain that no longer dominated his every thought.

Humility had never been his strongest suit, but he knew a miracle had occurred during the night, and that this woman in the prim gingham gown was responsible. Charity was silent yet smiling as she held half a steaming, buttered biscuit so he could take a bite of it.

She watched him eat four biscuits, three eggs, and a half a pound of bacon between gulps of coffee. His whiskered face was shadowy—almost sinister—beneath his unkempt hair. His bloodshot eyes searched hers as he ate, but Charity was determined that he would speak first. She deserved that much, after all he'd put her through.

Dillon sat straighter against the headboard. Groveling wasn't his style, yet he owed her his gratitude—and he hoped he didn't drift off before he discovered the reason for Charity's catlike grin. "So . . . once again I told you to leave, and once again I'm beholden to you for ignoring me," he began in a low voice. "Was it my gracious send-off, or my impeccable housekeeping that convinced you to stay?"

Charity unfolded the newspaper she'd carried in on the tray. "Neither. I was at the station, ready to board the train," she replied with a perfectly straight face, "when this caught my eye. I knew you'd want to see it."

Devereau shot her a suspicious glance before focusing on a boldly outlined column printed in large letters. "Well, I'll be—read it. My eyes are playing tricks."

With a demure smile, Charity began. "To Dillon Devereau, who I know damn well has followed me, colon. We'll settle your mistaken notion about your father's death one week from today, Friday, July nineteenth, at the Pacific Club. I'll see you at nine o'clock sharp, with your bankroll and your accountant in tow. Erroll Powers."

Devereau's head clunked against the headboard. "*Damn!* What's that bastard up to?"

"Sounds pretty straightforward to me," Charity replied with a shrug. "Maybe he thinks you're going to sic the authorities on him, and he's enticing you to meet him privately instead."

"Powers is *never* straightforward," Dillon grunted, "and I haven't contacted the police because I'm betting he's assumed a new identity."

"Probably so. Which is why he'd feel safe signing his own name to that ad."

Devereau studied the young woman beside him, puzzling over the ad's ulterior meaning. Gambling had been outlawed in San Francisco, which was why Powers hadn't mentioned poker specifically. But Erroll's intent was implicit and his name was known to anyone who recalled his father's death, and he was obviously planning a winner-takes-all confrontation. Dillon read the column again, chuckling as he laid the paper aside. "Powers'll just have to be disappointed, because I'm not falling for it."

Charity scowled. "But—it's the perfect chance to—it's exactly how you planned to bankrupt him, isn't it?"

"That was before Marcella ruined my hands. She'll see that ad, too, and they'll both jump me."

"Not with the crowd this is bound to attract," Charity reasoned. "Erroll probably set it up at a men's club for his own protection. Mama'll be *peeved* if you win all his properties, Dillon."

He looked at her from the corner of his eye, wondering how she came up with such astute comments. "No dice. They'll have to settle it between themselves, because I won't be there."

Charity stacked his dishes on the tray. "What'll you tell Abe, then?" she asked cautiously. "I wired him, asking him to come to San Francisco with your money and deeds. I thought I'd better contact him so—"

"You *what?* Littleton's coming *here?*"

"—he could find somebody to run the Queen and make the train ride, by Friday." She challenged the anger she saw rising in his eyes by staring boldly at him. "I was looking out for your best interests, Dillon. Figuring you wouldn't pass up the chance to win Erroll's millions. You were in no shape to send the telegraph yourself."

"Well you figured wrong! How dare you . . ." Scolding her took more energy than he'd anticipated, and he fell back onto the mattress. "Get over to that telegraph office and tell Littleton not to waste his time."

"*You* do it! I have a history of not listening to your commands, remember?"

Devereau glowered. "I suppose you signed my name to that message?"

"Of course. Why would Littleton believe *me?*" Charity looked him steadily in the eye, reminding herself that he deserved to be squirming this way. "Besides, he'll be someone to drive you to the Pacific Club, a cool head in case Powers gets ugly. No one needs to know your hands are injured—you can wear these over your bandages."

She pulled out the pair of large kid gloves she'd concealed in the biscuit basket and dropped them proudly on his chest. "We'll cut your hair and have Abe shave you, and you'll look as cunning and formidable as ever. A gambler has to have *presence,* you know."

He had to give her credit for trying, but he wasn't at all pleased. "As always, my dear, you've considered every angle except the obvious one," he stated coolly. "I can't *hold* a damn deck, much less deal or play out a hand."

"That's where I come in." Charity paused, and then gave him a confident smile. "You're going to teach me to play poker this week, Dillon. I'll hold the cards for you, and you'll indicate which ones to play by a set of signals we'll set up."

"*You?* I've seen how you shuffle and—"

"My clumsiness will be the perfect foil—"

"—I'll be *damned* if the Crystal Queen and my other holdings are going to ride on *your* game."

"—and Powers will be so distracted, assuming I'm fouling you up, that he'll mess himself up instead." She flashed him her brightest smile. "It'll work, Dillon. You've said yourself we make a helluva team."

He studied her freckled, guileless face and wondered how best to tell her this plan was a bust. "Powers won't buy it. He'll say it's another way to cheat, by—"

"How could an awkward, fumble-fingered preacher's girl cheat?" she demanded coyly. "And if you tell me what to look for, we'll catch *him* at it. He certainly won't let Abe sit in for you—"

"Well, that's a point, but—"

"—and after all the attention this game will attract, he can't refuse to play. Especially when word gets out to any spectators at the club that his opponent's *wife* is shuffling and dealing," Charity insisted. "He'd be laughed out of town for not accepting such a sure bet."

Devereau was half ready to believe her, ready to fall for the sparkle in Charity's jade eyes. And it *was* the situation he'd dreamed of for sixteen years: settling his old score with skill rather than weapons. "I . . . it just won't work. Too many ways to slip up."

Charity stood up suddenly, dumping the tray on the bed, and stalked to the kitchen. *So that's the man behind the facade,* she thought bitterly. *No gratitude, no gumption. No faith in how we can outfox Powers if we work together. This is MY life we're playing for, too, Mr. Devereau.*

Dillon stared after her. He understood her deep disappointment in him—hell, he was disappointed with himself—and he was truly touched by her valiant efforts to make his biggest wish come true. But there was more money and property at stake than she knew, and that advertisement might be a front for the most colossal con Erroll Powers had ever pulled.

And yet, as he considered the way Charity's reasoning made the pieces fit, he had to admit the situation was . . . terribly tempting.

With great effort he wriggled to the edge of the bed, giving his legs a chance to quit shaking. He shuffled very slowly, and had to rest against the kitchen doorway, which was just as well because Charity was indulging in a little cry. Devereau smiled ruefully: being married to a bastard like himself would reduce anyone to tears. And he sensed that the future of their marriage was as much an issue here as avenging his past. "Charity?"

She shuddered and wiped her face with her sleeve.

"You wrote that advertisement yourself, didn't you? So I'd get my pitiful ass out of bed and be a man again. *Your* man," he added softly.

Her lack of response was all the answer he needed. Dillon crossed the kitchen and wrapped his arms very carefully around her trembling body. She smelled like lilacs and bacon and that indescribable freshness that belonged solely to Charity. "I should have known you'd go to any lengths to save me from myself," he murmured against her ear, "yet again I underestimated you."

Charity's heart was hammering against the arm that held her. "That's a dangerous mistake for a man in your profession, Mr. Devereau."

Dillon felt a blessed vitality bubbling within him again, and he turned her so she could see his sincere, if haggard, smile. "And we'll be sure Erroll Powers makes that same mistake next Friday. We'll whip the pants off him, honey. You and I together."

Chapter 26

Devereau's spirits rose daily as he explained the intricacies of poker to his wife. Her memory was phenomenal; she asked excellent questions and posed situations in which Powers might corner them. His fingers itched to hold a hand so he could test her more thoroughly, but he had to settle for talking her through the proper moves as he sat close beside her.

Charity delighted in his praise—and in the way he nibbled her ear as he studied the cards. "This'll never do come game day, Devereau," she teased when his kisses made her squirm. "Powers is bound to object. So think of a simple system that won't give away which cards we're discarding."

Dillon considered her suggestion for a moment. "We'll play five-card stud, so let's number each hand from left to right. If you're to get rid of that deuce and the eight, for instance, I'll murmur 'one' and 'four.' "

"That's easy enough. Then he'll deal me two new cards," she said as she picked a pair from the deck. "I really think this'll work, Dillon. Except maybe for my shuffling."

He watched her clumsy attempt at mixing the deck, shaking his head as cards slipped out and flipped over. "Nimble as your hands are from playing the piano, I can't understand this problem," he said with a sympathetic smile.

"My fingers aren't as long as yours. And they certainly aren't as sensitive," she said ruefully. "I could practice with these shaved cards until the Second Coming and I *still* wouldn't be able to tell an ace from a three."

His fingers twitched with the memory of that fractional difference. "There are ways around that," he replied patiently. "And like you said before, who would expect a preacher's girl to be a card sharp? *My* question is how you propose to get into the Pacific Club in the first place."

"Through the front door," she quipped. "Mr. Acree will be eating out of my hand. You'll see."

"Mr. Acree? How do you know him?"

Charity shrugged. "I pounded on the Club's door the other day, and when he politely tried to throw me out, I asked him if he remembered your father. He was pleased to reserve you a room—said he always suspected foul play and was glad the issue was finally being resolved."

Devereau remembered the Club's butler as a pudgy fellow with a temper that snapped like a bear trap. Charity would no doubt ply her innocent magic come time to enter the exclusive club's male domain, but her halfhearted effort at shuffling told him something else was bothering her.

"What is it, honey? You're not getting cold feet only two days before the showdown, are you?"

She thumped the deck facedown on the parlor table and looked at him. "What if Powers doesn't take the bait? What if Mama's told him about your hands and he knows we're setting him up?"

"That's possible. And he might shy away because he thinks Kansas Pacific detectives saw his name in the paper," he replied in a thoughtful voice. "But the chance to ruin me financially will appeal to him. We'll attract an audience who'll be betting among themselves on the outcome of this contest, and Erroll can't resist playing to a crowd."

Charity nodded, hoping he was right. How foolish she'd feel if, after all her scheming, she and Devereau and Abe were the only players to show up!

Devereau slipped his arm around her. "Quit your worrying and kiss me," he murmured, "because on the slim chance that we lose to Powers, we'll still have each other. That means more to me than any fortune, Charity."

Charity succumbed to a kiss that indicated Dillon was his proud, passionate self again. She missed his caress, but his inquisitive lips found the places where she loved to be touched. His hair was longer, thick and soft when she wove it between her fingers, and as he moved his mouth firmly over her breasts, her intense longings made her squirm against him.

"Honey, it's been so long," he whispered. "Can we find a way—"

A pounding on the door startled them apart, and a young male voice called out, "Delivery for Mrs. Devereau, from Carter's."

Charity gave her husband an apologetic grin and rushed to the door. "Yes—please bring them in. I can't wait to see them!"

The husky lad carried two large white boxes to the parlor table, his eyes widening when he saw his tip.

"Thank you! And be sure to tell Mrs. Carter how much I appreciate her promptness." Charity nearly burst waiting for the delivery boy to leave, because she was about to give herself a rare treat. She lifted the lid of one box and then eagerly opened the other. "Oh, Dillon . . . they're lovely."

He wasn't sure what was exciting her, but he loved the way it lit up her face. "And what wonders have you wrought now, my love?"

She turned to him, her eyes a vibrant green. "I've had two dresses made. I—I hope you like them."

Devereau savored the sight of his wife, who was

unfolding a lavender silk gown with gleeful reverence. As she held the dress up against her body, he congratulated himself for choosing such a perfect color. "Try it on, sweetheart," he murmured. "I can't wait to see you in it."

Charity rushed off, and after hearing a hurried rustle of silk in the bedroom, Dillon watched her emerge like a fairy princess. The gown flowed about her, beribboned in purple with white lace at the throat and sleeves. Her transformation from waif to society woman was startling and extremely gratifying. "You've never looked lovelier," he whispered. "If only I could . . . touch you."

His poignant wish made her stop turning about. "You will, Dillon. Someday soon. I—I'll try the other one now."

Devereau swore at himself for dousing her excitement, but damn, it was difficult to experience her newfound glory with only his eyes! He wanted her desperately; sitting beside her as they practiced poker drove him to the edge of insanity. And as she floated before him now in a more daring dress of green stripes, he knew precisely why she'd chosen its design. "Powers won't be able to sit still on Friday, much less look at his cards," he murmured.

She was demure yet dazzling, adorned in a princess-style gown that made her eyes shine like gemstones. The bodice dipped provocatively, displaying her soft, peachlike skin above a column of ivory buttons that rose and fell with her breathing.

Dillon rested his wrists on her shoulders. Why, after years of chasing well-heeled women, did he suddenly have to possess this woman with the freckled nose and hair that was mussed from changing dresses? "Charity," he breathed, "Charity, I'm going to love you now—going to take this dress off you with my *teeth* . . ."

His kiss rocked her head back, and Charity reeled

with the intensity of his longings. Dillon's lips followed the curve of her neck, leaving a trail of moist heat in their wake. She sucked in her breath, grasping him for balance when his tongue slithered beneath her bodice to tease each of her breasts. And then he was indeed unfastening her dress with his insistent mouth.

The power in his lips made her pulse pound. She drove her fingers through his silky hair, watching him gnaw at the ivory buttons and the flesh underneath as though he were a dog with a delectable bone. It was dangerous, this burst of animal passion. Charity gazed down at her gaping dress, suddenly concerned about what was coming over him. "Dillon, stop—please," she begged in a ragged whisper.

Thinking he'd nipped her too hard, Devereau glanced up at his wife's urgent face.

Charity prayed for words that wouldn't wound him. "I—I want you Dillon," she stammered, "but if you keep on this way, you won't be able to look at this gown without remembering how you took it off me."

"What's wrong with that? You're my wife."

His puzzled tone made it hard to continue, but she had her reasons. "Think of how much rides on our game—how much you stand to lose over a stray thought. Distraction is your worst enemy, Dillon, because you won't have the *feel* of the cards to fall back on."

"Honey, I've had other beautiful women around me when I played, and I'll control my thoughts—"

"But they didn't have anything to lose," she pleaded. "What if I drop the cards when you wink or look at me that . . . *that* way? You know how clumsy I can be!"

He studied her for a long moment, suspicious of her sudden mood change. "Are you saying you don't want to be loved by a man with maimed hands?" he asked stiffly. "Don't lie to me, Charity. I'll know."

Charity closed her eyes and swallowed hard. "I'm saying that you don't even have to be in the same room to make me quiver," she breathed. "Your body's like a powerful engine, Dillon, and once it's got me going I can't just shut it off."

Devereau stood up slowly, wondering where she'd acquired this talent for bluffing—a talent he had little room to condemn. "I never realized how profoundly you were affected by my attentions," he said in a flat voice. "I don't enjoy being halted halfway through an explosion, but I'll try to keep myself in check."

He'd assumed his gambler's facade again, and Charity couldn't tell if he accepted her excuse or if he was seething. But she'd made a valid point, and her little ruse had saved them both embarrassment: this morning she found out she wasn't pregnant, and it seemed an . . . indelicate time to lead him on. She hoped he would forgive her, and be even hungrier for her after they confronted Powers.

Abe Littleton's arrival the next day gave them more important things to think about anyway. Devereau's partner stepped into the house, his bearded face registering contempt for Charity's calico dress and then horror when he saw Dillon's wrapped hands. "Good God, what happened to—how do you expect to play—"

"Won't you have a seat? Charity's made us some lemonade," Dillon said with a gracious gesture. He looked his friend over, grinning suddenly. "Damn, but it's good to see you! How are things at the Crystal Queen?"

"Fine, but had I known—"

"This won't be a waste of your time, Abe. After my run-in with Marcella Scott, Charity concocted a scheme to fleece Erroll Powers. She saved my life," he added as his wife went into the kitchen. "She's not the clingy fortune hunter you made her out to be in Kansas City."

"Run-in? *Charity* was behind that telegram?"

Dillon smiled. "We met up with Charity's mother and Powers in Dodge City, and Marcella caught me off-guard on the train ride out here," he explained, displaying his bandaged hands. "But Charity—she's my wife now, did I tell you?—pulled a very creative fast one, and we're set to challenge Erroll Powers tomorrow at the Pacific Club. Damn glad you could make it, Abe."

His partner's jaw dropped. "Devereau, that's the most—insane! You're *insane* to let her lead you into this—like a lamb to the slaughter!"

"What a biblical analogy," he quipped, fondly watching his wife carry a tray of lemonade and cookies to the parlor table. "But when I catch you up on all that's happened, you'll see that once Charity sets her strategy, her opponent doesn't stand a chance."

As they approached the Pacific Club, Charity longed for some of her husband's optimism. What if Acree didn't let her in? All their practicing would be for nothing, and Dillon would be the laughing stock of San Francisco. She clung to his elbow as the portly butler swung the door open and extended his hand.

"Mr. Devereau, sir, you're the *image* of your father—God rest his soul," the old gentleman added. "*So* glad you're here to show Powers what a real man's made of. He's already making a nuisance of himself with his bodyguards and his infernal instructions."

Charity kept a polite smile on her face. One worry

was behind her, but the next few moments would determine the success of their scheme.

Devereau smiled ruefully at Acree. "You'll have to excuse me, but I'm unable to shake your hand. I've had a nasty accident." He held his two gloved palms up and watched the butler's eyes widen.

"But sir, how ever do you plan to—"

"I'm going to handle the cards," Charity replied quietly, "while Dillon makes all the decisions. It's the only way he can play, since Mr. Littleton can't sit in for him."

Acree batted his eyes. "That's impossible. Ladies—even well-intentioned ones—are never allowed within these walls." The butler glanced nervously behind him, where Charity saw several nattily dressed club members watching them with expectant faces.

At Dillon's purposeful look, she put on her most charming, wide-eyed smile. "What my husband is too modest to say is that Power's own lady-friend *caused* this accident. She held his hands against a boiling stock pot, knowing full well the two men were to play out their fortunes at the game table."

Charity paused to let the butler's horrified stare intensify. "We're counting on your sense of decency and justice, Mr. Acree. Dillon may have lost his very *career* because of this treachery, and if I can't hold his cards, he can't avenge the loss of his father."

Acree fidgeted. "This is highly irregular, sir. I don't think I can—"

"Ask those men behind you," Devereau suggested. "Charity will be beside me during the entire match. No one's privileges or privacy will be compromised by her presence."

Looking befuddled, Acree went to confer with the crowd of onlookers that was gathering in the foyer. Devereau kept his grin to himself as Acree spoke of his dilemma; it was obvious that several members saw their own sport for the day vanishing if this showdown wasn't played out. And moments later, with a prim smile, the Pacific Club's butler was escorting Charity to the upstairs room he'd reserved. Only one hurdle remained, and Dillon hoped fervently that Power's greed was greater than his desire to cry foul play.

The salon was arranged as he'd anticipated: a circular oak table stood ready in the center, with desks for the two accountants on either side. Erroll was conferring with his henchmen, who would undoubtedly stand inside the door and pass word about the game's progress to their counterparts in the hallway. Devereau had a hunch they all sported a weapon or two, just as he knew Erroll had arrived early to rig the room.

When the door closed, Powers looked up with a condescending grin. "Already breaking the rules, I see. Young lady, this is no place for a pretty little wench to—"

Powers's attitude was more than she could tolerate. "I wouldn't be here if Mama—*Maggie*—hadn't scalded Dillon's hands," she asserted. "And for all I know, you put her up to it. So you'll either let me hold his cards, or we're on our way home."

The bodyguards fell silent, while a slow, cocksure grin spread across the shyster's face. "So *you* penned that ridiculous column in the newspaper," Powers replied coolly. "The only reason I dignified it with my appearance was because you and Devereau did me a big favor in Dodge. Scared the bejesus out of me at first, but it was the perfect chance to ditch Maggie—or whatever the hell her name is. A cunning woman, but she suffers such delusions. Thinks I'm enamored enough to overlook her ulterior motive for latching on to me."

"Well, I don't suffer my mother's delusions,"

Charity stated as she sat down next to Dillon. "So either you allow me to play, or you explain to Mr. Acree and the others that you're renegging on the challenge you issued in the paper."

Erroll's face hardened slightly when he realized he was cornered. "Doesn't your little consort know her place, Devereau? A man with any pride wouldn't allow his lady to state his conditions for him."

It was plain that Powers intended to insult them for the entire match—a common method of distraction. "It appears my wife *has* assumed her rightful place—beside *me,*" Devereau replied firmly, "so let's stop this quibbling and get on with our game. My accountant, Abe Littleton, has come, prepared with a substantial sum of money and the papers to my holdings. Not that I'll need them. I suggest we play until one o'clock, with a short recess around eleven."

Powers made a show of pulling out his gold pocket watch. "Fine by me. Four hours should be more than sufficient time to ruin you."

"And to compensate for your earlier arrival," Devereau continued in a businesslike tone, "I insist we play with new cards from the club's bartender." His insinuation was met with the briefest flicker of disdain, which confirmed Devereau's suspicions about the deck being stacked and marked.

"All right. Bart—" he instructed a man wearing a brown suit, "go get us four sealed decks. Although I doubt Mrs. Devereau can handle even one of them."

"How *astute* of you," Charity remarked sweetly, accenting the word's first syllable. "We'll do our best not to try your patience, Mr. Powers."

Erroll sat down across from them and pulled an expensive cigar from his pocket. He took his time lighting it, letting his eyes wander along her revealing neckline. "You've got your mother's mouth," he said with a hint of admiration. "If I'd known she had one like *you* waiting in the wings, I'd have—"

"Dumped her even sooner," Charity finished. "She knows you pretty well, Mr. Powers. And if you thought *she* had a tenacious streak—ah, here come our cards. What's the ante?"

"Five hundred dollars. Ladies deal first."

His barbs were taking their toll, and when she broke open a fresh deck, her hands felt even more awkward than usual. Dillon had warned her to remain calm above all else, because even with unmarked cards Powers could bring all sorts of other devices into play. On an impulse, she divided the deck, cocked the edges against her thumbs, and let fly with a force that sent several cards tumbling off the table. "Oh, dear! I'll just . . ."

She retrieved the stray cards, giving Powers an ample view of her cleavage while she confirmed Dillon's predictions: two holdouts were stuck to the table's underside, secreting a queen of hearts and its ace, as well as other face cards. Charity righted herself and smiled coyly. "I believe the cards got a better shuffle that way than I could have given them in fifteen minutes! Five card stud, Mr. Powers?"

Erroll sucked on his cheroot until the end glowed like hellfire. "Take off those damned gloves, Devereau. If this is a hoax, my men will be escorting you and this bubble-headed hoyden to the street."

Anticipating this challenge, Dillon had left his right hand unbandaged. He peeled the glove off slowly, wincing with the pain.

The sight of his red, ravaged skin made Erroll grimace. "How in God's name—"

"Marcella clasped my hands to a boiling stock pot," Devereau replied as he replaced his glove. "So now that your obvious advantage has been established, we'll continue."

He scooted closer to Charity and glanced briefly at their cards. As he'd hoped, the con man was glowing with overconfidence—the only weapon he and Charity could count on if they were to carry this challenge off. "One and four," he murmured.

Charity discarded, after replacing two of Powers's cards. The seven and five she drew did nothing to improve their paltry hand, and Charity suddenly realized why Dillon's unreadable expression was such an asset. Even if her husband did his damndest to bluff Powers, Erroll could read *her* face at a glance!

"Two thousand dollars."

"I'll see your two thousand and raise it one more," Dillon stated, and the two accountants came forward to place the bundles of money in the center of the table.

Charity nearly fainted. They'd invested thirty-five hundred dollars on the first round, on nothing higher than a nine! It was all she could do to hold the cards, and a warning glance from Abe told her how desperate she looked.

"I'll double the wager, to six thousand. Are you with me, Devereau?"

"Absolutely."

His voice sounded as cool as a glass of lemonade, and the thought only made Charity thirsty beyond belief. Why had she assumed a daring dress and a few artful smiles would carry her through? As things were going, it wouldn't take but half an hour to lose everything Dillon possessed, and she choked when she reminded herself that this game was her idea.

"Are you all right, Mrs. Devereau?" their opponent asked with an acidic smile.

"Thank you, yes," she stammered.

"Fine. Seven thousand."

"We'll fold." Devereau waited a moment and then nudged his wife. "Lay out the cards, Charity."

They fell to the table in a jumble. Powers took his

time separating them with a lean finger, and then displayed the pair of tens he'd won with. She could practically hear his laughter as his accountant collected the winnings. Why hadn't she been prepared for the reality of this card game? Six thousand dollars lost, all because she'd shied like a rabbit and—"

"Relax, sweetheart," Dillon murmured against her ear. "It's good strategy to let him win first—and I would have lost on that hand anyway. Have I told you how beautiful you look today? Keep smiling. It's your best weapon."

Charity took a stabilizing breath while Powers shuffled. Dillon wasn't blaming her for the loss—they had another chance.

"Looking at you certainly calls up the memory of your father." The dapper con man gazed at Dillon with eyes as blue and cold as china plates while he made the cards whisper between his hands. "But I never understood why you held me responsible for his death."

It was another of Powers's ploys, and Devereau forced himself to remain above it. "Where there's coal oil and gunpowder, there's bound to be fire, Mr. Powers."

"But I didn't shoot *him,*" Erroll insisted. "I was only calling a halt to a crooked dealer's—"

"He died as a result of that chandelier landing on him," Dillon stated. "And he took my mother and the family livelihood with him. Enough table talk. Deal the cards."

Charity could hear him controlling the anguish that had squeezed his heart for sixteen years. She arranged the cards in a fan so her husband could see them, incensed that Powers would bring the subject up during play. Their hand was better—two jacks and two nines—and Dillon replaced the other card in hopes of forming a full house.

She glanced up and saw their opponent reaching

stealthily beneath his checked frock coat. "Are you scratching your fleas, Mr. Powers?" she blurted. "or do you have cards concealed in your vest?"

Powers slammed his cards onto the table. "If you can't control your wife's tongue, then by God—"

"She asked a perfectly legitimate question." Dillon, too, had suspected Erroll's covert movement and was pleased Charity had called him on it. "We have witnesses to my complaint," he said, glancing at each of Powers's bodyguards, "and the next time I suspect cheating, I'll require you to either show me the object in question, or you'll forfeit the contest to me. Shall we go on?"

Their policing kept Powers in his place, but it didn't prevent him from winning. Round after round went to the man whose merciless blue eyes made his victories even harder to stomach. When he wasn't studying his hand, he was ogling Charity's neckline or gazing at Dillon with an egotistical contempt that made her boil. Why had Mama pandered to such an insufferable bastard for ten years? Erroll Powers made Papa's overbearing ways seem agreeable by comparison.

But of course Powers had more money, and his dark hair, startling blue eyes, and deeply tanned complexion made him a natural magnet. The luck that had enabled him to dupe Kansas Pacific officials for so long was obviously working for him today, because by ten after eleven Powers had won all of Dillon's cash and bank bonds, plus a row of Kansas City rental properties and part ownership in a steamboat business.

Charity was appalled. Had she known about her husband's various business ventures she wouldn't have *dreamed* of printing that ad in the paper. As they retired to the hallway for fresh air, she was surprised he even wanted to stand beside her.

Abe joined them, looking somber. "The bastard

can't seem to lose. It's not smart to leave him in there unsupervised."

"We're letting him tie his own noose." Devereau kept his voice low, because they were attracting a crowd of men eager for a glimpse of the day's celebrities. "Have you seen any more evidence of cheating? He seems to be playing a square game since we caught him with his hand in his vest."

"He—he has two holdouts stuck under the table," Charity whispered.

Dillon considered this information and Littleton shrugged. "The presence of such devices doesn't constitute cheating unless we catch him using them," Abe said. "And we don't have much time."

Charity shriveled with apprehension as she watched Dillon nod. He and Abe were so kind not to blame her for this fiasco. She glanced at the curiosity seekers, who stared at her in return. Where had she seen the gentleman in the tattersall suit?

"We're down to the Crystal Queen, aren't we?" her husband asked quietly.

Littleton nodded.

Charity felt the blood drain from her face. "Oh, Dillon, I had no idea I'd cost you—"

"And I had no idea you were such a crack actress." He brushed a stay red tendril from her temple with a gloved finger, wishing for some magical way to erase the worry from her pale face. "Every card game has a loser, Charity, and sometimes the luck of the draw overrides even the best professional's skills," he insisted. "Keep a straight face and a cautious eye. If we lose, we'll go out proud—and we'll demand a rematch."

She gazed up at him, her heart filled with gratitude. Dillon held her close and kissed her full on the mouth, oblivious to their audience. There *must* be a way to win his properties back! If she had to resort to trickery, by God that pile of deeds and money wouldn't remain in front of Erroll's dour accountant much longer.

As they entered the game room again, Charity sensed something was amiss. Erroll's henchmen were watching them with chilly, secretive grins, as though the battle were already over. She sat down and noticed that Powers had left his bandanna lying on the table . . . an odd choice of handkerchiefs for a wealthy man.

It was his turn to deal, so she pointedly handed him a sealed deck. She wanted to check the holdouts, but leaning over on a second lame excuse would be too obvious. Erroll was shuffling—Dillon's fate rested in this shyster's tanned, sinewy hands, and he obviously had no qualms about ruining them. As nonchalantly as she could, she extended her leg.

Powers stopped shuffling to glare at her. "I beg your pardon, Mrs. Devereau, but placing one's foot in the crotch of the opponent is *not* acceptable game behavior."

Charity quickly straightened in her chair. "I—I was just stretching. Sorry."

The holdouts were still in place, but who could tell which cards might be concealed there now? A villain like Powers might have royalty of every suit stashed in places she'd never even thought of.

"Ante up," he said as he sent the cards sailing neatly across the table. "What's the bid, Devereau? I must admit I'm impressed with the variety of investments you've amassed since you were a towheaded youth."

Devereau looked directly into Erroll's ice blue eyes, feeling the tight flutter of butterflies—more pronounced now, because this round affected not only his future but Charity's as well. He hoped she didn't flinch when she looked at the cards, because he planned to bluff to the hilt. Anything to stay in the game for two more hours, or until, by some miracle, he managed to bankrupt Erroll Powers. "I'm putting up my Kansas City casino, the Crystal Queen."

"Am I correct in assuming this is your last piece of property, Mr. Devereau?" His smile oozed the wicked assurance of a crocodile who'd cornered his dinner.

"Yes, it is. What comparable wager will *you* place, Mr. Powers?"

Their opponent smoothed his ebony waves, considering the many deeds and holdings on his accountant's table. Then he rearranged his cards with maddening slowness. "How about my estate in Leavenworth?" he ventured in a low, modulated voice. "Or—what the hell? If I lose this hand, it's *all* yours. No sense wasting two hours passing bits and pieces between us, on the chance you're holding a few good cards this time."

Charity picked up what he'd dealt, careful to maintain the poker-faced expression she'd watched Dillon wear so often. But once again their hand was a motley assortment of low numbers and a jack. Her head throbbed, and she wished there were some way to slip the high cards from Powers's holdouts into their own hand.

"Two and four," Dillon whispered.

She nodded, forcing herself to speak confidently. "We'll take two, please."

Powers passed her the two top cards, smirking. "I don't need any. Are you still in, or do you fold?"

Charity fought the tears that threatened to run down her face: they *still* held only random, uncombinable cards. It looked like the Crystal Queen, and the opulent lifestyle it represented, was on its way into Powers's possession. And there wasn't a damn thing she or Dillon could do about it.

"Still in," her husband announced.

Erroll's chuckle was muted. "I'm feeling generous, Devereau. Shall I make the wager more interesting by extending a loan of say, ten thousand dollars? You could repay—"

"Shut up and play," Dillon ordered. "Either you've got the best cards or you don't."

Powers sat back in his chair, gazing at his cards as though they were women he was trying to decide between. Then his nose crinkled. "Going to—ah! ah!—excuse me!"

The sneeze was real but Charity sprang from her chair when he reached toward his lap rather than his handkerchief. "Don't touch that queen of hearts, Mr. Powers! I have her twin sister in my hand," she cried out. "I won't watch Dillon lose everything to a cheat who—"

Bart's pistol took the rest of the sentence out of her mouth. He now stood at Powers's shoulder, aiming toward her chest—as were Erroll's accountant and the bodyguards by the door. "Enough of your paranoid accusations, woman!" Erroll thundered. "Show your hand! This game's over."

"As the accused, you'll show yours first." Dillon rose, placing himself in front of Charity. "Call off your damn guards. Neither of us is armed."

Powers stood suddenly, knocking Bart off-balance as he reached into his trousers for his own snub-nosed weapon. A wild shot rang out and the room became a circus of men dodging the bullet, all clamoring about who was cheating whom—until the door flew open and an authoritative voice ordered, "Police! Guns to the floor! Hands in the air!"

The pandemonium ceased immediately. During the muffled clatter of firearms falling to the rug,

Charity hazarded a glance at the newcomer. The man in the tattersall suit was holding them all at gunpoint, looking as though he made such dramatic entrances every day. She studied his swarthy face, trying to recall . . . he'd requested a song in the parlor car, and—and he'd been on her very first train ride from Leavenworth to Abilene!

Now he was directing men in policemen's uniforms to stand beside Powers, Bart, and the accountant. How had all this happened so quickly? "Mr. Powers, you're under arrest," he was saying, and we're taking you—"

"Who the hell are *you?*" Erroll demanded. "I'm going *no*where until these hustlers have been—"

"I'm Detective Cantrell," he replied calmly, "and I've been on your trail since Leavenworth. Thanks to a recent advertisement, we were finally able to pin you down. I have altered ledger sheets and witnesses to testify that you embezzled Kansas Pacific funds in Leavenworth, Abilene, Wichita, Dodge, and numerous stations in between. You don't have a leg to stand on, Powers. Come with me."

Erroll's blue eyes glittered accusingly. "I'm not leaving until I see her cards," he said darkly. "All my properties are hanging in the balance, and I'll be *damned* if Devereau gets them by default."

"You first, Mr. Powers," Littleton said in a purposeful voice. "Our agreement was that if we caught you cheating again, you forfeited. It's not Charity's fault you got greedy and stupid in the final hand."

Hearing the approval in Abe's voice gave Charity courage again. "He has two holdouts stuck under the table," she said quietly. "He's hiding the queen and ace of hearts, among other things."

Cantrell gave her a quizzical look but he squatted, and then pulled the two spikes out of the table's underside. "Who would have guessed I'd find such an angelic organist here in a men's club, telling me her opponent was concealing—"

The bottom fell out of Charity's stomach. The detective pulled a king and ace of spades from one spike, and the queen and ace of diamonds from the other. "I . . . I *saw* it—"

"You think I was stupid enough to keep the same cards there after you pulled your shuffling stunt?" Powers jeered. "I—"

"You were stupid enough to keep cheating," Devereau said calmly, "so the game—and everything you own—is ours. Fair and square."

"But I—"

"Get him to the station," Cantrell directed his men. Handcuffs came out of their pockets and two officers locked each of Erroll Powers's wrists to their own.

"You have no right to take me away before I see her hand!"

But the detective ignored him while gathering up the guns from the floor. "You other men can claim these after you answer a few questions. Nice to see you again, ma'am. You must have a manner as delightful as your voice, seeing's how you foxed your way in *here.*"

Charity smiled, but it wasn't because of the detective's teasing compliment. Erroll's bandanna had landed on the floor during the scuffle, and she chuckled as she held up the ace and queen of hearts it concealed. "She always was your lucky card, right, Dillon?"

"No, *you* are, you little . . ." He crooked his elbow around her and planted his lips on hers, an exuberant kiss that had Abe and Acree and the others chuckling good naturedly. "What the hell would you have done if Cantrell hadn't barged in when he did?"

Charity shrugged. "What did we have to lose? He

really did hide her under the table the first round—"

"You mean you didn't have her *twin sister?*" Littleton quipped.

"We haven't held a queen this whole blessed game," Devereau crowed. "Had *you* fooled, didn't she?"

With a gloved finger, he flipped over the cards Erroll had been holding. "Well I'll be goddamned," he breathed, and he gazed at his wife with profound gratitude and love. "Powers had the makings of a royal flush in spades, all but the ace he was reaching for. I knew he had some sort of system going, but we couldn't have kept bluffing long enough to call him on it. You just saved my life again, you know that?"

Charity felt a rush of joy, and when she threw herself into his arms she was laughing and crying at the same time. Fate had dealt them a miracle: they'd retained Dillon's holdings and acquired Erroll Powers's magnificent estate and his business ventures as well. Abe Littleton was actually grinning as he gathered up their papers, but that was nothing compared to the way her husband was studying her. Intense affection, unrelated to wealth or winning, lit up his light brown eyes.

"In all fairness, we should repay what Powers bilked from the Kansas Pacific," he suggested. "I'd hate to see them go bankrupt because of his escapades."

"I'm all for being fair," she replied with a giggle. "It won us a card game, didn't it?"

He glanced about the room, where only Abe remained with them, and caught her up in his arms once more. "But before we do that," he crooned, "we're going back to the cottage so you can change into your new lavender dress, and then we're going to celebrate until all hours of the night. We can afford such an extravagance, can't we, Mr. Accountant?"

Abe looked up from his papers with a knowing smile. "I'll see you in the morning. Enjoy yourselves."

All the way back to Winthrop Street they rehashed the most desperate moments of the poker showdown for the carriage driver. Charity couldn't believe their good fortune—surely this was all a dream, and when they woke up tomorrow Dillon would once again bemoan his injured hands. But she kept her doubts to herself, memorizing the sight of his golden, grinning face as the sunlight glistened in his hair and mustache.

Devereau held her close against his side as they walked up the stairs to the little house. It was time to declare his love: Charity deserved to know where she stood with him, yet he couldn't resist stringing her along for just a few hours more. "The time has come," he said in a mysterious voice, "so you'd best enjoy yourself to the hilt today, Mrs. Devereau. After dinner, we renegotiate."

"Yes, we do," she replied saucily. "And we'll see who gives in first."

Charity stepped into the house, thinking of a dozen ways to torture him with her body until he *had* to say he'd keep her. But her chuckles caught in her throat.

Mama was standing in the parlor, watching them with her calm, catlike gaze.

Chapter 27

"Well—Mama." Charity knew precisely why her mother was here, just as she suspected that a woman brazen enough to enter the house in their absence would have no qualms about rifling through their belongings. Still holding Dillon's elbow, she walked a few steps farther into the entryway, where she had a better view of the parlor.

Devereau's game box stood open upon the marble-topped table, just as they'd left it. Charity couldn't see if his weapons were still inside, but the fact that her mother was watching them with both hands in her skirt pockets suggested that she might be armed with more than her own pistol. "We weren't expecting you," she continued in as confident a voice as she could muster. "Last time I saw you, you were leaping off the train on the back of Jackson Blue's horse."

Devereau concealed his surprise. Charity sounded familiar with this situation, so he let her handle it as their visitor swayed a few steps closer to him.

"I—I can understand why I wouldn't exactly be welcome here," Marcella began in a silky voice, "but I came to apologize, Dillon. I was out of my head—had no idea how *serious* an injury I was inflicting when I burned your hands that way."

Devereau merely crossed his arms, listening.

Mama's eyes shifted continuously between the two of them as she slowly maneuvered herself into the doorway, where she was silhouetted by the afternoon sunshine. She fixed her feline gaze on Charity, her expression softening.

"It was an eventful train ride for all of us," she said in a beseeching voice. "I—I know I deserved it, but imagine my heartbreak when I heard my only child singing about never missing her mother until she was dead and gone. You have a haunting voice, Charity."

How many years had she longed to hear such praise from Mama? Yet she managed a short, mirthless laugh. "You were so heartbroken you maimed my husband and then tampered with the train's brakes? Spare us, Mother."

Marcella scowled. "What are you talking about? Why would I risk killing my own daughter and the only man who could snare Erroll Powers?" she protested. "I hope you stuck him good today. That pig deserves it, for running out on me."

Devereau took a step toward her. "You're talking in circles, Marcella," he said coldly. "You had no qualms whatsoever about injuring me, and you know damn well by the way we returned here that we didn't lose to Powers. The door's behind you. Use it."

Mama hung her head. When she looked up again, Charity sensed a shift in strategy as her mother focused pale, tearful eyes on her. "All right, I'll go," she mumbled, "but not before I say some things that have gone unspoken for far too long. I've been the worst sort of mother, Charity, and I apologize. I can't imagine what you must think about my despicable behavior these past ten years."

Charity raised an eyebrow. "Until a few weeks ago, I thought you were gravely ill and then murdered. Since I learned those lies were designed to fool a little girl, I've been much too busy to think about you even *being* my mother." The callous words startled her, but they were true. And as she saw a smile spreading across her mother's face she warned herself to beware of its artificial warmth.

"You *have* been busy," Mama agreed. "Your new dresses are quite becoming, and you've picked up enough poker to assist Dillon today. You were always quick to catch on to new things."

She paused, studying Charity as though she couldn't soak in enough of the daughter she gave up so many years ago. "You're pretty, and intelligent, and you've married a wonderful man. You've surpassed my fondest dreams for you, Charity. I regretted leaving you with your father, and I thought about you every single day. I've kept your dear letters, daughter, from the ones where your printing was large and blocky to the best ones, which revealed what a delightful, caring young woman you'd become. I missed you more than I can say."

Despite her best intentions, Charity felt herself weakening. Mama was dressed in a soft white blouse and a dark skirt, exactly like the photograph of the sainted invalid Charity had gazed at for more than half her life. She longed to believe her mother loved her, despite the cruel, selfish separation she'd enforced for ten years. Was it naive to think Mama's words didn't contain a single ounce of truth? Was it childish to want to embrace the woman she'd yearned for since she was eight years old?

When her mother opened her arms, Charity rushed into them, bridging ten years with five hurried steps. Mama's hug was warm and tight, stronger than she'd anticipated from a woman of her own height and build. It felt so different to be crushed against another set of breasts rather than clinging to skirted hips, as she had when she was eight. She clung to her mother's shoulders until awkwardness set in, and then stepped back to look into the face that was so like her own. Mama's eyes had the silvery sheen of tears, and even though she knew this reunion wouldn't be permanent, Charity mumbled, "I missed you, too, Mama. Every day you were away felt like forever, and I . . . I was devastated when I thought I'd never see you again."

Dillon saw Marcella's mouth twitch. He sensed she wasn't misrepresenting the truth entirely, but her spiderlike intentions were quite clear—and her power over Charity made him extremely uncomfortable. He tempered his words with suave patience, hoping to catch her in her own web without endangering his wife. "Charity has indeed grown into a fine woman," he said. "In fact, it was her ingenuity that saved me from ruin and brought the law down on Powers today. So now that he's been jailed for embezzlement, what will *you* do?"

A flirtatious smile played across Marcella's lips. "As you've guessed, I've come to talk to you—to *implore* you to consider my plight. I'm not asking for any of Erroll's properties, but more than once I risked my life to help—"

"That's an interesting perspective on theft," Devereau interrupted, "but Charity and I have already agreed to repay the Kansas Pacific. The future of the whole state will be bankrupted if her railroads fail."

Disdain flickered in Marcella's pale eyes. She released Charity, keeping a loose hand at her daughter's waist, but her gaze and voice remained intense. "Right or wrong, I devoted ten years of my life to Erroll Powers," she protested. "All my worldly possessions are in that Leavenworth estate, and now I don't even have train fare to return there and claim them."

Devereau chuckled. "A woman of your diverse talents should have no trouble raising money. But you won't get any from me," he added brusquely.

"You're damn lucky I'm not turning you in as an accessory to Erroll's crimes."

"But what will I *do?* I'm divorced, I've been abandoned—"

"And after the way you treated your family, you deserve to scrape for the rest of your days." Their voices rang in the small room, and he despised Marcella for ruining their afternoon—for taking advantage of his wife's childlike loneliness. "And I won't fall for blackmail, so don't even consider it."

The emotional timbre of the conversation brought Charity out of her brief euphoria and made her step back. She sensed that Mama, who again had her hands in her pockets, would stop at nothing to get what she came for. "Isn't it enough that you probably ended Dillon's career?" she demanded in a wavering voice. "Why don't you just leave us alone?"

In the pause that followed, Charity heard hoofbeats that halted in front of the house, but Mama didn't acknowledge them. She was staring them down, calling up yet another underhanded strategy, so when a treelike figure came silently to the door behind her, she wasn't aware that her shadow was now considerably longer.

"Dillon Devereau is a very wealthy man," Mama retorted. "He'll never have to pick up another playing card to keep food on his table. I'm destitute, I tell you! Powers left me penniless, and—"

Charity was too busy hiding her fear to listen to her mother's rantings. The dark, buckskinned man behind Mama was grinning demonically; the finger he laid atop his lips was unnecessary, because she couldn't have talked to save her soul! She'd never told Dillon about Jackson Blue's presence on the train, so her husband had no idea that his best friend could have been planning his demise, and might be helping Mama get ahold of Erroll Powers's estate.

Devereau kept this second surprise in check and stepped closer to Charity, though he had no idea how he'd protect her if things got nasty. Blue's loyalties were hard to gauge from one minute to the next, and this tinderbox situation would explode with a single inflammatory remark. The scout was turning the doorknob with the skilled stealth of a burglar, his dark eyes watching Marcella's backside.

Dillon focused his attention on Charity's mother, whose hands were now tensing beneath the folds of her dark skirt. "I've told you I won't be a party to blackmail," he repeated. "If I give you train fare now, you'll find another trumped-up excuse to demand more."

"You blackhearted bastard!" Marcella lunged for Charity and pulled her forcibly against herself as she backed toward the door.

Devereau's heart stopped. The hand that held his wife hostage was ringed with the dull gleam of his knuckle-duster; its short silver blade rested just below Charity's ear. How the hell could he rescue his wife? Unless he could convince Blue to disarm Marcella before she realized the scout was behind her, Charity would become the ultimate sacrifice to her mother's monumental greed.

Marcella wore a feral grin as she tightened her arm around her daughter. With her other hand she pulled the pistol from her pocket. "You've got one more chance! I want a fair cash settlement, and I want my clothes and jewelry from Erroll's estate, and—"

"Souls in hell want ice water, too," the man behind her stated with deadly calm. Blue had eased the door open without Marcella being aware of it, and he gripped her wrists. "Didn't I warn you not to harass these people? Let her go, Maggie. Drop the gun."

When Mama shrieked, Charity writhed free and dropped to the floor. As she scrambled toward Dillon, a bullet shattered the parlor window. Her mother was attacking Blue with the fierceness of a startled animal, but the Indian caught both her arms in his huge, dark hands.

"Devereau's pistol *and* his knuckle-duster?" Blue demanded. "Let's suppose you managed to kill Dillon or Charity. How would you collect what you claim he owes you?"

"That's none of your goddamned—"

"Well, these *weapons* are my business," Jackson declared above her outcry, "so *drop* them, before I have to hurt you." The buckskinned scout held her firmly in his grasp and turned toward Devereau. "You'll have to excuse Maggie. For ten years she's been salivating over Powers's money, and—what the hell happened to your hand?"

Dillon grimaced as he peeled the glove from the chafed, unbandaged palm that throbbed to life when he'd grabbed Charity. "That she-dragon you're tangling with held both my hands against a stock pot in the train's kitchen, so be careful. She's lethal even without any weapons."

Charity thought the Indian seemed alarmed enough about Dillon's injury to have been unaware of it. And he *had* rescued her from her mother's death grip. But as she watched him squeeze her mother's wrists until she gave up the pistol and then the bladed knuckle-duster, she had to hear some straight answers. "After seeing you leap from that livestock car to join my mother," she began pointedly, "why do I have a feeling our runaway train ride was partly *your* doing?"

Blue's face furrowed. "I can understand why you'd assume that, after the way I baited you and let your mother remain one town ahead of you. But far as I know, the train brakes were just strained beyond their limit, or improperly applied. And wasn't I right about Maggie?"

"That's beside the point. You're obviously in cohoots with her."

"Obviously—to everyone except Maggie." The Indian put a halt to his hostage's struggling by turning her until she rested against him with her arms crossed in front of her. "She was too busy ingratiating herself to Powers to consider me a serious contender. I was good enough to have some fun with—to make Erroll jealous—but not wealthy or refined enough to be thought of as a potential mate."

Devereau raised a teasing eyebrow. "You consider yourself husband material? Marriage was always an inconvenience, as I recall."

"It was—until I watched my closest friend assume a whole new purpose in life when he took a wife." Jackson Blue's dark face eased into a serious smile as he looked at them over the top of Marcella's head. "You've suffered a few setbacks since you put that shiner on Charity's finger, but you look pretty damn happy, my friend."

Charity felt her husband's satisfied chuckle as his arm tightened around her, but she remained skeptical. Was this the same savage who had called her mother a whore, and who so crassly interrupted their wedding night?

Blue's obsidian eyes lingered on her dress and hair, all signs of his former belligerence gone. "It probably sounds farfetched, coming from a reprobate like myself," he admitted, "but when I saw you and Dillon playing in that stream, easing each other's pain after your ordeal in the Cheyenne Camp, I realized what I'd been denying myself. At my age, I need someone to talk to now and then, to—"

"*Talk?*" Marcella piped up. She'd stopped struggling, but she was obviously tired of being discussed as though she weren't there. "You're too damn busy chasing buffalo ghosts and riding that black stallion to the ends of nowhere to keep a steady woman."

"But I promised I'd be here for you when Powers put you out, didn't I?" the scout replied earnestly. "He's done that rather often over the years, and who did you run to?"

"That doesn't mean I'd consider—"

"Why not? Because of my heritage?" the burly Indian turned her to face him, his broad hands gripping her shoulders. "My dark skin doesn't bother you in bed, Maggie. And you never hesitate to be seen in public with me."

Mama looked every bit as dumbfounded by Jackson's change of heart as Charity felt, watching this intriguing scene play out before her. "Things are different now," her mother stammered.

"Yes, they are," Blue replied. "I've learned that you're a woman with secrets and motivations every bit as underhanded as my own. And instead of being strung along by a handsome huckster, you're being wooed by a man with as much pride and money as Powers ever had. What do you suppose I've *done* with the fortune I earned hunting buffalo and gambling and guiding wagon trains?"

Marcella chuckled, looking away. "You certainly haven't spent it on clothes."

With an exasperated sigh, the Indian lifted her up until her face was even with his. "Maggie Wallace—because no matter who you once were, you'll always be Maggie to me," he said in a deep voice. "If I buy out San Francisco's finest menswear store, and replace the gowns and gems Powers bought you with, and promise you'll never have to behave like a conventional wife, will you marry me?"

The little house quaked with silence. Then, in a plaintive voice, Marcella said, "Please . . . you're hurting me."

Blue set his hostage on her feet, and after a moment's consideration he released her.

Marcella was flushed, and as she smoothed her hair she mumbled, "Jackson, really—that's my *daughter* you're spouting off in front of. I—"

"And since you had a hand in making her such a fine woman, I'm convinced the right man could turn you into a decent wife. Not that I'm a champion of decency," he added quickly, "but I think you were seeking Erroll's companionship as much as you wanted his—"

Marcella bolted, and within seconds she was down the front steps and racing along Winthrop Street atop Satan. Dillon and Charity joined Jackson at the door, their stunned silence broken only by the retreating hoofbeats of the Indian's horse.

Devereau cleared his throat. "Looks like she gave you the slip, ole buddy."

Jackson chortled, his dusky face creased with admiration. "I'll give her a head start, as usual. Maggie's an independent sort, but she'll come around once Satan and I take her for another swim." He smiled at them, reaching for the doorknob. "Mark my words, when I see you back home, she'll be my wife. And she'll never need to hurt either of you again."

Blue took the stairs two at a time and then loped in the direction of the Bay, his strides as swift and graceful as a gazelle's. Charity moved to the broken parlor window for a better view, still amazed by the scene they'd just witnessed. The man she'd despised had saved her life and turned a potential tragedy into a romantic comedy. Who would have thought Jackson willing to perform such a miracle?

"This is too good to miss," Devereau murmured.

He went to his trunk, grasped the binoculars between his wrists, then returned to stand beside his wife. Blue had cut across hills and lawns and was now catching up to the stallion as Satan cantered near the shoreline. "Watch this," he said, chuckling as he offered the binoculars to Charity.

She focused on the distant pair, her mouth ajar. Mama was laughing, steering Satan in wide circles around the tall Indian. Jackson, too, was enjoying the sport, and then Charity realized why: he was gesturing to the stallion, and the horse began to follow his master's commands rather than Mama's. He stopped suddenly, and with a grace amazing for such a massive beast, he raised his front quarters and walked toward Blue on his hind legs.

Charity gasped, because had Mama not clutched Satan's neck, she would have tumbled backward onto the street. Dillon hugged her shoulders, still chuckling. "Blue calls that stunt dancing with the devil."

"Well, *I* call it—oh my Lord . . ."

Once again the horse circled the buckskinned Indian, and this time Jackson sprang onto his back and reached around Mama for the reins. Satan bolted into a gallop then, heading toward the wharves. Charity gaped, horrified, as Blue charged down a narrow pier at such a startling speed they couldn't possibly stop before they reached the deep, sparkling waters of the Bay. "I can't watch this," she murmured. "He's really going to kill her this time, even if he doesn't intend to."

Devereau held his wife against his chest, squinting to follow the drama on the docks. Just when it looked as though the horse would go hurtling into the Bay, he took a sharp turn. "Well, I'll be—I had no idea Blue was in the shipping business. They jumped on to that last boat, but I can't read the name on its side."

Cautiously Charity lifted her face to peer through the binoculars. She found the vessel with the black horse on board and watched its white sail flutter as it rose up the mast. "It . . . it's called the *Maggie Blue,*" she whispered. "Jackson must be serious."

"No doubt in my mind. He goes after what he wants until he gets it."

As he gazed at the auburn-haired woman in his arms, Devereau was struck by the appropriateness of Blue's philosophy. He was captured in the liquid green loveliness of Charity's eyes, as he'd been captivated since the moment she first sang on the Crystal Queen's stage. He had encouraged her dependency, and then had abandoned her and sent her away, yet she'd followed him across the country and through the depths of a depression that could have killed him. Did such a strong woman *need* a man? God knows it was Charity who'd seen to every detail of their life since he'd lost the use of his hands. "It's time to talk," he breathed.

Although she'd anticipated this moment since they had struck their unholy deal, Charity bit her lip. The triumph she felt after they'd defeated Erroll Powers was gone now, the material winnings unimportant. Dillon Devereau had been a proud, wealthy man before she'd led him on this goose chase, and perhaps he'd resent a wife who just took over his affairs. "You first," she murmured.

Devereau shut his eyes against an acute attack of speechlessness. When he opened them again, Charity was still gazing steadily at him. She'd come so far from being the preacher's girl in threadbare calico; she was indeed the queen he'd envisioned when he first caressed the beauty beneath her muslin nightgown. She deserved his honesty and respect. And she would accept nothing less.

With his gloveless hand, Dillon reached for the tempting juncture where Charity's neck met her shoulder. Bless her, she didn't flinch. The heat of her skin seared his raw palm, but he'd be damned if he'd spend whatever time they had left together without touching her! Ironic, how they had started this wild journey with her depending on him for everything, and now the tables had turned. When he realized this, he understood the uncertainty that was now etched upon her slender face.

In all the times she'd longed to peek beneath his gambler's mask, she never imagined Dillon *grimacing* at such an important moment. Why was he so hesitant to speak his mind, unless . . . "You might as well be honest," she mumbled. "Circumstances have changed since we agreed to renegotiate. I—I've said and done things—"

"You did what you had to," he whispered, gripping her as firmly as his inflamed fingers would allow. And then they came to him, the words that would free her to make a decision. "You've complained—and rightly so—that I've left you without asking what you wanted, without any choices. So the choice is yours now. Ask, and it shall be granted. Though God knows I'm a far cry from the man you married, and you might never want me to touch you again."

How many times had she longed for such an open invitation to freedom? Yet now she felt overwhelmed by the burden of this momentous decision, and by what it cost Dillon to offer it. Charity let out a long sigh. "I can have anything I want? Forever?"

"Those are the terms I'm offering, yes," he replied in a tight voice. Where was the woman who'd tricked her way into his private car and trapped Erroll Powers with a clever advertisement? Her hesitation was killing him, and as the minutes ticked by, he knew Charity was considering options other than staying married to him.

Then, with childlike simplicity, she looked into his eyes and said, "I want a man who loves me."

Joy shot through him—and then he choked on it. How many times had he laughed with her and made love to her and complimented her and defended her honor? Yet the only time he'd expressed his love, she'd been too drugged to comprehend. Three simple words. And now that she had to beg the issue, such an endearment lost its power and sincerity. "I—I've been an insensitive—"

"Dillon, that was a presumptuous—"

"—cad, and I can certainly understand why you'd assume I don't—"

"—self-serving remark, because I could just as easily have said that I—"

"—love you—"

"—love you—"

They stared at each other, awestruck, until Charity felt a giggle bubbling up from the bottom of her soul. She laughed so hard she shook, and when Dillon joined her, their voices echoed around the cottage walls in the sweetest duet they'd ever shared.

Devereau embraced her, delighting in Charity's warmth as he realized he'd just won the greatest gamble of his life. He kissed her fervently, until they both quivered with the need for more. "This marriage got off to a shady start, dealing behind the backs of God and your father," he reminded her, "and after only a few weeks we've already had to renegotiate."

"*You* did. I went along with it . . . because I had no choice," she added wryly. "If I lost you, I'd be letting go of everything I ever wanted."

"I wish I'd said that." Dillon grinned until his dimple winked at her. "So what I'm really proposing is—well, why don't we stick with it, at least until we're back to Kansas City? We'll have uninterrupted days on the train to discuss what's important in our lives, and what we expect of marriage, and—"

"And what we want to do to each other in bed," Charity teased. "Be honest, Dillon. You came upstairs and fondled me that first night at the Queen. And I haven't been able to sit still since."

Devereau's jaw dropped, but then he laughed and clung to the preacher's daughter who'd forced him to face his own feelings—all of them. "You're stalling, young lady, and I demand an answer," he whispered. "It seems our marriage thrives from one crisis to the next, so let's enjoy the ride back, and renegotiate whenever we need to. Because I *do* love you, honey."

Charity smiled, this time looking behind his cool facade to see a man as vulnerable to the ups and downs of life as she was, and loving him for it. His heart had healed beyond worrying over the fate of his hands; his hold on her remained firm despite his bandages. And to Charity, that was the nicest touch of all.

"There is one condition, my love," he murmured, running his tongue along the shell of her ear.

"What's that?"

"I won't swim the Weber River again. And I can't carry you across the bridge," he added apologetically, "so you'll have to make your own way. But I'll be there to help you."

She felt laughter and a serene confidence swelling inside her, a confidence born of the trust they'd shared these past frantic weeks. Charity grinned and leaned back against his arms to gaze into amber eyes that melted her with their passionate warmth. "I can always make my own way? No strings?"

Devereau dropped his gaze to the column of ivory buttons that rose and fell with her quickened breathing. "No strings—except the ones I'm about to pull from your underthings. With my teeth."

Chuckling, Charity reached for him. "It's a deal."